Chapter # 13

SAGEBRUSH, WATERCRESS, AND CHOKECHERRY JELLY

From the Journal of a Homesteader

By

Maurice Vaughn Hansen

Bloomington, IN Milton Keynes, UK

AuthorHouse™
1663 Liberty Drive, Suite 200
Bloomington, IN 47403
www.authorhouse.com
Phone: 1-800-839-8640

AuthorHouse™ UK Ltd.
500 Avebury Boulevard
Central Milton Keynes, MK9 2BE
www.authorhouse.co.uk
Phone: 08001974150

First published by AuthorHouse 6/29/2006

ISBN: 1-4208-3150-X (sc)

Printed in the United States of America
Bloomington, Indiana

This book is printed on acid-free paper.

COVER PICTURE
Taken by the author, it is one of few remaining building in what was once
Dehlin, a town of around sixty five families, a school, a church, a post office,
and a store some twenty miles near due east of Ammon, Idaho.

Acknowledgments

First, and of course most importantly, recognition must be given Miranda Campbell Stringham whose attention to detail and whose perseverance in bringing together stories about these pioneers in her book *People of the Hills* has provided a base upon which to build. Her compilation was an invaluable resource and without it, this book would have been neither possible nor interesting to write.

Enthusiastic Julee Collins, wife and former owner of the Bone Store, ran down several sources of information for me.

Duane Jones, Miranda's nephew, was gracious enough to drive me around the area and helped me put communities "back on the map".

Lois Empey Shelton provided her father's (Ernest's) dictated story of his kidnapping, and surprisingly, a photograph of the kidnapper.

My sister, Eula Baldwin, helped me avoid loose ends and put me back on track a few times. She was honest in her comments.

Michele Kronenfels, a native French lady and my neighbor provided help with my lack of knowledge of French.

After my sister finished with me, I hired a professional editor, Bruce Coggin of A1 Editing Services, who further destroyed my precious manuscript and made it into a decent story.

Recognition must be given to my parents and teachers who unconsciously instilled in me an interest in writing, a curiosity to learn, and a degree of determination that forced me to stay with the job even though there were times when it seemed overwhelming.

And finally, I must recognize my wife, Hilde, who waited patiently while I pounded at my keyboard to record a story of little personal interest to her. She's an Austrian lady and I hesitated to ask her to read it. But she did, and then she had the audacity to tell me she enjoyed it. Thank you my dearly beloved, patient, and lovely Hilde.

Author's Preface

Although I grew up less than twenty-five miles from Bone, Idaho, I'd never been there. One aborted search for the town led me to within five miles of it but the paved road ended and I was sure I had taken a wrong turn somewhere.

Nevertheless, the desire to see Bone led me to a second attempt. Armed with the knowledge that it was beyond the end of the paved road, I found it. The Bone store, which is all that remains, was a somewhat dilapidated cinder block structure tucked into a corner between a small creek and a curve in the road at the bottom of a grade. Two windows with awnings and competing neon signs advertising Coor's Light and Bud Light on either side of a door centered between them gave the place a look of a sleepy-eyed hangover. Someone had carved a huge wooden bone and stuck it in the ground in front of and slightly to one side of the building.

At the time of my first visit, I was more intrigued by the place than interested in its history. I was, however, curious enough to ask where the name came from but received an answer that convinced me that it, like many other places in Idaho, was originally a French name, and if traced to its roots was spelled *"Beaune"*. Later I learned that wasn't so. It was named after the first postmaster, Orin Y. Bone.

I left the Bone Store after an hour or so and a cola, still wondering about its reason for existence. Two years went by and during that time, I stumbled onto a book written by a former resident of the area, Miranda C. Stringham. She provided a volume of collected stories written by most of the pioneers who had lived in a much larger area. Her book, *The People of the Hills,* fanned my interest from idle curiosity to a passion to put the story into a different format. And so this book was born.

The prospect of using Mrs.. Stringham's efforts as a reference to the personal lives of those pioneers, inventing a ficticious character to interact with the real ones to show the good times and the bad in the life of a homesteader, fascinates me as a writer. A splash of my own background with impressions of my wanderings through the area she and so many others loved helped me invent the story. I hope this book has some appeal to others as well as to the people whose forebears lived those lives in Miranda's book and to whom such a written record is deeply emotional and important. What I have *not* done is to rewrite Mrs. Stringham's book, so many of the personal experiences gathered by her are either omitted, expanded by further research or pure fiction based on fact.

And there was also another personal reason. As I read Miranda's record, I saw names that were familiar to me. Names of my friends, my neighbors, even my family name (although none in her story were related to me). Two of those names were Ludwig and Carrie Franck who's son, Dan, was one of my best friends when we were growing up in the Lincoln townsite.

I spent many days traveling around that area — about fifteen by forty-five miles — of farm land, range land, abandoned and decrepit old school buildings, ghost towns, tumble-down, weathered, remnants of houses, concrete foundations, abandoned basements, flat places where a building used to be, swaybacked barns, rotting fences with rusty barbed wire, old houses imprisoned by new-growth aspen trees, and ghosts. Ghosts of a people the last of whom were the age of my parents, but who have become as real to me as if they were living relatives. Ghosts of people who pioneered an area in high hopes of success; homesteading, grubbing sagebrush, plowing where no plow had ever plowed, planting crops where none had ever grown, and harvesting them. I watched their dreams disappear one by one as drought and the Great Depression took away from them what they had built in two generations. That's the sad part. There was another part, full of the joy of accomplishment, neighborliness, faith, and love of life. And that's the story I will tell.

AUTHOR'S NOTE

This is a fictional story about real places and real people, but it is fiction. John Fountain never existed, and because he never existed, anything he ever did in the story wasn't done, every relationship he, and other ficticious characters he associated with, never happened, The people who lived and homesteaded with John were real. They came from Miranda Stringham's compilation of stories of those same homesteaders. John's and several other fictional characters' association with them is entirely fiction.

John's interaction with his neighbors demanded that I portray them in a manner that, in all probability, was not true. Although I have portrayed them as I needed them to be to write a story, the story is fiction, the neighborliness and helpfulness of those people, as a whole, was not fiction. So, although the story is entirely fiction, John's neighbors were real. I knew some of them personally.

Because this story is fiction, I feel safe that my portrayal of their characters and personalities will not be construed as fact. It is not. I felt compelled to tell the story I have told. I hope the descendants of those homesteaders will understand and accept what I have written about their forebears is pure fiction.

...to the descendants of those homesteaders

Chapter One
Jean-Pierre Lafontaine

"I'm sorry, son, if you can't read or write or do sums, I can't use you." The boy's handsome face and clear brown eyes bespoke an intelligence that belied the storekeeper's words, and he seemed out of place in this farming community.

He picked up a deerskin sack and turned to leave. Henry Monson, a local farmer, looked him over. He wore jeans and a shirt that looked almost too small. The rolled up sleeves revealed muscular forearms. "Wait a minute." Henry said. "Can you handle horses?"

He turned, surprised. "Yes, sir, I had my own horse at home."

"Where's home?"

"A Shoshoni village between Fort Hall and Blackfoot, sir."

"You don't look like an Indian."

"My mother is Shoshoni; my father was French-Canadian, sir."

"A half-breed. Can you drive a team of work horses?"

1

"I never have, but I don't think it would be much harder than one, sir."

"Have you ever done farm work before?"

"No, sir. What kind of work is it?"

"Just plain hard work, animals, fields, everything from the crack of dawn till after dark. Have you ever done hard work?"

"Sir, I'm strong and I don't get tired quickly. I think I can work hard."

"Look, I'm not really looking for hired help, but my oldest son is only thirteen and one thing he isn't, is strong. I could use some help on the farm, but I can't pay anything. Would you work for room and board?"

"Sir, I don't know what room and board is."

"I don't give you money, but I give you a place to live. It won't be fancy, but if you've been living with the Indians, it'll probably be better than you're used to. We don't have any place in the house, but I can arrange something in the barn. You'll eat at the table with us. What do you think?"

"I think I would like to work for you for room and board, sir."

"You don't have to call me, *sir*. My name is Henry Monson. Just call me Mr. Monson. What's your name?"

"Jean-Pierre Lafontaine, sir."

The neat yard and garden set against a backdrop of a small orchard at the farm impressed Jean-Pierre. The outbuildings, some of them sheltering equipment, and the large barn were painted red with white trim on the corners and around the doors and windows.

The house, white with green trim, welcomed people passing or stopping by. Inside he met Lydia, Henry's wife, showing in addition to her obvious pregnancy a beauty, somewhat faded, not often seen in farm women; James,

2

a sickly-looking lad of thirteen; Susan, eleven, thin and freckled; and Sam, four, the youngest.

Jean-Pierre quickly learned how to do the ordinary things and never had to be shown a second time. Often he didn't need instruction. Within a week, Henry knew he was getting much more than he bargained for.

One day, while Henry showed Jean-Pierre how to irrigate, they sat together on the ditch bank. "At the store, Levi said you couldn't read or write, how come?"

"I've never been to school, sir."

"Not ever?"

"No, sir. I never expected to go to school. There wasn't one in the village where I lived."

"How old are you?"

"I'm sixteen, sir."

"Your name's French. What's the story? It's none of my business, but I'd like to know."

"According to my father, my grandfather was a nobleman in France and fled to Canada to save his life. I don't know much about him, except he was very rich and wrote books. I don't think my father ever told me even what part of France he lived in."

"I'm surprised you speak so well. If you didn't go to school, how did you learn that?"

"My father taught me, sir."

"Do you have any brothers or sisters?"

"No, sir. My father told me once he left his wife and her son and daughter in Quebec, because he couldn't get along with her, and came to Fort Hall to trap beaver, but the market for beaver had almost disappeared, and he could barely stay alive. He lived with my mother's Shoshoni band, and she convinced him to join her family."

"What happened to your father?"

"He died a few months ago, sir."

"How come you came to Ammon?"

"After my father died, my mother told me I should go live among the white men because he had changed the lives of the Indians and it would never change back. She gave me a deerskin sack with some things in it and these clothes and told me to leave. I didn't want to leave, but she insisted. I didn't know where to go. I knew there was a town named Blackfoot, and farther north was Eagle Rock. There were so many white men in Eagle Rock, I was uncomfortable, so I came east to Ammon."

"Jean-Pierre, I'm glad I found you. What would you have done if I hadn't been in the store?"

"I would have looked somewhere else, sir."

"How would you keep from starving?"

"Sir, my father taught me to use a slingshot. I could have killed some rabbits or birds with it. There is almost always something to eat, somewhere. I learned a lot about surviving from the Shoshonis."

Henry Monson turned to look at the lad full in the face. He was a tall, slender boy, too good looking to be real but intelligent, intent, and surprising. He seemed to flow through his work with the ease of a well-oiled machine without getting tired.

Henry was medium height, stocky, suntanned, with a somewhat round, clean-shaven face, and strong as a bull. His thirty-four years had left only a few laughter lines on his face, and a slight graying at the temples. He was impressive, and he was his own man. "Jean-Pierre, I think I'll just call you John. I don't like your double name. Okay?"

"Yes, sir."

"Damn it, John, call me Mr. Monson. I don't like to be called *sir*"

"Yes, sir, Mr. Monson."

Henry smiled in spite of himself. "John, I think dinner's ready."

Having never planted a seed or even seen a farm, Jean-Pierre's amazement grew with the crops. The greening of the fields, the role of water and sunshine raised many questions Henry couldn't answer. He wanted to know how a seed germinated, so he filled a glass jar with earth, planted several wheat kernels next to the side, and kept it damp. The entire Monson family watched as the seeds sprouted and grew.

One Sunday the Monsons returned from Sunday school, Jean-Pierre was out in the field when they called him to dinner. "Don't you get enough of the farm during the week?" Henry asked.

Jean-Pierre ignored the question. "Mr. Monson, sir, how fast does a sugar beet grow?"

"Well, I plant them in the spring and harvest them in the fall. Why?"

"I know that, sir, but I mean every day. Every day everything in the field gets bigger, but I'd like to know how much bigger."

"I've never even thought about it. I just plant and harvest, that's all."

"Mr. Monson, sir, will you teach me to be a farmer?"

"What do you mean?"

"I mean, I love the life you have here, and I want to do the same thing."

"I'm already teaching you, except when you're teaching yourself. All I can say is just keep on the way you are now."

"I am thankful to you for what I've already learned, but there are many more things than just plowing, planting, irrigating, and harvesting."

Jean-Pierre's curiosity surprised Henry. "You can't read or write or do arithmetic, John. Those are important things to know, and I don't know how to teach them to you."

"I remember that from the store the day we met, sir. I guess I will always have that problem."

The rest of the year went by, and Jean-Pierre proved his love of farming. He was seldom in his room in the barn, a converted granary, more or less separate from the animals, but warmed by their nearness. When he wasn't working, he was either staring at the fields or walking in them. That fall, the harvest in, and frost announcing winter's coming every morning, Henry and Lydia were enjoying a few minutes after the kids went to bed.

Henry broke the comfortable silence, "Lydia, I like that kid. I *like* that kid. I want to do something for him."

"What?"

"I don't know. Maybe send him to school."

"He's too old to start school."

"My dear wife, you're thirty-three. Are you too old to learn anything?"

"But he's a half-breed Indian."

"If he was half a man, he'd be a better man than a lot I know. Do you know he speaks the Shoshoni language *and* French?"

"Where in the world did he learn French?"

"He told me his father taught him. He was French-Canadian."

"But will they let him go to school?"

"I'll see to it."

Henry didn't tell Jean-Pierre till early the next spring. At first, Jean-Pierre hesitated, but his excitement grew until school started later in the year.

Uncomfortable at a desk made for someone much younger and smaller, he stood out among the other pupils. Miss Edwards, his first teacher, like Henry Monson, soon realized she had an exceptional student, and challenged him. She included him in every lesson, regardless of grade. She asked him how various things were said in French and Shoshoni. He was surprised, but complied, much to the amazement of his fellow pupils. His maturity and naturally inquisitive mind soon grasped the concept of learning, and before the school year was over he reached reading and writing levels even the fifth graders had problems with, and he understood what he read.

Miss Edwards asked him if his name had an English equivalent. "My first name, Jean is pronounced a little bit different from John in English, and it's not spelled the same. Mr. Monson calls me John all the time, because he said he doesn't like my double name. My middle name is really part of my first name. I don't know if it has an English meaning. Lafontaine means *the fountain*. Why, Miss Edwards?"

"I was just curious. At some time in the future, you might want to adopt the English version of your name to make it easier for people."

"Can I do it right now? I could be called John Fountain."

Surprised at his quick response, Miss Edwards said, "Well, I see no reason if you haven't been widely known as Jean-Pierre Lafontaine, and there's nothing binding you to a contract, maybe now would be a good time to change your name."

And so Jean-Pierre Lafontaine became John Pierre Fountain, later spoken with great respect by those who knew him.

When he announced the change at supper at the Monsons, Susan Monson burst into tears. "I loved the other name. I wanted to be Mrs. Lafontaine some day." John was simply amused.

On their way home from Idaho Falls a few weeks later, Henry said, "I'm sure you won't stay with me forever, but I hope you'll stay till James can take over some of the hard work. Have you thought about what you want to do?"

"Mr. Monson, sir, thank you. I haven't thought about leaving, but now I'm going to school, I want to be a farmer."

"I'm sure you can. Have you thought about where?"

"You homesteaded your place. I'd like to do that, too."

"But I started several years ago. I doubt if you can find anything, now."

"Maybe some day I'll go up into the hills east of here and see if I can find a place. I've heard there's still open land."

"That's pretty ambitious. You're only seventeen. Homesteading in the hills is hard work, even harder than farming in the valley. You know how much work there is here, but clearing the land and getting it ready to plant is a whole lot harder than what you're doing for me. Besides, you'll need equipment and horses and a cabin and, well, everything. All you have now is the clothes you're wearing and what we bought today."

"Mr. Monson, sir, what did you have when you started out?"

Henry thought a couple of seconds and said, "I didn't have a pot to piss in, and I had a pregnant wife. I fell into this deal. I was working for a dollar a day, and I knew I had to have something better, so I went to the land office in Blackfoot to see if there was a chance I could get some land of my own. I met a man there from Rhode Island, I think, who came west to homestead. He expected to get rich in a hurry. He offered me his homestead for a dollar. I had exactly $1.13 in my pocket. I gave him the dollar, and he gave me his relinquishment on the spot. We filled out the papers, and that was it. I still had to clear the crap off about twenty acres, and the first few years were hell.

"I admire your idea, but think about it. It's a rough life. Up there you'll have to depend on the weather, and that's never a sure bet. When my crops get dry, I can irrigate them. Up there you can't. But from what I know about you, if anybody can make it up there, you can."

"Thank you, Mr. Monson, sir."

"Damnit John, will you quit calling me *sir*?"

"Yes, sir."

After three years of prodding, pushing, and coaching, mostly by Miss Edwards helped by Mrs. Spring, his second teacher, he graduated from the eighth grade in May, 1914. He was almost twenty years old and ready to start his own life.

With intensely mixed feelings he told Henry, "Sir, I think I'd like to leave now. I love this place, and you and your family have been good to me, but I need to get started."

Two days later, he left. His departure from the Monson family brought emotion he'd not seen in them before — nor from himself. Henry shook his hand and seemed to hold it too long. Mrs. Monson hugged him, the first time she ever intentionally touched him. There was a catch in her voice as she said good-bye. James, now seventeen but no match for John at the same age, shook his hand and said, "So long, John."

Susan, a gangly, freckled fourteen with a broomstick figure hugged him till her mother's look of disapproval stopped her. At seven Sam didn't quite know how to shake hands and finally mumbled, "S'long". Freddy, a three-year old stomped on John's foot according to their ritual, bringing a fake howl of pain and much limping while the boy giggled out of control, then grabbed John's leg as if to keep him from leaving.

"John, I've got a horse you can have."

"Thank you, Mr. Monson, sir, but I plan to start out just like you did." Mrs. Monson convinced John he should take a bar of her homemade soap to wash his clothes, and he accepted her package of sandwiches, both of which he put into his deerskin sack and tied the drawstrings.

Leaving the Monsons was hard. He felt as if he was leaving a family he'd never see again, but the excitement of taking out a homestead overcame his sadness.

Just as John turned to leave the first white family he'd known, Henry said, "Here's ten dollars. You've more than earned it. I didn't quite tell the truth when I said I didn't have anything when I started out. I had a family to help me over the rough spots, and I know there are some pretty rough spots ahead for you. Please take it. It won't help you over every hump, but it will help you get started."

Then John left, but he went to say farewell to Miss Edwards. "Ma'am, I just want to say thanks for teaching me." Although Miss Edwards was ten years older than John, he found her attractive, and he thought of her often, though he had things to do before he started a courtship.

"You've renewed my interest in teaching. It was such a pleasure to see you move so fast. I'll always have stories to tell about my best pupil. Just so you'll have something to remember me by, I've got a little gift for you if you'll wait a minute." She left and returned with two books, one a worn, dog-eared *Holy Bible*, the other, Charles Dickens' *A Tale of Two Cities*. "Here," she said, "take these. I know you'll like Dickens. The Bible takes a little study sometimes, but it's the word of God. Maybe some day you can teach me more about the Indians' religion, but the Bible will tell you a lot about mine. I'd give you my *Book of Mormon*, but I'm afraid two religious books might be too much for now. And here's an empty notebook for you to keep a journal. Please write in it as often as you can. It will keep you company while you're alive, and it's the greatest gift you can leave behind. I've kept mine since I started teaching, and I often read it and remember the good *and* the bad times. Next time you're in Ammon, please come to see me."

At first, John was reluctant to take the books, but agreed and promised to return them as soon as he could buy his own. Then he opened the notebook and wrote:

May 8, 1914 Miss Edwards gave me this notebook to keep a journal.

He thanked her, smiled, and left.

Chapter Two
Sunrise on a new day

It was still morning when John Fountain turned his back on his past and looked to the hills to find his future. He dogtrotted east on the road till he reached the foothills, then left the road and walked cross-country. Spring was everywhere. The gray-green hip-high sagebrush, like miniature trees above the bright green undergrowth, gave evidence of good soil. As he moved among growing things, his spirit soared and he sang a Shoshoni song to welcome spring. His footsteps drummed the beat.

In mid-afternoon he arrived at Ozone, a cluster of buildings nestled in a broad cove with a small creek running through it. A long building with a barn beside it looked like a store. It was cramped inside, but it appeared one could buy just about anything he needed. Mrs. Otteson approached him, "Need something?"

"Mostly information, ma'am. I'm looking for a place to homestead."

"Most of the land around here is taken up if it's any good. You'll have to go farther east or south to find anything. Are you with your family?"

"No, ma'am. I'm alone. I don't have a family."

"Where do you come from?"

"I worked for Mr. Monson in Ammon for about four years."

"I don't know him personally, but I've heard he's a good man. How did you get here?"

"I came on foot, ma'am."

"You don't have a horse, or wagon, or anything?"

"No, ma'am, all I have is in this sack."

"I don't suppose you have a tent, either. You'll need shelter. Do you have a gun?"

"No, ma'am."

"Food?"

"I have a few sandwiches and a bar of soap Mrs. Monson gave me to wash my clothes and my blanket and a knife, and a coat."

"The sandwiches won't last long. You might find yourself eating the soap. It'll take some time to find a piece of land, but even then, you'll have to have food. How do you expect to survive without a gun to shoot game?"

"I can trap small animals and birds, and I'm pretty good with a slingshot, and I can make a bow and arrows for larger stuff, ma'am, if I have to."

"Those are Indian things. You don't look like an Indian to me."

"My mother is Shoshoni, ma'am, and I grew up among them. I know a lot about surviving."

"I hope you do. Do you have any money?"

"Mr. Monson gave me ten dollars, ma'am. That will last a while."

"Not long enough. Look, if you find a homestead and get it registered, we might be able to help you with food at first, but you have to pay it back when you get on your feet. You'll need seed and all kinds of things. Maybe you can get a job in the valley during the winter to buy those things."

"Thank you ma'am. I think the first thing I have to do is to find some land somewhere. Mr. Monson always said first things first. You said there might be land east and south of here. Can you tell me who to talk to?"

"Well, if you go east to Dehlin, you can find Jack Dehlin or Jed Rockwood. Both have homesteads there, and a lot of people are going into the area around Dehlin. Or you could go south to Canyon Creek and Seventy Creek, Pine Mountain, and Sheep Mountain. I've heard there's a lot of open land down there. There are also a lot of people."

"I'll try to be a good neighbor. Thank you, ma'am. I think I'll go to Dehlin first. Good-bye, ma'am."

John started out the door but stopped when Lenore called, "Young man, you come back here! I can't let you go out there with nothing but a few sandwiches. Let me put some stuff in your sack."

"Ma'am, I really. . ."

"You won't be sorry, and I don't want you to be sorry." Reluctantly, John handed her the sack. "What's so heavy in here?" She opened the sack. "A Bible? And Dickens? Son, you've got a lot of good reading with you."

"Yes, ma'am, I know. My teacher in Ammon gave them to me. And she gave me a notebook to keep a journal in but I'm, not sure what to write in it."

"A journal is a record of your life the way it happened. Like a diary. You write what you did, how you felt, people you meet. It's a record you keep about the important things."

"I guess I did it right, then. I wrote in it when she gave it to me."

Lenore opened the cover and read John's short statement. "That's right. If you keep writing in it, after a while you'll read it yourself, and after you're gone your kids will read it and know they've opened your heart. Can you cook?"

"Yes, ma'am, but I'm not used to using all the pans and stuff you use."

Mrs. Otteson walked around the store picking food easy to carry, yet nourishing. She put a tin plate on top. "There's a can of beans that'll give you something to boil water in, and you can cook and eat in the tin plate. The rest of the stuff is good, solid, dry food so it doesn't weigh much, and it'll keep, What's your name?"

"John Fountain, ma'am."

"Glad to meet you, John. I'm Lenore Otteson. I run this store, and I'm the post mistress here. My husband and I homesteaded this place several years ago, and the town is growing. There's seventy-three cents worth of stuff in the sack. You don't have to pay for it. It's yours. But when you sell your first crop, I hope you'll remember who helped you out."

"I'll put it in my journal, ma'am."

"If you're going to Dehlin, turn right toward Last Chance about two miles north. Be careful when you cross Willow Creek at Kep's Crossing. It's pretty high this time of year, and the bridge might be out."

"Yes, ma'am."

"Please call me Lenore."

"Yes, ma'am."

The loaded sack slowed John down, but he put his arms through the drawstrings and carried it on his back. He got to Last Chance in about half an hour. The place was pleasant with trees around a pretty spring, so he decided to camp there for the night. He wrote, "I got to Ozone in the middle of the afternoon. I stopped in Ottesons store. Mrs. Otteson asked a lot of questions. She gave me a lot of stuff. She told me it was 73 cents worth, and I do not have to pay it back but I will. I have stopped for the night at Last Chance. It is pretty, with trees around a nice spring. I ate one of Mrs. Monson's sandwiches."

A small herd of deer at the spring woke John the next morning. Peering over the edge of his blanket, he counted five, and watched them till they moved away.

He trotted along a wagon trail, the sack bouncing on his back. Long before he reached it, he could hear Willow Creek, a cacophony of rushing water. When he came to Kep's Crossing, he stared at it, intimidated. The bridge was gone, swept downstream. The raging stream ramming its spring load of debris sent a chill through him. At Kep's Crossing, it was wider, but still a furious, boiling mass of muddy water. Downstream it was even worse where it entered a narrow canyon gnawed through lava beds. Lenore was right; it might be hard to cross.

He walked downstream a way, then upstream where he found a place that looked like the easiest crossing. Raising his sack above his head, he jumped into the churning water and struggled across. The icy current pulled him diagonally downstream till he came to a small island. It was only a few square feet, but it gave him a chance to catch his breath and figure out his next move. From there the water was deeper but slower, and the channel was narrower. He'd have to swim. Tying the drawstrings as tight as he could, he plunged in. The cold water renewed his energy and, using the sack as a float, he kicked his way across.

After climbing a steep hill, the wagon track reached a broad, nearly flat area. As he trotted along the wagon track to stay warm, he ate another sandwich. Greening fields of winter wheat amid patches of snow looked like the pattern on a pinto pony. By the time he reached Dehlin, his clothes were dry, and the sun was high.

First things first, he said to himself. I have to find someone who can show me where some open ground is. Another wagon track branched off to the right toward a small barn and corral. Smoke rose from a cabin's chimney.

A man a few years older than he answered his knock on the door.

"Hello, sir, my name is John Fountain. I don't want to disturb you, but could you give me some information?"

"I'm Jed Rockwood. Come in." Inside, the single room, the afternoon sun made a pattern from its two south-facing windows. John felt a friendly atmosphere.

"Where's your horse?" Jed asked.

"I don't have one yet, sir. First I have to find a homestead and file a claim on it. Then I'll look for a horse."

"Well, there's still some open land around here. Where'd you come from?"

"From Ammon, sir."

"Today? On foot? That's about twenty miles."

"I left yesterday and camped at Last Chance."

"How did you get across Willow Creek?"

"I waded part way, and swam the rest."

The niceties of two strangers getting acquainted went on for an hour or so, Jed asking most of the questions and telling some of his experiences homesteading with his brother, Amos. John's excitement grew.

"I'm alone for a couple of days. Why don't you stay here for the night? Tomorrow, we'll ride out and look around. Tomorrow's Sunday, and I promised my wife I wouldn't work."

"I don't want to be any problem, sir. I could…"

"I'd like to have the company. It's not very lively here alone."

"I could pay you, sir."

"No, you can't. The food's not very fancy, and the cot sags a little in the middle, but you'll be more comfortable here than sleeping under a bush somewhere. Besides, there are no rattlesnakes in the cabin."

The sun was still high, so Jed took John out to show him his field. The winter wheat was just recovering and appeared like a bright green ocean. Patches of rapidly retreating snow made the landscape a green and white patchwork. As they walked, John knew homesteading was a way for him to live in nature, be what the Shoshonis had always been, though owning land and planting crops was not part of their culture. After supper, John asked more questions.

May 9, 1914 Five deer woke me up this morning. I watched them till they went away. Mrs. Otteson was right. Willow creek was very full, and the bridge was gone. I waded part way but had to swim the rest of the way. I got to Dehlin in the afternoon. I met Mr. Jed Rockwood. We walked around his field full of new wheat. He told me it was winter wheat. They plant it in the fall so the snow can wet it in spring.

The next morning, Jed brought two horses and saddled one of them. John told him he'd rather ride without a saddle.

"I don't know. He's never been rode without a saddle before."

"I've never used a saddle, sir."

Easing himself up onto the horse's back, he spoke to it quietly. The horse shuddered, looked around at the new rider, and then stood still.

"I really expected him to try to throw you. You must have a way with horses," Jed said.

"You have to give them a chance to know you, sir."

"I think we should ride down to Hell Creek, then back across Tex Creek, down Pipe Creek, and up Bull's Fork. It'll fill up the day, and you'll get a good idea of the country. That's what Amos and I did before we settled here."

"I think I'd like that," John said.

It did take all day. Jed stopped often to explain which land was taken and who homesteaded it. The greening grain, remnants of snowdrifts, sagebrush, stands of willows and bushes in the draws, and plowed ground on the rolling hills looked like a patchwork quilt thrown over an unmade bed.

Jed explained a homesteader had to show he meant business by clearing the land, farming it, building a cabin, and living on it for at least five years. "Does it cost anything, sir?" John asked.

"Well, the law says a dollar and a quarter an acre, or less for 160 acres."

"I have only ten dollars."

"You don't have to pay till you get a patent."

They followed Hell Creek upstream, then climbed out and headed almost due north, across low hills, and around aspen groves, finally coming to a small basin. "This is Pipe Creek. This little basin looked good to Amos and me, but it was too far away from everything, so we went back to the Dehlin area."

Their ride took them down Pipe Creek to Bull's Fork just below Tex Creek, and up Bull's Fork, a small stream in a narrow valley between rolling hills. As they rode they passed coves filled with aspen, chokecherry, willows and tall grass. Scattered sagebrush stood like beacons announcing fertile soil.

"Is that a cabin up there?" John asked. "It looks small. Whose is it?"

"George Fogelsong's, or Fogelson. I'm not sure which. Actually, it's a dugout with a roof. That's why it looks so small. He's a widower with two boys and a girl. They live there."

Minutes later the tiny valley opened up, and the stream widened, too, hosting a dense thicket of cattails. A half-finished cabin caught John's eye. "Do you know whose cabin that is? It looks pleasant."

"It belongs to a man named Franck from some place in Utah. He comes up once in a while in summer and works on the cabin and clears a little bit more land. I haven't talked to him yet, but Jack Dehlin knows him."

"I like this area, sir. I'd like to find a place here. We passed a little building back there beside the road. It looked empty. What is it?"

"It was the Bull's Fork School. I've always liked the area, too. Let me show you my first choice when we came here. It's next to the Franck place."

They rode a short distance to a small brush-filled cove where water flowed from a watercress-filled spring. Fragrant white fingers of chokecherry blossoms scented the air. "This is it!" John exclaimed, "This is where I want to homestead. Do you know which direction the land runs?"

"Sure. The farmland is on top of the ridge, and most of it is nearly flat. Bull's Fork is almost at the eastern edge. Plenty of room for a cabin and outbuildings. It's a great place, but it was claimed when we looked at it.

"Oh," John said, disappointed. "If it was mine, I would have done something by now. You said you homesteaded three years ago, and it was already claimed?"

"Yes, it was about three years ago. Come to think of it, you're right. I wonder why it looks like nobody has done anything. Let's take a closer look."

While they rode around the cove, then up to the flat area above it, there seemed to be no sign that anyone had done any work on it. Jed said, "You know, John, sometimes people will stake out a homestead, then lose interest or something, or maybe the land office is too far away. Blackfoot is over twenty miles, and it might have been too far to bother. I still can't believe a place like this is still open, though. You have to clear it, grow a crop and build

20

a cabin. With less than two years left, I don't think there's time for anybody to do that. Let's look for posts."

There were posts all right, but they appeared to have been put in hurriedly and many of them had fallen down. "John, I think this land is still open."

"Does that mean I can stake it?"

"Yes. If you want, I'll come up tomorrow and help you."

"But what if it's been registered?"

"The only way to find out is take the information to the land office and ask. The worst thing that can happen is that it still has a valid claim on it."

"Mr. Rockwood, I'd appreciate your help. I really like this place."

They rode back to the cove. John dismounted and walked around it, tasted the spring water, then ate a handful of watercress while he climbed through the aspen to the top of the ridge. It was perfect. A broad expanse of sagebrush as high as his hips spread before him. The thought of the work required to remove the native plants never crossed his mind. He could see nothing but green fields of grain waving in the spring wind like ripples on a lake.

He returned to Jed. "What do I have to do now?"

"Well, you have to stake out 160 acres and locate it in the land survey and take the information to the land office and file your claim. If there's already a valid claim on it, you have to start over."

In spite of Jed's offer of another night of hospitality, John remained in the cove and Jed led his brother's horse back home. Alone, John looked at everything again. A sage hen startled him when he almost stepped on her. This was where he'd make his home. He was sure it was still open.

May 10, 1914 Mr. Rockwood took me all over the area and finally we went to Bull's Fork. He showed me where he wanted to homestead first. It was a pretty little cove with a good spring. I walked to the top of the cove to look at the land. The sagebrush is quite high. I am very glad. My mother told me the white man's medicine is strong, and now I will own land just like him. I will clear the land and plant it and have crops of wheat. I will build a cabin and find a pretty wife, and we will have many children. We will be happy. I ate the last of Mrs. Monson's sandwiches.

The next day Jed helped John stake his claim. Most of the original posts were close enough they were able to stand them up again in a slightly new position. Finished, Jed wrote a description of the land on a piece of paper and gave it to John.

He interrupted John's frequent thanks reminding him being a good neighbor meant helping others, and John realized his desire of total independence wouldn't work. He needed his neighbors.

The same day he caught a rabbit to eat, and took its skin for a winter coat.

Chapter Three
Threatening Weather, Then Sunshine

The next day John headed southwest, crossed Gray's Lake Outlet and the headwaters of Willow Creek and camped in the forest on his way to Blackfoot. At the land office, he handed the numbers Jed gave him to a middle-aged woman. A sign on her desk said she was Rose Gerrard.

"Ma'am, I'd like to know if someone has filed for a homestead on this land." She took the numbers, opened a thick book, looked intently at several pages, then returned to the counter.

"No. Nobody has filed on this quarter section. Do you want to file?"

John's heart skipped a beat. "Yes, ma'am."

Mrs. Gerrard took a printed sheet and began her question. "Your Name?"

"John Fountain, ma'am."

"Are you a citizen of the United States of American?"

"Yes, ma'am."

"You look a little dark. Who is your father?"

"Jean-Claude Lafontaine, ma'am."

"That's French. Is he French?"

"French-Canadian, ma'am."

"And who is your mother?"

"A Shoshoni woman named Rosemary Gibbons, ma'am."

"You mean you're an Indian?"

"I am half Shoshoni, ma'am."

Rose glared at him. "A half-breed! The worst kind. Indians are not citizens of this country. Sorry, we can't record your claim."

"Ma'am, I *am* a citizen of this country. I was born here."

"That doesn't make any difference. You mother was an Indian, and Indians are not citizens."

"I don't understand, ma'am. The Indians were here before there *was* a country."

Rose's voice got louder. "Listen. You are *not* a citizen. You cannot file for a homestead, understand?"

"No, ma'am, I don't understand."

"Listen carefully. You are *not* a citizen of this country. You're an Indian, and Indians are not citizens of this country. Do you understand that?"

"No, ma'am, I don't understand that. It makes no sense. I'm half Indian. My father was white. Doesn't that make a difference?"

"Your father wasn't a citizen, either. He was a Canadian. If you want to file for citizenship, you can come back. Until then, you are not eligible to file for a homestead. Now please leave!"

A man came out of another office behind Rose. When he learned what the problem was, he assured Mrs. Gerrard anyone born on United States soil was a citizen, except Indians. John's father was white. That's all it took.

Calmer, Mrs. Gerrard continued. "Have you ever borne arms against United States of America?"

"I'm not sure what that means, ma'am."

"It means, have you ever fought United States of America in a war with a gun. I think you might have, being an Indian."

"No, ma'am. I don't have a gun."

"I'll bet you've shot arrows at soldiers, though. That's the same thing."

"No, ma'am. The Shoshoni Indians are peaceful people."

The questions continued, and John, now sure he could qualify, answered them.

"I'm sure you're at least twenty-one years old, but just to make the record complete, are you twenty-one?"

"No, ma'am, I'm twenty. I'll be twenty-one next year."

"Aha!" A crooked smile of satisfaction creased her face. "All you Indians, especially you half-breeds, are trying to get something for nothing from the government. You cannot file a claim on a homestead unless you're twenty-one years old or the head of a household. Now, that that's settled, don't come back here till you're twenty-one years old."

John stood helplessly while his dream crumbled around him. "Isn't there some way I can file, ma'am?"

"No. Good-bye and good riddance."

John turned to leave, then went back. "Can I talk to the man in the office?"

"It won't do you any good."

"Ma'am, please."

Mrs. Gerrard gave him a frozen stare and went to the door, talked briefly to the man inside, and returned to her desk without looking at John.

Alan Denning came to the counter. "I'm sorry, what's your name?"

"John Fountain, sir."

"John, there's really nothing we can do for you till you're twenty-one. Do you have any relatives you could arrange something with, someone twenty-one or over who could file and turn it over to you when you're twenty-one?"

"No, sir. My only family is my mother, and she's an Indian. The lady told me Indians are not citizens of this country. No, sir."

"Anybody else who isn't a relative?"

"Sir, I don't know anyone except Mr. Rockwood close to my . . . the land I wanted to homestead, but he's used his homestead right. I worked for Mr. Monson in Ammon for four years. He told me about homesteading, and I decided to do it, too. Isn't there anything I can do?"

"There really isn't anything you can do except to get a year older. Mrs. Gerrard thought you were already old enough. Maybe you should have let her go on thinking that. Where is this piece of land you're interested in?"

"It's about twelve miles east of Ozone, sir."

"A lot of people are interested in that area. Too bad you'll have to wait. The land will be taken up fast, especially now spring is here."

"Thank you, sir."

A thoroughly dejected John left, his hopes splintered. His dream of homesteading had become a nightmare. After he closed the door, Alan turned to his assistant, "Rose, that boy is serious. Too bad he's a year too young."

"He's a half-breed. We don't need people like that homesteading in this country. They're a nuisance. They're sluggish, lazy, foul, heathens, and thieves. They should all be rounded up and put in a pen."

"Yes, Rose, I've already heard your story."

John retraced his steps walking steadily all night. Bitter disappointment killed his appetite. Early in the morning, he turned toward Ozone and arrived at the store in midmorning. He insisted he pay the seventy-three cents, saying he'd not be a customer after all.

He was tired, and it took till almost dark to get back to "his" place. He ate the can of beans since it needed no cooking. His purpose gone, he moped around the little cove, daydreaming of what might have been, his shattered hopes dangling like a white flag of defeat. He slept little that night.

Early the next morning, he ate a handful of raw oatmeal and ripped out the stakes he'd put in three days before. Slinging his deerskin sack over his shoulder, he walked toward Ammon, his energy and enthusiasm gone. Early in the evening he arrived at the Monson's. They were just sitting down to supper, and were glad to share with him. Although they were glad to see him again, his tale of defeat at the land office made conversation difficult, and they spent most of the evening in silence.

Just before bedtime, Henry said, "Rose Gerrard hates Indians, and I suspect she'd put up any obstacle she could to stop you from owning land. She's been in that office since it opened, and she probably knows all the rules, as well as how to bend them once in a while. She's a good woman, but she can be tough. I never thought about the age requirement when you left here. And the part about citizenship. I had no idea Indians aren't citizens. Seems unreasonable. I don't know this Denning, he must be new since I was there last. Do you want to come back to work for me? Same deal, then try again next year."

"Thank you, sir. No, I think I'll go back to my mother's people. Why does age make such a big difference?"

"It's not the age, John. It's the rules. They get in the way sometimes, but without them, civilization wouldn't be civilization."

May 14, 1914 Two days ago I went to the land office. A lady named Rose Gerrard asked many questions. She told me I was not a citizen of United States. That is impossible, I told her, and she got very angry. Then a man came out and told her I was a citizen because I was not all Indian and I was born in this country. Then she found out I wasn't twenty-one and stopped making the application. Then the man told me he was sorry but the rule could not be broken. I walked all night on the way back and stopped to pay Mrs. Otteson the 73 cents.

Although back in a familiar bed, John slept fitfully. At breakfast, he toyed with the familiar pancakes, unable to eat. His discouragement grew as he noted the family he knew so well seemed unusually happy, as if glad he didn't get his homestead. Their excitement grew till Henry, grinning broadly announced, "John, you can have your homestead."

"They told me I'm not old enough."

"Lydia solved the problem last night. She asked me if she could take out a homestead. I hadn't thought of it, but she can, and so we decided she'd file and relinquish to you next year."

John stared at Lydia. "Would you do that for me?"

"Of course. I had no idea I *could* file until Henry told me. So we'll do it."

Everybody laughed then, including John. They promised to come to look at his chosen area on a weekend as soon as possible.

May 14, 1914 I stopped on the way back to my homestead and told Mrs. Otteson what happened. She was glad it all worked out for me. David Campbell was in the store and we talked a little bit. Then I stopped to tell Mr. Rockwood. He said he found all the posts down and put them back up. He thought somebody was trying to jump my claim. When I got here, I walked around thinking what I would do. The first thing I need is a new shelter, and I think I'll make a teepee as soon as I can. I wish Willow was here.

Alexis Johnson's uncle gave her the name "Willow" when she became a woman. She was a beautiful girl with uncommon features. Her face was narrower than most, like John's mother's, and her lips formed a pleasing bow under a slender nose and bright, shining, almost black, eyes. Her long black hair hung in two braids over her shoulders. She was the main reason John was reluctant to leave the Shoshoni camp. She and John met often on the banks of the Snake River. At first, they just talked, but as time passed, their meetings became more than just friendly.

A real homesteader now, John went to his field to see what it would take to clear it. Clearly, he needed an ax. He returned to Ozone the next day and bought one for $1.24 from his precious hoard of money. By May 20, he'd made some progress, but the job looked overwhelming. He wrote, "The land I have cleared is very small. It will take a long time. I paced the distance I have cleared. It is 100 steps wide and 150 steps long. I will be glad when I have my homestead."

He worked two more days, eating grouse and rabbits and tanning the rabbit skins for a winter coat. He cooked some oatmeal from the food Mrs. Otteson gave him. It took two meals to eat the first batch because he didn't know it swelled when it cooked.

He smoked the flesh of two rabbits the way he'd seen his mother smoke meat. It was edible, but he decided to wait till later in the year when the rabbits would be fatter.

As he whacked through the brush, he carried it to a pile and his journal showed he hadn't completely lost his Indianness.

May 22, 1914 I set fire to the sagebrush after I worked all day. The fire went very high in the air. I felt like dancing the way we used to dance. I didn't have a drum so I made a drum noise with my mouth. I wanted to sing, so I stopped the drum noise and sang. It was very late when the fire went down. I wish I could see Willow. When I finish I will go back to my mother. Maybe Willow will be in the village.

May 23, 1914 I got a big surprise today. The Monsons came in the middle of the afternoon. They knew where I was because the fire from last night was still smoking. I have cleared a piece 250 steps wide and 250 steps long. Mr. Monson said it was a lot. Mrs. Monson walked around the cove and showed me where I would build a house and where a garden should be. She was excited about the wild plants and the spring. Mr. Monson said they will go to Blackfoot in the week, and asked if I would like to go with them, I told them no if I didn't have to. They stayed with some friends in Ozone.

A few days later Jed came to see how John was doing, and invited him to come to his place to eat. John accepted and reported, "We had some pig meat and potatoes and gravy. It was very good." He killed a sage grouse on the way with his slingshot. Jed, impressed that John was so accurate with his simple device, wanted to try it. John wrote, "Mr. Rockwood had not seen my slingshot. He was surprised I could throw a rock so good with it. He tried it, but he needs a lot of time before he can use it." (Later John reported that Jed told Lenore Otteson, "I couldn't hit the broad side of a barn with it, but John hit a sage hen in the eye.") Jed gave him some potatoes to take home.

In the afternoon of May 30, Jack Dehlin and Arthur Schwieder paid him a visit. Although he learned a lot about the Mormon Church from the Monsons, he'd never been asked to join. This visit was friendly but clearly intended to lure him into their fold. He wrote of it, "I had two visitors today. Mr. Jack Dehlin and Arthur Schwieder came. We talked for a long time. They told me some day Dehlin would be a big town. I think they want me to be like them. I want to be like the white man but I don't think I have to go to his church just because he thinks so. They told me there are many families around Dehlin who are Mormons and they were thinking of getting a church started. Mr. Dehlin said I should come to some of their social things to get acquainted with the people. I should know more people who live here. I didn't get much land cleared today."

The visit disturbed John, but it also inspired him to try to read Miss Edwards' Bible. His journal entry for May 31 reveals his frustration. "While I worked today I thought a lot about Mr. Dehlin and Mr. Schwieder's visit yesterday. I decided to read Miss Edwards' Bible. It is very hard to understand. Adam and Eve were the first people. They had two sons. Cain killed Abel, and then went to the land of Lot and found a wife. If Adam and Eve were the first people. where did the people in Lot come from? I decided it was too complicated for me to read."

After his attempt to read the Bible, he turned to *A tale of Two Cities*, and found something he considered funny. "I got out the other book to read. I liked the way it started. Everything was opposite each other. I laughed when I read about the two kings with large jaws. One of them had a pretty wife and the other one had an ugly wife. They were from England and France. I am not sure what the next part means. There are a lot of strange words about things I have not learned. It's a little bit hard to read but I think it will be easier after a while."

After getting wet several times in rainstorms, he realized he needed canvas for a teepee. Reluctant as he was to go into debt at the Ozone store, he needed some other things as well. His tin plate was badly bent, and he needed something to replace the tin can.

June 1, 1914 I went to Ozone today. I asked Mrs. Otteson if she had some canvas. She told me no, she only had tents but she could get canvas in town. I told her I wanted canvas for a teepee. She wanted to know why I couldn't use a tent, so I told her snow would slide off a teepee real easy but on a tent it gathered and some times the tent would fall down. I know because I have seen it happen in the white man's camps. When I told her how much canvas I needed, she did some arithmetic and told me it would cost me 3 dollars and 54 cents. She offered me a used tent in good condition for two dollars and a little stove for fifty cents. The stove is tiny but it would keep me warm on cold nights and I can cook on top of it. I told her I needed a frying pan and a cooking pot. She told me I could take the stuff and pay when I have the money. All together, they cost seven dollars and fifty-six cents. I think I will have to find a job in the winter time.

I agreed to buy them. Mr. Otteson helped me make a pack with the stove and the tent, but there was no room for the stove pipe or the pans. It was very heavy to carry. I got back home when it was getting dark. I didn't have time to work in my field after I put the tent up. I asked where I can find work in winter, and she told me a lot of the farmers worked at the sugar factory in Lincoln in the fall. I have to go back in the morning to get the rest of the stuff, so I can't work in my field.

The load he had to carry the next day wasn't as heavy as the day before, but it was awkward, especially the stovepipe which was in three pieces. Arthur Schwieder gave him a ride. "Mr Schwieder came by in a buggy and give me a ride. I wish he was here yesterday."

He added, "I forgot something. I saw a track of a wolf at my spring. It was a big wolf and an old one. The coyotes are howling now."

John's days were full from the moment the sun brightened the eastern sky till darkness swallowed the last light. For the next week, he chopped, whacked, pulled, and burned brush. Daily he opened more land, but he would not be satisfied until the whole quarter section lay naked in the sun. He was getting tired.

June 10, 1914 I am working too hard I think. I quit this afternoon and rested and cooked a grouse with some fried bread. I also made some potatoes in my new pot. It tasted very good. I decided to clear a path all the way to the end of the homestead. I paced the area I have cleared. It's 493 steps long and 250 steps wide. It's wider where I started though. I think if I clear a stripe to the end of the homestead, it will be about 890 steps long. I will not finish this summer. I carry water in my new pot and I have to drink from it often.

This morning I saw the wolf's track again. I wish I could see him but he's afraid of me. I am writing this in the sunshine in my tent. I am very tired. Maybe I should take a day off and rest. The Monsons always rested on Sunday. Tomorrow is not Sunday but I won't work anyway.

Mr. Fogelsong came by and told me who he is. He said Mr. Franck would probably come this summer again to work on his cabin. He said I should plant some vegetables so I could have some to eat. He said he had some seeds left. He said it was a little bit late in the year but I could get something from them anyway. He will come tomorrow to help me make a garden. He has a shovel and I don't. He said he would sell me a couple of sacks of wheat for seed when he threshes this year.

Some day I will have a cow and a riding horse and a team of work horses and some pigs and chickens. I miss Mrs. Monson's cooking.

The next day George Fogelsong came with his children and helped John prepare and plant a garden. They took turns using George's shovel to prepare the soil. All the seeds he had left over were planted with the help (or hindrance) of the children. John wrote of the oldest son, "Conrad tried to help, but most of the time he was in the way. I hope I can have some sons some day. I would like to see Willow again."

After seeing the wolf tracks near his spring, he watched for him. On June 13 he recorded, "I got up early and went to the spring. I think I saw the wolf when he went in the trees but I am not sure. There were new tracks, too."

June 20, 1914 The patch is getting bigger. I stopped today before it got dark. I would like to have some tame chicken to eat. The frying pan is a lot better than the tin plate but I'm getting out of lard. Washing clothes with hot water from the new pot is a lot easier. Mrs. Monsons soap is lasting very good. Mrs. Otteson said I might have to eat it. I tried a little piece. It tasted very bad. I would have to be very hungry to eat it.

June 21, 1914 I decided to not work today because I am very tired. I got up early and saw the wolf. He started to run away then he stopped and looked at me. I think he has been eating the bones I leave in my dump. He is very big and very old. I will see if he will eat some fried bread. In the afternoon, I read my journal. It does not sound like I talk. It sounds very funny. I don't know what's wrong. I will take it to Miss Edwards next time I go to Ammon. I have to get some lard and salt.

At the Ozone store, John asked Mrs. Otteson to read his journal and tell him what was wrong because it didn't sound the way he wanted. He wrote, "She wanted to know who Willow was. I told her she was my Indian girl friend. She said if I talk to my journal and then write what I said it would be better."

Not having any way to get around except walking cost John clearing time. "Mr. Monson said debt is a killer. I don't have any money so I can't buy a horse without going into debt. I guess I'll just have to wait till I have a crop."

John and the wolf were friends after several encounters although each gave the other plenty of space. "I threw some fried bread to him, and he ate it and then came a little bit closer and lay down."

The howl of coyotes was an inescapable part of John's childhood, and sometimes he wrote of his concern for what he was doing. "I hear the coyotes howling and it makes me wonder what they are thinking about me. I am taking their hunting land away from them. When the white man came and took our hunting lands away from us, we felt the same way. The whole valley along the Snake River is full of white men and they have made towns and schools and built churches and have governments and they have left the Indians out of it. Maybe that is why Indians are not citizens."

Still seeking help with his journal, John wrote two letters, one to his former teacher. "Miss Edwards, What I have written in my journal does not sound like me. Will you help me?" and the other to Henry Monson saying he wanted to visit them. He wrote them on the backs of calendar pages which he took to Ozone. Lenore took his two letters, folded them and addressed them to Miss Edwards and Mr. Monson using simply Ammon, Idaho for the address, and sent them on their way. After paying a nickel for the postage, John returned to his camp.

June 26, 1914 I mailed two letters today at Mrs. Otteson's store. They were the first letters I ever mailed. It always seemed complicated to me that a letter mailed from any place could go to any place else, but Mrs. Otteson told me how it happened. It is really simple.

My garden needed water so I gave it some from my kettle. Every thing is growing except the potatoes. I think something is eating the lettuce.

I read a little bit more of Dickens. I wonder what the message meant when it said RECALLED TO LIFE. That is a strange thing to say but it was getting dark and I could not see very well so I quit reading. Tomorrow I will read more.

June 27, 1914 I worked so late I did not read more of my book

John read *A Tale of Two Cities* as often as he could. Sometimes he had amusing comments, "Dickens was a good story teller but he tells stories much better than I read them." He often had to read chapters twice or three times to be sure he understood them.

His friendship with the big wolf continued, and he sought ways to get him to come closer. One entry said, "He stood and watched me while I watched him. Tomorrow I will leave some fried bread for him closer to my tent. He will not be like a dog friend but it is wonderful."

Near the end of June, Jed told him about a Fourth of July celebration in Ozone and urged him to attend. At first John was reluctant because he remembered what happened in Blackfoot at this celebration. However, Jed convinced him to attend to get acquainted with his neighbors, and assured him the people in Ozone didn't get drunk.

His work was going well, and by the first of July, he'd cleared more than a third of his land. One more strip and he'd be nearly half finished. Encouraged by his efforts, he almost decided to stay on the job and not attend the celebration, but he needed a rest and this was a chance to get away for a while.

Chapter Four
Sunshine and flowers

At the Fourth of July Celebration, spirits were high, anticipation filled the air, and little clumps of people discussed the things that mattered: their church, the crops, the weather, the price of wheat. Kids filled the air with screams and dust. Farmers and ranchers brought stock for riding and roping, and a large corral was prepared for a rodeo. Logs provided seating. Horses raced on the main wagon roads, and people lined up to cheer their favorites. Ladies served food from a temporary kitchen. Cloth covered pies awaited the pie-eating contest. A shaded bower built of posts covered with leafy aspen branches provided shade for the tables where people ate, visited, or just rested out of the sun. A man played a piano accompanied by a violin and a Jew's harp on the speaker's stand near the bower. It was a welcome celebration where there was little entertainment outside the church or school or home.

As John watched, John Molen, master of ceremonies, bellowed, "Ladeees and gentlemen, and you kids! It's time for the sack races. The first race will be for boys six to eight years old."

Eagerly, ten flushed little boys rushed forward to be fitted with sacks and lined up. The announcer shouted, "All ready?" Immediately, one boy fell down in his eagerness to be first off the starting line, and had to be set back on his feet.

"Ready? One for the money, two for the show, three to get ready, and four to GO!" Like ten inexperienced frogs, they hopped toward the finish line. None made it. One little boy tried running with short steps instead of hopping, but when he started to fall, he let loose, ran out of his sack, and fell down.

The sacks were gathered and the next age group called with only slightly better results. Most of the sixteen-year-old boys made it.

The three-legged race caused almost as much confusion and at least as much shouting and laughter. With left legs tied to right legs, two boys staggered to the finish line on three legs. The winners, although not truly on three legs, arrived at the finish line with one boy more or less carrying the other.

The main foot race, the "way up there and back" race, about a quarter of a mile, took the steam out of all but the most unlikely winner, a fat lad from Canyon Creek. As he crossed the finish line, red faced, arms and legs pumping, his grim expression exploded into a smile. When Mrs. Larsen handed him his prize, a bottle of soda pop, he slumped to the ground and said, "I didn't think I'd make it, but I just kept goin' and goin' and goin', and I made it." Those near enough to hear him cheered, then laughed when he announced, "Now I'm ready for the pie-eatin' contest."

The smells from the food lured John to buy a roast pork sandwich for a nickel from Mrs. Holmquist. "In Norway, we grow pigs. The biggest and best pigs in the world. Much better than the pigs here. Where do you come from?"

"I have a homestead on Bull's Fork, ma'am."

"Is your family with you?"

"No, ma'am. I don't have a family. When I have a crop and a cabin, it will be time to find a wife."

"You need a wife now. I can help."

"No, ma'am. All I have is a tent to live in. That's no place for a woman."

"Do you have a spring? I wish we had a spring. The boys carry water a mile."

"Yes, ma'am, I have a small spring."

"That's good. Do you have livestock?"

"No, ma'am. I still have to build a place for them."

"Have you not got a horse to ride?"

"No, ma'am."

"I don't know if it is true, but I heard a man from Gray's Lake brought a horse. He says it never has been rode. He'll give it to anybody can ride it."

John was interested, but he had no place to keep animals. Regardless, he asked, "Where is it? I'd like to see it."

"If it *is* true, it's probably down by the rodeo some place. You sure you don't want help to find a wife? I know some pretty girls waiting for you."

"Thank you for the sandwich, ma'am. I'll go take a look at the corral." He'd gone only a few yards when he met Henry Monson. They shook hands and helloed each other. "I see you took the day off. Good. How's the clearing coming?"

"Pretty good, sir. I think I'll finish this year, and Mr. Fogelsong said he'd sell me a few sacks to plant winter wheat. Is Mrs. Monson with you?"

"Yes, she's somewhere gabbing, probably with Mrs. Campbell. They've been friends for years. Freddie is with her. The rest of the family went to a church doings in Ammon. Where are you headed?"

"I heard about a horse I can have if I can ride it. I was on my way down to the corrals to look at it. I'd like to know what you think of it, if you have the time, sir."

"Sure, glad to. You missed a good show when we filed on your homestead, Alan Denning was glad you were able to get something. But Rose just about exploded. 'We don't need any half-breed parasites homesteading anywhere in this country.' When she found out there was nothing she could do about it, she stalked back to her desk and sulked. You sure hit a nerve with her."

"Mr. Monson, sir, why does she hate Indians so much?"

"Well, it's kind of a weird story. Several years ago, her father got drunk in a beer joint in Blackfoot. An Indian, stone sober, came in to buy a soda pop. Rose's father decided to pick a fight, so he went over to the Indian and tried to push him away from the bar. The Indian resisted and grabbed the edge of the bar. Jack pulled a knife and began slashing at the Indian. The Indian just stayed out of the way and it made Jack mad, so he raised the knife up in the air and stumbled just as he tried to stab the Indian. He fell on the knife, and it went through his heart. End of Jack. When all the witnesses got through in court, the Indian was set free. Rose didn't like that and tried everything she could think of to put the Indian in jail for killing her father, but everybody just laughed at her. She's been down on Indians ever since. There's Lydia."

Before John had time to turn, he felt a small foot stomp hard on his. "Ouch! That hurt!" he exclaimed according to the ritual and, hopping on the other foot, turned to the giggling boy at his leg. "Now it's my turn." He missed and the boy laughed louder than ever.

Freddie turned. "Mamma! Here's John!" he shouted.

Lydia and Mrs. Campbell joined them. Lydia held out her hand and a smile lit her face. "Hello, John. We were hoping to see you here. We were so happy when we got your letter. You're welcome any time."

Questions about his progress followed until Henry saw an opening and said, "John asked me to take a look at a horse. We'll see you later." With Freddie holding fast to John's hand, they left.

A group of men were talking at one corner of the corral. Short introductions brought John and Henry into the conversation. James Sibbett pointed to a haltered horse tied to a corral post. "That's him. Beautiful horse, isn't he? But he's the meanest one I've ever had anything to do with. I think he's too good a horse to just throw away, but we haven't got the time to fool with him. That's why I'm offering him to anybody who can ride him."

Immediately John knew the shiny black gelding with a white star in his forehead was the horse he wanted. Without turning he asked Henry, "What do you think of him?"

"Looks like a damned fine horse to me. Do you think you can ride him?"

"I won't know till I try, will I? It would be awful nice to have a horse, though. It takes me almost three hours on foot from my place to here."

"Have you got a place to keep him?"

"Not yet, sir. I'd have to build a corral and a shelter for him.

John turned to Mr. Sibbett. "When can I try him?"

"Well, there's a couple guys already. The rodeo committee thought the best time would be at the end of the rodeo. Sort of like saving the best till last."

Henry and John, with Freddie hanging onto his hand, left to see what else the celebration offered. The pie-eating contest was next, and the fat boy was in position, ready to start. John Molen mounted the stand, stopped the music, and bellowed, "Ladees and gentlemen! The tables are set. The pies are cut into four pieces to a pie. The seats are mostly full. The contest is about to begin. Gather round for the fastest, funniest, messiest, most fulfilling of all contests! All the pie you can eat in ten minutes. We have six boys and two girls. There's still room for two more."

A teenage boy and a girl from Sellars Creek took the empty places. "Is everything ready, ladies?" A voice said everything was ready. "Then let's begin. Ten minutes to eat all you can hold. One for the money, two for the show, three to get ready and four to GO!"

Pieces of pie were shoved into wide-stretched mouths like wood into a potbellied stove. The fat boy put his first piece in all at once, then gagged. A tall, skinny lad from Ozone ate in huge bites.

The teenager couple fed each other resulting in pie-smeared faces. Some contestants looked as if they dove face first into the piece in front of them. And some of them did.

A quiet kid from Dehlin ate steadily, stopping only to breathe. The Empey girl couldn't finish her second piece. The leaders eyed each other, and started another piece. The others, realizing they didn't have a chance, slowed or stopped. Laughter, in bursts and spurts rang in waves through the crowd. By the time Dehlin had eaten nine pieces, Ozone picked up his ninth, but couldn't open his mouth. He dropped it on the table, turned green and left. You could hear his mother shouting above the retching, "That was a dumb stunt. All that good pie going to waste! You ought to be ashamed of yourself. Just look at your clothes. I have enough to do without washing clothes all the time. At your age, too." The kid from Dehlin won.

The scene was chaos. Uneaten pieces of pie were gathered and taken away. Remnants were dumped from the planks resting on sawhorses to serve as tables, then wiped with damp rags to complete the job, and the food servers resumed their efforts.

The rodeo was the main event, and the stock was calves to be roped or ridden. When the announcer called, many of the boys and a few girls scrambled to the corrals. The calves were to be ridden as caught, and each contestant drew a number to determine his or her turn. Although most parents wouldn't allow their children under eight to ride, one six-year-old boy carried number three.

On his way to the corral, John heard his name called. "John Fountain! John!" Mrs. Holmquist, leading a very nice looking girl, shouted from about ten feet away. "I want you to meet someone. This is Delia Stewart. She teaches school in Rigby, and she's here for the summer. I thought you two should get acquainted because you will be coming to Ozone once in a while. Delia, this is the boy I told you about."

The girl blushed and muttered, "Glad to meet you."

Put off by Mrs. Holmquist's forwardness John replied, "Hello," and then didn't know what else to say. His mind was on a black gelding, not a pretty school teacher. After an embarrassing pause, he stammered, "I'm on my way to the corral with Mr. Monson. I think the rodeo is about to start. Maybe I'll see you later."

Mrs. Holmquist didn't give up. "Why don't you go with him?"

"I don't know, he's with somebody."

"That don't matter. Go ahead."

The young woman followed the two men and Freddie down to the corral. When they reached the log seats, Henry excused himself, and took a reluctant Freddie to join his wife sitting not far away.

John, more uncomfortable than ever, turned to Delia and asked, "Have you been to many rodeos here?"

"Only one. John, I. . . I'm sorry. Mrs. Holmquist has been playing matchmaker ever since I got here. She's embarrassed me several times. I'm sorry. I'll go now."

John's manners returned, and he turned to face Delia. She was about his age, most shapely and very pretty. "No, don't go. I was surprised, too. Mrs. Holmquist sold me a sandwich when I first got here. She asked a lot of questions when I told her I don't have a family. I don't even have a horse. That's why I'm going to try to ride Mr. Sibbett's horse. I don't have anything except my land." Again he looked at Delia and their eyes met. "Do you live in Ozone?"

"I'm spending the summer with my aunt and uncle. They live on Rock Creek. It's about four miles or so south of Ozone. Where is your homestead?" Again she blushed, surprised at her question.

"On Bull's Fork. It's about eleven miles from here."

"Oh, I've been there. It's a pretty stream in summer. Do you know where Fogelsongs live?"

"Yes, Mr. Fogelsong is my neighbor about a mile downstream."

The conversation went on. The rodeo came and went, cheers and moans unheeded, and neither John nor Delia knew who won what. But John heard the last announcement: "Ladeees and gentlemen, I have the pleasure and honor to announce we have a wild horse for someone to ride, if he can. The first candidate, or should I say victim, is Reuben Donan from over Cliff Creek way. The second victim is Glenn Gould from Ozone. And then there's John Fountain from Bull's Fork, if the horse is tame enough by then."

Some people started to leave, but stopped. This wasn't part of the rodeo, but it sounded interesting, so they returned to their seats. The horse was brought resisting into a chute, blindfolded to quiet him, and saddled. A confident, but nervous Reuben eased himself onto the saddle. The blindfold was removed, the gate opened, and the horse leaped out. In less than three seconds, Reuben was sitting on the ground. Glenn had seen enough. The horse did a crazy dance jumping into the air and shaking. Glenn decided he didn't even want to try. The horse was just too wild.

"Still want to try, John?"

A cheer went up when John waved his hand but he paid no further attention to what went on in the crowd. He thought only of the horse. He'd watched the horse during Reuben's short ride and thought he knew what to do. When the horse was wrestled into the chute again, John asked that they take the saddle off. One of the cowboys exclaimed, "What? Take the saddle off? You're nuts! You can't ride this thing even *with* a saddle. He'll kill you if you try it bareback."

"I have never ridden with a saddle, sir. I can tell more what he'll do if I can feel him. But I'd like to have a longer rope on the halter, in case he throws me."

Mr. Sibbett heard John and said, "Okay, take the saddle off. Somebody get a longer rope. I'd like to see what this guy can do."

The cowboys took the saddle off and tied a twenty foot rope on the halter. John coiled the rope in his hand and lowered himself onto the horse. He gave the signal. The horse sprang from the chute and after a series of jumps and shakes, disposed of John in about six seconds. But John landed on his feet and hung onto the rope, running with the horse and keeping constant pressure on the rope until the animal stopped. Slowly coiling the rope, he moved in speaking softly. The gelding stood still until John had coiled half the rope in his hand, then reared up and struck out with his forefeet. Staying out of the horse's range, John began again with his constant pressure. Again and again, the horse reared up and tried to get him, but he was always out of range. After several minutes of coaxing and pulling, John

46

got close, the horse keeping his eyes on his new enemy. When John reached its side, the horse turned his head toward John just as he grabbed its shoulder, and, like a spring suddenly released sprang onto its back. The crowd thought he had bitten John on the butt and laughter rippled through it. Screaming, the horse leaped straight into the air, shaking himself like a whip. John tightened the rope, pulling the horse's head to one side. Turning, bucking, jumping, whirling, rearing, he could not shake the thing loose. Once John almost fell, but pulled himself back up quickly. Slowly the wild horse tired and began to run, jumping and bucking, unable to look straight ahead as John held the halter rope tight. When the bucking stopped, John jabbed his heels into the horse's side, relaxed the rope, and yelled, "EEEEEE Yaaasaaaaa! Haaaaaaaaaa!" Suddenly free, the gelding flew around the corral, tired, frightened, and beaten. Knowing the horse would attempt to jump out of the corral, John pulled hard again on the halter rope. Every time the horse slowed, John yelled and kicked him to make him run some more. Mr. Sibbett and the three cowboys watched with a mixture of fear and admiration while John gained control of the wildest horse ever born on the Sibbett ranch. When the horse slowed, John urged him to run some more, and when he refused, guided him, lathered with sweat, blowing and panting, to where the owner waited. The audience stood up and cheered.

"That's the goddamnedest ride I ever saw! Where the hell did you learn to break horses? I swear you could read that horse's mind," James Sibbett exclaimed.

John, himself winded, puffed, "I never learned, sir. I just had to do it once with my own horse."

Mr. Sibbett looked at his cowboys. They nodded. "How would you like a job on my ranch? A dollar a day and food and a bed. We could use you."

"No, thank you, sir. I'm homesteading on Bull's Fork. Is the horse really mine to keep?"

"Jim Sibbett never went back on his word. I need a piece of paper to make it legal." One of the cowboys found a stray piece of paper and produced a pencil. He wrote, "I, James Sibbett sold this black gelding with the white star in his forehead to. . . What's your name, again?"

"John Fountain, sir."

"to John Fountain on the 4th of July, 1914 for a good price. James Sibbett." He handed the paper to John. "Keep it in case you ever need it. I still think you'd make a good hand on my ranch, and if you ever change your mind, come and see me. What a ride! I thought he had you once, but you got back up. *Can* you read his mind?"

"No, sir, but without the saddle, I could tell about what he was going to do by the way he moved. Thank you, sir. Does the horse have a name?"

"Not one you'd tell your mother."

"I'll call him Shoni. How old is he, sir?"

"He's just about four. By the way, you can keep the halter and the rope. I don't know who the rope belongs to."

The crowd thinned out, most of them homeward bound. The others, nearly all Ozone people, sat around visiting. John turned to look for the Monsons and nearly bumped into Delia.

"You were magnificent, John!" And then, "I hope we can see each other again," and blushed.

John's complexion didn't provide for blushing, but his face got very warm. "Now I have a horse, maybe we can. I have to go now to tell the Monsons good-bye. And good-bye to you, ma'am." He left Delia with a smile on her face.

"Well, well, John. It looks like you have a lady admirer. How did it go with her?" asked Henry.

"She's a nice lady, sir."

Mrs. Monson had to know more. "What did you talk about? I don't think either of you saw any of the rodeo. Every time I looked over, both of you were talking. Come on now, what did you talk about?"

"Mostly me, I think. She had to know everything."

"Did you tell her you're part Shoshoni?"

"Yes, ma'am."

"What did she say?"

"She said she was part English, ma'am."

"Will you be seeing more of each other?"

"I don't know, ma'am. We might."

"John, you're disgusting. That pretty girl is crazy about you, and you act like she's some guy you just met. Don't you have any feelings for her after spending the afternoon in a huddle?"

"What kind of feelings, ma'am?"

"Good feelings. You know, like she's the girl for you, or you can't wait to see her again. Nice, warm feelings."

"I think she's a nice lady, ma'am."

"John!"

Henry ended the exchange. "Didn't you see how embarrassed she was when that older lady brought her to meet John? I think we should just let things take their course. John, where will you keep your new horse?"

"I have to build a corral. I've got a lot of aspen and an ax, but I'll have to borrow Mr. Fogelsong's shovel to dig post holes."

Henry looked at Lydia. "How would you like to go camping tonight?"

"What? Where?"

"At John's homestead. Then I can help him build a corral tomorrow. I've got a shovel in the back of the buggy. Besides, you haven't given him your little gift or the soap you're so proud of. The neighbors are still here. We can ask them to take care of the kids tonight and tell them we'll be home tomorrow. I think Freddie would like that, wouldn't you, Freddie?"

Freddie's sudden smile said more than words, "Can we, Mamma?"

Lydia tendered a few halfhearted objections but gave in. They bought some food, and talked to their Ammon neighbors. They invited John into their buggy, but he said he'd rather ride Shoni if he could. Rested, Shoni resisted but John's soft words calmed him enough so he could spring onto his back. He bucked half heartedly but finally settled down to being obnoxious. He tried to bite the man on his back, and got a slap in the nose. When he settled down, they left.

About half way home, John let the halter rope loose, yelled, EEEEEEYaaaaaa HAAAaaaaa, and Shoni took off down the wagon road free to run. John let him go, feeling in his legs every move the horse made, in case he got contrary again, until Shoni tired. Then they returned to the buggy, both panting.

"Gee, John, you sounded just like a Indian," Freddie exclaimed.

"Gee, Freddie, I *am* an Indian. Didn't you know that?"

"Yeah, but you don't act like a Indian most of the time. Will you teach me to yell like that?"

"Sure, but not while I'm riding Shoni."

At the camp, John staked Shoni out in a grassy area near the garden, and they ate what Mrs. Monson brought, then talked till late and went to bed. Freddie started the night under John's blanket outside, but when the coyotes howled, he left and spent the rest of the night safely between his parents in the tent under the quilt Lydia brought to John.

Henry and John started chopping poles at sunrise, and by early afternoon had a small corral around the horse. Lydia marveled at John's garden. She praised his pleasant little cove and everything in it, then launched into questions about the "cute little school teacher."

John's answers were just as noncommittal as the day before, but she persisted noting how much nicer the place would be with a woman's touch until Henry told her John would make up his own mind. John killed two sage hens with his slingshot, and gave them to the Monsons before they left. Lydia gave him two bars of her homemade soap and a simple, hand-tied, woolen quilt.

July 5, 1914 I am glad I went to the rodeo in Ozone yesterday. I won a beautiful fast horse. He threw me off once, but I knew why and when I got back on him I rode him till he quit. I named him Shoni. The Monsons came with me and they had Freddie with them. Mr. Monson helped me make a corral for Shoni today. Mrs. Monson gave me a quilt and two more bars of soap. I don't know if I should put this in my journal. I met a nice lady named Delia Stewart. We talked during the rodeo and she watched me ride my horse. She said she wanted to see me again. Miss Stewart is a very pretty lady. I must go back to work."

Every day for the next few weeks, he rode Shoni, and spent as much time as he could getting acquainted. Having the horse also provided an incentive to work harder. He wrote, "The work seems to be easier than it was at first." His plans included visits to Ammon and to Delia Stewart, and to his mother. His world was expanding.

July 13, 1914 I saw Wolf again this morning. He's not so afraid of me as he was at first. He came in my camp from the hill. I threw him a piece of bannock and he grabbed it and ate it.

I ride Shoni every day. I had to move him to more grass yesterday. I think he has decided to be my friend. He lets me get on his back every time. I think I will ride him to Ammon next weekend. I have three strips done now. It is 890 steps long and 350 steps wide. I think another strip will make it about half done. I think the part I haven't cleared should be easier to finish than what I have done so far. I have read more of the two cities story. The third chapter started with something I had not thought about. How each man and woman in the world is different. In the mind of every single man is a different kind of thought. Even in big cities and in small teepees each of us is different. The Monsons are nice people but they are different than I am and each one of them is different than each of the others. I never have thought about that before. I think it is a wonderful thing. I will talk to miss Edwards about that. I did not understand the rest of the chapter. I don't know how any body could be buried for 18 years and then be dug up. I think Mr. Dickens didn't know much about dead people but he kept saying it over and over. "Buried how long? Almost eighteen years. You had abandoned all hope of being dug out? Long ago." Maybe that is what the message is RECALLED TO LIFE. I have read that chapter two times but I don't know for sure what it means. I must think about it.

Displeased with his journal entries, John rode his horse to Ammon, stayed with the Monsons, and took his notebook to Miss Edwards. She read his entries and showed him how to improve them. On July 20, he reported, "I went to visit Miss Edwards and she helped me a lot with my journal. She told me there is a difference between how to say you are happy. She told me I was happy on my homestead, and I should be glad I have it. That isn't a big difference, but it is different. And she said I could use contractions instead of two words. I couldn't remember exactly how to do it, so I didn't before. I went back and changed most of them.

"She teased me about Miss Stewart on the 4th of July. She said she knows Miss Stewart but not very well. She was surprised I had won Shoni at the rodeo when I told her about it. I am very glad I went to see her."

John reported that Mrs. Monson started asking again about Delia Stewart, and it made him wonder himself what his feelings were. He told her, "I don't know how I feel about her. I just talked to her for a couple of hours."

That night he burned a pile of sagebrush, and danced and sang around the fire. His Indianness would not be suppressed.

Chapter Five
Indian Summer

July 23, 1914 Today four Shoshoni Indians came to my camp just at noon. I cooked a rabbit for them and gave them some bread. I knew two of them were from Fort Hall. The other two were strangers to me but they were very friendly until they got ready to leave. Then they said they would take Shoni with them.

The Indians came to John's tent when they smelled food cooking and asked for something to eat. They were surprised when he answered in Shoshoni, and they ate together. They left nothing John offered them. After two hours, they got ready to leave but told John there were four of them and they would take his horse and there was nothing he could do about it. John was sure Shoni wouldn't tolerate them and sat back as they expected him to. The surprise came when the first one entered the corral. Shoni reared and charged the Indian, who ran around the corral with the horse chasing him. Finally he jumped between the poles to safety. The other three laughed at the circus in the corral until the leader pointed to another and told him to get on the horse.

He ran into the corral and grabbed the halter rope, but Shoni bit his arm when he tried to mount. He ran screaming and bleeding and sat on the ground outside with Shoni watching him. The third managed to sneak close enough to jump on Shoni's back but lasted just long enough for the horse to jump into the air and shake him off outside the corral. He lit on his face in a pile of Shoni's leftovers. The horse stood still while the leader himself entered the arena. Shoni offered no objection when the last Indian mounted him, stood still for a moment, then threw that one out of the corral with one mighty heave.

Painfully, the four of them got back on their own horses and told John he could keep his wild horse. They didn't want him anyway. As they rode slowly away, John took his slingshot from his pocket, filled the empty pocket with rocks, opened the corral gate, leaped on Shoni and, yelling EEEEEEYaaaaaa HAAAaaaaa! lit out after them. When the Indians saw him coming at them on the back of the very horse they tried to steal, they prodded their own horses but couldn't outrun Shoni who was probably having more fun than John. He seemed to know exactly what to do. The barrage from John's slingshot found its mark, on an Indian's back or his horse's rump. As he pulled up to the last rider, Shoni reached down and bit the Indian's horse, which jumped to kick at Shoni, and unseated its rider.

John chased the other Indians till he ran out of rocks. On the way back, the unseated Indian was sitting in the sagebrush. Shoni snorted. He jumped to his feet and ran toward his retreating comrades.

All the way back John talked to Shoni and at the corral took the halter off to let him free. He sat on the top rail and watched Shoni roll in the grass and dust. The horse stood up, shook himself, and walked to John. The bond between man and horse was sealed.

Confident he'd gained the friendship of his horse, John let him loose without the halter. He wrote, "When I got back to my tent I took the halter off and let him free. I know I took the chance he might run away. He didn't. He stayed close to me at the tent eating the grass. Then I went into his corral and he followed me and waited while I closed the gate."

When the wolf showed up at the end of July, John wrote he didn't seem to be well. He hesitated to eat, and probably wouldn't live much longer.

He continued clearing his land even though the heat had become intense. "The weather was hot today and I drank two pots full of water. I quit for a while, and waded into my spring and splashed water on me. It was very cold, but I was able to work almost till dark."

John wrote often of his growing interest in Delia Stewart, and went to visit her. She wasn't home but her aunt said she'd be there the next weekend. He stopped at Otteson's store on the way home and found out his credit had reached $18.24.

August 4, 1914 I have more than half the field cleared now. I have finished two more strips. That makes 550 steps wide and 890 long. The homestead was 890 steps by 890 steps altogether. The work is going much faster now I have learned a few secrets of chopping down sagebrush. Sometimes I can just hit it with the back of the ax and it breaks off and I don't have to chop. Taking it to a pile to burn takes most of the time. I have nine black spots in the field where I've burned it. Maybe it would go faster if I burned it more often. I'll try it tomorrow.

Today a rattlesnake tried to bite me. There are quite a few rattlesnakes and mostly they just crawl away, but I surprised this one. Every day I take Shoni out for a run. In my camp I let him loose, but I keep him in his corral when

I work. He always stays close and I can call him to me. I pulled a few small carrots today and fed them to him. He sure likes carrots. I hope he doesn't learn how to pull them. I ate a small cucumber this morning. It was the only one that was very big. There are a lot of very small ones but they will grow. I wonder if Mrs. Otteson would like to have some of them. My potatoes are growing very well, but I haven't dug any up to see. Next year, I'll start my garden earlier with more things in it. Day after tomorrow, I'll ride over to see if Miss Stewart is home. I think about her a lot. She is very nice, and I think she likes me, too. Maybe she would be a nice wife for me some time.

August 7, 1914 I have a wonderful life! Every day I can see what I did during the day. Clearing the sagebrush off my fields seems to have slowed down but I know it hasn't. I am past the middle, and when I look back at what is clear, it is bigger than the rest. I worked hard today and quit before it was dark. Shoni was waiting for me. When I got to the corral gate, it looked like somebody had tried to open it. If the Indians came back, I hope they had the same surprise. Maybe I didn't close it right. Tomorrow I will ride Shoni to Rock Creek. I am anxious to see Miss Stewart. She is a very nice lady.

Now I'll read Chapter 4 in my *A Tale Of Two Cities* book, again. I want to be sure I understand what Mr. Dickens is writing about. It should help me write in my journal too. But I won't ever write the way he does. He spends too much time without saying very much.

I am happy I might see Miss Stewart tomorrow, but I am afraid. I don't know how to talk to her. She will probably think I am stupid.

Although John had talked to her during the rodeo, she asked the questions and he answered them. He just didn't know how to start a conversation with this fascinating girl.

Chapter Six
Lightening Strikes

All the way to Rock Creek, John thought about what he would say to Delia Stewart. She had sparked a curiosity and it had to be satisfied, but he was afraid he'd say something silly or stupid.

He arrived about eleven and saw her barefoot and bare-legged sitting on an overturned bucket in the yard. She was wearing a loose, flowered, cotton dress hiked above her knees, and her hair hung in random locks over her face as she bent over her work. The apron in her lap was full of new peas she was shelling into a pan beside her, and the sight of her startled John. A sudden, warm rush took his courage away. He rode past without stopping.

Delia, intent on her task, heard John's horse, but she didn't look up till he was almost out of sight. Oh dear, she thought, I didn't expect him till this afternoon. Look at me. I have to comb my hair. Not as shy as John, she hailed him, "John, I'm here. Over here!"

Turning his horse, he shouted, "Hello, Miss Stewart." As he came closer he told a small white lie to hide his embarrassment. "I guess I wasn't paying attention to what I was doing."

"I was sure you'd come this weekend, but I didn't expect you till this afternoon. I'm sorry, I must look a mess."

"You look fine to me."

Delia blushed. "Then you don't know much about how a girl feels when she's caught doing chores. Thank you, anyway."

"You weren't home last Saturday, so I decided I'd come again today. It doesn't take very long, now that I have a horse."

"Come in." John followed Delia into the house, a simple two-room cabin with a wood floor. It was clean and neat. A huge stove, a table, and four chairs dominated one end of the first room, and light from a window over the kitchen counter cast the filmy shadow of its lacy curtain onto the table. Another window next to the door lit the rest of the room. A narrow bed provided sitting space. "I'll call my aunt and uncle so you can meet them."

"I met them last Saturday when I was here."

"Oh, yes, of course. I'll let them know you're here anyway. You'll have to stay for dinner."

Delia left, and John watched her as she walked toward the barn. In a minute she returned. "Uncle Bill's mare is having a colt, and they're busy right now. They'll come soon. Isn't the miracle of birth wonderful?"

"Yes, ma'am."

"My name is Delia, not *ma'am*. You're not one of my students, you know."

"Yes, ma. . . I mean Delia. I'll try to remember." John felt his face grow warmer. "I. . . I guess I'm not used to talking to girls."

"That's kind of sweet. You mean you've never had a girl friend?"

"I had a girl friend, sort of. She was a Shoshoni girl named Willow."

"Let's go pick some more peas, then we'll finish shelling them. But first I have to comb my hair. It's a mess." John watched, fascinated and flushed, watching her breasts rise and fall when she combed her hair. Out in the garden, they picked more peas. Realizing her dress was open at the neck when she bent over, Delia pulled it close and picked with one hand.

They shelled the rest of the peas, and in a few minutes, Mrs. Rawlins came. "It's nice to see you again. I guess Delia has already invited you to dinner. Is that the horse you won at the rodeo?" Once more, John explained his horse's name. She said, "You're so polite, and you speak so well. Where did you learn that?"

"My father taught me."

"I wish some of the fathers around here would teach their sons the same things."

Dinner was hearty, ending with apple pie. Afterward, they all went to the barn and looked at the new colt, wobbly on spindle legs, seeking its mother's teats and swaying as it sucked, its tail signaling everything was in order.

Delia turned to John. "Let's ride over to Canyon Creek. I'll get my horse."

Her aunt added, "You can meet several people there if the store is open. You must have met a lot at the rodeo, though."

"Yes, ma'am, I met a lot of people. One of them was Mrs. Holmquist. She introduced me to Delia."

"Oh, yes, Mrs. Holmquist. She's a fine woman, but sometimes she tries too hard to make people happy."

John was surprised at how easily Delia saddled her horse. Finished, she turned to him. "Don't you have a saddle?"

"No, I've never ridden a horse with a saddle. I like to feel what he's doing. That's how I was able to stay on Shoni at the rodeo."

"No bridle either?"

"No, but some day I'll get one. I really don't need that kind of control for Shoni. I guide him with the halter rope and my knees."

They rode in silence at an easy lope for a few minutes, Delia leading. John watched her as they rode along. She made him feel warm all over, and she was much easier to talk to than he feared. Yes, he thought, she might be a good woman to have for a wife. "How far is it to Canyon Creek?"

"Oh, about four or five miles, I guess. They've moved the schoolhouse from Birch Creek to Canyon Creek to use for a store. A man named Orin Bone bought it."

"They moved a school house?"

"Yes, but it wouldn't fit in the dug way going down the hill to Canyon Creek, so a bunch of the neighbors dug and blasted a space big enough to get it through."

Only the sound of the horses' hooves broke the silence. John wasn't the only one thinking about the other. Delia reined her horse in slightly to let John get ahead and watched as he swayed on his horse. In her imagination, she took off his shirt and saw a body with muscles like wire stretched around an armature. His buttocks and legs seemed to be a part of the horse, and the shape of his back was. . . . erotic. Mrs. Holmquist was right when she said he was a good man.

Delia rode up beside John and said, "It must be hard to clear 160 acres of land alone. How do you do it?"

"With an ax mostly. Then I pile the brush up and burn it."

"I mean, do you just go out and cut down whatever you come to, or do you have a system?"

"I guess I have a system. I clear strips about a hundred steps wide. I don't know if that's the best way, but it works all right for me."

"What are your plans when you finish?"

"Well, I hope to finish before winter and get a crop planted before it snows. Then after I've got a cabin and a barn and a bigger corral built, I guess I'll start a family." They covered the rest of the distance at an easy lope.

Orin Bone met them at the Canyon Creek store, and with introductions complete, they spent half an hour wasting conversation on each other. A huge, bearded man wearing a stocking cap came in and bought a small sack of potatoes and some sugar. Orin introduced him to John. Delia already knew him. Delia said, "Mr. Rudolph, how are you? We don't see much of you. I guess you're pretty busy these days."

A deep voice, thick with a German accent, rumbled from somewhere down in his huge body. "Ya, I been busy. I haf cows to feed and pigs to swill and work in the fields. I haf enough to do to keep myself from trouble."

"Oh, come now, Mr. Rudolph, you never get into any trouble."

"I try not to. The people sometimes need some help. So I help. It is good for me and good for them, I think. Nice to see you again Miss Stewart. Mr. . . Ah, Ah. . ."

"Fountain, sir. John Fountain."

"Mr. Fountain, I not see you before. You homestead here, ya?"

"Yes, sir. I have a homestead on Bull's Fork."

"Hey, you the guy rode the horse?"

"Yes, sir. He's the black one tied outside."

"Mighty fine animal. You ever race him?"

"No, sir. I never thought of racing him."

"You should. He look like very fast horse. Good-bye."

As he closed the door behind him, John turned to Delia. "He's a giant. Where did he come from?"

"He came from Germany several years ago. He's pretty rough on the outside but has a golden heart. He's a character, but everybody likes him in spite of his smell and the way he looks. He's one citizen people can depend on. Sometimes he shows up at church socials and eats his way through a mountain of food. Shall we go? I'd like to ride down to Willow Creek."

A few minutes later, they sat together listening to the, gurgling, splashing, sometimes quiet, sometimes not, song of Willow Creek. They chose a place where spots of sunshine freckled the ground. Delia, as usual, had the first word, "We talked during the rodeo, but it seemed I had to ask a question to get you to say anything to me. I know you're shy, and I am, too, around strangers, but we're not strangers any more, and I still have to lead you or you won't talk. Are you really so shy?"

"I guess so. I just don't know what to say to a girl."

"Then tell me about your Indian girl friend."

"We were good friends."

"John! I know that. Why do I have to pry every word out of you like some of my students? What did you do together?"

"Most of the time we talked about what was going on in the village."

"Didn't you go anywhere together? See other people? You see, I don't know how Indians socialize. I just want to learn."

"We weren't alone together very much. Indian mothers are pretty strict about their daughters."

"But you were alone together sometimes, right?"

"Yes, once in a while we'd meet down beside the Snake River."

"And?"

"We just met, that's all."

"Did her mother know?"

"Oh, no!"

"What did you do?"

"Miss Stew. . . Delia. That's too personal for me to tell you."

Delia blushed a violent red. "Oh, I'm sorry. I shouldn't have pried so hard. Forgive me?"

"OK."

This time Delia didn't know what to say. She'd learned a secret John had never revealed to anyone, and she knew it. She was ashamed and at the same time even more fascinated by him. "I truly am sorry for prying. Let's talk about your homestead." John's face brightened, and he told her in detail about clearing the land, trapping rabbits, killing grouse with his slingshot, and about the Indians who tried to steal his horse.

"Oh, I'd like to have seen that. I bet those Indians won't come back and try again. That must have been some sight. You chasing them throwing rocks at them. Shoni must be a wonderful horse."

"He's a lot better horse than my first one. He was a pinto about the same size as Shoni but not nearly as fast. He came to me when I whistled a certain way. I'm trying to teach Shoni to do the same."

"Your father must have been a good man, but what brought him to Fort Hall?"

"He was a sort of adventurer. He left Quebec and his wife and her two children and never saw them again. He was sixty-two when I was born. I guess to make up for not having any children in Quebec, he tried to make a gentleman out of me, even in the Indian camp. He taught me English and French and. . ."

"French? You speak *French*?"

"Yes. But I don't read and write French. I learned to read and write English in Ammon. Mostly Miss Edwards taught me."

"Say something in French to me."

"What do you want me to say?"

"Oh, anything."

"*Oui. Non.*"

"What does that mean?"

"Yes and no. Two words."

"Say 'I love you,"

"Why?"

"I just want to hear how it sounds."

"*Je t'aime.*"

"So little? I thought it took a lot of words to translate from English to another language."

"No. That's all. I feel funny doing this." Actually, John *did* feel funny. He'd just for the first time in his life ever told any girl he loved her in any language.

"I'm sorry. I don't want you to feel uncomfortable. It sounded so romantic. I'm just curious about everything. I promise I won't ask any more questions like that. What was it like growing up as an Indian?"

"It was different. Parents told their children legends about everything while they were growing up, and we had dances and sings and other celebrations. After my father died, my mother told me I should live in the white man's world, and learn to be like him. I'm trying to, but there are so many things I have never known before. For instance, you're the first white girl I ever knew who was about my age. At least I think you're about my age."

"I'm twenty-two."

"I'm twenty."

"Do you ever get the urge to go back to the Indian ways?"

"Sometimes. And sometimes I do. Once in a while when I've worked hard and I'm very happy, I dance and sing around the fire I build to burn the brush. It gives me a good feeling and I feel closer to nature."

"You sing and dance alone? Out in your field?"

"Yes. When I'm happy I love to sing of my happiness while I dance. It would be better if I had a drum, though. A drum makes the dance better."

"I'd love to see you dancing around a big fire and singing, while the flames leap into the sky and sparks fly all around. It sounds so. . . so. . . so exciting, romantic, so adventurous."

"I never thought of it that way. Last night I did it because I was coming to see you today." John felt his face get warm. "Maybe we should go, now."

"Not yet. Please. What can we talk about that will keep you here?"

"I don't know very much about you. Let's talk about you."

"There isn't much to talk about. I was born in Rigby, went to school there and to college in Logan, Utah. Then back to teach in Rigby. I'm hoping for a job in school administration before I die. I love to teach young minds and watch them grow. Would you like to come to my school some time and tell some of the Shoshoni legends to the students? I'll bet they'd be fascinated. Are there many?"

"I wouldn't know how to tell them. Yes, there are quite a few. Some of them shouldn't be told to white kids, though."

"Why?"

"Well, they're about things white people don't talk about."

"Like what, for instance?"

"Delia, please. It would embarrass me."

"Why would it embarrass you? If they're just legends, I don't see why you'd be embarrassed to talk about them."

"One of them is about how Coyote is the father of all people."

"What's wrong with that?"

"Nothing. It's a Shoshoni legend, and the Shoshonis know that, but it gets very specific about how it happened."

"What do you mean, specific?"

"Well, I. . . I don't know how to tell you."

"Just say it."

"Well, The. . . Coyote. . . You know how babies are born."

"Yes, of course."

"I. . . Well I don't want to say it."

"If it's just a legend. . ."

"Well, Coyote has intercourse with an old woman and her daughter and they had hundreds of babies the next day, and that's how it happened."

Delia's face reddened again, "Oh, good heavens! How awful!" She grew quiet and then said, "Yes, I guess we'd better go."

They rode a long time before John said, "I guess I should have told you something else. I'm sorry if I embarrassed you. The Indians pass these legends down from generation to generation, and the children hear them from the time they understand the language. They don't mean the same things to Indians they do to white men."

Delia was silent, nodding as John spoke till they were almost to her house. "John, can we walk the rest of the way?"

"Sure, I must have embarrassed you awful. You haven't said anything for a long time."

"It's really my fault. Ever since I was a little girl, as long as I can remember, I've been too curious about everything. That's why I've asked you so many questions. But I've gotten to know you very well, I think. And I like you — very much. You're so different from men my age. Jack Sweringen and I are supposed to be a couple in Rigby, but there really isn't anything between us. We go to dances and things like that together, but probably because people there expect us to. But he's not anything like you. I find you very exciting. Oh, I shouldn't have said that."

"I find you exciting, too, and I'm *not* sorry I said that." They had almost reached Delia's house when they stopped and turned to face each other. Excitement and anticipation fired between them. Suddenly Delia threw her arms around John's neck and kissed him fully on the mouth, turned, and leading her horse, ran the rest of the way home. John, shocked and elated, flipped himself aboard Shoni and let out a yell. "Eeeeeeee Yaaaaa Haaaaa!" and horse and rider streaked off toward Bull's Fork.

Chapter Seven
Thunder and Lightening but no Rain

August 12, 1914 I've worked very hard ever since I last saw Delia. I would go to see her Saturday but I think I should work in my field. All of my neighbors have finished threshing and I have two sacks of wheat I bought from Mr. Fogelsong. I think I will start planting in about a week. I probably won't finish clearing this year, but I will have a crop next year.

I read Chapter 5 of the two cities story. At first it was hard to understand, then I realized they were in Paris. They found the girl's father in a room at the top of a bad smelling stairway. Now I know what RECALLED TO LIFE means. The old man was locked in the little room for a long time making shoes.

August 14, 1914 I saw Wolf again this morning. He looks very bad. I gave him two bannocks to eat. I hope he doesn't die, but I know he will some time. It's nice to have Wolf for a friend. He knows I won't hurt him so he comes very close to me. I feel very sorry for him.

John thought often of Delia as he swung his ax and dragged sagebrush to a pile. If he only knew when she'd be home.

When John came into view, Delia's breath caught. She slowed her horse to a walk. She didn't have to take his shirt off mentally. It was already off. Even at a distance she saw his back glistening in the sun. It was just as she had imagined when they rode to Canyon Creek. As she came closer, she could see the paths his sweat made through the dust.

His unshaven face set in determination, John heard only the steady crack of the ax and the rustle of branches as he moved the brush out of the way. She was almost upon him before he knew she was near.

The soft plodding of hooves startled John, and he looked up. He hadn't thought of her for at least five minutes, and there she was, coming toward him. He dropped the ax and waited. Little puffs of dust exploded from her horse's hooves. Her face was flushed, her disheveled hair hung in wisps about her face, and her dress was hiked far up her legs. She stopped a few feet from him, swung out of the saddle, and walked toward him as if driven. She said nothing, and the sight of her there on his land took away John's ability to speak.

They stood facing each other for a long second, their eyes locked like the last time they met. It was excitement and desire waiting only for fleeting indecision. Delia flung herself at him. She hadn't planned it that way, but the sight of this half naked man out in the open field, shining with sweat and streaked with dust, aroused her beyond anything she'd ever known.

"Hey, you'll get all wet!"

"Yes, I know." Her hands ran over his back making muddy streaks. John, lost in innocence and not knowing what he should do to prolong the moment, just stood still. But passion breeds passion, and he returned her embrace.

"What. . . I. . . I never expected you to come here."

"For the past eight days, I've thought of nothing but our last visit. I waited as long as I could to hear from you, but you've been busy, I know, so I came to you. I had to."

"I'm glad you did. I'm still sorry I embarrassed you."

"I deserved to be embarrassed. I asked too many questions. Can we look at your place?"

"If you'll let me wash off first." On the way back to his tent, John asked, "How'd you know where to find me?"

"You told me, don't you remember? You said it was on Bull's Fork about a mile from the Fogelsongs."

At the camp, John headed for the spring, then remembered. She was a lady. "I've got to get this stuff off me. Why don't you go in the tent and wait?" When she was out of sight, he pulled off his shoes and pants and walked into the cold water.

But Delia peeked through the tent flaps, and saw the back of a naked man. Spikes of excitement shot through her. When he turned, she gasped. She'd never seen a man that way. The sight lasted only a second, but it would remain in her memory for the rest of her life. John put his pants on and came into the tent.

"Now I feel better."

Pillows of muscle rippled his stomach, and the sight of his nipples, still erect from the cold water, sent a shiver through her.

"Are you cold?"

"Oh, no. Turn around." Obediently, John turned around. "You missed a spot on your back," she lied. "Let me clean it off."

"There's a rag hanging above the stove, but it's probably dry. I'll wet it for you." He walked the few yards to the spring and returned with the dampened cloth and handed it to her. She wiped it over his broad shoulders and down the middle of his back, then tossed it back above the stove.

"You're clean now."

"Thank you. Let's go." He started to put on his shirt when she reached for him, her hands moving over his chest and shoulders. She pulled his head down and kissed him, again. Her hands flew around to his back and pulled him to her. He felt his passion rise and stepped back, afraid. Although he knew what might come, he didn't know how to act or what to do.

Delia, surprised, released him, "I don't know what to do. You are the very first girl I ever kissed. I. . . well, I just don't know what I should do. Let's go look at my land."

Still excited but also relieved, she said, "Yes, let's do that. That's what I came for. I need to relax a little after the ride out here."

John pulled on his shirt and they left the tent. Delia was as excited about the location as Lydia Monson. She pulled a handful of watercress from the spring and ate it as they walked about. Chokecherries, hanging like tiny bunches of grapes, bent the bushes low. "Oh, the chokecherries are ripe. Why don't you pick some and make some jelly?"

"First, I don't know how to make jelly, and, second, what would I do with so many?"

"Let's pick some anyway. They're good to eat right off the tree."

"I know that. Do you know why they're called *chokecherries*?"

"Yes. Just try one that's not ripe."

They went out into the field, John showing her the places where he danced around the piles of burning brush.

"You have a pile over there. Let's light it and dance around it."

73

"What? You're not serious."

"But I am serious. Let's do it right now."

"I only dance at night. It's much better then."

"Then let's wait till it gets dark."

"But you have to go home, and it'll be dark."

"Oh, John, I'm just too impulsive sometimes. I wanted to surprise you and spend a few hours here, but the sight of you out there working, it. . . it changed everything. I'm sorry. I think I should go, now."

"On the bank of Willow Creek, I said the same thing. You said, 'Not yet' and began asking more questions. I don't want you to go, not now."

They walked in silence several more minutes, each waiting for a magic moment when they could let their feelings lead the way. Delia, retying her shoe, let John get a few steps ahead of her and whispered, "*Je t'aime.*" John heard it but closed his eyes and walked toward the tent. She caught up and slipped her arm through his.

John's thoughts were confused. Delia's visit had sent him off in a new direction, a wild direction that had no direction.

Delia had the same problem. She thought about how her visit had turned out, and suddenly she was ashamed.

"John, I don't think we should see each other again for a long time."

Stung, John faced her. "Why?"

They'd reached the tent, and John held the flap open for her. She hesitated, then went in. "It's just. . . Things are moving too fast. I have to have a chance to let my head catch up to my feelings. I've done something I never, ever thought I'd do. I've been so forward. I've shown you a side of me I didn't want you or anybody to know, a side I didn't know myself and I'm not sorry, just ashamed."

"I don't want to stop seeing you. Let's promise each other we won't let things get out of hand."

"All right. Shake on it?"

Their hands clasped, but only for a second before their lips met. John took over against his own will. Their embrace lasted minutes. Both felt John's arousal, and pulled each other closer. John crooked his finger and lifted her chin. She answered the question in his eyes with a faint nod. He led her toward the bed. She followed. Suddenly, "John, I can't, I can't. I mustn't. John, please. I just can't. I have to go. I have to get away from you. This hasn't turned out anything like I planned."

"I'm sorry, Delia. It got out of hand."

"It's not your fault. I've been throwing myself at you ever since I got here. I don't blame you. I blame myself. I'm ashamed of myself and afraid. Scared silly."

"Of me?"

"Heavens no! Not you. I'm afraid of *me*! I can't handle it! I have to go now. I just *have* to."

Delia Stewart, ashamed, frustrated, and confused, mounted her horse and with a quick wave to John, galloped off.

All the way home and during the night, she railed to herself: How could I have done that? How *could* I? I'm not that kind of woman. I'm a twenty-two-year-old virgin acting like a whore. The teacher of little children. What would they think if they knew? What would their parents say? I'm so ashamed of myself. I *threw* myself at that man. And why? Because I peeked and I saw him naked. I'll never be able to look him in the eyes again. He was *naked!* I've ruined everything and it's all his fault. If he just wasn't so beautiful! Delia Stewart, you are an absolute *idiot*! Hours later, she managed to drop off to sleep.

John, ashamed for his actions, stood in his tent thinking about what had happened. He moped around the rest of a ruined day. He thought: I wish I knew more about white women. Delia seems so. . . *complicated*. I was just getting to know her, and I ruined it. She said she didn't want to see me for a long time. Does that mean *never*?

August 18, 1914 Another sad day. I found Wolf dead near my tent. Maybe he came to me for help. I took his coat to make myself a coat for winter and buried his body. Now we will be real brothers. It was cloudy but it didn't rain. My work is going slower. I keep thinking about yesterday and Delia. I wonder if she's as sad as I am. I hope she lets me know when I can come to see her again.

August 19, 1914 I've worked so hard to take my mind off Delia, I let my garden get dry. I hope it recovers. I watered it with my cooking pot, but it was a lot of work. I dug a ditch from my spring so I can water it in rows.

Shoni and I went for a ride again, but I didn't feel much like yelling for him, so we didn't go very far and we didn't go very fast, either. I've thought a lot about Delia and I think she really wants to see me again, but I'll have to wait till I know. I don't feel much like going to Rock Creek to see her if she doesn't want to see me.

Chapter Eight
Cloudburst and Flood

The next day, August 20, 1914, John sharpened his ax in the morning and started working. His mind was on Delia and what had nearly happened and not on where his ax was headed. The death of his wolf friend was also on his mind, and when he swung the ax at a sagebrush, it glanced off and cut two inches deep between his right great toe and the one next to it. Had a stone just under the surface of the ground not stopped the ax, he would have lopped off his great toe. The blood spurted, sprinkling the brush and puddling on the ground. John's first thought was not the pain, but now he'd have to buy a new pair of shoes. The next was he might not be able to plant his winter wheat. The realization he was seriously injured came when he tried to walk and his cut shoe flapped against the wound. He sat down on the ground and looked in awe at the red flood coming from him. Seeing how serious it was made him sick. He took his knife and cut off the lower part of his pants leg and bound his foot together slowing the blood somewhat. He knew he had to have help and remembered with horror he'd left Shoni locked in the corral, and his corral was a quarter of a mile away.

He tried hopping on one foot toward the tent, but the blood started to run again. Knowing he'd pass out if he lost much more blood, he sat down. Placing his fore fingers between his lips he blew the scream of an eagle, hoping Shoni could hear him. He could feel himself getting weak. Twice more he whistled to Shoni. Minutes dragged by. The blood slowed but was still a steady seep, soaking the pants-leg bandage. "Come on, Shoni, Cone *on!*" he said aloud.

Again he whistled then lay down on the ground, his ground, his field, his farm. I guess if I bleed to death it will be at home, he thought. Still no Shoni. Again he whistled and lay back down and waited with the side of his face against the ground. Faintly he could hear in the earth the sound of horse's hooves. He sat up again. In a few minutes that seemed an eternity, Shoni galloped to him and stood, waiting.

John got to his feet but couldn't get enough leverage to mount the horse. Every effort cost him more blood. He dropped to his hands and knees. "Shoni, down. Down, boy." He'd never taught Shoni to kneel, and though the horse sensed something was wrong, he stood over his master, listening for a familiar sound. John reached the halter rope and pulled. "Down, boy, down." Still the horse stood, but bent his head. "Down, boy, down."

As if their closeness imparted understanding, Shoni bent his forelegs and lowered himself to the ground. John struggled aboard. A weak yell sent the horse running. He steered him to the Rockwood farm where John called as loudly as he could, "Mr. Rockwood! Mr. Rockwood, I'm hurt!"

Jed wasn't there. John steered Shoni out toward the fields, but saw no sign of Jed. Growing weaker, he pointed Shoni toward Ozone. He bled with every step Shoni took. After almost an hour, Shoni and John got to Otteson's store. By then he was so weak he couldn't call out. He lay face forward on his horse and waited. From somewhere, whatever remained of his consciousness heard a familiar voice, "It's John Fountain. He's been hurt!" Jed shouted, "John's been hurt. We need a buggy, quick!" John muttered incoherently until Jed hoisted him off his horse and laid him on a quilt in the back of Aaron Judy's buggy. He felt someone take off the makeshift bandage and tie on a new one. "Tie it tight. He's lost enough blood already." His head was on someone's lap. "Shoni. . . please."

"Don't you worry about your horse. Jed took him."

On the way to Idaho Falls, John knew they were moving as fast as two horses could pull a buggy. He bounced around a lot, but the quilt helped cushion him. He woke when the buggy stopped and heard voices and scrambling as people moved all around him. He was lifted onto a stretcher and carried into a brightly lit room.

A voice said, "That's a nasty cut. How did he do it?"

Another voice he faintly recognized said, "He was clearing his land and I guess he cut it with an ax." Then he lost consciousness.

It was morning, and the sun shone into the room. Still not completely awake, he turned his head to look around. Three other patients were there. There was also an antiseptic smell he neither recognized nor liked. He tried to stretch. Pain stabbed his right foot, and brought him up, but made him lie back down. My foot, he thought, I cut my foot. Looking down, he saw it was bandaged and elevated a few inches.

Breakfast came, but he was too weak to eat. His head swam and he couldn't think. He lay back and tried to remember. Shoni. What about Shoni? Who'll take care of him? A dim memory of someone saying Jed Rockwood had him eased his mind.

A nurse entered the room, looked the other patients over and came to him. "Good morning." He answered automatically, but it sounded like someone else's voice. His mouth was sticky, and his throat felt as if it had healed over. The nurse gave him a pill and a glass of water, which he welcomed and drank at once. Nausea swept over him. The nurse barely got there in time with her little tin dish. "You shouldn't drink so fast."

That's like telling a starving man not to eat steak, he thought. She brought another glass of water and offered him the pill again. This time he was more cautious and the pill went down.

"Dr. Mellor will be here in about half an hour. He wants to talk to you," she said and left.

John had just dropped off to sleep when Dr. Mellor's voice, more of a Harvard University English professor than a country doctor, said, "That was a nasty cut, but it was clean. You nicked one bone a bit, but you'll heal. How did it happen?"

He was not yet up to answering questions and this one seemed to recur. Doesn't anybody listen? He thought, then answered, "I cut myself."

"Well, we'll have you back on your feet pretty soon, but we'll have to hobble around on crutches for a while. We can't take chances with that kind of cut, can we?"

He thought: How can you say *we*? It's *my* cut. The doctor listened to John's heart, and, when a nurse came in to change the bandage, he examined the cut. John looked at it too and thought it was somebody else's foot, swollen huge, and purple with stitches like insect tracks holding it together.

A man two beds over looked, too and remarked, "Damned fine lookin' piece o' rotten meat you got there!" That made John chuckle, the first light moment since the day before. The doctor left him with the nurse.

"Hold still, Mr. Fountain," the nurse warned, "or you'll make it bleed again. You've already taken two pints of blood, and that's really not enough. You have to build yourself up."

"How much blood do I hold?"

"About six pints altogether. You lost a lot, and you still need more, but you can make it up yourself now."

"Where did it come from?"

"You mean the transfusion?"

"I guess so. I don't know what you mean."

"Oh, we had one pint here that matched you, and one of the student nurses donated another."

"Does that mean I have somebody else's blood in me?"

"Yes, exactly."

"I didn't know that was possible."

"It's a relatively new technique, but we have it here, and it probably saved your life. You didn't have much left to keep you going."

"I would like to thank the student. Can I, ma'am?"

"Probably. I'll tell her when she's here next time."

John couldn't remember ever being so tired. He lay back on the bed and had just closed his eyes when, "Hey, you Okay?"

He looked up through half-closed eyes and saw the character who commented about his rotten foot standing next to the bed. He couldn't have been more than five feet tall. Several days' growth of whiskers bristled among wrinkles that made his face look like an old hide that laid out in the weather for ages. His bald head reflected the overhead lights. John thought he couldn't have weighed more than ninety pounds. "Yes, sir, I'm better now. But I'm very tired. I need to sleep."

The man smiled and revealed a mouth that looked like a broken picket fence. What few teeth he had didn't meet; they meshed. "What happened to ya?"

"I cut my foot while chopping sagebrush."

"Oh, a sodbuster, huh?"

"I don't know, sir. What's a sodbuster?"

"He's one a them bastards always plowin' up the country an' buildin' fences."

"I'm homesteading a piece of land. Does that make me a sodbuster?"

"Sure does. We don't like sodbusters."

"Who're we?"

"The cattlemen. We need open range for the cows t'eat on an' fer. . . fer. . . Hell we jist need open range. Don't you understand that?"

"There's a lot of open range left."

"Yeah, but you bastards keep fencin' it off so we cain't go through."

"I'm sorry, sir. I'm very tired. I don't want to talk about your problems. I have enough of my own."

"Jist thought I'd let y'know where I stand."

John slept for the rest of the day and woke up at supper time. He was hungry and put it all away. He had just taken a bite of cake when the old cowboy returned.

"Say, kid, what's yer name?"

"John Fountain, sir. May I ask yours?"

"Sure can. I bin wranglin' cows since I was ten. Hell, I know cows better'n they knows theirselves." I wrangled cows all over the country and fer a while even in Hywaii. I knows cows an' horses an' sheep better'n most anybody. I don't know pigs, though. They's a mystery t'me. Dumber'n hell."

"If we're spending time together in this room. I'd like to know your name, sir."

"We all have our own likes an' things we don't like. I don't like onions, 'specially raw, but the damned camp cook serves 'em that way jist t'git me riled up. Hate raw onions. They sting. One time a guy in a resternt put raw onions on my hamburger, an' I socked him in the nose. Started a hell of a fight. He beat the shit outta me. I can jist barely eat 'em cooked. I was once in a cow camp where the cook made cooked onions ever' damned way they is, an' I got t' likin' them a little bit, but then I went to Montana, and the cook wouldn't cook onions. Hell, I quit that job."

John realized he had to be direct. "Look, I'll ask you once more. If you don't give me a straight answer, just leave me alone. What. . . is. . . your. . . name, sir?"

"Tiny. They call me Tiny. Guess it's cause I'm so little. I never growed very big. But, hell, I can fight. I lose most all of 'em though. I had a fight with a midget one time and beat the hell outta him."

"Do you have a last name?"

"Sure, Tiny George. That's me. I bin wranglin' cattle since I was ten, an' in spite of my size, I'm pretty damned good at it. I knows cattle better'n they knows theirselves."

"Tiny George. Is that your real first name?"

"Nope. My first name is George, but nobody calls me that. Why?"

"Because I just wanted to know who you are. If George is your real first name, what is your real last name?"

"Evans."

"George. . . ah. . . Tiny, you don't seem to have much wrong with you. Why are you in the hospital?"

"I tried t' rob a bank over in Alpine, Wyomin', and got caught cause I was jist layin' there."

"I don't understand. You are in a hospital because you tried to rob a bank and got caught lying down. Tiny, that doesn't make any sense."

"Oh, I fergot t'tell ya. I took this little stick an' put it in my pocket an' walked into the bank. I never did try t'rob anything ever before. I was so damned excited I almost shit my pants. Well, I went in, an' there's this guy in a cage, an' I stuck the stick in my pocket at him, and said, 'This here's a hold up. Give me fifty dollars.' Well, he said, 'Is that a gun in there?' and I says, 'Yer damned right.' and he looked at me fer a couple seconds and said, 'I don't believe it. Show it to me.' Well, I pulled it out and showed it to him, and he laughed. Then it happened. I had a heart attackt. Hell, it hurt. I doubled up an' fell on the floor, an' they called the sheriff, an' he come and took me in a ambulance to here. I guess I'm better now, though an' they'll probly come an' put me in jail most any time, now. I bin here four days now. I like the food they serve. It don't have no raw onions in it."

"Do they just leave you here alone without a guard?"

"Hell, no. They's a guard outside the door right now. If I started out that there door, I'd git caught on the spot. I cain't go no place without that damned guard. Not even to the can. I try to stink up the place to get him t'leave, but he jist stays there. Bastard's probly got a tin nose."

Another doctor walked in and took Tiny back to his bed and checked his blood pressure and pulse. Tiny dressed himself in his shabby clothes, and a few minutes later the sheriff came and took him away. He waved to John. "So long, kid. Bin nice talkin' to ya. Maybe I'll see ya agin. Usually do see guys agin even after severl years have went by."

The two other men in the room heaved a simultaneous sigh.

"Boy! Am I glad we got rid of *that* guy," said the man next to John, "I'm Rupert Jones. I had a little heart attack, too, and they put me in this room as punishment, I think. You're John Fountain?"

"Yes, sir."

The other man spoke. "I'm Harvey Smith, from Tetonia. Glad to meet you, John. Sorry I can't come over and shake hands. I broke my leg."

"Glad to meet you gentlemen. We'll shake hands later. Where did the little guy come from?"

Harvey answered. "I tried to find out but gave up when I couldn't get a straight answer. All I know is what you know. He came here from Alpine. After the first question, I was afraid to ask another one. You got more out of him than either of us."

There was idle chatter for a few minutes more, then a pretty girl came into the room to take the dishes away. She stopped at John's bed. "You're Mr. Fountain, aren't you?"

"Yes."

"Mrs. Jackson said you wanted to see me. I gave you a pint of blood when you came in."

"Thank you very much. I didn't know they could do that, but thank you again. Who's pint of blood do I have in me?"

"Oh, I'm Helen Whittle. I'm a student nurse. I work on the floor twelve hours a week. I'm glad I could help you out. Dr. Mellor said he wasn't sure you'd make it even after the transfusion. That's an awful nasty cut. You kept saying something that sounded like Shoni. Can I get you anything else?"

"Shoni's my horse. No, Helen, and thank you again for the blood."

"How about you gentlemen?"

"A bottle of beer would be nice," Rupert said.

"Afraid not, Mr. Jones. Have you got a second choice?"

"No, thanks, I'll just suffer the consequences of being here." Helen wheeled the cart of dirty dishes out and closed the door.

The conversation slowed, then stopped, and the men fell asleep. The next morning after breakfast, bandage changing and a visit from the Harvard English professor doctor, Jed appeared at the door.

"Mr. Rockwood! How's Shoni?"

"John, please, call me Jed. He's fine. He sure wanted to follow you though. It was all I could do to hold him back. All the way to my place, he kept trying to turn back. He must think you're God or something. He settled down and he's been no trouble since. How's the foot?"

"It looks awful, but I guess it's healing. What brings you to Idaho Falls?"

"You. I knew you'd want to know about Shoni."

Jed told him Aaron and Mary Ann Judy brought him to the hospital but didn't stay, because they had to get back home.

John asked Jed to tell Mrs. Otteson he might not be able to pay his bill soon. Jed said, "I just wanted to tell you about Shoni. You were pretty worried about him at Ozone. I have to get back. We finished planting our winter wheat, and we're getting ready to move to the valley for the winter."

"I guess planting winter wheat is out of the question for me now. Oh, Jed, one more thing. Would you make sure the stuff in my tent is all right? There are a couple of books and my journal I'd like to have. If you can take them to your place, I'd appreciate it."

"Sure. Well, I'm glad to see you made it. I'll pass on the good news to the folks in Ozone. They'll be glad to know. So long, John."

John leaned back, relieved Shoni was all right. Then thought: Good grief! What if Jed reads my journal?

The first five days lying in bed were almost as bad as having a cut foot and far more monotonous. He read newspapers and cast-off magazines and talked to his roommates. A stroke victim who couldn't talk replaced the heart attack, and the broken leg hobbled out on crutches, leaving him virtually alone in the room.

The morning of August 24 brought a pleasant surprise. He finished eating his breakfast, and cast about in his mind for something to chase away the monotony when Helen Whittle came in carrying a pair of crutches. "The doctor thinks you can go to the toilet now without making your foot bleed. Can you get off the bed by yourself?"

"I think so." Getting off the bed was easy. Holding that crazy hospital gown closed so he wouldn't be exposed, wasn't. As he slipped to the floor, the gown didn't, and he half stood, half sat looking at the evidence of his maleness. So did Helen. He tried to cover himself, but just made things worse. His face hot, he mumbled, "I'm sorry."

"That's all right, Mr. Fountain, I've seen worse. Here, try these." He took the crutches and put them into position.

"They're a little short, I think, but I can use them."

"I'll stay close just in case you get a little dizzy." John *was* a little dizzy. As he tried to rise on the crutches, he listed to one side and the crutch slipped. Helen caught him. "Whoopsy daisy!" John turned to face the bed and stood slowly but got faint. Attempting to regain his balance, he caught his gown with his hand, and broke the tie. His hands flew around to his rear, but too late. Helen spoke up again, "Don't worry, I've seen worse." He had the fleeting thought: Does she mean it's the best of the worst or the worst of the best?

"Mr. Fountain, if you don't feel like it, we can wait another day."

"No, I think I can make it. This outfit isn't made for getting in and out of bed. If you'll help me back onto the crutches, I'll give it another try." Helen walked backward in front of him moving slowly. After only a few steps his foot hurt, but he ignored it and made it to the toilet. Getting down was easy. Getting back up and onto the crutches wasn't. Back on the bed, he fell asleep.

Dr. Mellor's deep, soothing voice woke him. "Well, now let's see how the foot is doing." Mrs. Jackson was with him and changed the bandage while the doctor examined the foot. "It's healing nicely. We'll be up and around before we know it. Does it hurt?"

"Not so much now, but it hurt when I was on the crutches."

"That's because the blood ran down when you stood up."

"How much longer will I have to stay here?"

"We'll see," said the doctor.

After they left, he wondered where he would go when he got out. He had only the tent, and the weather was getting cooler, cold, in fact. Chopping stove wood on crutches didn't seem likely. Besides, he had to find the ax. And what about Shoni? Now he had more problems than he ever thought he'd have. His land wasn't cleared. That wasn't too important. He could plant what was cleared with the two sacks of wheat he had, but how could he do it on crutches? And how could he pay his bill at Otteson's, the hospital bill, a new pair of shoes, hay and oats for Shoni, and what about a job for the winter? Everything that seemed so clear last May suddenly wasn't. His whole future was a wreckage of problems.

He remembered the joy he felt as he swung the ax, the *thunk*! it made when it cut into a stump, the rustle of the branches as he dragged them to the burn pile, the fire reaching high in the air, sparks flying around when the pile collapsed, dancing around the fire. . . And Delia saying, *"You have a pile out there, now. Let's light it and dance around it together."*

He wished he *had* lit it and danced with her, even in the daytime. His thoughts returned to her visit. He remembered her sudden departure with only a wave of her hand. He thought: I wonder what she's doing now.

There seemed to be nothing to break the loneliness. No, not just loneliness; it was the helplessness. His world had become so small he could see all of it, and all of it was wreckage. Lunch came and went. John fretted into the afternoon: How? How can I do it now?

Chapter Nine
Clearing Skies

Henry, Lydia, and Freddie Monson broke his dismal reverie. "We heard about your accident and came as soon as we could. The other kids wanted to come but they had to go to school," Henry said. "How's the foot?"

"I guess I'll live with it. The doctor said it was a clean cut and no bones were damaged. He took the stitches out yesterday. Do you know what day it is? I've lost track of time."

"It's the twenty-fifth. How much longer will you be in here?"

"The doctor said about a week."

They filled the while with small talk. Henry asked how it happened, and Lydia asked if it hurt. They reported the childrens' progress and how things were going on the Monson farm. Henry ended the visit with, "Well, we'd better be getting back. It'll be time to do the chores before long. James and Susan will start them, but they can't do it all. Sam can't do much yet, either." They shook hands all around.

Freddie said, "Please get better."

"I will, Freddie, I promise."

After they left, John thought: Oh, I'll get better all right, but then what? What do people do in a case like this? I just wanted to be like the white men. If I'd stayed in the Shoshoni village, I wouldn't have all these problems. I wonder what my mother is doing. I'll have to go see her as soon as I can.

Another restless night followed, and the next morning he had another roommate, a boy about nine years old. His parents brought him in with Dr. Mellor. After many reassurances about getting all the ice cream he could eat afterward, they left. He came over to John's bed.

"I'm gonna have my tonsils out. Are you gonna have your tonsils out, too?"

"No, I cut my foot, and I have to stay here for a while."

"Let me see!"

John smiled a little. "I don't think the doctor would like me to show it to you. It's pretty awful."

"Show it to me anyway. I want to see it."

"No, I can't."

The kid walked around to John's injured foot and roughly began unwinding the bandage.

"Hey, leave that alone!" The kid didn't stop. "Look, when they take your tonsils out, they use a knife. I'll tell the doctor to cut your throat and let you bleed to death if you don't quit." John leaned forward far enough to grab the boy's arm, dragged him closer, and said, "Now go back to your bed and leave me alone." The boy tried to pull loose. John pulled him nose-to-nose. "I mean it, kid. Leave that bandage alone!"

As if in answer to his unspoken plea, a nurse came in, hustled the boy out, and closed the door. John got unsteadily to his feet, took the crutches, and hobbled to the toilet. The trip was much easier than before. When he returned, he sat on the edge of the bed instead of lying on it. The hospital gown was still embarrassing, so he didn't leave the room until he had to.

The tonsillectomy returned, but remained very quiet, refusing to eat any ice cream. He left the next day. A very old man came in soon afterward and filled a bed two places away. He was unable to speak, just looked at the ceiling and wheezed. John went to him in a futile attempt to relieve the deadly boredom, "Sir, my name is John Fountain. May I ask yours?"

No verbal response. The old man's eyes moved around wildly and seemed to have trouble finding the speaker. The round hole of his mouth, white tongue slithering in and out like a snake's, told of his frustration at not being able to speak. He left the old man.

He was getting better on the crutches. Helen found a screwdriver and he lengthened them to a more comfortable height and found he could wander around the hospital easily. But there wasn't much hospital, and he soon returned to the bed.

The next day he started another halfhearted tour of the place. He went to the door, opened it, and stood face to face with Delia. Surprised, both of them said the other's name at the same instant. John reached for her and dropped a crutch. She picked it up and handed it to him at arm's length. He was disappointed. There would be no greeting kiss, however fleeting.

She asked, "Can you make it out to a place where we can talk?"

"I was just now going out to see something more than the four walls of my room and here you are! I'm glad to see you. Very glad."

Walking slowly beside him, she led him to a small table where she sat in a single chair across from a bench. "Please," she said, pointing to the bench. "How is the foot?"

"It's getting better every day. I think it'll be a lot better now that you're here."

Ignoring his comment, she said, "I'm a college-educated woman, but I have trouble saying some things to you." John reached for her hand, but she pulled it back. "Please, John, please try to understand this. I'm twenty-two years old, and I have things to do. I want to teach young minds to know, to grow, to open them up to the wonders of the world. That's why I asked you to tell them some of the Shoshoni legends." She blushed. "I still think some of them would be a good thing for them to hear. For the past couple of weeks, I've thought too much about you. I can't let that happen. Not now. I have too many things I want to do, and I can't get deeply involved with a man until they're done, and that was about to happen. When I heard what happened to you, I had to fight the urge to come to you right then, but school was about to start, and I had to get ready. I don't want to live the way so many other women have without ever doing anything anyone noticed. That's why I left you. I wanted to be sure you know that, and that's why I came today."

"I was destroyed." John said. "I kicked myself all over for what I did. I have something I want to do, too. And I want you to share my homestead, but I want it to be finished before I take you there. I want that as that much as you want your dream."

"That's so sweet of you. I knew you'd understand. You do understand, don't you?"

"Almost. What I don't understand is why you want something most other women seem not to care about."

"I want to be different. Mother is devoted her life to just being another wife in a farming community. There are a lot of joys in such a life, but there are other things I think are better. Please try to understand."

"I guess that's something I have to learn. I'm trying hard to be a part of something that's so different from my early life I make mistakes. Maybe some day?"

"Yes, John, maybe some day, but not yet. I should go now." She reached across the table and took his hand and shook it. "Good-bye, John." And she left.

He watched her leave, and then watched the door, hoping she'd come back. She didn't.

After Delia's visit, John was in worse emotional condition than if she hadn't come at all. He had almost resigned himself to never seeing her again, or at least not soon, and then she showed up and told him she couldn't be part of his life.

Aaron and Mrs. Judy came in to visit the next morning. More routine questions and routine answers. Then, "Jed Rockwood dropped by the store and asked if anyone was coming to town. He had a package for you. We were coming today, so we brought it."

The package contained John's journal and the two books Miss Edwards gave him wrapped in old newspapers. Now he had something to do besides stare out the window. The walls and ceiling of the room were impressed upon his memory so well he could tell which dots were spiders and which were flies and which were flecks left by the painters. If it moved, it was a spider. If it disappeared, it was a fly. If it did neither, it was a spot.

"Thank you so much, Mr. Judy, sir. I've wanted something to take my mind off this place for a little while. It isn't very exciting after the first day or so. The food is a lot better than I can fix and they take pretty good care of me, I guess. It's the first time I've ever been in a hospital, and I hope it's the last." Mrs. Judy agreed with him. She had to stay there ten days when her last baby was born.

"What's in your journal, John?" Mrs. Judy asked. John told of the things he wrote about and mentioned his experience with the old wolf.

"You were friends with a wolf?" Aaron asked.

More routine questions and more routine answers about his friendship with the wolf, and the fear most of the homesteaders had of them.

"The Shoshonis have a lot of legends about wolves. Some of them are very funny."

"Come to think of it, no one has ever been attacked by one. Jed said to tell you Shoni got out of his barn some way and disappeared. They hunted all over the hills and finally found him at your place in the corral."

As the Judys prepared to leave, they asked John what he planned to do.

"I can't do much on my place on crutches. I wanted to plant my wheat and get a job in the valley this winter, but I guess that's not possible now."

"Your neighbors got together and planted your winter wheat. I heard there were three grain drills, and they did it in a hurry. They ran into some stumps, but they got it all in. They had to find a few more sacks of seed, but they got a lot of the cleared land planted. I heard about it yesterday at church."

John was stunned. "They planted my winter wheat?"

"Right. It didn't take long, and they had a party afterward. There was a whole bunch of them: Jed and Amos, George Fogelsong, Ludwig Franck, Jack Dehlin, Tom Doman, Art Schwieder, and a few others. The wives cooked in your tent on the littlest stove any of them ever saw. I don't remember now who all was there."

John's voice broke when he said, "Mr. Judy, sir, I'm a stranger to most of them. I haven't even met Mr. Franck or Mr. Doman. Why would they do that for a stranger?"

"They knew you were laid up and you have a good friend in Lenore Otteson. She thinks you're one of the finest young men she ever met. Do me a favor, John. Call me Aaron. We're almost the same age, and when you call me Mr. and *sir*, it makes me nervous. Well, I've got to be going. Mrs. Judy, are you ready?"

"Yes, Mr. Judy, *sir*, I'm ready." She winked at John.

Alone again, John grabbed his journal. The pencil was where he left it, a reassuring sign probably no one had read it. He began to write.

September 3, 1914 I haven't written anything for a long time because on August 20, I got in a hurry to finish clearing some more land and plant some winter wheat. I was sure I could finish before winter, so I sharpened my ax and began working very fast. It turned out to be too fast and I missed my mark and the ax glanced off the stump and cut my foot. At first I thought it was awful because I'd have to buy a new pair of shoes, then I knew how awful it was when I started to walk and part of my shoe with my big toe in it flapped against the rest of my foot.

John was still writing when Mrs. Jackson and Dr. Mellor came in. Reluctantly, he closed his journal. She took off John's bandage and the doctor looked intently at the wound. "It's healing nicely, John, I think we can go home tomorrow. How do you like that?"

"I'd like it a lot better if I had some way to *get* home."

"I'll leave a note at the entrance for anyone who might be going that way. We want you to stay off your foot for another month or six weeks. What will you do now?"

"I just don't know, sir. I had planned to find work in the valley this winter, but now. . . I don't know what I can do. Every job I ever heard of means walking around."

"All I can say is stay off that foot for a while. Try to find a job that lets you sit."

September 4, 1914 The doctor came in just as I finished writing, and told me I could go home tomorrow. I think I can make at least one crutch when I get to my tent and it will keep me off my foot. I don't think I can get on Shoni from crutches. though. I'll have to figure something out. I don't feel any pain any more unless I bump it so I guess it's getting all right. The big problem right now is how to get to my tent.

I walked around the hospital a little bit more. It's called the General Hospital but I don't think it was built to be a hospital. I think there are only two rooms for sick people, one for women and one for men. But now I don't care. I can leave tomorrow. But how?

September 5, 1914 I was getting ready to leave when Mrs. Otteson came in. I told her I could leave but had no way to travel. She came to see how I was and offered me a ride to Ozone. I owe the doctor and the hospital $75. I don't know where I can find that much money. But I can pay a little bit at a time. Now I owe people about $100. I hope I can do something at the Lincoln sugar factory. I don't know what they do there, so I'll have to go see

When I went to give the crutches back, they said to keep them till I don't need them any more then bring them back.

We got to Ozone kind of late and I slept on the floor. I bought a new pair of shoes and pants on credit while I was there. They told me Mr. Judy was the new bishop of the Ozone ward. I guess it has something to do with their church.

September 6, 1914 It rained all night last night. Mr. Dehlin came to Otteson's about noon and brought me to Jed's place. Shoni almost knocked me over when I went to him in the barn. Jed told me about him getting away and then finding him in his corral at my tent. Jed helped me get on him. I tried to let him go faster but it hurt my foot, so I slowed him down. I had to get him close to the corral so I could get off.

When I went into my tent, it was all nice. My ax was there and the quilt and blanket were folded. The stove was all ready to light, so I lit it. I'm too excited about being back to be hungry. I hope they have something I can do at the sugar factory. I feel finally free from the hospital and the four walls of the room I was in.

September 9, 1914 Yesterday and today, I went up to look at my field. There was nothing showing above the ground, but I dug up a couple of kernels and they were starting to sprout. I will have a good crop.

Chapter Ten
Clearing Skies

John found out in Ozone that the sugar factory usually started late in September or early October. He decided to go there to find out more. He tried to clear more brush, but soon quit.

Lincoln was a small village, a store and a few blocks of houses, most with a barn and an outdoor toilet, and was generally known as the townsite. The Utah-Idaho Sugar Company built a sugar factory in the early 1900s and added a school and about fifty houses along the main east-west road, to house some of the employees. This part of the town became known as the "line". The houses were identical east of the factory. Those west of the factory were better houses for the staff and supervisors. The best houses were brick; the others, frame. All had indoor plumbing.

Sand Creek divides Lincoln east and west. The sugar factory was built a short distance west of it. The tall chimney vented smoke from its steam generating plant during operating months, and the *chug, chug, chug* of the steam engine could be heard for almost a mile. That single steam engine sent power throughout the factory along belts, pulleys, and gears. John was intimidated by what he saw.

September 17, 1914 I went to the sugar factory yesterday. They were running it to be sure everything was all right. It's a big place with a lot of noise that sounds like drums. It was the biggest building I ever saw in my life. It had many windows and a tall chimney, the tallest I could imagine. I didn't know how to ask for a job, so I asked the first person I saw. He said to go to the office, but they said they didn't have any jobs right then, and asked me what I could do with a broken leg. A man named Mr. Weaver came in and said he thought I could sharpen the knives that cut the beets into strips before they go to the main part. He said maybe there would be an opening in a few days, and told me I might be able to stay in Denning's boarding house. They had a barn where I could put Shoni. He told me I should be close by in case an opening comes. I went to the place, and found out they could keep both of us, but it would cost a dollar a day. When they asked if I had a job, I said no, and the man said he didn't think they should take us if I don't have a job. He said to come back when I know for sure. The people around Bull's Fork are a lot more helpful. I rode back to my tent and got here very late. I had to stop to let Shoni eat some grass on the way. My sore foot got cold at night and hurt.

John rode about twenty-five miles back to his tent for the night. He could as easily have stayed with the Monsons, but he was worried, worried about his bill at Otteson's store and the hospital, and worry made him forget Ammon was more convenient. The next few days were very discouraging. He rode again the next day to Lincoln, only to be told to return the next day. But the next day was Sunday, and when he showed up, there was no one at the factory who could tell him anything. Dejected, he returned to his camp and spent another uncomfortable night, his foot aching in the cold. He noted in his journal on September 20, "I found out they work for twelve hours every shift. That's less than I worked here, so I can do it all right."

When John got to the sugar factory on Monday, Clarence Weaver was at the office asking if he'd been there. "Boy, am I glad to see you. You can go to work right now. The guy I hired didn't show up, and I can't wait for him. We start cutting beets tomorrow."

"I have to take care of my horse first, and find a place for myself." John returned to the Dennings' boarding house, and they agreed to take his horse but had no room for him. Mrs. Denning suggested he might find a place about a quarter mile down the road but said it might not be very nice. That night he wrote, "Mr. Weaver showed me what to do and told me to keep the place clean. He said the beets are washed but there is always a little bit of dirt left and the knives get dull. He told me at first I would get $3.00 for working twelve hours. The place I found to stay isn't very nice. I'll ask the man where Shoni is tomorrow." Life seemed more stable the next day.

September 22, 1914 Last night I figured I would get almost $80 for each month of work. I have to work from 7 in the morning till 7 at night, and I will have Wednesdays off. First, I will pay Mrs. Otteson and then pay the hospital and Dr. Mellor. My foot is getting better, but when it gets cold, it still hurts a little bit. The work is not very exciting, but Mr. Weaver said it is important. I got a place to stay at the boarding house. The number on my room is 7. It's a very big white house with two floors. From the outside, the house looks like a long box with windows. The kitchen and dining room and the place where the Dennings live are on the ground floor. There are only two rooms to rent there. Upstairs, there are six with two bathrooms like the one at the Monsons. A little way away is a red barn for up to eight horses. A haystack is next to it. Sand Creek runs next to the barn, and that's where they water the horses.

Mr. Weaver asked me to work tomorrow instead of taking the day off. When things work out, the white man's ways are good. I was feeling very bad a few days ago, but now I am happy. I have a job and a place for Shoni and me. I'm kind of mixed up. I've never been paid for working before, and I'm not sure I know what to think. I'm happy I can get out of debt, though.

John's new job created new problems. At the homestead, he could ride Shoni whenever he wanted, but in Lincoln, he couldn't. At first, he accepted he'd be doing the same thing over and over, but as time passed, he grew frustrated. He wondered what was going on at his place. Shortly after he began working, he returned to his land, took down the tent, wrapped the tiny stove and simple utensils in it, and stowed everything under some quaking aspen. There was snow on the ground and it was very cold.

October 1, 1914 I've been standing for a little while on my foot and it doesn't hurt much. I think in a few more days I can walk on it without crutches all the time. It still hurts when it gets cold.

Today Mr. Weaver brought me my first pay. They pay the crew on the 1st and the 15th day of each month. I am very happy to have a job. I'll be glad when I don't owe any more money to anybody.

I paid Mrs. Denning $10 for Shoni and me for ten days. She said I should pay on the first of every month, and it would be $30. Then she said she'd make it $25 for the both of us for a month. It still seems a lot of money, but I guess that's about what I should expect.

The next Wednesday, John rode to Ozone and paid ten dollars on his debt there. but commented he still owed almost half a month's pay. Frustration with the routine hung heavy on his mind.

October 13, 1914 I almost wish I hadn't decided to take this job. I use a file with three corners to sharpen the shredder knives, and I use about two files every day. They get dull or full of junk, and I have to throw them away. They're about 16 inches long, and usually with one stroke, I can sharpen two sides of a cutter. I ask myself often, isn't that exciting? Payday is the only good thing I can think of about this job.

October 19, 1914 Tonight for supper, Mrs. Denning served cooked carrots. I asked her I could have one or two for a treat for Shoni, and she gave me three.

On his next day off, John went to Ozone and finished paying his debt at the store. The snow was about three inches deep and it made the countryside look like a dreamland.

Lenore told him, "The first snow came at just the right time to cover the new wheat so it won't freeze."

"I hope I can stay on my land next winter. I don't think I want to work in the sugar factory any more."

With little time after work, John tried to read Dickens. "I read some more of my two cities story. It's about the only thing that's interesting in my life any more."

Next payday, he paid for his room and board. Twenty-five dollars was a lot but he was satisfied. "It's nice to have a warm bed and good food to eat and to know Shoni is where I can ride him and take care of him. That and reading, which I don't have very much time for anymore, are the only things that make life interesting."

His foot was almost completely healed, so he took the crutches back to the hospital and rode up to Ozone for Lenore's report on the snow.

"What brings you up here?" Mrs. Otteson asked.

"Well, ma'am, I took the crutches back to the hospital and paid them ten dollars. It was such a nice day, I just decided to ride on up."

November 14, 1914 I got another check for $36.00 today because tomorrow is Sunday and there would be no one in the office to make the checks. On Wednesday, I'll pay the hospital $15.00, and I think I should have a new coat for winter.

November 17, 1914 Today a kid about 14 fell off a long pipe that carries the pulp from the factory to the pulp pit. He broke through the frozen surface and nearly drowned before he got out. They said he was a sorry, stinking mess. Some other kids dared him to walk out on the pipe and he wanted to show how brave he was. Brave is when you do something scary when you have to. Stupid is when you do something scary when you *don't* have to. I've been over there only once and it smelled awful bad. I imagine what the kid felt like.

Mr. Weaver invited me to come to his house for Thanksgiving dinner. It was a big surprise. He said he would find someone to take my place for a few hours, or if I had enough knives sharpened, I could leave anyway. I'd like to see how he celebrates this holiday. Mrs. Monson always made so many good things to eat I felt ready to explode at the end of the meal.

Tomorrow is my day off work and I'll take Shoni out again. I wish I could get to my homestead, but they say it's impossible to get around up there because of the snow. I haven't read in my *A Tale of Two Cities* for a long time, so I guess I'll read more of it. I wish I understood it better.

John agonized over the weight of debt at the hospital. "Now I feel a lot better. I rode Shoni in to the hospital and paid them $15 and I owe them $35 more. If I pay the rest in two payments, I'll be finished with them and my money is mine. I bought a good winter coat for almost $10 and I have a little bit of money left. The coat sure felt good on the way home."

On Thanksgiving Day, he arrived at the Weavers at about four. Mrs. Weaver had decorated the house with orange and green "things" and to John, it smelled better than at the Monsons. "Mrs. Weaver served the turkey from the top of the stove not at the table like Mrs. Monson did. They had about the same things to eat. Donald, the Weaver boy who is thirteen said the prayer, and it was almost as long as the one Mr. Monson used to say, and it sounded like a history lesson."

On his return to the boarding house, he had another surprise. Mrs. Denning routinely prepared holiday feasts for her boarders, and there was another meal waiting for him.

November 30, 1914 Last night I stayed up late reading Mr. Dickens' story. I have gotten so I can understand it a little bit better and I can almost understand why he spends so much time describing things. The handy man at the bank kept his son with him. The two of them looked exactly alike with their eyes too close together and when they sat close together they looked like a pair of monkeys. I wish I could write the way Mr. Dickens does.

A violent blizzard swept through the valley near the end of November leaving a dazzling landscape of rumpled drifts. By the second of December, most roads were again open, and people began moving about. John never missed a chance to ride Shoni, and he wrote of their trip together on this day. "It was such a beautiful day today I decided to ride on out the Lincoln road to the Ozone road. There was a terrible wind last weekend and the drifts were piled very high, but there had been traffic on the road, so I could get through. The snowy landscape at the edge of the hills was covered with ice crystals flashing like frigid sparks from an icy fire. I felt as if I shouldn't be there. I wanted to float above the ground and look down on it. Down wind snowdrifts stretched out in white streaks behind every bush and tree. In the little coves only the tips of trees and brush peered above the drifts. When I reached the road to Ozone, I stopped. There was no sign anyone had been on it. Before me lay a scene of the earth asleep under a dazzling blanket so pure it begged to be left alone. I didn't want to wake it up, so I turned Shoni around and we came back to Lincoln."

By mid December, he finished paying off his debt at the hospital. "Now I am free from debt. I don't owe anybody anything. My foot has healed and I have a job to give me money for my homestead in the spring. I've heard they can't keep the roads open even to Ozone. Several families stayed in the hills. I will stay when I have a cabin and a pretty wife and many children. We will grow enough food to last over the winter and we'll be like the bears and sleep and not come out until the sun brings the spring."

He wrote of Dickens' description of being drawn and quartered after reading of it. "It sounds to me like the Shoshonis butchering a buffalo, except they don't hang them till after they're dead and they don't cut out the insides and burn them while the animal watches. It almost made me sick."

All winter long, John thought of going home. He read *A Tale of Two Cities* at every opportunity and often wished he could write as well as Dickens. A comment in a scratched-out entry was, "But why should I write again what someone else has written. Let my grandchildren read it for themselves. Let them find themselves wrapped in the fantasy of a wonderful story wonderfully told."

December 23, 1914   The Lincoln School had its annual Christmas party tonight and I went to see it. The children acted out several of the Christmas stories. In one of them, a boy had to turn a somersault. His shoes were too big for his feet and they crashed on the stage like firewood dropped onto the floor. It looked like he got dizzy and staggered to the edge of the stage and fell into the audience. I'm sure he wasn't supposed to.

I lived with the Monsons long enough to have an idea what the Mormon Church believes, although I don't believe it's any more realistic than some of the Shoshoni rituals. What I don't understand is that the white man uses only one day a week and days like Christmas for his religion. It doesn't seem to be a part of his life like with the Indians. This gives me great problems.

Although the Weavers and the Dennings invited John for Christmas, he accepted the Monson's invitation. They greeted him like a son, including Freddy's ritual foot stomping. And there was somebody new, a girl named Lillian — pretty, about eighteen. Her first words made a deep impression on John. "I'm glad to meet you. I've heard so much about you I feel as if I already know you. What's it like to be a half-breed Indian?" You sure don't look anything like any Indian I ever saw. From your name, I think your father must have been white and your mother an Indian. Was she pretty?"

His response to such an overwhelming greeting was, "Hello Lillian."

During dinner, Susan left the table in tears after a short argument with Lillian. After she left, Mrs. Monson talked a lot about what John was doing and how she admired him. Lillian listened carefully.

John wrote of it. "I decided Mrs. Monson was trying to find me a wife just like Mrs. Holmquist did at the Fourth of July celebration in Ozone. I didn't like it because I want to choose my own wife, and I don't think Lillian would be a good choice."

He left about eight, and all the family except Susan came to say good-bye. Lillian kissed him on the cheek and promised to see him again.

Henry stayed when the others went inside and started to say something. "John, Lydia. . . Oh, never mind. Good night. I hope you had a good time."

John was on Shoni when he heard, "Jean-Pierre!" Susan stood shivering in the cold beside the gate.

"Susan, you shouldn't be out here in the cold without a coat."

"I know. I had to say good-bye to you." John dismounted. "I'm sorry for the way I acted. But Lillian is so pretty, I felt left out. That's why I left. I didn't have anything to do with her when she lived here. Mother arranged the whole thing. I'm so ashamed."

"Susan, please forget it. I was surprised when you left the table, but don't worry about it. You're still pretty special to me."

John rode back to his room at the boarding house. All the way, he thought of the pretty girl who asked so many questions. She was just the pretty kind of girl he wanted to share his homestead. He thought: How could she ask what it feels like to be a half-breed? I think I feel like any other person. What a question! She's awful pretty, but I don't think I could stand to live with her. His mind made up, John slept and the next day returned to his job.

One of John's coworkers invited him to the New Year's Eve dance at the Lincoln School where he was promised he'd meet a lot of pretty girls. John went.

January 1, 1915 The beginning of a new year. I hope the new one is better than the old one. I got paid yesterday because today is a holiday. After I paid Mrs. Denning, all the money I have left belongs to me and I won't have to pay anybody anything. I must think about what I'll need when I go back to my homestead.

I went to the New Years Eve dance at Lincoln School last night. There was a man who played some drums but they didn't look like the ones at the Shoshoni village. One was very big and sounded a lot like the ones we use, but the others were smaller and made a funny sound. This was the first time I have ever gone to a white man's dance and everything was strange. Men and women danced together and sometimes went in circles. I have never seen men and women dancing together before. In the Shoshoni village, men danced and women danced, sometimes at the same time, but not together.

Then a girl came to me and sat down and asked me why I didn't dance. I told her I didn't know how. She said we should try. She called it a waltz and pulled me onto the floor. She said I just had to count, one, two, and three and do what she did. I tried, but it seemed she was on two when I was on one and on three when I was on two. We finally sat down and soon she left.

One time I went to the punch bowl and the girl behind me started to talk to me. In a few minutes a guy came up to me and pushed me and I spilled some of my punch. He said she was his girl and I should stay away from her. I didn't know what he was talking about, so I ignored him. Then he grabbed my arm and told me I should go outside with him. The girl tried to make him calm down but he kept on. I was getting angry and I went outside. He tried to hit me with his fist but he wasn't quick enough and I stayed out of his reach. He smelled like my uncle used to smell when he came back from Blackfoot sometimes.

The bully who planned to bloody John had no idea of his distaste for violence. John kept just out of the bully's reach, letting him flail the air with his fists until he tired and got crazy mad. Then he backed up against the building and raised his hands as if in surrender. The bully charged head first from ten feet back. John stepped aside and let his would-be executioner smash his forehead against the stone foundation of the building.

When John returned, the girl was headed outside. She stopped only long enough to say, "Every time he drinks he gets nasty. He's really a nice guy. Please don't be too angry with him." John told her to get a coat for him.

"Is he hurt?" she asked.

"He bumped his head. He's resting now, but he really needs a coat." John never saw either of them again that evening.

Later he met Paul Schwartzkopf towing a very pretty girl to the refreshment table. "John!" Paul shouted, "This is Julia Sanders, my cousin."

Although by now, John was used to peoples' matchmaking, he didn't always like it. "In a little while, Paul Schwartzkopf called me and brought his cousin to see me. She was a very pretty girl named Julia Sanders. Paul left us together. It seems everybody wants me to meet somebody else and it's usually a girl. Julia and I talked while we drank a glass of punch and ate a couple of cookies, but she seemed not to know anything at all and it was hard to talk to her because she kept trying to change the subject, and she couldn't understand why I didn't belong to her church. She was pretty but I don't think I'd like to be around her very much."

Chapter Eleven
Bad Weather and Deep Snow

January 15, 1915 The weather has been awful bad. Every time it gets a little warmer, it snows, and then the wind blows and the snowdrifts are very high and it's very cold. When I take Shoni out, I'm afraid he'll get sick or maybe fall. His barn is quite warm because there are several other horses in it.

Today was payday and I have more money than I ever had in my life. I have to think about the things I need to build my barn and cabin. I'll have to buy some work horses and a plow, and probably a wagon, too. I think I should talk to Mr. Monson about what I should buy. He's a very wise man.

January 20, 1915 I am so tired of this job I think sometimes I'd rather be with my mother at the Shoshoni camp. At least there, every day can be different. Here it is always the same, sharpen knives, sharpen knives. Sometimes a rock will get stuck in the roots of a sugar beet and ruin the edge of the knife and I have to grind it till it's straight then give it a new edge but it's about all the excitement I find. Today was my day off and all I can think of is getting back to my homestead.

January 31, 1915 I sat today on my stool and thought about what I'm doing. Will I ever be like the white man? No. I don't think so. Too much of my life was spent as an Indian.

I remembered the first time I saw my homestead with Jed, and how much I wanted to have that piece of land. I was very disappointed when we found it had been staked, but so much time had passed, I was sure whoever had staked it should have done more in about three years than had been done. Jed gave me the description, and I was very happy when Mrs. Gerrard said it was still open. But I will never feel the disappointment that I felt when I found out I was too young to have a homestead. I remember when I spent the night at the Monsons on my way back to the Shoshoni village and everybody seemed so happy the next morning, I felt like even the Monsons were against me. The Monsons must like me very much for Mrs. Monson to take out a homestead in her name for me. I almost cried for joy.

Mr. Monson is like a real father to me. But I will never forget my own father. He was a very gentle man, but also very strict. He took me on long walks along the river and out in the hills and taught me all he knew. I'll never know anybody who speaks French. I would like to go to France some day to see where my grandfather lived. I wonder if it was in Paris. Mr. Dickens' book says Paris is an awful place.

I think I was about four years old when my father made me a slingshot.

Young Jean-Pierre listened to his father reading his French Bible. The story of David slaying the giant Philistine with a slingshot brought the young man to full attention. What sort of weapon could a boy use against a giant? What

112

did it look like? Was it heavy? His father made one for the inquisitive boy. The first time Jean-Pierre tried it, the rock flew backwards bringing laughter from his father. But with practice, he was able to use it effectively. Later, at a contest shooting arrows, he heard his father call out in French, "Make sure it doesn't go behind you, Jean-Pierre."

When John was born, his father was an old man but he was lively. They often ran foot races, and the old man always won. When John was about fourteen, he won the race. His father said, "That's the last time I will race with you."

"Why?"

"You beat me, but I won because you did what I wanted you to do. Remember, if you work hard enough you will always win." Jean-Claude was seventy-six years old.

About two years later he died and left John and his mother alone. John's heart was heavy for a long time.

"I must go back to visit my mother when I am through here and spring has come. I will take her some food and some presents. I have some money now for my homestead, and I can share what I have. My father always taught me I should honor all women. My mother is a pretty woman and I remember her with a blanket over her shoulders in winter and her long hair in braids hanging over her shoulders. She liked a little fur cap my father made from a rabbit skin for her. Sometimes she even wore it in summer."

His childhood was filled not only with the games Indian children play, but the seriousness of survival as well. Depending on the season, their searches sometimes took them far afield, often for weeks at a time, but for the young Jean-Pierre, it was also a game to be played, a new adventure to be lived, a fun time for his family and for the tiny band he lived with.

A few months after his father died, John's mother told him he should live with the white men. "The way of the

113

Indians is hard, and the white man's medicine is very strong. You must learn the white man's life and be a part of it."

She gave him a leather sack containing a knife, a coat, and a blanket, and gave him some white man's clothes to wear. Leaving was difficult. Mostly, he didn't want to leave his mother, but leaving his friends, and especially Willow, made his departure doubly difficult. He was only sixteen, far more an Indian boy than white, and his mother told him he must enter a new life about which he knew almost nothing. Honoring his mother's wisdom, and having no idea where to go, he left and started walking. Henry Monson found him at the Ammon store.

"At first, I felt very lonely at the Monsons and I think a little bit scared, but after a few months, I was less lonely. The Monson family was very good to me and taught me many things about living on a farm. Sometimes it's a hard life, but mostly it was much better than living in the Shoshoni village. I missed my mother a lot at first and I missed seeing Willow, but I got over it."

February 15, 1915   Today was payday again. I heard yesterday a farmer delivering beets last October, got his coat caught in the hook they use to dump the wagons at the beet dump and it lifted him up in the air when the beets were dumped. He would have been OK, but his coat tore loose from the hook and he fell down and broke his leg.

It's snowing again today, and will probably snow for several more days. All I've been able to do to keep from dying from boredom is read my book.

February 24, 1915   I read my journal from the start to the end. I have written so much that says nothing I'm ashamed of it. Mr. Weaver came to me today and told me I have a job again next season if I want it. I didn't tell him yes or no, but he promised it would be a different job. I haven't spent very much money because I want enough to build a new corral and a barn and I have to finish clearing the land. I think I will pile the sagebrush all together and then set it afire and dance and sing around it all night. I will make a drum to keep me company. I will be happy. I wish there was somebody to share my happiness with. Maybe Delia will, but I don't think so. The last time she saw me, she told me she didn't want to be a homesteader's wife. I wonder if I could find Willow. She'd dance with me. I remember Willow so much now I've been so lonely for so long. I wonder what she's doing. I will go to see her when I go to see my mother in the spring. Willow is so beautiful, and so nice to be with. When I first saw her, I was only ten years old and she was only nine, but she smiled at me with her dark eyes and I knew I would know her better. When I was fourteen and she was thirteen, we slipped away from her mother's attention and went down to the river. When we returned to the camp, we came into it from different directions. We did this as often as we could and her mother never found out about us. I am surprised she didn't, though. I think sometimes we got a little bit careless.

I don't know why I wrote that. I think it is too private. I wonder what Willow is doing now.

By mid-March, the campaign was nearly over. Clarence Weaver told John there would be only about two weeks left. The snow in the hills was still very deep but John was determined to get to his land. "I want to see my wheat growing and get back to real work that shows when I finish it. I hope I don't have any trouble getting to my tent and stuff. I've saved $132, but I need some new clothes."

As closing time came closer, John became more and more anxious to leave. His work had been messy, causing him to have cold hands much of the time because he had to rinse the knives in a bucket of water before he sharpened them. He couldn't wear gloves because they got wet and his hands got colder.

The steady heart beats of the steam engine ceased to bother him, and he'd grown used to the maze of belts and pulleys to spread the power around the factory. His lone hour of excitement came when a Frenchman visited him. His company supplied information about the processes to the Mormon Church before it build its first sugar factory in Utah, and now he was visiting all of them to gather information on improvements made to the processes. John reported the Frenchman told him his spoken French was very good.

On his next day off, he rode to Ammon to discuss his plan with Henry who suggested he build a barn big enough for a team of work horses, Shoni, and a cow or two. He was especially proud of Sam who'd taken John's experiment with seeds in a glass jar a step further to fulfill a science project in school. He showed that for each seed planted, thirty-five to fifty new ones grew. It won him first prize.

March 29, 1915 Today is not a very happy one for me. The factory is closed, but I can't leave here because an awful snowstorm came up. I'll just have to sit here and wait until it's over.

March 30, 1915 It's still snowing and everybody says we're in for a real blizzard. Mr. Denning has a radio in the boarding house and we listened to it almost all day, but all the news is about more snow and blizzards.

March 31, 1915 It's still snowing. Everything is covered up to three feet, and the wind is starting. I wonder how much longer I have to wait.

April 1, 1915 Snow is blowing so thick I can't see farther than a few feet in front of me. I've never seen snow blowing so thick. Sometimes, I think the wind is blowing in all directions at once. One of the other boarders wants to go home to Rexburg, but he can't leave, either. All I can do is read. It keeps my mind off the blizzard.

April 2, 1915 The storm seems to be blowing itself out, but the drifts are higher than the windows in the house. I hope it isn't so bad on Bull's Fork. I'd hate to remain here any longer than I have to.

April 3, 1915 The storm stopped and the sun is shining but it's bitter cold and nobody is moving. They can't move anyway because of the drifts blocking every road. I can't believe the white man's god is so angry with him. Here it is April and we're snowed in. Bruno Stositch, he's the guy from Rexburg, prays a lot and always before we eat. Today he asked his god to send warmer weather and a whole bunch of other things. I hope it works.

April 5, 1915 I got a surprise visitor today. Streeter Wallace who has a homestead near Ozone, came to visit me. He told me he'd worked at the sugar factory for several years in winter and on his homestead with his brothers in summer. But he also told me spring comes very late in the hills. He said I shouldn't be surprised if I can't get to my place for another couple of weeks. Maybe more. I didn't like the part about the late spring. He told me he'd heard about me in Otteson's store but never was able to meet me.

April 9, 1915 Bruno's prayers must have convinced his god of something because today was nice and warm. Shoni and I rode out to Ozone but the road up the hill and all around was awful muddy where there wasn't any snow. We had to go out far off the road to get around the mud. Mrs. Otteson said she wished she'd moved to the valley, too.

When I got back to Lincoln, I read some more of Mr. Dickens' story. I had to read the last chapter several times before I understood it.

April 10, 1915 At last the weather is getting warmer and a warm wind is blowing. If this continues, I'll be able to return to my homestead in a few days. I've heard the road to Ozone is passable with only a few mud holes. I will ride out tomorrow to see how far I can get.

April 11, 1915 Mrs. Otteson told me no one had been able to cross at Kep's Crossing, yet. Willow Creek was very high and the bridge was gone, again. I didn't dare try to cross it. She said they'll rebuild the bridge this summer, after the water gets lower. The warm weather and wind has melted so much snow water has become my enemy. She told me I might be able to cross it if I went up to the headwaters, but she wasn't sure. I think that's the route I took when I went to Blackfoot. I'll try it tomorrow. I am spending so much money at the boarding house I'm afraid I won't have enough to make my homestead. Every day costs me nearly eighty-five cents.

Chapter Twelve
Weather Improving

April 14, 1915 Day before yesterday, I got to my homestead by crossing Willow Creek over its headwaters. It was still very high but Shoni was able to make it through. As we got closer to my homestead, I could see the winter wheat in the clear patches and I felt very happy. The place where I'd put my tent and stove was still covered with snow and I had to dig them out with my hands. I put the tent up in a spot where the snow was melted and started a fire in the stove. Shoni went in his corral and stayed there without the gate closed. I have to build a barn the first thing. The days are quite warm, but it gets cold at night and the snowdrifts freeze till I can walk on them. Shoni grazed on some new grass and I had a sandwich Mrs. Denning gave me, but we had to go to Ozone today to get some food. I should have thought of that on the way up, but I guess I was so anxious to get here, I just forgot about food. I bought a shovel and a big hammer and some big nails to start on a barn. The next day, I chopped down 15 of the straightest aspen trees and started to cut them to make a log barn. I have the first logs laid on the ground now. I worked so hard yesterday all my muscles are sore this morning. I just finished my breakfast and I'm waiting for the sun to get higher. I think I've never been happier than I am now.

Being back, after being imprisoned at the boarding house for so long, and able to do what he wanted to, erased the memory of his monotonous job at the sugar factory. Within a week, he had the walls for the barn finished, and planned to add a sod roof.

April 24, 1915 I finished the barn yesterday. The aspen logs were not as straight as I thought, so it took a lot of mud to fill the cracks. The real work was putting the sod on the roof. Shoni walked right in but it looks kind of funny, sort of like a very long toilet. I'll build one big enough for a team of horses and Shoni later. I'm so excited about being able to work on my place, I find it hard to believe I'm really doing it. This morning I went to Ozone again for food and a kerosene lamp. I'm writing this in its light. I also bought a sack of oats for Shoni. He's eaten the new grass about as fast as it grows. It was a big load and it took almost all day. The snow has almost all melted from the field I've cleared, and the wet field shows through like huge rips and ragged holes in a worn white blanket. I bought a sack of alfalfa seed to plant the new cleared part when I've finished some of it.

April 26, 1915 The sagebrush here isn't so thick, so I can clear it faster. It made me think of the last time I worked in my field when I cut my foot.

John continued clearing the land working carefully to avoid another accident. The rest went much faster, and he finished in about a month. He pondered the layout of the barn and cabin and planned every step in his mind as the ax struck and the brush fell. He decided to use boards from the sawmill instead of logs, as many others used.

He needed a wagon and horses too. He rode to Covert's sawmill to find out what lumber cost. Mr. Covert was shoveling snow away from the sawmill, getting it ready to start about the first of June. John described what he wanted to do and learned he could get poles for his corral just by cutting them on Pine Mountain. The barn he described would cost about a hundred dollars for the lumber. He was surprised at the amount, so Mr. Covert suggested a shed to be incorporated into a bigger barn in the future. It would cost about a quarter as much.

He returned and marked the location of the corral and barn, and the cabin on the ground. He hadn't seen his mother for five years, so the night before he left to visit her, he burned a pile of sagebrush and danced and sang around its roaring flames. His songs, sung in Shoshoni, told of his joy. He had done something he never thought of in his wildest dreams as a boy. He pounded two sticks together to create the rhythm, and his dance returned him to his childhood. The next day he went to his mother.

She seemed older and sadder, and not so pretty as he recalled. "Jean-Pierre, you look hungry. Don't you have enough to eat?"

"I have enough to eat and I have a piece of land like the white man. I will grow crops of wheat on it, and I will build a cabin on it. I will have a pretty white woman for a wife, and I will have many children. I will be a real white man like my father. I am trying very hard to be the way you told me. The white man's medicine is very strong, but I have been strong too."

"That is good. Why have you come to me if all is well with you?"

"I came to you because you are my mother. You are wise, and I want you to know I am all right. Is everything all right with you?"

"I am healthy. I have enough, but you are so hungry. Do you eat well?"

"I have enough to eat, and I am very happy. Do you know where Willow is?"

"She is with Tommy Johns, and they live in Fort Hall."

"Then I will not go to see her."

"My son, I know about you and Willow. It is better you do not try to visit her."

"How did you know?"

"Her mother told me."

"Then why did she not stop us?"

"She wanted Willow to be with you."

Looking back, he thought they should have known others in the village would notice them.

Alarmed at how his mother had changed, John looked around the teepee and saw little food, so he rode the few miles to Blackfoot and brought back a load of food for her. He prepared some of it for them and spent the night in her teepee. The next morning, he took a gold coin from his pocket and handed it to her.

"Here is twenty dollars. I am sure you can use it. Please take it."

She took the coin, and he thought he saw tears in her eyes. Everything looked bad, and the place where she kept her food contained almost nothing except what he bought for her. He wanted to tell her he would take care of her, but she had other family. Then he left. Many friends wanted to talk to him, but his visit had saddened him, so he didn't stop. He enjoyed the visit with his mother, but when he saw how she lived, he thought he was the richest man in the world. He knew he was no longer a Shoshoni Indian. He was a white man. His medicine was part of both, and he was very confused.

June 8, 1915 I have been thinking of my mother and how poor she is. The sparkle has gone from her eyes, and she is very thin. She looks so much older than I remember her.

On the way home, I stopped at the Ozone store to find out who might have some workhorses to sell. Mr. Otteson told me to go see Abe Day.

Abe recognized him immediately as "the guy that won the horse." He sent him with Tom Shurtliff to look at what he had for sale. "We've got some very good ones, but they'll cost you a lot."

"I don't need the best ones. I just need a team to haul stuff on a wagon right now, then for farming."

Tom said, "I've got a couple that ain't too well matched I can sell for seventy-five dollars. One of them is four years old, and the other one, three. They've been broke together, so I know they can work together." He pointed them out.

"The one with the blaze on his forehead is Mage, and the other one is Bud. Mage is three and Bud is four. Bud's a plodder. Mage ain't. He likes to have his way sometimes, but he's a good horse. They work good together. You got harnesses?"

"No, I forgot about that. Now, that's something else to take money. I'll have to think about all this for a while. Where can I buy harnesses?"

"Just about anybody that sells farm machinery sells harnesses. A new set will cost almost as much as the horses. If you can find some used ones, you'll get a better deal, but they might have to be fixed up a little. Leave a note at Ozone next time you're through there. Maybe somebody has a set for sale."

John thought: Seventy-five dollars! That will leave me only about sixty for all the other things, but I've got to have horses. Maybe an investment in a decent team is worth it.

He heard at the Day farm Ludwig Franck moved into his cabin the previous November, so he stopped to get acquainted.

A little girl five or six years old answered his knock.

"Hello, is this the Franck homestead?"

A tiny voice answered slowly, "Yeees."

"Is Mr. Franck home?"

Again, "Yeees."

"May I talk to him?"

"I don't knooow."

"Will you call him, please?"

"Yeees." But she never moved.

"What's your name?"

"Eyereeeen."

"Well, Irene, I sure would like to talk to your daddy."

A tall woman appeared behind the little girl. "Hello. I don't know you. Who are you?"

"John Fountain, ma'am. I'm your neighbor. I've come several times to get acquainted, but found no one here."

"Oh, yes. We've heard of you. Please come in. We don't get many visitors. Irene is kind of shy around strangers, but she always gets to the door first when someone knocks. Ludwig is in the other room feeling sorry for himself, He's got a cold."

"Thank you ma'am."

The woman called out, "Ludwig! John Fountain is here."

A voice that sounded all nasal came back, "I'll get dressed and come out."

"No, you stay in bed where you belong." She turned to John and said, "My name is Carrie, and that one is Eugene, and the little one is Lee. You've already met Irene. Kids, this is our neighbor, Mr. Fountain." The kids mumbled something and went back to what they were doing.

Mr. Franck's voice came from the other room. "And I'm Louie, usually the man of the house, but right now not worth anything. Carrie, bring a chair for John."

Mrs. Franck brought a chair and set it quite far from the bed. John said, "Mr. Franck, sir. I just wanted to thank you for helping plant my grain last fall and to get acquainted. I was in pretty bad shape after I cut my foot. You stayed here all winter?"

"We came early last November. It wasn't bad till January after the thaw. Then it got really cold. There were a few days when I thought we would freeze, but I've got a lot of wood, so we kept warm most of the time. When George Fogelsong told me about your problem, I decided to help. I know some day I'll need some help, so I'll get even with you. Besides, we had a kind of a party afterward. Then I went back to Utah to get the family."

Small talk filled another half hour.

Carrie asked John to stay for supper, but it seemed to him they didn't have any more to eat than they needed, so he thanked her and went home.

June 10, 1915 Today was very hot. When I walked out along my field, I could feel the leaves brushing against my hands. It made me feel very good. Later, I rode to Ozone to see if I could find a wagon to haul the things I need. Mr. Otteson said maybe Clark Barzee over on Noon Creek would have an old wagon to sell. I asked if he knew anyone who had a set of used harnesses I could buy cheap. He took me out to a barn next to the store and dug around in a bunch of old boards and sacks and other stuff and pulled out a tangled mess of leather straps. He said they belonged to a man who came, sold his horses, and didn't know what to do with the harnesses so he left them there in case somebody needed them. They were all covered with dust and bird stuff, but they seemed to be complete. He told me I could have them if I wanted them. He warned me they were dry and should be oiled. Well, that's one thing I won't have to buy. Mr. Barzee had a wagon with a grain bed on it. It needs a few new boards, but he offered to sell it to me for ten dollars, then said seven would be enough. He told me I'd have to soak the wheels.

Farming sure gets complicated if you don't have the equipment. That makes over eighty dollars I have to spend before I can do anything else. I don't have much more money. My wheat will be ready to cut about the first of August, and I have to build a corral for my new horses, and some kind of shed I can make into a barn. I think I like to solve this kind of problem, though. I just thought of something else. I have to have some hay for the horses.

John went back to see Mr. Day to buy the horses. "You have a crop coming, don't you?" Abe asked.

"Yes, but I think I'll have to sell it to pay for all the things I need to get started. It will probably take almost all the money I have."

"Look, if you want to pay for just one horse now I can wait till you sell your crop for the rest. It's only a couple of months. I like you, son. I think you'll be an asset to this area, and I want to help you. What else do you need?"

"Well, sir, I hadn't thought of it till yesterday, but I don't have any hay to feed them. Shoni grazes around the area but there's just enough for him."

Tom Shurtliff walked up leading a very nice horse. "Tom, John needs some hay. We've got a little extra now, don't we?"

"Yeah," Tom said. "How much?"

John was embarrassed. He had no idea how much. At the Monsons, it seemed to be quite a lot. "How much can I load onto a grain bed?" John asked. Both men laughed.

Tom said, "Not very much. We could loan him a hayrack can't we, Abe? He can load it up, take it home and bring the rack back. I guess that's something else you need."

John paid Abe forty dollars and led the horses behind Shoni to Otteson's store where he put the harnesses on them. The harnesses were complete, and he went to Barzee's to get the wagon. Mr. Barzee was gone, but his wife took the seven dollars and John started to hitch the horses to the wagon. There was no double tree or single trees, or neck yoke. He returned to the house and asked Mrs. Barzee about the missing things. She told him Mr. Barzee wouldn't be back till the next day, so John rode back to Otteson's store to buy the missing parts and left the team tied to the wagon. Mrs. Otteson laughed and said, "You sure are having a hard time getting things organized, aren't you?" She didn't have any single trees or double trees either, but did have a neck yoke. She told him she had an order to Idaho Falls on Monday, and she would include John's stuff on the order. It would cost five dollars. John rode back to Barzee's and asked if he could leave his team there for the night. Mrs. Barzee said, "Sure, put them in the barn. There's some hay you can feed them. Clark should be here by about eleven tomorrow morning. You're sure having a hard time getting things to go your way, aren't you?"

"Yes, ma'am, it seems just about the time everything seems to be worked out, it goes wrong. I'll come back tomorrow. Maybe Mr. Barzee can lend me an outfit for a few days."

John commented for that confused day. "I'm sitting here by my lamp writing this, and when I read it over, I have to laugh. What else can go wrong?"

June 12, 1915   I knew most of the people wouldn't want to work on Sunday, so I tried to get my wagon and take it to Mr. Day's place for a load of hay, today. Mr. Barzee was home when I got to his place and he laughed a little when I told him what had happened yesterday. He loaned me his rigging for the wagon, and I went to Mr. Day's place. The wagon was kind of wobbly and I drove very slowly. He and Tom helped me load the hayrack onto the wagon, and we loaded the hay and I drove home. He suggested I drop the rack off on Monday. I had no good place to put my team, but they didn't seem to mind sharing the tiny corral with Shoni.

I met Mr. Schwieder on the way home and he told me there would be a Fourth of July celebration in Dehlin on the fifth of July because the fourth was on Sunday. I should come and race Shoni. Maybe I will. I need a couple of days off and by then I should have my corral built.

After exchanging wagon beds at the Day place, John picked up his new rigging in Ozone and took the borrowed one back to Barzee's. The next day he began cutting poles for the new corral, and in about a week had it almost finished, but not without more tools. "I had to get a saw and a folding ruler and some more big nails in Ozone. It seems no matter what I have, it's never enough. I wonder if it will ever end."

His shed would be just big enough to keep his team and Shoni out of the weather with room for manger and a place to hang the harnesses. He went to look over Jed's and Arthur Schwieder's barns. Both were essentially the same: pole frameworks with sawed boards nailed to them. The roofs were different. Arthur had real shingles and Jed's roof was board and batten.

He finished his corral in a cool rain, letting it wet him through, and by the middle of June had most of the pole framework for the barn up. He wrote, "I'll go to the sawmill tomorrow to buy the boards for my shed. I have the framework up already. I think it's a little bit smaller than Mr. Covert figured.

"I walked out along my field again and felt very good. The heads are almost formed, and the leaves are almost to my middle. I wish Mr. Monson could see it. Even the alfalfa has started to grow, but it doesn't look so good. There are bare spots in it."

June 23, 1915 I thought Mr. Dickens had begun to make sense, but as I read farther in to the second book, it seems he's not so clear any more. In chapters 7 and 8, a Monseigneur Marquis shows up without a very good explanation of what he is. It's getting harder to read again, but I guess that's because I have to read each chapter at least twice before I think I understand it. I also think I should read it more often. When I work so hard I don't feel much like reading at night even with my new lamp.

June 26, 1915 I got a nice surprise when I went to the sawmill. Mr. Covert told me my shed was a lot smaller than he thought I would build and the lumber cost seventeen dollars instead of twenty five. He sawed the boards while I was there and I got a lot of wide ones and some about half as wide to nail over the spaces between the wide ones. I also chopped down some poles and brought them and finished the frame for the shed. One side of it is now finished. It's going a lot faster than I thought it would. I should finish it in a couple of days. I also had to buy some smaller nails.

I didn't know how many nails it would take. It seems like there's never an end to what I need.

By the end of June, the new shed was almost finished, and on July 4, he put the horses in it, fed them in their manger, and hung the harnesses on pegs behind them. It was a most happy day and it looked as if someone lived there.

July 4, 1915 I have horses and a wagon and a good crop of wheat growing in the field. And my garden is growing well. I tried the carrots and they are still small. I will go to the celebration in Dehlin tomorrow. I think I would like to race Shoni.

I hope I can meet another pretty girl again this year. Maybe Mrs. Holmquist will find another one. I don't much like her help, but at the same time, her matchmaking is kind of interesting. She introduced me to Delia.

At the celebration, John led Shoni around, and greeted many others, including one newcomer, Harlin Loveland. John and Harlin became friends at once, comparing notes on homesteading and laughing at John's problems when he bought the wagon.

He met Jed. "I hope you're going to race Shoni. I haven't seen a faster horse in this area."

"I think I will," John announced. He met many other homesteaders, and it seemed everyone knew more about him than he knew about them.

As in Ozone the year before, they erected stands to sell food and put a little money in the church coffers. He enjoyed meeting the people with whom he had so much in common, and decided it was time he did more visiting.

Then came the surprise. Mrs. Holmquist found him. "Have you got a wife, yet, John?"

No, ma'am, I've been very busy."

"What happened between you and Delia?"

He thought she shouldn't ask, but answered, "We got along all right but I guess I'm just not the right man for her."

"Then I find you another one," Although John didn't want her help, his curiosity was aroused. He bought another of her pork sandwiches, and had just started eating it when she caught up with him again, leading yet another girl. She wasn't very pretty, but kind of nice looking, anyway.

"John I think you should know Luella Loveland. She's a nice girl."

A hapless John said, "Hello, ma'am."

"My name's Luella," she said. "I'm glad to meet you, John. I see you've already met my father. We started our homesteading this spring, although he filed two or three years ago. You're standing on part of it now."

"When I first got here, I liked the place, but Jed told me it was already taken. How long have you been here?"

"We came this spring."

Mrs. Holmquist interrupted, "You don't need me any more. I go now. Good luck, and the same to you, Luella."

"I wonder what she meant," John mused.

"I think I know. While you were talking to my father, I asked her who you were. She said she'd find out if you were married. After you bought that sandwich you haven't eaten much of, she came and got me and brought me here."

John remembered the sandwich and took another bite. His mouth was full, so it gave him time to think of something else to say. Luella was very young.

"Excuse me, Miss Loveland, I'd almost forgotten my sandwich."

"My name is Luella. Daddy warned me she's a matchmaker. I heard you won a horse at Ozone last year, is this the one?"

"Yes. That's him. His name is Shoni. I'll race him this afternoon. He's never raced before, but he's a fast runner and I think he'll win."

"Where did you get such a funny name for him?"

"It's short for Shoshoni."

"Why Shoshoni?"

"When I lived in the Shoshoni village, I had a horse named Pony. When I won Shoni last year, I decided to name him after the Shoshoni Indians."

"Why were you living in a Shoshoni village?"

"I thought everybody knew. My mother is a Shoshoni Indian, and my father came from Canada."

"I didn't. Then you're not a Mormon?"

"No."

"You don't talk or look like an Indian. Do you believe in God?"

"Not the same way you do, Miss Loveland."

"Luella."

"Luella. The Shoshonis believe they're a part of something much greater than any one person."

"Then you must be a heathen or an atheist."

"I don't know what you're talking about."

"All atheists are bad people and so are heathens."

John didn't want to argue with her. He knew she'd been taught the "truth" in white man's terms and there was no use arguing. He said, "I know about your church because I lived with a Mormon family for four years before I started homesteading. I respect your church. Why can't you have the same respect for what I believe?"

"Because you're wrong, that's why." And she left. John finished his sandwich and tried to forget about her.

132

A woman sat at a piano on the platform and a man came out with a violin. As at Ozone the year before the stage was to be the center of activity. The proceedings were almost the same as in Ozone, except Mr. Schwieder called out the events. The children's races were all won by the favorites, and the fat kid won the "way up there and back" race, again. The pie-eating contest was won by the same kid from Dehlin, and John learned his name was Rulon Doman, the son of Mr. Doman he'd had met a while before.

There was one big difference. Two girls won the three-legged race, much to the chagrin of the boys running against them. They had to beg to be allowed in the race with boys, and were admitted with protest. "If these two girls want to race, why don't you boys just go ahead and beat them?"

When Mr. Schwieder announced the horse race would start, John took Shoni to the road where the race was held. There were seven men on saddled and bridled horses. A couple of them complained their horses had to carry a heavier load. John would either have to drop out or borrow a saddle. The race officials, three men John didn't know, said there was no rule about that, so John lined up beside Tom Shurtliff, ready to run. Shoni was excited and skittish. The race track, approximately a quarter mile slightly downhill, wasn't much more than a wagon track. Two lines scratched across the road marked the start and finish. The finish was in front of the announcer's stand.

Mr. Schwieder dropped the flag. Shoni was headed in the wrong direction, but John turned him around and he understood what he should do. John's Indian yell signaled Shoni to run his fastest, and he took off. Soon, he was far ahead of the rest of them except Tom Shurtliff. Everybody was yelling and clapping. John guided Shoni straight down the road, and they passed Tom just before the finish line.

"How much do you want for that horse? Just name your price." Tom said as they dismounted.

"I wouldn't sell him for anything," John said.

"That's the fastest horse I ever raced against. I thought Dan was the best, but yours has him beat for speed."

"How much do you want for Dan?"

"You ain't serious. I wouldn't sell him for anything."

"OK, Tom, isn't that what I just said about Shoni?"

"Yeah, I understand." They sat around for a while talking about their horses till another race was announced, and John lined up for it. The other horses were still standing when Shoni was ten feet down the road. Mr. Rudolph joined John after the race, and shook his hand so hard John thought he was trying to pull his arm off. "I congrat you, John. You got a fast horse there. Good horse. You ride good too. And you yell good. That's good. That horse know when you yell, he gotta go fast. I get *Gänsehaut* (goose bumps) when I hear you EeeeeeYaaaaa Haa!" The way he yelled it, made John laugh. It just didn't fit coming out of his mouth.

They talked for quite a while and Mr. Rudolph told John a lot about coming from Germany. He worked on the east coast for a while and found his way to Salt Lake.

From Salt Lake he headed north when he learned the land in the hills was open for homesteading. He homesteaded on Birch Creek. "Then you're a citizen of United States?" John asked.

"Don't know. I guess so. I live here, and I don't go back to Germany."

John told him of his citizenship problem. Rudolph said, "I just went to the land office and told them I staked a homestead, and they wrote it down."

John decided not to race Shoni again and was just ready to leave and ride back to Bull's Fork when Mr. Loveland and Luella came up.

Harlin said, "Go on Luella, tell John what you said you would."

"Oh, Dad, I'm embarrassed."

"Go on. You said you would."

John sensed she'd told Harlin about their talk. "Miss Loveland, do you think Mrs. Holmquist is a bad person?" John asked.

"No."

"Do you think she would have brought you to meet me if she thought *I* was a bad person?"

"No, I guess not."

"What did you want to say to me?"

She hesitated, and Harlin said, "Go on, Luella. tell him."

"I'm sorry I said what I did to you. I'm really sorry. Dad got angry when I told him about this morning and made me promise to apologize. Will you accept it?"

"Miss Loveland. . . Luella, I accept."

She said, "Thank you!" and they left.

The next day, John scratched the plan of his cabin out on the ground. Each room would be twelve feet square with a wooden floor. When he measured from corner to corner he was surprised his eyes could have deceived him so much.

He discussed the construction with several neighbors and started the work. His foundation was made of large rocks he had to carry a long way, then cement them together using sand from Bull's Fork. He wrote, "It's like Mr. Monson said, 'You have to have a good foundation, or nothing will turn out right.'"

On July 17, he finished the foundation, stood back to admire it, and planned his next move. It wasn't what he planned.

Chapter Thirteen
Clear Skies and Sunny Weather

July 18, 1915 I had to haul lumber in my grain bed for my cabin, and I'd just got the last load unloaded when Mr. Otteson rode up. He told me Ernest Empey had been kidnapped and was being held for $6000 ransom. I don't know Mr. Empey, but according to Mr. Otteson, I should volunteer to go look for him. I rode to Ozone where Sheriff Bob Oley deputized a bunch of us. I found out Mr. Empey was probably being held over on Sheep Mountain where I buy my lumber. The sheriff then told us to go home and wait till tomorrow.

My wheat is ripening.

July 19, 1915 I got to Ozone about eleven in the morning, and the sheriff and two detectives from Ogden came just after I got there. The kidnapper left a very threatening note. If we tried to find Mr. Empey, he was sure to be killed. The detectives warned us against running off into the hills to search because it would be a good way to get him killed for sure. They think a man named Baldy Dean is the kidnapper. He must not be from around here, I never heard of him.

Sheriff Oley told us to go home and wait till we were called before we did something wrong.

When John got back to the homestead, the Monsons were there. It was John's twenty-first birthday, and they came to give him the homestead. All the papers were made out, and John was finally the owner. Mrs. Monson hugged him and told him how she liked what he'd done. She was excited about everything, even the shed.

Both of them were surprised to see the cabin would have three rooms. John explained he would finish two of them, then add the other one later.

"Henry," Lydia said, "this is so exciting, I almost wish we were starting over again."

"Not me, I envy John what he's done, but I've already done it, and I can't think of any reason I'd want to do it again."

July 26, 1915 Mr. Franck came by today on his way from Ozone. He told me Mr. Empey got away from his kidnapper. The kidnapper was a man named Baldy Dean, and he'd been taken into custody.

Ludwig looked around and said, "John, your place is starting to look like something. You've got a real good layout here. Your cabin looks like three rooms. Why so big?"

"It doesn't seem to be a lot of extra work, and if I can find a pretty wife some day I might need three rooms."

"Got anybody in mind?"

"No, sir, I had one I thought would be right, but she decided she didn't want to be a homesteader's wife."

"Please, John, just call me Louie. Everybody else does. Have you seen many rattlesnakes?"

"No. A few showed up while I was clearing the land, but no more than I expected. Why?"

"Well, some time ago my boys saw one crawling out of the grain patch and thought it was a big worm. Scared the daylights out of Carrie, and she pounded it to death with a big stick. A day or so later, Dave Rushton came by and told her to be careful because its mate could be close by. She's been scared out of her wits ever since."

"You can tell her not to worry. Rattlesnakes are loners. When a female is ready, the male finds her and they mate, then go their separate ways. They won't bother you unless they feel threatened. I just let them crawl away."

"You don't kill them?"

"No," John said. "Why? Rattlesnakes and hawks and owls are the best insurance against mice the farmer has."

"I guess so. Bishop Judy says you can remove a rattlesnake's fangs and then it's not dangerous any more but can still catch mice."

"He shouldn't say such things. A rattlesnake depends on its poison to kill mice, and it can't poison mice without fangs. It'll starve to death unless the fangs grow back."

"How come you know these things?" Louie asked.

"I grew up as a Shoshoni Indian. We know these things."

Louie was silent, then said, "I'll tell Carrie. It should make her feel better. About the rattlesnakes, I mean. How come you grew up as a Shoshoni Indian?"

"My father was from Canada, and my mother is Shoshoni. I thought everybody knew that."

"But you don't look like an Indian."

"What does an Indian look like?"

"Just. . . different," Louie said. "Well, I guess I'd better be getting on home. Carrie is waiting for some mail I got at the post office."

139

After Louie left, John thought about living in nature, not ruling it. He was doing just what the Indians don't do; ruling nature by clearing away sagebrush and planting wheat. He was trying to be a white man.

By the end of July, John's cabin was framed, but it would be a long time before he could work on it again. Harvest season had started, and according to the custom, the farmers banded together to help each other thresh. Mr. Hammon cut the wheat and stacked it a few days before the thresher came. Being John's first harvest, his excitement grew and the prospect of seeing his first success as a white man set him thinking about all the things he had to do to get ready. Up till then, he hadn't thought about storage, so he quickly converted Shoni's tiny barn to a granary — not a good one — but perhaps adequate for his needs. Then came the big day.

August 11, 1915   All my neighbors showed up today to help. Joe Empey brought his threshing machine to my place yesterday. It will take about three days. I expect a good crop.

I wrote the first part this morning before I started threshing. I have to write how I feel. I stood in the wagon when the first load came off the thresher and I felt my medicine growing. I was so happy, I yelled, "I did it! I did it!"

Joe Empey grinned at John and said, "It makes you feel good doesn't it? Is this your first crop?"

"It sure does make me feel good. Yes, it's my first crop. A little over a year ago, I never thought about actually harvesting a crop. All I could think of was getting the land cleared, and then I cut my foot really bad, and I thought I would never have a crop, but my neighbors planted part of what I had already cleared. Mr. Empey, sir, I've *never* been happier in my life."

"You're not the first one I've threshed the first crop for, and all of them have the same feeling. As if they'd created something. I felt the same way."

John wanted to strip naked and roll around in the wheat kernels and wiggle in them. He dipped up both hands full and let them run between his fingers, then held his hands higher and let them fall farther. He sat down on the wheat and thought about what he'd done. He'd done something white men do. He wrote, "My life has started. I have a crop of wheat. I will be a good neighbor. I will be a good farmer. Soon I can find a pretty wife and start a family with many children!"

August 12, 1915 I had to have some sacks for my wheat, so Jed loaned me forty, but said he'd have to have them back for his threshing in about a week. The threshing crew filled the sacks while I took the load I had in my wagon. I left my homestead just before it was light and got back home very late at night. It was a very long day.

I had to stop and let the horses rest several times on the way up out of Kep's Crossing. When I got to the elevator in Ammon, I had to shovel the wheat out of the wagon, and when it was weighed, I had almost a ton. I hope I can get it all hauled before winter.

I bought fifty used sacks at the elevator. They cost $2.50. When I got back to my place there were another thirty sacks full of wheat. I left the new sacks and loaded twenty of the full ones onto the wagon.

John managed to haul four loads of wheat to Ammon before he had to help his neighbors. One day the threshing machine broke down and he got a fifth load to the valley, but the job seemed endless. He was discouraged. By the time he finished helping his neighbors thresh, he had a full granary and over a hundred sacks out in the open that had to be hauled to Ammon. Rain became his greatest worry. He worked from the time he could see in the morning till he couldn't see at night. Two rooms of his cabin were framed up waiting for the walls but it looked like he wouldn't get it closed in before winter.

August 31, 1915 I hauled the last of the sacked wheat yesterday and I'm a little over half finished. Today I took the day off and put the canvas back in the grain bed and loaded it from my granary. There's so much more to haul. I should have my winter wheat planted by now. I'm tired.

September 1, 1915 The weather is holding out, but Bud and Mage are getting tired. I decided to stay home today and let all of us rest. I needed some food, so I rode Shoni to Ozone to get some and some oats for the team. I felt like I was robbing myself because I wasn't getting my grain to Ammon.

At the Ozone store, Mrs. Otteson said, "You look so tired. You must be working too hard"

"I have a lot of wheat to get to the elevator and I have to work hard to get it there before bad weather comes. I've been hauling a load every day."

"Every day? No wonder you're tired."

"I know ma'am, but I can't think of any other way to do it."

John hadn't thought about the distance, only that it took about an hour and a half longer to go than to come back. He had to plant his winter wheat soon, and finish hauling the grain later. The field had to be prepared, and he didn't have even a harrow so he could broadcast the seed and harrow it in. He needed so many things.

September 12, 1915 I just quit hauling wheat and planted most of the newly cleared part by hand. I hope it wasn't too late. It gave Bud and Mage a chance to rest though. I borrowed Louie's harrow and dragged it over the field. I might have about fifty acres planted. There are a few kernels showing, but I didn't expect the harrow to cover all of them. I need a disc or a plow or something to prepare the soil. I don't like what I'm doing, but I have to have a crop next year.

September 19, 1915 During the past week I got six more loads of wheat to the elevator. Each load has been about a ton, so I've sold about 12 tons. I asked the man at the elevator how much it was worth so far. He told me between $500 and $525.

Debt was John's great enemy. At the elevator, he asked, "When can I get paid for it?"

"Any time you want. Do you have much more?"

"Yes, I have a lot more, but I don't know how much more I can haul before I have to quit. I have some debts to pay, but I've been so busy hauling, I haven't paid anybody anything. I think I'll take payment now."

The elevator operator gave John a check for $494, which excluded $7.50 for 150 sacks. He cashed the check and paid Mr. Hammon and Mr. Empey for the harvest work, and Mr. Day for the last payment on his team. Free of debt, he thought: Now everything I get is all mine. I just have to work very hard from now till the weather gets too bad.

September 26, 1915 Another six loads. I'm so tired I fell asleep on the wagon on the way home. When we come close to Bull's Fork, Bud and Mage almost run. They're tired, too. I wish I dared to take a whole week off and just sleep. What am I doing? Why do I want to be a white man? My mother told me the white man's medicine is strong. I wonder if it is if he has to work so hard and so long every day. In the Shoshoni camp we looked for food together. White men search alone. When I lived with the Monsons there was always enough to eat, and there was always hard work, but the work wasn't as hard as what I'm doing. I am tired and sad together.

October 3, 1915 I got another six loads of grain to the elevator last week. I haven't had time to work on my cabin. I could leave what I have in my granary, but Mr. Fogelsong said it would be a bad idea unless I could mouse proof it. If the mice get in it, I could have trouble selling it. I heard the sugar factory is about to start. I don't want to work there, but I think I should. I'd ride over today except it's Sunday and there wouldn't be anybody to talk to. I'll go tomorrow.

October 4, 1915 I went to see Mr. Weaver today. He was expecting me. He told me I could work on the spinners this year and I should be ready to go to work next Monday. He told me I would get five cents an hour more, which would be $3.60 a day, and my day off would be Friday.

He must have been expecting me. He'd already arranged with Mrs. Denning for my room and board and space for Shoni, but didn't know I had a team of horses, too.

On the way home, John stopped in Ammon to see Henry. He was plowing and the first thing he said was, "You look like something the cat dragged in. What have you been doing?"

"I'm trying to get all my grain hauled before the weather gets bad."

"How much to you have to haul?"

"I've hauled twenty-two loads and I'm about three quarters done."

"I knew your crop would be good when I looked at it a few months ago. Is it in sacks or bulk?"

"Bulk, sir. I couldn't put it all in sacks, and it's in a sloppy granary. I don't think it's in a good place."

"Tell you what. I can finish this plowing later, and I can help you get your grain out of the hills."

John felt as if he'd already slept for a week. The problem wasn't solved, but he had a better chance. Henry said he'd be up in the morning to help.

Together, they hauled eleven loads to Ammon. The weather cooperated for a while, then it rained or snowed and sometimes the loads got a little wet in spite of the canvas they used to cover them. There was still wheat left in John's granary when weather made them quit.

During a rare rest period, John said, "I have another problem. I have to work in the sugar factory again. Mr. Weaver told me I should come to work on Monday. I need so many things."

"Well, the sugar factory will give you an income. Maybe sacrificing a couple of loads of wheat will be worth it. Besides, you might be able to haul some on your days off."

Henry had to get back to his plowing, and John went back to work in the sugar factory. He rode Shoni to Lincoln to find a place for his work horses.

John wrote, "I was lucky. Someone I don't know at the boarding house told me a man named Charley Johnston moved into a house in the town site. He had no livestock and there's a barn."

John asked Mr. Johnston about using his barn, and received a warm welcome. After introductions, Mr. Johnston said, "Well, I have a few chickens and a pig in it but it has horse stalls. Let's go out and look at it."

It turned out to be just right. "How much do you want for it?"

"Son, you can have it for nothing if you don't burn it down and you can stand the pig and the chickens."

"Do you know where I can buy hay?"

"There's hay in the loft you can use. I can't do any more than pick my teeth with it, and that won't take very much. I'd like to get rid of it anyway before it rots." If you need some more, I'm sure you can find it."

"I'd be happy to pay for the space and the hay."

"You must be just starting out. I know how damned tough it is. I homesteaded south of town thirty years ago and worked my butt off for ten years before I ever saw light out of debt. If I can help you with your horses, you're welcome to it. You'll have to do the feeding though. Damned near broke my back a few years ago, and I don't dare climb any higher than two or three steps. You'll have to take them to water. The canal is just across the road. They tell me it freezes tight in winter."

Back at his place the next day, John took another load of wheat to Ammon, took horses to Lincoln, and put them in the barn. He could haul grain to the elevator on Fridays.

Chapter Fourteen
Mixed Weather

Thus began a second winter at the sugar factory. not so different from the first. After he delivered the last load of grain to Ammon, John collected $628.84. Having no experience with banks, indeed, with that much money at all, he was reluctant to leave it in the bank, afraid he'd never see it again. Clifford Reims, the man at the elevator, told him the bank was far safer than his pocket. Still not satisfied, he went to see Henry. A short conversation with Henry convinced him and he opened an account at Anderson Bros. Bank.

Running the spinners, the centrifuges that remove the molasses from the crystallized sugar, was new and his first experience using a machine for which he didn't provide the power. Clarence taught him the fundamentals and left him on his own.

October 23, 1915 I will be very glad when I don't have to listen to the heart beat of the steam engine of the sugar factory. This year, they don't expect as many beets as they had last year, but I think I probably won't be able to get back to my farm much sooner. I don't like to work here, it's too monotonous, but I need the money. I know I'll have to buy some equipment for the farm, and maybe even a new wagon. And I need hay for the horses. The alfalfa I planted last spring just got started and I didn't even bother to cut it. I have to buy some new clothes. I want to finish my cabin and live in it.

October 29, 1915 I went to a Halloween dance at the Lincoln School tonight. I hoped to find a pretty girl for a wife, but I didn't. I guess it's because I don't dance I have trouble meeting girls. I did see the girl friend of the guy who wanted to fight me last winter, though.

The girl came to where John was sitting and asked, "Aren't you the fellow Alex started a fight with last winter?"

"I don't know. Who is Alex?"

"When we were in line at the punch bowl, he came up to you and wanted you to go outside with him. When I found him, he was lying in the snow and his face was all bloody."

"Oh, yes," John said, "he ran into the side of the school building."

"My name is Ruth Wright."

"I'm John Fountain." He didn't know what else to say, so he just looked at her. She was different from other girls. She wasn't especially pretty, but pleasant looking, and she seemed to be easy to talk to. "Do you live in Lincoln?" he finally asked.

"No, I live in Iona, but I have an aunt here, and I come to visit her as often as I can. I happened to be here today, so I came to the dance. I haven't seen you dancing."

"I can't seem to get the timing right, so I just watch."

"May I watch with you?"

Surprised, he said, "OK." She seemed smart enough not to ask stupid questions. He liked her.

John went to dances or programs at the Lincoln School or the Mormon Church as often as he could, but was always somewhat uneasy because he wasn't a Mormon as most of them were, but Ruth seemed to be truly friendly. "What do you do when you're not out having such a good time?" Ruth asked.

"I'm working in the sugar factory for the winter. The rest of the year I'm homesteading on Bull's Fork."

"Where did you live before you started your homestead?"

"When my father died, I came to Ammon, and Mr. Monson gave me a job. My mother sent me away to live among the white men."

"Why?"

"My mother is a Shoshoni Indian and my father was a Canadian. She told me I'd have a better life among the white men. I was only sixteen when I left."

"John — I hope you don't mind my using your first name — I have to leave. I wish I could stay and get better acquainted, but I have to get back to my aunt's place." She looked him full in the face and smiled as she said good-bye. John thought she was nice looking.

November 19, 1915 I took a little bit of money from the bank for some new clothes while I was in town. My old winter coat was getting thin and I needed a new union suit for winter. I also bought a new pair of shoes and some overshoes and a warm shirt. Mrs. Denning told me to be sure to be here for Thanksgiving dinner this year. She's a nice lady.

I'll finally have time to read Mr. Dickens' story again. I've forgotten where I left off, but I have it marked. I really enjoy reading it. I still think he spends a lot of time explaining things but I'm sure that's one of the things that makes it so interesting.

November 20, 1915 Mr. Monson came to the sugar factory and invited me to come to their place for Thanksgiving dinner. I told him I already had an invitation at the Dennings. He was disappointed and so was I. It's almost a family reunion when I visit them and to me, it's really home, but I had made a promise I thought I should keep.

Then I thought of my mother and her life. I have to go visit her again when the factory closes. I'm sure she could use some more money. I hope the family is taking care of her. Sometimes I wish I were still there in the camp. We didn't worry about money like the white men.

November 26, 1915 Yesterday was Thanksgiving and Mrs. Denning had all the things to eat that others have this day. A boarder named Willie Peabody from Shelley gave the prayer before we ate. It was a lot shorter than Bruno Stositch gave last year.

Today when I went to feed and water Bud and Mage, I stopped at the Lincoln store. I'd never been in it before, but I thought I'd like to have a soda pop. I was surprised to find Ruth in the store. Her uncle is the owner, and she'd come to visit again. She seemed glad to see me, so I asked her if she had time to take a little walk. She agreed, and we walked down the road toward Ammon. We walked for about a mile and turned around.

John was enjoying the friendship of this girl. She asked him, "Is it hard to homestead a piece of land?"

There was only one answer, "Harder than I expected." He told her about his visit to the land office and Mrs. Gerrard.

"What a nasty woman!"

"Well, she was just doing what she was supposed to do. I guess she was right, but it was pretty disappointing for me."

"How did you finally get your homestead if you weren't old enough?"

He told her about Mrs. Monson and what she did, and how they came on his birthday and gave him the relinquishment papers.

"Then you're just twenty-one since last July. I was twenty in July. What day?"

"The eighteenth."

"That's a coincidence! My birthday is July 18, too. Where were you born?"

"According to my mother, I was born on the bank of the Snake River"

"I remember you said you were half Indian. Which half?"

That took John by surprise. "My mother is a Shoshoni."

"I know that. I was just being facetious." She looked at him out of the corner of her eye with a cute little smile, "As if I expected you to say the top half or the bottom half or the right or left half."

That struck John so funny, he laughed long and hearty. And so did Ruth. It was a very pleasant laugh. He thought she was almost pretty when she laughed.

"Does anyone call you a half breed?"

"Sometimes. Why?"

"I don't like that. It sounds like a barnyard accident. I prefer mixed blood, but only when it's necessary to make a point. Where did your father come from in Canada?"

"From Quebec. The city of Quebec. My grandfather came from France."

"I'm asking too many questions. Forgive me, but you're so interesting. Something drives me to know more about you."

"When you're not in Lincoln asking me questions, what do you do?"

"I'm trying to become a school teacher. I help the teachers in Iona part of the time. I've heard about the homesteaders, and some day I'd like to teach in one of the schools where the homesteaders' kids go. It must be a challenge to teach all eight grades at once."

They said good-bye at the store, and she squeezed John's hand. He liked Ruth. She wasn't so pretty, but he thought she wasn't dumb like so many others he'd met. He told her he was reading *A Tale of Two Cities*. She looked surprised and said she'd read it twice. She said she'd be back in Lincoln in a month or so. He hoped she'd be at one of the dances they have in the Lincoln schoolhouse.

November 30, 1915 I hope the snow at my homestead doesn't ruin the frame and the floor of the cabin. I wish I could have built a roof over it. But my wheat was more important at the time. I think I still owe Mr. Covert some money. I'll have to look it up.

Then I thought about Ruth. And I thought about being half Indian. Which half? I started to laugh again. It was something I never, ever would have thought of if she hadn't said it. Then I thought about how she might fit at my homestead. She's very nice to be with.

December 2, 1915 For the past week, I've been reading my book every day. I still have to read some chapters twice to be sure I know what they say, but the story is very interesting like Ruth said. She said she read it twice. I'm reading it twice too, but at the same time.

There was an accident at the factory last Wednesday. A man fell from high up onto a big crate and broke his back and fractured his skull. His name was David Bogle. He's paralyzed from the waist down. With a fractured skull, it might not be the end of his troubles. Mr. Weaver told me a few years ago, a man running the spinners caught his sleeve and it twisted his arm off. This is a dangerous place to work. So is homesteading if you don't watch out all the time.

December 10, 1915 I expect the Monsons will invite me for Christmas this year. I didn't go to their Thanksgiving dinner and I'd hate to miss a chance to go there for Christmas. I haven't seen the boys or Susan for a long time. About two years, I think. I'll ride over there some time and see what's going on.

December 13, 1915 I rode Shoni to feed and water my team, but the streets are so slick from snow I didn't go anywhere else. I have to chop the ice out of the canal and carry water to the barn for Bud and Mage.

December 17, 1915 This job is so boring that if it wasn't for the two cities story, I think I'd get sick.

December 20, 1915 I haven't heard from the Monsons so, even though it was quite late to go visiting, I rode to Ammon. No one answered my knock, so I came back. I'd really expected to hear from them by now. I hope everything is all right. But I'm worried. There is almost always somebody at home. They have relatives in Utah, but I don't think they'd all go down there. I think they'd let me know if they did.

John had just returned from his chores in Lincoln townsite, and was putting Shoni in the barn when Henry showed up. He said, "Lydia is in the hospital. She developed gallstones and had to be operated on."

"When can I go see her?" John asked.

"Well, we took her in last Monday, and they operated on Tuesday, so she'll be there for about another week. She was pretty worried about what you'll do on Christmas this year."

"I'll go visit her next Friday," John promised, "How are the rest of the family?"

"Well, James is just James, as usual. Typical kid, I guess. He seems to think if you get half way through a job, you can consider it done, and he drops his tools and goes away. Sam is the opposite. He's so thorough it's disgusting. Everything is done completely, and the tools are all back where they belong. Since he won the science contest in school with the bottle and the wheat, he's always got something growing in a bottle or a pan or a can or something. Freddie is disappointed you won't be with us for Christmas. He seems to think his mother got sick on purpose.

"Susan's having a hard time. She says the other kids make fun of her because she's so skinny and has pimples. I never had any sisters, so I don't know what it's all about. Lydia is waiting in the hospital for me. I'll tell her you'll come to see her."

"Please give my hellos to the boys and Susan. I'll see Mrs. Monson next Friday."

December 26, 1915 After Mr. Monson left me last Friday, I went to the Christmas show at the schoolhouse. It was about the same as last year. The different rooms in the school put on their own little shows and the kids forgot what they were supposed to say. Just like last year, one boy was supposed to turn some somersaults on the stage, which he did OK, but his shoes were far too big for him and they hit the floor with an awful thud, but he didn't fall off the stage.

As I was leaving, I saw Ruth. We talked a few minutes and she said she would be in Lincoln till the school Christmas vacation was over. We agreed to meet next Friday night at the New Year's Eve dance at the school.

The prospect of seeing Ruth again made him happy. "I still haven't learned to dance," he told her.

"That's OK, I'll help you sit them out."

"What about your friend from last year?"

She looked disgusted and said, "I haven't gone anywhere with Alex since that night. He could be pretty nice, but if he had something to drink, he always got nasty and I don't like it. I like somebody like you. You're a lot easier to be with."

December 29, 1915 The work is still boring, but the time passes a little bit faster because I think about seeing Ruth again on Friday. I wonder what we'll talk about. She said she thought I was interesting. She's interesting too. Maybe I should ask her more questions about her.

December 31, 1915 I went to see Mrs. Monson today. She was out of bed and looked tired and she was kind of pale, but she was happy to see me. We talked about the family and how bad she felt because they couldn't invite me to Christmas. We talked for about forty-five minutes, and she told me again about Sam's growing things in bottles and cans and stuff, and how unhappy Susan was because she was never invited to dances or anything. She said she was getting over it a little bit, though. Freddy blamed her for getting sick so they couldn't invite me. That makes me feel good. He's really a little brother to me. I don't remember how we got started on the foot stomping routine, but it's fun to make him laugh. She said they'd let her out in a couple of days. I know what it's like, so I understood how she felt in that room.

When I got back to the boarding house, I got ready to go to the dance. I was anxious to see Ruth again. She sure is nice to be with. I'll see her again in about three hours.

January 1, 1916 Last night, I thought I had found the girl to share my homestead. Ruth came just a few minutes after I got there. She was dressed in a very pretty dress, and her hair was combed so her face looked like a bright light. She really looked wonderful. We sat down to watch the others while they danced. They had the same band as last year with the big drum that made a lot of noise and the little ones that made a funny noise, and a man who played an instrument I'd never seen before. Ruth told me it was a saxophone. And there was a piano and a trumpet, too. The music was good, she said. But I guess I'll never get used to white man's music.

Determined to lead the conversation away from him, John asked her, "Have you always lived in Iona?"

"I was born in Iona, and I've always lived there. I went to Rick's College in Rexburg to learn to be a teacher, but that's the only time I've lived anywhere else. Why?"

"I guess I just want to know more about you. You asked me a lot of questions about me and I thought I should get even. You know a lot more about me than I know about you."

"But you're so much more interesting than I am. Just think about it. You've lived two very different lives. Mine is all Iona. When you were growing up, did you do all the things the Indian boys did, like going hunting for buffalo and elk and deer and all those things?"

Again, she started the questions. John thought about what she said. His life might have been interesting to her, and he really had lived two very different lives. She didn't ask dumb questions, and it seemed she really wanted to know. "Yes, I've gone hunting for game, but not for buffalo. They were mostly gone when I was a boy. Mostly we hunted for small game and roots and berries and things like that. Other things were not so easy to get."

"Did you speak Shoshoni all the time or English? By the way, your English is much better than I hear from other white men."

"Did you just call me a white man?"

"I know you're part Indian, but you just don't look like any Indian I ever saw. You're a handsome man, and I've never seen an Indian I would call handsome. Does it bother you?"

At first, he couldn't think of anything to say to her, but then remembered her question. "Most of the time in the Shoshoni camp, I spoke their language. My father taught me English and French."

'Have you ever spoken French to anyone except him?"

"Last year, a Frenchman came to the sugar factory, and we talked together for a little while. I was surprised we could. I'd never spoken French to anyone but my father."

"He must have taught you well. You're lucky."

"Yes, he was a good teacher, but sometimes too strict. Sometimes I had to repeat something several times for him. He wanted me to say everything perfect."

"Perfectly," she said.

"Thank you," John said.

"How about your mother? She must have had an influence, too."

"Yes, I watched her do all kinds of things. One of the things most useful was tanning hides. I have several now I will take to her to make me a winter coat. Even my father learned those things from her. She kept me entertained with Shoshoni legends, too."

"What kind of hides do you have?"

"Mostly rabbit, but I have one a wolf gave me."

"A wolf *gave* you a hide?"

"That's not *exactly* what happened. I fed a very big, old wolf for a while, and when he died near my tent, I took his hide and tanned it. In Indian legend we're brothers."

"I thought wolves were dangerous. How come you fed one?"

"I noticed the bones I'd thrown away were disappearing, so I watched for him. When I finally saw him, he just stood and watched me, and after a few days I began throwing him pieces of fried bread. We never got very near each other, but we were friends."

"Now do you see why I think you're so interesting? You know so many things I never even dreamed of. How many legends do the Shoshonis have?"

"There must be hundreds of them. My mother told me a different one almost every time. Mostly they explain how things came to be."

Her eyes lit up and she insisted he tell her some. The dance had reached the intermission and they went through the line for food. When they sat down again, she turned her face him. She looked pretty. Although her features were plain, he thought she seemed to glow. Maybe he was interesting to her. He'd never thought of himself as interesting; just a homesteader trying to build a farm. He felt very confident talking to her. She was special.

After they ate, she asked, "Do the Indians have a legend about the creation of people?"

He remembered how Delia blushed when he told her, but Ruth seemed to have a genuine interest, "Yes, but you probably don't want to hear it."

"Why not?"

"The coyote is the father of all people." He hoped that would be enough. It wasn't.

"How could that be?"

He learned at the Monsons white people don't like to talk about reproduction except in the most general terms, yet she was so easy to talk to he told her the story he told Delia.

Her response was surprising. "Oh how fascinating! But I couldn't tell that to any of the children in school. I'd never get a job teaching anywhere."

"It didn't bother you to hear it?"

"No. Why? It's just a legend."

The dance went on and they talked about the dancers. He told her about dancing around a sagebrush fire and singing and how it was so different from the white man's dance.

"You danced around the fire? Alone?"

"Yes, why not? I was happy and I make up songs as I dance."

"What kind of songs?"

"Mostly just words that say how happy or how sad I am. They don't rhyme the way yours do. They're just an expression of feelings."

She looked a little surprised but agreed it seemed the natural thing to do. She pointed to a couple dancing on the floor keeping time with the music so grotesquely it resembled the way John danced around his fire. They laughed about it for a long time. Then John made drum sounds with his mouth to match their movements and she laughed even harder. She was so pleasant to be with and she could talk without sounding stupid or dumb. He liked her very much.

Finally midnight came and everybody stood around waiting for the second when 1915 became 1916. At the stroke of midnight, everybody shouted "Happy New Year!"

Ruth looked at him and he kissed her, not a hard kiss, their lips barely touched. She said, "Happy New Year, John Fountain."

"Happy New Year, Ruth Wright."

As they parted after the dance, she took both of his hands and squeezed them, then looked into his face expectantly. He kissed her, this time hard.

He wrote after the dance: "I think Ruth Wright would be a good wife. I really enjoy being with her."

January 4, 1916 Mr. Weaver said today I could be a foreman on the middle section next year if I wanted to work here. I work in that section now. I told him I'd think about it, but sometime I wanted to stay at my homestead.

January 7, 1916 Today it was very cold. Mr. Denning said it was forty degrees below zero. When I went to feed the team, I put Shoni in the barn while I watered them. I had to chop the ice out of the hole twice. Working in the sugar factory was OK at first when I needed the money very much. I still need money for equipment, but the farm should be able to stand on its own.

I wonder what Ruth is doing. I enjoyed our visit on New Year's Eve very much.

January 17, 1916 Mr. Weaver told me today that last night another man was hurt at the sugar factory. He fell on a slippery floor and broke his arm.

January 21, 1916 Today I stopped at the Lincoln store. Mr. Wright teased me a little bit about Ruth. I asked him when he expected her back in Lincoln.

"Hard to say," he said. "She told us she really likes you, but didn't say when she planned to come back."

It was a little bit warmer today, but still not pleasant.

January 28, 1916 Last Monday and Tuesday were so warm almost all the snow melted. I didn't need my coat. The sun was so bright on the snow that hadn't melted sometimes it was hard to see. It was almost as if the white man's god had decided in my favor. I wished it would stay that way, but by yesterday, everything was frozen again. Some of the fields that filled with water are lakes of ice now. Fog froze on everything it touched. Tiny twigs looked like overgrown white fingers sparkling in the sun. Small branches were swelled by frost to the size of an arm. I felt as if I were trespassing in a fantasy land. I wonder if Ruth enjoyed it as much as I did. She sure is nice.

February 2, 1916   Today is what the white man calls Groundhog Day. He comes out of his hole and if he sees his shadow, he goes back and sleeps for another six weeks. Well, he didn't see his shadow. It snowed all day and it's snowing right now.

February 4, 1916 After I did my chores, I rode toward Ammon. I wanted to go to Iona, but I knew Ruth was probably teaching school and I wouldn't see her. It's a beautiful day, but it isn't beautiful. I look at what I'm doing. It's the same thing day after day. I want to be a white man, but is this the kind of life a white man has? I never thought about it when I was at the Monsons, but now I see my worlds are very different. To the white man, money means survival; to the Indians, food is survival. What different worlds they are! We find what nature provides for us. The white man *decides* what nature will provide. I learned many things in my childhood the white man doesn't know. And since then,

I've learned many things the white man knows. Many of them are opposite each other. Which is right?

I should ask Ruth what she thinks. She understands much more than other whites. I wonder what she is doing now. I really like to be with her.

February 11, 1916 Mr. Weaver told me the factory might finish by the fifteenth of next month. Mr. Wright said Ruth might come at Easter time, or sooner. I hope sooner. She's not as pretty as I would like, but she's easy to be with. I like her very much. She is a teacher. Delia was a teacher. Do they have the same ideas about being a homesteader's wife? I have to find out. I'm not so sure Ruth is the girl I want, but maybe she is. I still don't know how she feels. I hope I can see her before Easter.

February 16, 1916 I heard today the situation in France is getting worse. The Germans have marched almost to Paris. There is more and more talk of United States joining the war. I hope not. It makes no sense to me that neighbors can't get along with each other.

February 18, 1916 It's nice to have a day off once in a while, but when it snows like it is today, I feel like I'm in a prison. I read some more of Dickens.

February 21, 1916 Yesterday one of the men who works in the factory went to Mr. Weaver and asked what he could do about a sugar boil he had on his arm. Mr. Weaver told him he should go to a doctor and have it cut open. One of the other men told him to take a soda pop bottle and fill it with hot water, then pour the water out and put the opening over the boil. Today, I heard he used the soda pop bottle and when the bottle cooled, it got stuck and he couldn't get it off. His wife jerked it off and out came everything. He's better now.

The snow stopped on Sunday but it left a new layer so deep it comes up to my knees. I guess the next thing will be a blizzard. The sun was shining all day today, so if it thaws enough and freezes, it won't blow around when the wind starts.

February 25, 1916   This morning the sun was shining. I wanted to just keep on riding to Iona. After the factory closes I'll try to get to my homestead. I need some new clothes and a stock of food to take with me.

It seems the closer I get to the end of this job, the slower the time goes by. I felt the same way near the end of the season last year. There are about seven more days before the end of the sugar beets.

Now I have some money, I can buy a lot of things to finish my cabin, so I can live in it. Then I will look for a wife.

I think Ruth and I could get along. She's at least as pretty as the other homesteaders' wives. I hope I can see her again before I go to the hills.

March 3, 1916 Mr. Weaver told me there wouldn't be any more molasses after the sixth, but he wants me to stay here till the ninth to learn more about the middle section, so I can be the foreman. I didn't tell him I would or wouldn't. The money I earn is important, but I'm not so sure I would like to leave my farm another winter.

I asked Mrs. Denning when Easter was. She looked on her calendar and said it was the twenty-third of April. I'd like to see Ruth again, but I don't want to wait that long. I think I'll ride over to Iona after I'm through on the tenth and see her if I can.

March 10, 1916 It was a little bit windy during the past week, but today the sun shone very bright, and it was quite warm. After I fed and watered Bud and Mage, I rode on over to Iona. I didn't expect to see Ruth, but she was walking down the street toward me.

As John rode closer, Ruth called, "Well you're a long way from home. What brings you here on such a beautiful day?"

"I just wanted to see where you live. I've never been here before. I expected you'd be in a schoolroom somewhere."

"If you'd been a few minutes later, I would. I help teachers mostly in the afternoons. How much time do you have?"

"I guess all afternoon. I finished at the factory yesterday, and today would have been my day off, anyway. Why?"

"If you're willing, I could use your help this afternoon for about an hour or so."

"I'm not a teacher. How could I help you?"

"On Friday afternoons, we try to do something different. The fifth and sixth grade students are learning about Indians and I planned to tell them a couple of the legends you told me, but you tell them so well, I wish you'd tell them to the students. Will you do it for me?"

She looked from the corner of her eye at John and said, "Please?"

"I'll try," he answered. He tied Shoni to the gatepost, and they went into the school. No one was there yet, so they sat in two of the desks.

"I told the children about you already, but I never expected to see you here. You said you grew up as a Shoshoni boy, and you speak the language. I'd like them to hear you tell one of the legends in Shoshoni. I think they'd get a kick

164

out of it. Just a short one, and then you can tell it in English so they'll understand it."

"Do you want me to talk all afternoon?"

"Heavens, no. Just two or three or four legends. You must have some favorites. Just tell them."

In a few minutes, the students trickled in like drops of water from the eaves. They looked curiously at John. He remembered sitting at a similar desk in Ammon where he sat sideways. Ruth left the room and returned with a chair for him. By the time all the students were seated, there were only two empty desks.

When Ruth stood up, the room got quiet. "Boys and girls, we're lucky today. We have a man with us who lived his first sixteen years as an Indian boy. I told you about him a few weeks ago, and today I met him on the street on my way to school. He's agreed to tell you some of the legends his Shoshoni mother told him when he was growing up. Now, I know he doesn't look like an Indian, but that's because his father came from Canada. And now Mr. John Fountain will tell you a few Indian legends he heard at his mother's knee."

John felt all those young eyes looking at him. He greeted them in Shoshoni and smiled. Their eyes widened and a few mouths dropped open. He told the story of the coyote who let the animals out. He made all the sounds and movements his mother used, but made the story shorter than the real version. When he finished telling it in Shoshoni, he looked at Ruth. Her eyes were wide and her mouth was open, too.

He repeated it in English. The kids clapped and smiled, and John told three more that were a little bit longer.

When he finished, Ruth clapped, too, and asked the class, "Do you have any questions?"

One little boy who wore glasses and who hadn't shown the same enthusiasm as the rest, asked, "Where can I buy the book?"

"The Shoshonis don't have a written language. The legends are passed down from parents to children all the time. They've never been written down. I remember them from my mother telling them to me. And that's the way it always was."

The boy raised his hand again. "Is there a legend about where people came from?"

He looked at Ruth. Ruth looked surprised and sucked in her breath. "Yes, of course there is, but it's very long and I think Miss Wright would like to end the class before I could finish it."

She nodded and said, "I think we should all show Mr. Fountain our appreciation for taking the time to tell us these stories."

There was more clapping and a girl about twelve asked, "Where did you get a funny name like Fountain if you're an Indian?"

"My father's name was Jean-Claude Lafontaine, and mine was Jean-Pierre Lafontaine. When I started to school, my teacher suggested I change my name to John Fountain."

"Why did you change it? I like Jean-Pierre Lafontaine."

She pronounced it correctly, but John told her it was easier for people to remember and easier to say.

The students were excused, and Ruth went to John with her eyes shining. "That was wonderful! You should be a teacher. They'll never forget this afternoon. You sidetracked the people legend quite nicely. I had just a moment of fear." She was almost pretty again.

Outside, John untied Shoni and started to mount, but Ruth asked, "Can we walk a little bit? It's still early. . . unless you have something to do in Lincoln."

"Just do my chores and eat my supper is all."

They walked together to the edge of town and stopped. She stood close and he put his arm around her shoulder. She didn't resist. "Will you be in Lincoln again, soon?" he asked.

"I hadn't planned to come until Easter. Why?"

"I'd like to see you again before I go to the homestead for the summer."

"When will that be?"

"Soon, I hope. The factory is finished for this year, and I'll ride up tomorrow or the next day to see if I can get all the way. The road to Ozone is open, but I'm not sure if it's open out to Bull's Fork."

"Homesteading sounds so romantic. Like pioneering. I've always been fascinated by the stories of pioneers going places where no one ever went before and building towns and growing crops."

John almost said it was also very unnatural. "It's anything but romantic. It's just plain hard work all day, every day."

"John Fountain, I like you. You're a nice man. When I first saw you, you talked to me until Alex butted in. The reason I went back to Lincoln this year was just to see if you might be there, so maybe I could get to know you better." Her head tilted a little. and she looked at him from the corner of her eye, and smiled. "You know I'm not as pretty as some girls, but you didn't seem to mind. You pay attention to what I say. It's nice to have a handsome man do that. And you kissed me when the year changed. Thank you. I liked it."

He kissed her again. "I think we'll see each other again."

167

He got on Shoni and waved to her as he left. She was still smiling at him.

It was March 15 before John got to the homestead. Everything was where he left it and only about a foot of snow remained on level ground, but the bushes and trees below the brow of the cove were still buried. Mice had gotten into his granary, and what was left wasn't good for anything but seed. He decided to wait a while before he moved back.

After returning to Lincoln, he went to Idaho Falls and bought some new clothes to wear to social events. Up till then, he wore clean work clothes like most other men, but he saw others dressed in nicer clothes with low shoes.

Again he rode out to his place, but decided there was nothing to do for a week or so and returned to Lincoln. He had time to visit his mother again before he moved to the farm.

Chapter Fifteen
Dark Clouds

March 23, 1916 I got up very early this morning and took care of my team. Mr. Denning agreed to take care of them for a couple of days while I visit my mother.

It took him longer to get to the Shoshoni village than before, and he didn't arrive till very late in the afternoon. He found his mother sitting wrapped in blankets hunched over a smoky little fire in the middle of her teepee. She was thin, and her face showed a weariness he had never seen. He sat across from her.

"Jean-Pierre, you are hungry. Do you have enough to eat?" She looked as if she hadn't eaten for days.

"Yes, I have plenty to eat, but you do not. You look like you are starving. What do you eat?"

"I have enough," she said.

He looked at the place where she kept her food. It was empty. "My mother, there is nothing there. What do you eat?"

"I have enough."

He looked a long time at the shriveling woman who was his mother and felt ashamed. She needed him. As he watched, her face contorted in pain and she laid on her side and moaned.

"Rosemary, what is it? Are you sick?" he asked.

After a long time she said, "It's the pain. It comes and it goes. It is going now." She sat up again and smiled at him. He was relieved to see that. She didn't often smile.

"I will go to my uncle." He left her and want to talk to her brother, Herman. He was gone but would be back soon. John returned to his mother.

"What is wrong with you, Rosemary?"

"My son, my time is nearly over. I must tell you something you never knew. Not even your father knew. A long time ago, when you were born, I knew there was something wrong in here (she pointed to her belly), and when you came out, there was another one, a tiny one. She was your sister. But she was dead. I don't know how long she had been dead, but it must have done something to me. I had no pain for many years, but I never was able to bring you a brother or another sister. I think the reason has come back now, and it will end my life. Are you living well among the white men?"

"You cannot be more than forty years old. You are too young to die. I will talk to my uncle. Maybe something can be done. Have you been to see a doctor?"

"No doctor can stop what nature intends, my son. Just let it be. Are you living well among the white men?"

The second time she asked. He answered even though the answer made him feel ashamed. "Yes, I am living well among the white men."

He went then to see his uncle. On the way, all he saw was poverty, poor people trying to stay alive in a white man's world — a world he was a part of. He was a part of the strong medicine that left his kin so poor.

His uncle waited for him in his teepee. "My son, it is good that you have come. Your mother is very sick, and she will now die happy that she could see her son again."

"Can nothing be done to save her? She is too young to die. Is there no food for her?"

"Jean-Pierre, your mother gets the best care we can give her. It was hard in winter, but now that spring is almost here, we can find food for her. We will make her as happy as we can. Do not worry about her. She is content."

"Uncle, she is *dying*. I don't want that. My father is dead, and now my mother will leave me. I don't want that."

"My son, the white man's medicine is strong in you. You know that our lives come and go, and others replace us. You must not feel bad about that."

"The white man's doctor healed my foot. I would have died if I had not gotten to a white man's hospital in time. Can't we take my mother to the hospital?"

"I fear it is too late. And the white man's hospital costs more money than we have all together."

"My uncle, I have money. I will pay for my mother. Please let me take her to the hospital."

"My son, you are young and you live with the white man. You can think only the way the white man thinks now. If you were still living among us, you would understand. Your mother will not agree to go to a white man's hospital."

"Then I will ask her. Please take this money. It will help the village. I live in the white man's world, but part of me is still Shoshoni. Please take it."

John gave him fifty dollars. He said, "Thank you, my son. You will always be one of us."

His mother was lying on her side, moaning, when he returned. When she sat up again, he sat beside her and put an arm around her and hugged her. "Your father used to do that. It made me feel safe and happy. He was a good husband. Have you found a wife, yet?"

"No, not yet. As soon as I finish my cabin, I will seek a pretty wife, like you."

"I was pretty when I met your father, and he was as handsome as you. When you were born, you looked exactly like an Indian, but as time passed, you began to look more and more like your father. You will find a pretty wife, and you will be as good to her and to your children as your father was."

"Rosemary, I want to take you to a hospital. I think they can make you live longer. I will pay whatever it costs."

"No, my son, it is too late. What have you done among the white men? Are you living well?"

Once again, a question about him. He was ashamed to answer. He had done very well, and was proud of it, but now he was ashamed. He was richer than the entire village, many times richer. He thought of the rich man in *A Tale of Two Cities* and he wondered if he was becoming like the Monsignor the Marquis.

"I have a piece of land and a crop of wheat. For the past two winters, I have worked in the sugar factory. I have become acquainted with two white girls I liked very much, but one of them said she did not want to be a homesteader's wife. The other one is very nice, but I don't know how she feels about me. Maybe I don't know how I feel about her, either.

"I have become a white man, but I'm still part of your life and you are a part of mine. I cannot just let you die alone. I must do something."

"There is nothing you can do. Go back to your new life and live it until your circle is complete. You are a white man, and you cannot do anything about that, just as you cannot do anything about my sickness. I am getting cold."

Indeed, the teepee was cold. The fire had almost died, so John found more wood, enough to last a long time, and brought it inside. He put some on the fire. John's uncle brought food: *camas*, something he'd not eaten for almost six years.

He stayed that night with his mother. Twice during the night, she moaned and twice he woke and listened till her breathing was normal. He hated himself for becoming a white man.

John tried again the next morning to get his mother to let him take her to a hospital, but still she refused. As he left, he stopped to say good-bye to his uncle. Herman promised to tell John when his mother died. John asked him if he knew where Bull's Fork is. He said, "Do not worry, my son, I will find it."

March 29, 1916 For the past week, I haven't had either the interest or the feeling to write in my journal. I haven't even read in my book. I am so sad about my mother. I have just done my chores and rode Shoni around. Once I rode to Ammon to see the Monsons, but I didn't even stop. I turned around and come back to Lincoln. And I haven't thought of my homestead because it makes me sad to have so much and my family and friends in the village are so poor. But I must come out of this sadness and go to my homestead.

April 1, 1916 I rode up to my place day before yesterday and the snow is almost all gone around the cabin and barn. I put the grain in my granary in sacks and stored it in the barn, and started tearing the granary down. The wheat wasn't as bad as I thought, but it still smelled like mice. The floor in my cabin was a little bit warped, but maybe it'll straighten out when it gets dry. I pitched my tent on the floor and put up the stove. I killed a sage hen that was awful thin but it tasted good with some fried bread. It made me think of Wolf who died close by. My mother will not be able to make me a coat, now.

April 2, 1916 I brought my team to the boarding house to get ready to go to the hills tomorrow. They seemed to be happy to do something besides stand in the barn. I asked Mr. Johnston about keeping them there next winter in case I decide to spend another boring winter at the factory. He said it was OK with him. I'd kept the place clean and the horses didn't seem to mind the smell of the pig, but he still refused to take any pay for it. I will have to get more hay for next year though, and I think I should feed them some oats, too. They didn't get many this year.

John stopped writing and answered a knock on his door. It was Ruth. She was flushed and excited. "John, I have wonderful news," she said. "I've got a teaching job in Ashton next year. I couldn't wait to tell you! It looks as if I was just in time. I see a wagon outside. Are you leaving soon?"

"Yes, I'm leaving in the morning. But I wanted to come back to Iona to see you again."

"Oh, John, I'm going back to Rick's College in a few days for summer school. I would have missed you for sure. I'm glad I came today."

John thought she'd be in Iona forever. His feelings were so mixed he stammered. "Are you staying with your aunt again?"

"Just for tonight. I have to be back in class tomorrow afternoon. Have you got some time now? It's only five, and we can walk somewhere."

He wanted to and he didn't want to. His mother's condition weighed on his mind and now Ruth was going out of his life, maybe forever. "Yes," he said, "I'd like that."

As they walked, she talked excitedly about her new job, but John heard only that she was leaving. "Will I ever see you again?"

"I don't know. Ashton is a long way from here, and I don't know if I'll have time to come to Lincoln any more. But I'll miss you."

That sounded so final. He wanted to beg her to stay. Finally he decided to tell her. "Ruth, since I met you, I've thought of little else except you. I have a homestead that needs a woman, a wife, and I've thought of you. I think you're the most interesting girl I've ever met and I'd like to share my life with you."

She stopped, turned looking him fully in the face, and said nothing for a long time. Then quietly asked, "John Fountain, are you proposing to me?"

"I don't know, I guess so. I like you so much, you can't imagine it."

"I've never known anyone like you, man or woman. You're wonderful, and whether it makes any difference to you or not, I think I love you — but not enough to marry you. You are the nicest thing that ever happened to me, but I'm not ready to get married. I want to be a teacher, and the only way I can is to take this job. I'm disappointed you're not more enthusiastic about it, but if I've disappointed you, I understand why. I'm truly sorry. I can't marry you, now."

"I've met several girls and got serious about one of them. She was a teacher, too. She didn't want to be a homesteader's wife, and told me that very plainly. Well, that's what I am. . ."

She put her fingers on his lips. "Stop! I'd love to be a homesteader's wife. Your wife, perhaps. I've already told you I think it's romantic. And just so you know it, I've been very flattered that such a handsome man has paid me as much attention as you. I'll never forget it. It's just that I'm twenty years old, and I want to do something else first.

175

And while I'm doing something else, I don't want to feel as if I've taken something from someone who's waiting for me to make up my mind."

They came to the Lincoln store. He turned to face her and took her hands in his. She looked at him and said, "Kiss me John, and say good-bye."

The next day John went home to Bull's Fork.

April 6, 1916 I've been here for three days and haven't done anything that shows. I almost wish I had some more land to clear. I have to work harder on my cabin. I have to get Ruth out of my mind. For a plain-looking girl, she was wonderful. That's enough! It's over John. Get back to work! You have a cabin to finish and then you can look for a pretty wife!

John took the boards from inside Shoni's tiny barn, and nailed them to the cabin frame, then rode to the sawmill to arrange for some more lumber. Jack Dehlin was there with Mr. Covert, discussing buying the sawmill. Mr. Dehlin didn't plan to start the sawmill for about a month, but there was a pile of lumber already cut that John arranged to buy.

He stopped at the store in Ozone and bought some things he needed including a few sacks of oats and returned to his camp. The tent had been cut down and stuff scattered around, but a closer inspection indicated that nothing was missing. He went to Louie Franck's place and told him what he'd found. Louie told him he saw four Indians on horseback leaving the area just fifteen or twenty minutes earlier.

He knew who it was. Collecting a pocket full of rocks, he jumped on Shoni, and took off after them, and in a few minutes caught up with them. The sadness of seeing his mother in such condition and then losing Ruth caused an anger John seldom felt. The Indians hadn't done anything except cut his tent down and scatter things around, but he was bent on revenge.

The first rock hit the last one, the leader of the band, in the back of the head, and he fell to the ground. A second one hit the rump of the horse in front of him and when he jumped, he threw his rider. The third one fell when Shoni bit his horse in the flank and he bucked. John let the fourth one go and went back to clean up on the leader. Intensely angry, he jumped off Shoni and ran after the Indian. He caught him easily and twisted one arm against his back. The Indian drew a knife but John's was already at his throat. The Indian dropped his knife when a little bit of blood stained John's blade. He almost cut deeper, but stopped when he heard his mother's voice, "Jean-Pierre! Don't!"

With his knife still at the Indian's throat, he yelled in Shoshoni, "Take your ugly band out of here and don't you *ever* come back. If you do, I'll kill all four of you." The other two on the ground started toward John, but thought better of it and stood some distance away. John's knife pricked the skin under the leader's chin and a drop of blood ran down the blade. He shouted into his face in Shoshoni from an inch away, "Get out of here and don't forget I'll kill you if ever you come back!" To emphasize his point, John's knife pricked his chin a little harder, and a trickle of blood dripped from his chin. John let him loose and he ran, and so did the others.

It was so against John's nature, he hated himself. Back at the tent, he trembled because of what he'd almost done.

He hauled all the sawed boards from the saw mill, and nailed them on the cabin framework. Louie Franck helped him put on the shingle roof and install the stove. He would cover the inside with beaver board. Standing at the door looking at his handiwork, he thought: It looks good but empty. I guess I should get a regular bed. I'll look for one next time I'm in Ozone.

Only scattered patches of snow remained. The earth, awakened by spring, thrust its emerging life toward the sun.

He wrote, "My hand-broadcast crop looks better than I expected, but I think I need a disc to turn the soil, It's faster than a plow and doesn't go so far into the ground."

New homesteaders arrived weekly, and on April 27, he wrote, "People are coming in quite fast, and they're building new schools. The little log school house in Dehlin is filled and they're planning a new one."

The next day he rode to Ozone, bought a cot and a pad, paid four dollars for them, then went to pay for the lumber, At the sawmill, Jack Dehlin asked him what color he planned to paint the cabin.

"I don't know. I hadn't even thought of painting it."

"You'd better. Otherwise when it gets wet, it'll expand and warp, and after a while the outside will leak and let in the cold."

"It seems there's always something else I need."

April 29, 1916 Today, I picked up my bed and bought some seeds for a garden and I probably bought too many seeds. Mrs. Otteson told me I should have some flowers, so I bought two packages of flower seeds. I don't know what good they are, but one package was sunflowers. She said the seeds are good to eat. I already knew that, but these are bigger than the wild ones. She also told me I should plant some strawberries and raspberries, but they don't come from seeds, you have to have young plants. She suggested I ask at Dick Prophet's place on Chicken Creek. He has both strawberries and raspberries, or at Jones's on Sellars Creek Then she said I should plant some apple trees. That seemed like a good idea, too. By the time she was finished, my head was swimming. I'd never thought of many of the things she suggested. I think my place can be a lot like at the Monsons.

My bed looks and feels a lot better, and now I must plant all those seeds. I think I saw a place in Idaho Falls that sold young apple trees. I have to go to CW&M (Consolidated Wagon and Machinery) to look at machinery, so I'll see if I can find the place where they sell apple trees.

May 2, 1916 Today I am very sad. My uncle came and told me my mother lay on her side in great pain and said, "Tell Jean-Pierre," and she died. It is not the way of the Shoshonis to grieve. It means only that the cycle of life is finished. But I am a white man, and the death of my mother brought me great pain. Perhaps even more than when my father died. After my uncle left me, I took my shovel and went to my garden place. I tried to work the pain away and now I have all the area almost ready for seeds. Seeds that will start a new cycle. It makes me feel better to know that.

John planted his garden, and cleared brush to make a yard. He took Lenore Otteson's advice to build a root cellar to store part of the garden produce. On a trip to Idaho Falls with Henry Monson he bought a disc and a harrow. He could use the disc to keep the weeds down during the summer fallow periods, as well as to prepare the field for planting. His journal recorded this trip. "Mr. Monson and I discussed buying a grain drill. He said hand broadcasting works, but you get a lot more even distribution with a drill. When I added up all the things I need the price was almost $400 including a few smaller things. I decided not to buy some of the more expensive things like the drill. They also had beaver board. I don't know how to get this stuff up to the farm, but I'll figure it out. I bought a bucket for water and looked at their water pumps. We also looked at harnesses for my team and at a new wagon. Just those two things would add over a hundred dollars. I'll get along with what I've got as long as they don't break down completely, or wear out.

"When I got home, for the first time since I visited my mother, I thought of what she said. That I had a sister born dead at the same time. I wonder what she'd be like. Would she have tried to live in the white man's world? Maybe she would have been a teacher, too. I think it would be nice to have a sister, but her life cycle ended before it even began."

May 13, 1916 I had some cattail shoots today, and I caught a fish in Bull's Fork. I never even thought of looking there for fish. Monday I'll go to Idaho Falls to buy some of the other things I need. The list seems to get longer every day. I have to get the beaver board on the inside of the cabin before winter. And I've been thinking of installing a water pump in the house.

May 15, 1916 Last Thursday, I drove the wagon to CW&M and brought back enough beaver board to cover one room of my cabin. I had to have a lot of nails and some strips to cover the joints, too. The next day I started nailing them on. It sure makes the place look a lot nicer. Some time I'll buy some calcimine to cover it and make it look cleaner. But that comes after I get all the inside walls covered.

My crop is growing nicely, but there are a few spots that seem dry, and there don't seem to be as many plants as I thought. A good rainstorm would help a lot.

May 18, 1916 There was a little bit of rain today, but mostly clouds, then they went away and the ground is about as dry as it was before. My crop needs a lot more rain. Hot weather hasn't even got here yet, and if it doesn't rain, I don't know how my wheat will survive.

May 24, 1916 My wheat is half way to my knees but it's dry. Some of the stalks are turning yellow already. The alfalfa patch is also dry, and I think I can cut it in a couple of weeks. It didn't do very well. I hope it rains soon. I feel so helpless. All I can to is hope it rains.

May 26, 1916 Today I bought two gallons of white paint and a big brush to paint my cabin. Mrs. Otteson said it has lots of linseed oil in it to keep the boards from getting wet. When I got home, it was late in the afternoon, but I started anyway. I have to do something to take my mind off my problems. I didn't get much done but it seems to go fast. The boards are rough and they take a lot of paint. I'll probably have to put on two coats.

When John went Otteson's to buy a scythe to cut his hay, he was still picking paint off his hands. He asked, "What can I use to get the paint off me and out of my brush?"

"Turpentine. I forgot to tell you. Haven't you ever painted anything before?"

"No, ma'am, but the cabin looks so good I think I'll paint the barn red. I put the brush in a can of water. Do you think it's too late to clean it?"

"You can try."

"OK, I'll take a can of turpentine, too."

As soon as he got home, he put the brush into some turpentine, and started cutting hay. Out of about 15 acres, he got one small stack — about enough for Shoni over the winter. His journal noted, "I thought it would rain yesterday, but it just stayed cloudy and today was clear and hot again. I'm worried about my wheat. It's only up to my knees and the heads are very small. While I was in the store, I saw a

181

poster that said there would be a three-day Fourth of July celebration at Canyon Creek. I think I'll go. Maybe I can find something good. My bank account is down to less than $700. I have to be careful how much I spend from now on."

Chapter Sixteen
The Rains Came

June 12, 1916 I had some radishes from my garden today and they tasted pretty good. I wish I had a spring out in my field. It's so dry, I'm afraid the kernels that have formed will be shriveled. I started to disc the summer fallow ground and got about a fourth of it done. I should finish by the end of the week. Still no rain, but off to the west some clouds were forming at nightfall. I hope it rains.

June 16, 1916 Lightning slashed through the clouds I saw yesterday and thunder rolled over the hills, but left nothing but a lot of noise. It was cool, but not wet. I walked through my field and felt helpless as a baby. My grain is dying from thirst.

I cooked a meal, and I thought of my mother and how her family lives and it made me sad. I don't remember days when I was as intensely unhappy as I am today.

June 17, 1916 Again the thunder came during the night, and then I heard the sound of rain on my roof. I went outside and ran around in it naked holding my hands to the sky rubbing it on my chest, my hair, my back, singing. Flashes of lightening lit me up in the darkness like a ghost gone crazy.

This morning, a slow drizzle filled the air. I am so happy. In the late afternoon, the rain stopped and a beautiful rainbow painted the sky with color. My thirsty grain looks greener already.

Back in my yard, I looked into every little puddle and saw life, not crawling or swimming life, just life. My medicine is strong.

John spent the next week digging a root cellar into the bank on the north side of the cove where he thought it wouldn't be buried completely by snowdrifts in winter. He wrote, "I think the Shoshonis should have learned about root cellars."

June 29, 1916 The sun has been high and bright and hot. My wheat doesn't look the same as it did last year, but the heads have filled out a lot since the rain and so the crop should be better than I expected a week ago. My alfalfa field shows signs of growing and maybe I will be able to harvest one more crop of hay.

July 3, 1916 My wheat has revived from death. The heads are not quite full, but there will be a crop.

Tomorrow, I'll go to Canyon Creek to the celebration. I think I'll try to ride a bucking horse. I like the challenge. Maybe Mrs. Holmquist will have another pretty girl. She probably will. I'll buy one of her sandwiches, and give her a chance.

At the Canyon Creek rodeo. John rode two bucking horses and won ten dollars.

From the crowd congratulating him, came a voice from his past. "John Fountain!" It was not Mrs. Holmquist;

it was Delia. "I'm so glad to see you. I was sure you'd be here. Meet my husband, Ralph Johnson. We were married three months ago."

Ralph said, "Glad to meet you. You won the horse two years ago in Ozone, right?"

"Yes, sir, and just in time. I had no way to get around except walking."

"Delia told me you were pretty spectacular the way you handled him, and without even a saddle."

"He's kind of a one-man horse. Jed Rockwood took care of him while I was in the hospital."

Small talk continued, Delia said, "By the way, Ruth Wright is a really nice girl, but she has nearly the same ideas as I. Don't feel too badly about her. She'll make a good teacher. I envy her one thing, though. She got you to tell some Shoshoni legends to her kids."

"How did you hear about her?"

"News travels fast among us teachers. She was pretty excited about you. She said you were the first smart man she ever met."

"Yes, maybe, but not smart enough to keep her." The talk changed to crops and work and rain. After a few minutes, John went to see Mrs. Holmquist for a sandwich.

"I wish I had some Norway pigs here. They're the best in the world; not little and puny like the ones here. They have real flavor, and they taste good, too. You don't have a wife yet, no?"

When John said nothing she continued, "Then I find you one, a good one. You just wait."

"Mrs. Holmquist, ma'am, all I want is one of your delicious sandwiches. I can find myself a wife. Thank you."

"Men have not got sense when it comes to women. Women are a lot smarter about other women. I'll help you find a good wife."

"Thank you, ma'am, but I think I should find my own." He paid for the sandwich, and went to watch the kids' races. The little fat boy who won the "way up there and back" race for the past two years seemed specialized in that race. He'd grown up and slimmed down a lot. He still had the unmistakable round face, but he was much faster than the competition and easily beat a field of eleven others.

Generally, the celebration was the same as the previous ones. The kids' contests were won and lost while their parents talked in little clumps or wandered about looking for something else.

The pie-eating contest had a new champion: Lillian Butler from Deer Creek. She smiled weakly when she was given her prize, a bottle of soda pop, and ran behind a tree and emptied her stomach. The retching made her drop her soda pop and she lost that, too. All she had left was the dubious fame of being the only girl, ever, to win a Fourth of July pie-eating contest in the hills.

Mr. Bone was the master of ceremonies. A musical group behind him played when he wasn't announcing. A tinny piano, an accordion, a Jew's harp, and a violin played by the only woman in the band, completed the ensemble. The music they played, sometimes something less than expertly, provided welcome relief. During a lull between events, they played "Turkey in The Straw" so vigorously a few people started an impromptu dance in the dusty grass. When they played "Silver Threads Among The Gold," the grandfathers and grandmothers caught dance fever, too.

Out of the din, John heard Mrs. Holmquist call to him. She was leading a dark haired girl. "John, I want you to meet Ida Prophet. Ida, this is the boy I told you about, John Fountain. I think you two should get acquainted."

"Hello, John," Ida said.

"Hello, ma'am." Ida was kind of pretty, and looked pleasant, but John wasn't convinced he needed Mrs. Holmquist's help.

"Well, I'll leave you two alone and get back to my stand."

Ida said, "Aren't you the one who won that beautiful black horse two years ago in Ozone?" The question seemed to be repeating itself.

"Yes, ma'am."

"Hey, if we're going to be friends, please call me Ida. That's my name. Why so formal?"

"My father insisted I always call him *sir*, and women *ma'am* and I did. I can't seem to get out of the habit."

"Tell me about the horse."

"What do you want to know? I don't really know how to tell anyone about a horse."

"Let's start with his name."

"Shoni. It's short for Shoshoni."

"Mrs. Holmquist told me you have a homestead on Bull's Fork."

"Yes, I've mostly finished a cabin and a shed, and I've had a crop. And that's about all there is to tell."

"She also said you cut your foot and had to go to the hospital for a long time."

"Yes, I was there about two weeks."

"Mrs. Holmquist is a nice lady, but she can't stand to see anyone unmarried. I'll bet she told you she'd find you a wife."

Clearly John wasn't the only one who'd run into Mrs. Holmquist's matchmaking. "Yes. This is the third time she's found someone for me. I don't mind too much, except I think I'm better qualified than her to find someone."

"I agree. She's done the same thing to me four times now. A couple of the boys were nice, but others are leftovers. What do you do with them? She also told me you're part Indian."

"Yes" he said, "My mother was a Shoshoni Indian."

"You said *was*. Did she die?"

"Yes, about three months ago. What about you?"

"Me? There's not much about me to tell. I was born in Rigby and came here with my folks. This is the third time they've homesteaded. I hope it's the last."

"Why do they keep doing it? I think once is enough. Someone told me it sounded romantic. I wish it was. I feel like I've really done something, but once is enough. and it's *not* romantic."

"Dad is always looking for the pot of gold at the end of the rainbow. That's all right, I guess, but first you have to find the end of the rainbow and it seems to keep getting farther away. I love it here, though."

"Mrs. Otteson told me you have a lot of berries at your place, and maybe I could get some starts. I'd like to have some on my place if you would let me have a few."

"They're all over the place. Let's go find mother and tell her. She's here somewhere." It took about two minutes. Ida introduced John and told her mother he wanted some berry starts.

"So you're John Fountain. I'm glad to meet you, finally. I keep hearing the name, but I didn't have a face to go with it. Yes, of course, you can have some berry plants. They grow fast and send up shoots all the time. You live on Bull's Fork, don't you? That's quite a ways from us. You can come any time. Bring something to carry them in. There's always somebody home."

"Thank you, ma'am. I'll probably come next Saturday if that's all right."

He and Ida walked for a while, and he heard his name, again. Mr. Bone motioned for him to come to him.

"Jed Rockwood says you're pretty good with a slingshot. How about a demonstration?"

"What kind of demonstration?"

"Just show the crowd what you can do with it. Have you got it with you?"

He wasn't eager to show anything so ordinary, but a small crowd urged him.

"What do you want me to kill?"

Somebody hung a crude cardboard target on a tree trunk. John picked up a rock about the size of a thistle bud and hit the target square in the middle. He threw a dozen more and wound up with half the kids there gathered around asking questions. He showed them how to make one for themselves, and let a few of the older ones try his.

The sun was getting low, so John said good-bye to Ida. "Will you be here for the program and dance, tomorrow?" she asked.

"I don't know how to dance."

"Well, the program is mostly local talent and is sometimes very interesting. It's also sometimes not. But I'd like it if you came."

John attended the next day. He felt good with the people.

The celebration on July 5, was mostly a program of local people doing something. He particularly enjoyed one lady who gave what was called a "reading". Only she didn't read it. It was very funny, telling about the joys of being a homesteader's wife.

Later in the afternoon, the crowd thinned as people went home to do chores and get ready for the dance which started about eight o'clock in the schoolhouse. John rode home and took care of the team and gave Shoni a hand full of little carrots and some hay and oats. He dressed in his new clothes with the low shoes and ate a fried bread and leftover sage hen. He didn't know Mrs. Holmquist would sell sandwiches at the dance. Just as he walked in the door, Ida appeared.

"Wow, you look good! I'm glad you came," she said. "Mrs. Holmquist was worried her matchmaking didn't work."

"Has it worked?"

"That's not what I mean. She caught me as soon as I got here and started asking questions about us. I was embarrassed."

"Maybe we should have a fight in front of her," John suggested and Ida laughed. They sat down together to watch the people dancing. Several other men asked her to dance, so they talked between dances. She asked him why he didn't learn to dance and insisted she show him how. When he tried, he demonstrated his inability to the whole room. That satisfied her. He told her the only dancing he did was the Indian way.

"How do they dance?"

"It's a simple step. While I was clearing my land, sometimes I'd burn a big pile of sagebrush and dance around it at night, and sometimes I sang, too. I was happy and I was singing about it. That's not what I see here."

"What do you see here?" she asked.

"Men and women struggling with each other."

"Struggling?"

"Yes, it looks like they're wrestling."

"Oh John, you're being silly."

"Just watch them. I know they're happy, and that's why they come here, but I dance *because* I'm happy. Do you remember a couple of weeks ago when it rained so hard during the night after it hadn't rained for weeks? My wheat was dying and I was almost dying too. The noise woke me up, and when I saw all those big raindrops, I went a little crazy, and ran out and danced in it, naked."

"You didn't! Not *naked*!"

"Does it shock you?"

"I guess so. I don't know. I just never heard of it before. You must have been very happy."

"I was, and I still am. That rain saved my crop. Well, almost. Without it there wouldn't have been very much. Now I'll get *something* at least."

Ida sat quietly for a long time, but finally said, "In some ways, you seem strange, but when I think about what you say, it makes sense. Sometimes, when I was a little girl it rained a warm rain, and I used to just stay out in it and let my clothes get wet. I didn't stay there because I was happy. I stayed because it felt so good. My mother used to scold me for it, but it was worth it."

Punch and cookie time came followed by more dancing, and at midnight there was potluck, and then still more dancing. They talked a lot, but to John she was just a nice girl. He liked her, but not the way Mrs. Holmquist thought he should. He rode home at a slow lope under a moonlit sky. The coyotes were howling.

July 8, 1916 I went to the Prophet's place today and got some plants. Mrs. Prophet insisted I keep on digging them up. She talked all the time, and I learned more about her and her family and the third time they've homesteaded than I ever thought possible to learn about anybody in such a short time. When I left, she gave me a big sack full of strawberries. They weren't in very good shape when I got home, but I ate them. I hope mine taste as good.

By the middle of July, John had calcimined the beaver board interior a cream color, looked it over, and was satisfied. He wrote, "I'm not sure what to do next. I think I need some shelves, maybe with doors for kitchen things, but I don't know how many or where to build them, and I don't have very many things to put on them, either. I need a wife to help me now."

Out in the field, John rubbed a few heads of wheat between his palms to release the kernels, noted they were shriveled at the tips of the heads. He estimated what his yield would be. "The whole field looks like a lake in a golden sunset," he wrote.

He had time before harvest began to get some boards from the sawmill and install a floor in his barn. He outlined his plans for the future in his journal, "I'll be glad when I can have a cow and some pigs and chickens and ducks and other things running around the yard looking for food. I'll be glad when I have a family of boys and girls. But I'm ahead of myself. I have to have a wife, first."

July 25, 1916 I think I made a good friend today. Mr. Schwieder came by and told me Mr. Hammons would start heading in the Dehlin area tomorrow, and asked me if I wanted him to cut my grain again this year. I told him I did. He said Mr. Empey would follow the header by about three days.

They hunkered down in the field and Arthur changed the subject, "All your neighbors think a lot of you. Not a one of them has said a word against you. We've agreed you would be a welcome addition to our church. Please come to our services next Sunday."

"Why?"

"Just to know what we believe."

"I think I already know what you believe," John answered. "I lived with a Mormon family in Ammon for four years, and I learned from them what your church teaches."

"Were you not inclined to join us?"

"No, sir."

"Why?"

"I couldn't think of any reason why it was any better than the way I live now, or any better than what the Shoshonis believe. I really don't think being a member of your church would improve my life any. I'm very happy the way I am, and if my neighbors think a lot of me as I am, then isn't that mostly what counts?"

"That's my point, John. You could make a real contribution to our church by being a member."

"Mr. Schwieder, sir, is it important to you or to anybody else I do something I'm not ready to do, or want to do? I live my beliefs every day of my life. I'm already part of something that's bigger than I am, and I'm happy with what I believe."

A big stink bug crawled from between John's feet. He picked up a straw and teased it to make it expose its stinker. The bug turned and crawled past Arthur, who stuck out his foot and dropped it on the bug smashing it into the dust. Then he said, "I agree we're all a part of something much greater than us as individuals, and the Bible makes it clear from the creation. But man's purpose on earth is to bring it into fruitfulness. From what I and your neighbors know of you, we know you should join us."

"Mr. Schwieder, sir, just now you killed a stink bug, and you didn't think anything of it. That's something that never even *occurred* to me. As an Indian, I take only what I need from nature, and I leave what I don't need. Killing something just because it's there and we think it's useless, is not a part of our beliefs. Right now I'm doing something I'm having trouble with. I've cleared off a piece of land, and I've taken control of it to raise wheat — much more wheat than I'll ever use. But I'm doing it in a white man's world to provide others in his world with the things they cannot get for themselves."

"Are all Indians like you?"

"Mr. Schwieder, my father and mother taught me to respect the rights of others, and that's what I'm trying to do. As a homesteader like you, I have accomplished a lot, perhaps more than I would have as an Indian, but the Indian background and beliefs I grew up with are deep within me, and I can't change that. That's why I can think of no reason to join your church."

"I think I understand you, John. You'd be a good member anyway, and if you ever decide to join us, you'll be welcome. I just came to find out about your plans for heading and threshing, and I wound up being a poor missionary." He got up and brushed the dust off his pants. "I have to go home, now. My wheat's waiting for me."

July 30, 1916 Today is Sunday, and I did a few chores and put the wheels I soaked in the spring back on my wagon before I read in my book again. A revolution started in France and the Bastille fell to the revolutionaries. They freed the prisoners and then killed an old man who treated people badly, and Madame Defarge cut his head off. There was a lot of killing. The people were after revenge.

August 6, 1916 We finished threshing my grain in two days. Mr. Empey came with his threshing machine last Tuesday instead of the second as originally planned. I was right. I got 916 bushels off 60 acres. That's a little more than 15 bushels per acre. That's about what everybody got because of the drought. I got one load to the elevator on Wednesday. The price was up to $2.20 for a hundred pounds. I had 2,200 pounds and my first load was worth $48.40. I got less for a hundred pounds last year. The trip still took almost sixteen hours. I wish there was a place closer to me.

I think I should take the job in the sugar factory again this winter.

August 13, 1916 I'm so tired I could go to bed and sleep for a week. I have to get up before it's light and load the wagon then go to Ammon and back. I get here long after dark and I still have to take care of my team. They're getting tired, too. I had to buy a lot more sacks and I've got the filled sacks under a big canvas to keep the rain off. So far, it hasn't rained, but if I don't finish soon, it will. I wish I had a permanent granary. I'm sure if I farm long enough I'll have more money invested in equipment than the farm will ever be worth. There is always something more I need.

On September second, John finished hauling his grain and took his pay, a little over $1200, bought a few things, and reported he had $1,151.52 left in the bank. He immediately started discing, and planned to plant about sixty-five acres, leaving about the same acreage fallow. "I look out over my farm and I feel good. I've had two crops off it, and I have a small bank account and some of the machinery I need. But I need a hayrack, and I hope I have time to build one before I go to work in the sugar factory. Louie Franck said he'd help me."

He started broadcasting his next crop a few days later. "I started spreading the seed wheat yesterday. It would be a lot easier and better if I had a grain drill. I'm sure after I harrow it in, it will be spread a lot better. I thought about buying a drill, but I don't have a way to haul it up to Bull's Fork, and when I went to CW&M, they didn't have one, anyway. But I'm happy. I remember the same kind of work on Mr. Monson's farm. There was always something to do."

September 16, 1916 Most things in my garden are ready to harvest and I'll put them in the root cellar. I finished planting my wheat last Wednesday and started to harrow it in. I had dust all over me and the horses were all dusty when I finished. It still bothers me that some of the kernels end up on top of the ground. A grain drill will be the next thing I buy. Now I need some rain. And I've got to get a hayrack built.

Chapter Seventeen
The Sun Breaks Through

September 22, 1916 I went to Ozone today and Mrs. Otteson told me there would be dance tomorrow night. I haven't been to any of the social things since July 5, and I think I need a change from what I'm doing, so I decided to go.

"Ladies choice! And no husbands or boy friends," came the announcement from the stage. John had been watching the couples dance to the screech of a violin and a tinny piano. A beautiful girl with long, silky, brown hair reaching past her shoulders, and a shining face flushed with the excitement of dancing, sat across the small room from him. He watched her while she danced with many young men, all eager for her attention. Several times they made eye contact and once she flashed him a smile, but he turned away. When Bishop Judy announced ladies choice, she suddenly appeared in front of him.

"Jean-Pierre Lafontaine, will you dance with me?" John hadn't heard that name for a long time and he just looked at her. "Don't you recognize me?" she asked.

"No, I'm sorry, I don't. Who are you?"

"Susan Monson. You remember. Henry Monson's daughter."

"You. . . You're. . . Susan Monson?" He couldn't believe it.

"In person, and now I'd like to dance with you."

He took several seconds to recognize the beautiful creature in front of him. She had changed from an unattractive little girl into a breathtaking beauty. Her face had gone from freckles and very plain to beautiful. Her skinny body had filled out. She was a mature young woman. "You've changed so much, I didn't recognize you."

"May I have this dance with you, Jean-Pierre?"

"I'm sorry, I don't know how to dance."

"Then I'll show you. It's just a two-step. Come on, let's try it."

He didn't know if it was the shock of seeing a plain-looking child who had blossomed into beautiful woman or the pleasure of being asked to dance by such an attractive partner, but either way, he still couldn't get the rhythm. Finally they sat down next to each other.

"How is the homestead coming?"

"It's getting closer to what I want."

"What do you want?"

"So far, I have a shed for my horses and a corral, and I have a garden, and I've almost finished a cabin. I've been living in it for several months, but I still have to finish the third room. I bought a pump for the kitchen, but it isn't installed yet. That's the next thing."

"And then what?"

"I'll finish it."

"And then what?"

His next step was to find a wife, but he wasn't sure he should tell her. He knew she liked him a lot, but he wasn't prepared for what came next. "I. . . ah. . . I think then I will be ready to start a family."

"I want to help," she said.

"What do you mean, help?"

"If you're going to have a family, you have to have a wife."

He didn't know what to say. He remembered what Delia told him in the hospital. *"They become Mrs. Something-or-other and that's the end of their lives. They never leave anything behind; they're just a homesteader's wife."*

"What? Susan, I don't even know you. You're not the little girl I knew. I don't know what to say."

"Then let's get better acquainted."

"What do you mean?"

"I mean let's get together on dates and things. You know a. . . a courtship. That way we can learn a lot more about each other."

"Susan, I'm twenty-two. Isn't that too old for you?" He really didn't think so, but wanted to slow her down.

"Jean-Pierre Lafontaine, I'm seventeen years old, almost eighteen, and I know how old you are. You lived with us for four years. Remember?"

"Of course, and maybe that's why you are almost a little sister to me. I have a hard time realizing you're so. . . grown up, and so pretty."

Susan stood up, raised her hands above her head, turned around, and asked, "Do I look like a little girl to you?"

"No, Susan, you look like a beautiful woman to me. I can't believe what happened to you, but you still seem like a little sister to me. I can't help it."

"I'm sorry. I guess I hoped for too much. I don't want to embarrass you. Do you remember how I cried when you changed your name?"

"Yes, but I don't know why. After all, John Fountain is a lot easier to get used to than Jean-Pierre Lafontaine."

"Not for me. I don't care who John Fountain is. I will always call you Jean-Pierre." She pronounced it "pee-air," and John tried to correct her with no success.

They went on talking. When boys asked her to dance with them, she said, "No, I'm with John-Pierre." At midnight, potluck was served. Bishop Judy said a long prayer, blessing the food, the people, and the crops before he led his flock of believers through the food line.

As John and Susan ate, she said, "I love this part of a dance. It's so much fun to eat other peoples' cooking. Even the same recipes taste different when someone else cooks them."

"Yes, I know. It's a treat to eat something besides rabbit or sage grouse. I've planted gardens, but they don't last but a few months and they're gone. I'm sure your mother told you about the things growing on my place, but I can't keep them forever, so I have to eat them when they're in season."

"What's in season now?"

He was puzzled. She should already know. "The usual, cucumbers, a few tomatoes, carrots. You know. Your mother grows a garden. The chokecherries are ripe, but most of them have either dried up or fallen off the bushes. Some of the service berries are left."

"John-Pierre, would you mind if I came to visit you sometime?"

"Why? Hasn't your mother told you about my place?"

"Just to see it. Mamma says it's beautiful, and I'd like to see it."

John wondered: Should I say yes and take a chance, or say not to come. What if her visit turned out to be something we would regret? No, she was like a little sister. Nothing could come of a simple visit.

He changed the subject. "What happened to your friend I met at your place about two years ago? I think her name was Lillian. I don't think anyone ever told me her last name."

"Lillian Cross. She lives in Spanish Fork, Utah. We got into a fight over you, and Mamma finally admitted she'd made a mistake inviting her to come to our house for Christmas. She hoped you would find Lillian attractive and marry her. She left the next day. I haven't heard from her since."

"You two fought over me? Why?"

"Oh, for Heaven's sake, John-Pierre! She was trying to take you away from me."

"But I don't belong to you."

"Not yet, but we will be married one day. Now, may I come to visit you at your place?"

The attempt to sidetrack the issue didn't work. He knew although Lydia thought a lot of him, her attitude had changed. "Susan, I feel like I'm already part of your family. It's hard for me to realize the girl I considered a little sister has become a beautiful woman. Seeing you tonight as a grown woman I didn't even recognize made you another person. I don't know what to think. I would love to have a wife as pretty as you and children who look like you, maybe even like me, but you've changed everything for me. You've always been special, but I never thought of us as anything but brother and sister. I have to ask you something. What is your mother's objection to me? Having Lillian come from Utah so I would find her attractive, tells me something I don't like to think."

"Mamma really loves you, almost like a son, but she's a very strict Mormon, and you're not. That's the reason."

"I don't understand why it should make a difference. I don't think I'm a bad person just because I don't belong to your church. Anyway, I think I'd like to see you more often."

"John-Pierre! You *still* haven't answered my question. May I come to visit you at your homestead?"

"Yes, but let me pick the time. And your parents are invited too, if they want to come with you."

"I wouldn't *think* of visiting you alone, you dummy." She gave him an impish grin he hadn't seen before. "When can we get together again?"

He knew she was leading him but he didn't mind. "I don't know. I'm still working, and it's always late when I quit."

"Didn't you quit early today to come to this dance?"

"Yes, but that was different."

"How different?"

"Susan, I really do want to see you again. I'm so surprised by what happened to you, I can't think straight. But now you're asking me to make a decision I hadn't thought of making. When are you home?"

"I'm always home. How about next Saturday? There's nothing going on in Ammon, but we can take a walk or something. We've kept your room in the barn. Daddy has some help come in once in a while, and he puts them out there."

John was trapped in a lovely way. He wanted to see Susan now she had grown up and changed so much, but he was still torn by the feeling she was a little sister. "OK, I'll come next Saturday."

Susan kissed him squarely on his mouth. "I'll be waiting for you early in the afternoon."

The crowd thinned, and Susan met the Campbells and left with them.

September 27, 1916   Today and yesterday and the day before, I've thought of Susan and the change that has come over her. I've worked on my cabin as if she were here and I was building it for her. Maybe I just need to have something to make me work harder. She's pretty and when she smiles at me I feel a kind of tickle inside. Her eyes sparkle, and the whole room lights up like the sun coming up in the morning when she smiles. It shouldn't be that way with a little sister.

October 1, 1916   I tried to find some chokecherries to take with me to the Monsons, but they were all gone. I got there just at dinner time and they invited me to eat with them. Susan and I walked for a long time in the afternoon. She's the prettiest girl I've ever known. We talked about just about everything.

The afternoon was pleasant, and they talked of memories they shared, often laughing. And a few things they didn't have in common. "Will you ever decide to join the Mormon Church?"

None of the Monsons had ever mentioned joining their church before, so this time the question surprised John. "I don't think it would make me any different from what I am now. I am very happy with what I believe. Why should I change?"

Susan thought a while, then said, "Maybe you shouldn't. I can see your point. Like Daddy says, 'If it ain't broke, don't fix it.'" They laughed, and the subject seemed to be closed. But she said, "It would make it a lot easier to convince Mamma we should get married."

"Get married? I barely know you. Why are you bringing that up?"

"John Pierre, when we met at the dance a week ago, I kissed you because I wanted you to know I am not a little girl and certainly not your little sister. And you kissed me back. Not the way I wanted, but you did."

"That was different. I wasn't expecting it."

He wanted to kiss her again, but they were in the street and there were people around. They walked a little longer, and then he did kiss her. She didn't resist and put her arms around his neck. He found it hard to let her go. She smiled and he forgot the little sister problem. She was a beautiful woman, and he wanted her to share his life. He walked her to her door where she grabbed him and kissed him again. He ran to Shoni and galloped all the way home.

October 3, 1916   The sugar factory started, and I've got a room again at the Dennings. My team is again in Mr. Johnston's barn, but I need to get a load of hay for them. I have Sundays off work this year, and I think the job will be a lot more interesting because I can move around. I'm a foreman in the middle section, and I get forty cents an hour.

I think of Susan a lot and wonder how she'll like the cabin. I started to ride to Ammon today, but turned around and came back.

October 8, 1916   I just returned from seeing Susan. Her mother was all right, but seemed kind of cool to me. She must know Susan and I are getting closer to each other. Susan has known it for a long time, but I just found out today for sure. We sat in the Monson living room with the family and remembered when I was working there. It was nice sitting next to her on the sofa with the rest of the family joining in the conversation. Just like I'd never left, except I wished we were alone. When I left, Susan went with me to get Shoni and kissed me hard. I did too.

October 10, 1916 When I went to feed my horses, I thought how wonderful it would be if she was with me, and we were on our homestead. Her beautiful, smiling face is like a new beginning, a new day, a new world, a new anything. Why do I feel this way? My heart is heavy when I'm not with her.

October 11, 1916 I never thought about it when I started this job, but my day off is Sunday, and if I need something from Idaho Falls, all the stores are closed. I don't know of anything I need right now, but I'm sure I'll have to go some time.

October 13, 1916 I wish it was Sunday and I could go to Susan. If I wasn't working all the time, I might be at the Monsons all the time.

October 15, 1916 I went to see Susan again today. Her mother was very cool, but smiled and greeted me the usual way. I just felt something was wrong and when Susan and I went for a walk, she told me her mother was worried about me coming to see her and hoped it wouldn't go on.

John went to see Susan the next Sunday and got there just after dinner. He and Susan left the house and walked a long way in the direction of Ozone and when they turned to go back, she turned and kissed him. Then she turned and they stood for a little while with her back toward him holding his hands in front of her. He could feel her hair under his chin. He wrote, "I guess I got a little crazy. I moved my hands up and held her breasts. She didn't move them away, just said, 'John Pierre, please. Not until we're married.' I moved my hands and she thanked me."

They sat on the back door step after they returned. Lydia came out to feed the chickens, and Susan said,

"Mamma, John-Pierre and I will be married some day." She kissed his cheek.

"Susan! Shame on you." Then she went to feed the chickens.

When she disappeared into the chicken coop, Susan said, "John Pierre, maybe it would be better if you didn't come next week. Mother is against me marrying outside the church, and it will be hard to get her to understand. I'll be eighteen in November, and it will help, but if I have to wait till I'm twenty-one, I will. Do you remember when my birthday is?"

"No."

"It's November third. You always gave me a little gift. Remember the red beads you gave me when I turned thirteen? I still have them." He did remember. She was so happy her freckled face lit up like a rising sun. He left just as Mrs. Monson came back from the hen house.

After supper, Lydia sat Susan down across from her. "Young lady, what did you mean, you'll marry John?"

"Mamma, I love him and I'll be his wife some day. I want your permission, and right now you won't give it, but if I have, to I'll wait till I don't need it. You always say you like him, and you've shown it, too. Why are you suddenly against him when you found out I want to marry him?"

"I do like John, but not as a son-in-law. He's just not one of us. He's an Indian and Indians are heathens. I want more than anything for you to marry some nice Mormon boy in the temple where you'll be sealed to him for time and all eternity. John can't be married in the temple. Have you ever talked to him about joining the church?"

"Yes, Mamma. He has nothing against the church. He just doesn't see any reason to be a part of something that's not so different from his own beliefs. He's so honest about it, I have to agree with him. Mamma, he lived with us for *four* years. He's almost a part of the family already."

"My little girl, you still don't see, do you? If you're not married in the temple, you'll never get to heaven, and the family will be broken in the hereafter. I want something better for you."

"For me, Mamma? Or for you?"

"Young lady, I won't hear such talk from you."

"Mamma, we haven't decided when to get married. Can't we talk about this another time, with Daddy?"

"Can't you find a nice Mormon boy? Maybe a returned missionary?"

"I know lots of nice Mormon boys, Mamma, but they don't interest me. I want to marry John-Pierre. I've always wanted to, ever since he came to live with us. He was always nice to me. Other boys weren't. They called me names because I was so skinny and had freckles, and I was ugly. It wasn't until last year any boys even looked at me."

Susan's tears welled and her mother tried to comfort her, but knew what Susan felt. She'd gone through the same thing.

October 17, 1916 I heard today the snow in the hills is about six inches deep. I'm happy for that, but I wish I was living in my. . . I wish *we* were living in *our* cabin. I wonder what Susan and her mother talk about when I'm not there. Have I created a problem to make trouble between them? I think Susan can be strong sometimes.

October 20, 1916 We got a little bit of snow here today, but it wasn't very much. I can feel the winter coming and my job in the factory is getting to be routine, but far more interesting than the last two. Part of my job is making sure all the men have the things they need to work with. The mechanic in this part of the factory works pretty hard to keep everything running smoothly. His name is Bill Fans, and he comes from Shelley every year to stay with his sister in Lincoln while he works in the factory. He's a little guy, and is always dressed in very neat coveralls, and wears a tie. He knows his business though. I think he can fix just about anything.

I went down to the sugar purifier today and found a lump of melted sugar. I broke off a piece of it after it cooled and tasted it. It was pretty sweet, but tasted like caramel except it was very strong. I'll take a piece of it to the Monsons next time I go. I hope I can go soon.

October 22, 1916 The news from Europe doesn't sound good and German submarines have been seen near American ships. I hope President Wilson can keep us out of it. We don't need to be a part of it.

October 27, 1916 Today Olin Christi, the man in the carpenter shop, cut three of his fingers off on a saw. He was taken to the hospital. His foreman told me he'd been warned often about being too careless around his machines.

Chapter Eighteen
Clouds Gathering

October 29, 1916 It's getting quite cold and there's frost on the ground every morning, but the sun shines bright during the day. I wonder if the snow in the hills is holding out.

I had almost decided to wait another week to go to see Susan, but I couldn't wait any longer. Mrs. Monson answered the door, and looked at me. I couldn't tell what she was thinking, but she waited a second or so then said, "John, how nice to see you."

He hadn't expected that. "Hello, Mrs. Monson, ma'am. Is Susan at home?"

"No, she has a date with a fine young man who just returned from a mission to England. I don't know when she'll be back home. She left right after dinner." John felt smashed like the bug Mr. Schwieder killed with his heel. He didn't know what to say. Finally, he mumbled, "Please tell her I came." He rode back to his room. What had he done? Would he ever see her again? Mrs. Monson had tried once before to find someone for him. Now she was trying to find someone else for Susan.

Later that day, Mrs. Denning knocked on his door, "John, you have a visitor." He opened the door and Susan, angrier than he'd ever seen her, flung her arms around his neck. "My mother did it again. I hate that woman. I *hate* that woman! Hold me, please, John-Pierre." She was shivering.

Mrs. Denning said, "John, why don't you introduce me to your girl friend? I've never met her."

He introduced them, and they exchanged hellos with Susan still attached to his neck. He led Susan outside and turned to face her. "What happened?"

"My dear mother again. The Sunday school arranged a welcome home party for Grant Ensile, who just returned from a mission in England. I didn't really want to go, because I never thought much of him. He always seemed to be hiding, or something, but Mamma said I should go. I thought I'd just stay an hour or so, then come home because I was sure you'd come today. Well, Grant has changed, and about half an hour after I got there, he took my arm and led me into another room. He told me my mother said I wanted to marry a returned missionary, and he was the one. I started to leave, but he grabbed my arm again, and tried to kiss me. I slapped him, and he got a really strange look on his face, as if he couldn't believe it. He said all the girls wanted to marry returned missionaries, and he had picked me out because my mother told him I wanted one. I left then, and just after I turned the corner at the Ammon store on the way home to tell my mother what I thought of her little trick, I saw you riding toward Lincoln. I started running, but I couldn't catch up with you."

"Did you walk all the way?"

"Of course I did."

"That's nearly three miles. Then your mother doesn't know you're here?"

"No. John-Pierre, will you please take me home?"

"Sure, but are you sure your mother should see us together?"

"I *want* her to see us together. I'm so angry with her, I'd do almost anything to make her feel the way I do. Can we both ride your horse?"

No one had ever been on Shoni except John, and he had no idea what the horse would do with two on his back. He said, "I don't know, but I'd like it if he got used to you."

He led Shoni from the barn and told Susan to pat his neck and nose a little. At first Shoni was nervous, but calmed down when John talked to him. He mounted, and pulled Susan up behind him. The horse accepted the new load with only a slight quiver. "Where to, Miss?" he asked.

"Take me home, Mister," she said.

Shoni broke into an easy lope and covered the distance in good time. Susan held to John's waist a lot tighter than was necessary and laid her cheek against his back.

At her house, she dismounted. "Please come in with me. I want to show Mamma she can't just tell me who I should marry."

Mrs. Monson started to greet her daughter but stopped in mid-sentence when she saw John, "What? John? I thought. . . What happened? You were with that nice. . ." She got no further.

"Damn it, Mamma. don't you *ever* try to do that to me, ever again. That idiot proposed to me and said I was supposed to marry a returned missionary. You told him that's what I wanted. I don't want anything, ever, to do with Grant Ensile, again. I didn't like him in high school, and I never will like him."

"Susan Monson, don't you dare talk to your mother like that!"

"Like what, Mamma? Like I was supposed to let you decide who I'll spend the rest of my life with? You can be sure it won't be anyone *you* pick out. You knew I didn't want to go to that party, but I did just to please you. I am your *daughter*, Mamma. I'm not something you can trade off and arrange marriages for. I won't *let* you do it. John-Pierre, come and kiss me."

He was seeing a side of Susan he hadn't suspected. He was as surprised as Susan that Mrs. Monson pulled such a trick. But he wasn't as angry as Susan.

"Mrs. Monson, ma'am. I know I'm the cause of this. If I didn't love Susan, I'd leave right now and you'd never see me again, but I think she's right."

He couldn't judge her reaction from her face, a picture of disbelief, defeat, anger, hurt, or all of them. She turned and walked into the kitchen and closed the door. Susan kissed John and said, "Stay here, I've hurt her feelings very bad. I have to go talk to her."

John heard muffled voices from the kitchen. Susan tried to comfort her mother, perhaps apologize, but then he heard, "I wish he *would* go away and never come back! He's a heathen, Susan. A *heathen!* Don't you know what that means?"

"Yes Mamma, I know what a heathen is. Anyone who doesn't believe in God the same way you do." More muffled voice sounds, and then it grew quiet. After about ten minutes, the door opened and Susan came out.

John half expected her to tell him to go home and not come back. Instead, she said, "I made up with Mamma. She's crying, and she's so mixed up she doesn't know what to do."

"And I'm the cause?"

"Partly. But the real problem is you're so much a part of her life already, she's having a lot of trouble with her own feelings. You heard her say she wished you'd go away and not come back. It was hard for her to say. She didn't really mean it. She just has a problem because you have other ideas about religion,"

"Will it help if I joined your church?"

"Yes, of course it would help, but don't. I love you the way you are and I'd be disappointed if you did, just because someone else wanted you to."

He'd already seen one side of Susan he didn't know, and now he saw another. She was very strong, much stronger than he thought. "Will you be all right, now?" he asked.

"Of course, John-Pierre. I think we should say good-bye for now. Please, come back next Sunday."

October 31, 1916 More and more bad news comes from Europe. In spite of not wanting to be a part of any war, it seems the United States might not be able to stay out of this one. President Wilson is trying but the Germans are becoming more aggressive. They've sunk several American ships.

Just to take my mind off what happened the last time I visited Susan, I read again my journal. I have three notebooks full now, and the difference between them, especially the first and last one, is surprising to me.

November 3, 1916 Today is Susan's birthday. I should have bought her a little gift, but where? I can't get to town. Maybe I could have found something at the Lincoln store, but it's not open when I can go there. I wish I could reach her just to talk to her. I'm afraid Mrs. Monson will convince her to push me out of the picture. No, it won't happen. She's failed twice already to separate us, and I don't think she'd try again after last Sunday. Susan surprises me all the time.

November 5, 1916 Susan came outside and met me. "John-Pierre," she said, "let's go somewhere." She was already dressed for the cold. I agreed, but my mind was full of questions. After we'd walked a short distance, she took my arm, but didn't say anything. I could tell she was upset, but a week had gone by since she and her mother had argued. I thought it should be over by now.

There were other complications. John asked as they walked, "You're so quiet today. Has something happened?"

"Yes. Mamma got sick after you left last Sunday and was so bad she couldn't get out of bed. She's had a little problem since last Christmas when she had her operation, but it got real bad after you left. The doctor came out twice during the week and told her to stay in bed and be careful what she ate. She couldn't keep anything down. The doctor didn't say it, and Mamma didn't either, but I'm sure it's because of what I said to her. I feel so bad. I wish I could get sick instead of her. I was so mad at her for what she did I said things I'd never, ever, thought of saying before. I guess the shock was too much. I feel so bad about it. We made up, but I still feel guilty. Would you be angry with me if I asked you to leave. I'm worried about her, and when she learns we're together, it might make it worse. Please? John-Pierre?"

"Is there something I can do? I don't consider her my enemy. I owe a lot to her."

"No. It will just take time. I'll let you know when you can come again. I'll miss you, but I love my mother, too."

"I'll miss you, too, but if it will help your mother, I'll wait to hear from you. I'd do anything to make you happy again."

November 8, 1916 I wonder how Mrs. Monson is. I wonder how Susan will reach me. Is everybody angry with me? I'm

214

always thinking about what happened with Susan and her mother. I understand what Mrs. Monson's problem is, but she sure gets upset about it. I have never seen Susan so angry. I must stop thinking about it.

I went up the road toward Iona to a farm and bought a load of hay and put it in the barn. It was hard work, but it had to be done. The farmer's name was Jennings, but I don't remember his first name. I had to pay $2 for the load. He said he had plenty, so I can get some more if I need it.

A few days later John saw Susan. He told Mr. Weaver he needed some time off to go to Idaho Falls to buy some things. He came home through Ammon even though it was a little farther. He thought about stopping by the Monsons, but decided not to. As he passed the Ammon store, Susan came out. She almost dropped her bag of groceries in her hurry to get to him. He got off and she ran up to him. "John-Pierre! I'm so glad you came by. I couldn't find a reason to go to Lincoln and I didn't know how to reach you, so I just waited and hoped."

"I decided to come by your house, but when I got near, It didn't seem like such a good idea. How is your mother?"

She got over being sick, but she's still having problems. Yesterday she asked me if I'd seen you, and when I said I hadn't, she shrugged and never said any more. But you won't believe what happened last week. Mamma and Daddy were talking about you and she said she thought you were a very fine man, but she just couldn't stand the idea of me marrying a heathen. Daddy jumped right on it and told her if you're a heathen, it'd do the church a lot of good to have a lot of heathens like you in it. It started an argument I don't think has been settled yet. I've missed you so much."

"I've missed you, too. When can I come to see you at home?"

"I don't know. I'd hate for Mamma to get sick again, but I don't think she would. Please, let's give her some more time. I'll ask her if it will be all right when I think it's time. I've got to get home, now."

He returned to Lincoln a lot happier than he'd been for two weeks.

November 26, 1916   I finished reading my book, at last. It took me more than two years because it was so hard to read at first, and also I didn't have much time. I finally just decided to go on reading without being sure I understood everything. I didn't understand every word, but I understood the story very well. I'm very glad Miss Edwards gave it to me.

Mrs. Denning asked me if I'd be here for Thanksgiving next Thursday. I told her I wasn't sure, but she said she'd set a place just in case. She's a nice woman.

December 3, 1916   Mrs. Denning had a very nice Thanksgiving dinner last Thursday. I hoped the Monsons would invite me to come, but I never heard anything from Susan or anybody else in the family. I'll just have to wait, I guess.

John had gone back to reading an old magazine when Susan knocked on the door. She was all smiles. "John-Pierre! I asked Mamma if you could come to visit again and she said yes! I wanted you to come next Sunday, but we're leaving on the train for Salt Lake and we won't be here. But you can come on the seventeenth. We'll be gone on the weekend. Daddy wants to go to some sort of farmer's conference, and we decided to make it a family affair. It's our Christmas present."

"How did you get here?"

"I walked of course, why?"

"I guess that means I'll have to give you a ride home."

"I guess so," she smiled at him, "but can't we visit a little first?"

"Shall we go some place exotic? Maybe to our homestead, or we could stop in Ozone for some exciting conversation with other homesteaders."

"How about our homestead? I've never been there."

"I warn you, it's a long way from here."

"I'd go anywhere with you."

They walked to the Lincoln store leading Shoni, turned right and came to Ammon still walking. They parted at the Ammon store, and John returned to his room very happy.

December 7, 1916 Just knowing Mrs. Monson was well again makes my heart lighter. I know she thinks a lot of me, but her religious beliefs create problems for both of us. I wish I could wave my hand and make it all disappear.

Chapter Nineteen
Thunderstorms and Rainbows

December 16, 1916 The factory has been so busy this week I was surprised Saturday came so soon. I'm glad because I didn't have so much time to think about tomorrow. I hope Susan's trip to Salt Lake was interesting. I've never been there. It must be a big place.

December 17, 1916 Mrs. Monson met me at the door. She was very cordial; not what I expected after the last time I saw her. I gave her the melted sugar for the boys and she thanked me and said she'd take care of it. Susan was smiling as usual and I fell in love with her all over again. She led me to the living room. I thought something was about to happen but the visit with the family was normal. Mrs. Monson suggested Susan and I go for a walk, so we just took off walking. I offered to buy her a candy bar, but the Ammon store was closed.

They didn't speak of getting married until they started back to her house.

"John-Pierre, you haven't asked me to marry you, yet."

"I thought it was all decided. I *do* want to marry you."

"Then ask me proper."

At first, John was surprised, then grinning, he dropped to one knee in the middle of the street, clasped his hands under his chin, looked up at her, and said, "Susan Monson, I need some help on my homestead. Do you want the job?"

Susan burst out laughing, then looked disappointed. "How much does it pay?"

"All I can pay you is my love, forever. Will you be my wife, Susan Monson?"

"Yes. Yes! I'll be your wife, and the pay is just right." Then she grew serious again. "Mamma is against us getting married. She doesn't think she could stand what the other church members would think if we did, but I think what Daddy told her made her think a little bit clearer."

"What was that?" John asked

"Maybe our church would be better off it had a few heathens like you in it."

"What does your father think?"

"I'm sure he'll agree with us."

"I should easily have the cabin finished by next June, and we could move into it, and live there. Maybe even over the winter."

Susan turned her face to him. "I can't think of anything I'd rather do!"

Back at the Monsons, Henry and Lydia were reading. James was busy with a broken toy on the floor while Freddie watched. Sam was reading a big, thick book. Susan and John held hands and sat next to each other on the sofa.

As John was leaving, Mrs. Monson surprised him. "John," she said, "next Monday is Christmas, but you have to work. I'd like you to come to Christmas dinner, so I'll fix

219

it on Sunday, if you can come." He quickly agreed. Susan went with him to the barn. She opened his coat and hers and they kissed good-bye. She pressed hard against him.

December 24, 1916 Although it wasn't Christmas, Mrs. Monson fixed a dinner that was more than I remember while I lived there. Susan and I sat next to each other just like we did before and sometimes we touched as we ate. And sometimes she'd lean against me. Her parents didn't seemed to be disturbed.

We were all happy and I felt wonderful, but I wasn't prepared for what followed the meal. We sat around again in the living room after the dishes were washed and put away. (I helped.) Without warning, Susan announced, "John-Pierre and I want to be married as soon as possible. We don't want to wait another day. We want your permission and blessings. Mamma, Daddy, will you give us your permission?"

John was surprised. Everybody stopped what he was doing. The room grew intensely silent. Then Freddie shouted, "Yes! yes. I want John for a *real* brother!" Mrs. Monson started to cry. Henry frowned and the other two boys sat with their mouths open.

Through her tears, Mrs. Monson said, "No! no! *no*!

The frown disappeared from Henry's face. "John," he said, "Susan is too young to get married. Have you thought of that?"

Susan, still flushed with excitement, said, "Daddy, I've known John-Pierre since I was eleven years old. I know what I want, and I want to be his wife."

Lydia again said, "No!" John realized the time had come. It was time to ask to marry Susan.

"Mr. and Mrs. Monson," he began, "I love your daughter and I want her to share my life, my homestead, my future, have my babies, love me, be my helpmate, my friend, my wife. Please, may I marry Susan?"

Lydia Monson just stared. The tears were gone, and John was afraid of what she'd say.

"She's such a *baby!*" she wailed.

"Mamma," Susan answered, "remember when I had my first monthly? I was scared to death but you said, 'You're a woman now.' Mamma, that was three *years* ago." Then she stood and twirled around just as she had at the dance in front of John and asked, "Am I not a woman any more?"

"Susan, you shouldn't talk about such things in front of John and your brothers."

"Do you really think they don't know about it, Mamma? I'm *not* a little girl. I'm a woman, and I want to do what women do. I want to be John's wife." Mrs. Monson said nothing, but Henry Monson was ready to take over.

"Susan, are you pregnant?"

"No, of course not!"

"John, I love my little girl as much as you do, but she is awfully young to get married. Her mother was eighteen when we got married, and I know how tough it is to switch from living alone to living as a pair. You're twenty-two, she's seventeen."

"*Eighteen*, Daddy, last month. The same age as Mamma was when you got married,"

"And a woman," he added, as if to reassure her. "I think you'd make a great husband for her, but I'm still hesitant, probably because you're not a member of our church."

He expected this to come up, but he didn't expect what Mrs. Monson said next. "Henry, he's not only not a Mormon, he's a heathen. I don't want my daughter married to a *heathen*."

John had to say something. Her angry words made him angry. "Mrs. Monson, ma'am, you've known me longer than you've known Freddie. You've told me I was almost like a son, and you proved it when you helped me get my homestead. My father was a Catholic. He grew up that way, and when I was old enough, he read parts of his French Bible to me. But he never stood between my mother and her people and their beliefs. I think I'm a better person because he encouraged me to learn the ways of the Shoshonis. I've lived in two worlds. They are different, but in the end they are very much alike. I know a lot abut your church, and I don't think joining it would change my life very much. I respect your church and its principles. My Shoshoni background is deep within me. All I ask of you is you respect my beliefs as I respect yours. Does that make me a *bad* person?"

"But you can't be married in the temple, and I want that for Susan."

"Mamma, being married in the temple is supposed to make Mormons happy, but I know a lot who are not. The love between John-Pierre and me forms a far stronger bond than any promise of 'time and all eternity'. No one has ever come from there and told us about it. We have only the word of the church it's true. I've thought a lot about it ever since I first saw John-Pierre, and I have doubts. I would like to be married in the temple but I don't think it would add anything to our lives."

Susan came to John, turned her back to him, and pulled his hands around her waist. "I love you, John-Pierre."

Lydia finally spoke, "No, you're not a bad person. You've lived in two worlds. I'm torn between those two worlds. Maybe it's because I know only one of them, I want the best for Susan."

"So do I, Mrs. Monson, ma'am. Like my father, I will not stand in the way of Susan's wishes for our children.

I intend to teach them everything my father *and* my mother taught me. I don't intend to make Indians out of them, but I want them to know them."

Mrs. Monson took Susan by her shoulders, and stammered, "I. . . I. . . Susan. I just want you to be happy. It's hard to give up my little girl." She took a deep breath, sighed, and said, "I hate to lose my little girl. I. . . I. . . I. . . Yes, you can marry John. Henry, what do you think?"

"Hell, yes! We're not losing our little girl, we're gaining one hell of a good son."

The whole family exploded and danced around like they had suddenly gone crazy. Freddie stomped on John's foot, the cut one, three times and jumped up and down with joy. "Now, John's my *real* brother. Now John's my real brother," he shouted. James, always just James, shouted, "Whoopeeee!" And Sam, the quiet one, took John's hand in both his, and shook it so hard it surprised him, "John, welcome back into the family. Now I want you to teach me about Indians."

Henry seemed to be the happiest of all. "Welcome to my family. I'm proud as hell to have you in it."

Mrs. Monson, crying big, heavy, wet tears, wrapped her arms around John's neck and kissed his cheek. "John," she said, "I love you. Please take care of my little girl."

"Don't worry about Susan, Mrs. Monson, ma'am. I'll do everything I can to make her the happiest wife there ever was."

Susan glowed and gave him a kiss. "Welcome to my family, John-Pierre Lafontaine," she said.

John's medicine was very strong. He had really become a white man. "Thank you, Mr. and Mrs. Monson, for the most wonderful Christmas gift in the world."

"For hell's sake John, stop the *Mr.* and *Mrs.* stuff. We have first names and you know them. Either call us that way or," he said it quietly, "call us Mom and Dad."

223

Susan, stopped the mini-celebration. "When?"

"When what?" Henry asked.

"When can we get married, of course?"

"Oh dear!" her mother said, "I hadn't thought of that. When do you want to get married?"

"Tomorrow. This afternoon. Right now!" Susan cried. She meant it.

"My goodness! You're in a hurry. So soon is impossible. We have to make you a dress, we have to find someone to marry you, you have to go to the courthouse and get the license, and we have to arrange so much. We have to decide who to invite. We have to know what to feed them. We have to. . ."

"Mamma, all we need is someone to marry us. The rest is dressing."

Mr. Monson, grinned. "Susan, this 'dressing', as you call it, is not just for you. It's for your mother and me, and for your brothers and friends. And we do have to take care of the legal matters. You've waited a long time. A few days won't make much difference. You have the rest of your lives to make up for it."

Susan turned to John, "When do you want to get married?"

"Tomorrow. This afternoon. Right now," he echoed, and she brightened. "But your father is right. We can wait a few days. I have to get some time off anyway. How about New Year's Day? I think I can get Monday and Tuesday off, and we can do all the things we have to do in a week. I think we'll have to go to the courthouse together, though."

Susan put on a pouty face, but she knew John was right. "Can we get the license tomorrow? New Year's Day is so far away, but I guess I can wait. I'll try."

At the sugar factory the next day, Mr. Weaver congratulated John. He'd heard of Henry Monson and was sure John was marrying the right girl. "How did you arrange the church thing with them?"

"Susan said everything necessary. She has her father wrapped around her little finger, but her mother was another problem. She solved it, though. I have to get ready, and I'll need some time off, if it's possible. We plan to be married on New Year's Day and take the next day off, too. Can I do it without causing a lot of problems here?"

"That's all you need? Yes, of course. We can get along without you for a while," he said.

"Then I'll tell them tonight after work."

The next week seemed to flash by for both Susan and John. He spent much of his time accepting congratulations, and shaking hands with well-wishers. Susan was busy with her mother being fitted with a simple, but elegant, wedding dress. Both Susan and John suggested Bishop Judy to perform the ceremony because Ozone was where they found each other, again. Lydia was pleased Bishop Judy would marry them instead of "some legal person they'd never see again." Susan took John to J. C. Penney where he bought a new suit. In his words, "Susan reminded me I should have a suit to wear."

A day before they were married, Henry told John "You have a room at the Eleanor Hotel in Idaho Falls for two nights with our best wishes. Just be gentle."

"Thank you sir, uh. . . Dad. That's what my father told me, too."

In his anxiety, John forgot the traditional symbol, a wedding ring, but promised to buy one later. He kept his eyes on his bride when Bishop Judy performed the ceremony. He didn't hear him ask, "Do you, John Fountain, take this woman, Susan Monson to be your lawful wedded wife?"

Susan poked him in the side and whispered, "Say, 'I do.'"

"I do!" he sputtered. Then paid attention to the rest of the vows and gave the right answers.

About thirty people attended the ceremony held in the Ammon Ward chapel. The wedding guests enjoyed Lydia's homemade cake, and the guests congratulated the newlyweds, and trickled out.

Neither John nor Susan knew what they felt as they entered the lobby of the Eleanor Hotel in the evening of January 1, 1917. Anticipation? Excitement? Intimidation? Fear? The fact they were a married couple hadn't soaked in yet. Bundled in coats against the winter's frosty bite, John, in his new suit and Susan still in her white wedding dress stood out like shining lights as they cautiously approached the desk, taking turns moving a foot or so at a time. Although Susan had stayed in a hotel in Salt Lake a few weeks before, John never had. Neither was sure what to do. The clerk, a man of enough years his hair was gray, raised his head and looked down his nose at them.

"Well," he said, "what can I do for you?" He surveyed them like an eagle looking for prey.

"Well," said John, his voice making a noise he didn't recognize, "I think we're supposed to have a room here. For two nights."

"What sort of room do you want?"

"I don't know. I thought it was all arranged."

"You *thought* it was all arranged?" Don't you know? Who arranged it?"

"I think Henry Monson did." The clerk turned and fumbled with some papers.

"I don't have a Henry Monson staying here. Anybody else?"

"But he's not the one who's staying here. We are."

"Who are we?"

"Susan and I. Henry Monson said it was all arranged. Is this the wrong hotel?"

"I don't know. What hotel were you looking for?"

"The Eleanor Hotel."

"That's this hotel all right, but I don't have anybody named Monson registered."

"Mr. Monson *isn't* staying here. He arranged for *us* to stay here."

"And who, may I ask, is *us*?"

"Susan Monson and John Fountain."

"If you're not married, you can't stay here. This is a respectable hotel. Go to some other hotel if you want your fun with the lady, but don't try to stay here."

John, frustrated, somewhat angry, intimidated by the old hotel clerk, blurted out, "We *are* married!"

"Then why do you have different last names?"

"We *don't* have different last names."

"You just told me Susan Monson and John Fountain. That sounds like different last names to me." Susan saw an element of her father's wit.

"Did my father put you up to this?"

"Who is your father?"

"He did, didn't he? Where are the rest of them?"

A snicker came from behind a post in the lobby. John turned just as several of their guests of the afternoon rushed out and grabbed Susan and took her away.

"John-Pierre, we're being shivareed!" Susan called.

John, baffled his bride of only a few hours was being hauled away, rushed after them, but there were so many others in his way, he couldn't catch up. He returned to the grinning clerk. "What's happening?"

"Susan just said it. You're being shivareed."

"What does that mean?"

"You've never heard of it?"

"No. Now tell me what is going on. Why are they taking Susan away?"

"Your father-in-law just set you two up for the standard prank for newlyweds. It's an old trick. When a couple is first married, the bride is stolen, and the groom has to go find her. Now, go find your bride. Your room is waiting for you, and it's nice and warm."

"Do you know where they've taken her?"

"No, and even if I did, I'd be breaking the law of silence if I told you."

Without the faintest idea of what was happening, knowing only that his bride was gone, John turned and looked around the lobby. Deciding he'd just as well go along with it, he set out to find her. Tracking skills learned as a child came in handy. There were a lot of them, and the snow was relatively fresh. He spotted Susan's footprints among them and followed as fast as he could. But soon the footprints grew fewer until he was sure he wasn't following the fugitives. He doubled back and found Susan's prints again. Then *they* disappeared. They were carrying her!

The only thing to do was to look in every door he came to. Most were locked, and the few open were bars and restaurants. It wasn't likely a bunch of Mormons would go into a bar anyway. He was at the corner of C Street and Park Avenue when the thought hit him. Someone *else* had to be in on the stunt, someone who had a comfortable place to wait. But who? *Who*? John went back to the disappearing tracks, and recalled the guests. None had any connection in Idaho Falls he knew of. It had to be someone the Monsons knew. But who?

The clerk at J. C. Penney! When John bought his suit, Susan told him the clerk was the manager. How would she know that unless the Monsons knew him? And Henry took him there to buy new clothes once before.

John walked slowly past the front of the store, looking inside from the corner of his eye. Sure enough, he spotted a flash of light, as if someone moved a candle. And

228

he was sure he heard voices. He went to the back door. It was open! And he heard his bride's voice. He opened the door slowly, and slipped inside. Susan sat on a soft chair behind them, her back to him, watching the front of the store with the others. Without a sound, he crept up behind her, put his hand over her mouth, picked her up, and carried her out. Knowing it was John, she carefully closed the door behind them.

They ran all the way back to the hotel. The gray-haired clerk laughed and agreed to keep their secret, gave them the key to their room, and bade them well.

But they didn't go to the room. Instead, they stopped at the top of the stairs out of sight. The kidnappers appeared in less than five minutes. One of them said sheepishly, "We lost Susan. Has she come back?"

"No." The clerk's face was a deadpan. "That was Henry Monson's daughter. I hope she doesn't come to any harm. You guys might have a problem if she does."

"Where's John? Did he go looking for her?"

"Of *course* he did. Wouldn't you go looking for a bride as pretty as her?"

"I wonder what happened to Susan. It's awful cold out tonight, and if she doesn't come to the hotel, she'll freeze. Maybe we'd better start looking for her. Jim, why don't you wait in the hotel in case John comes back?"

Jim Samson, a man no sickness ever ignored, welcomed the chance to help by staying in the warm lobby.

As they left, the clerk called out, "You'd better find her. Her father and John will kill all of you if anything happens to her."

John and Susan were giggling almost out of control. They waited in their hiding place till the pranksters left before going to their honeymoon suite where Susan fell into John's arms. As they embraced, Susan began to shiver.

"Are you still cold?"

"No, I'm all right. I guess I'm just excited, is all."

"So am I, my pretty wife." The word "*wife*" brought the realization home to him. He was *really* married, and what they were about to do sent a chill up his spine.

"John-Pierre, I'm scared. I'm so scared. Please hold me."

Slowly the shivering subsided, and they spent the rest of the night oblivious to everything but each other.

Chapter Twenty
Sunshine and Flowers

The next morning, John mused, "I wonder if they're still looking for us." A knock on the door startled them, and he called out, "Who's there?"

"It's your breakfast, and I've got some news." Susan quickly slipped on her dress and John pulled on his pants and opened the door.

"Is it OK if I come in?" John opened the door wider. The clerk followed a tray of breakfast through the door, and set it on a table, "You'll never believe what you did to those guys. They were worried to death. The one they left here asked me if I had anything for a headache, so I gave him a headache powder, but I guess I got it mixed up with a sleeping powder, and he went to sleep in a chair. About midnight, they came back and I told them both of your were here. I think they were either scared silly or stupid. Anyone would have figured out the *only* place either of you would be is here. Idaho Falls isn't big enough for a grown girl to get lost in. They wanted to come up and complete the shivaree with a lot of noise, but I told them not so late at night. They took their sleepy friend and left."

"I guess we turned the tables," John said.

"Yes, and very nicely. You'll be telling the story for a long time."

After he left, they looked at each other. Susan burst out laughing first and John did, too. "Wait till I tell Daddy!"

They spent their first day as a married couple walking around, holding hands. They had lunch in a restaurant, and went to bed early in the evening. Early the next morning, John got the buggy and Susan sat beside him, holding onto him as if her life was in danger, all the way to Ammon.

The Monsons were eating breakfast when they arrived. John stayed only long enough to put the horses in the barn and get Shoni to ride to work. The boys looked at Susan as if they no longer knew her. Lydia hugged her daughter. "Are you all right?" she asked.

"Of course, Mamma. I've got the most wonderful husband in the world." Then she hugged her brothers and turned to her father. "Daddy, that was some trick you and the hotel man pulled on us. I didn't know what was going on because he acted so funny, but then I figured it out. They shivareed us all right, but John found me and took me away without them knowing I was gone. They were pretty scared guys for a while. They thought I was wandering around Idaho Falls alone and lost on a cold winter night. But I was really snug and cozy with John-Pierre."

When Susan finished telling her father about the shivaree, he admitted, "Gary Hausner gave me a key to the back door of the store, so you'd be inside. I've known old Jake Jacobs at the hotel as long as I've been in this country. I knew he'd give you a hard time."

"He did. We were so confused we forgot we were married."

John came back at 7:30. Susan greeted him with a loving kiss, and Mrs. Monson said, "I knew you'd be good to Susan. She's so happy."

"I hope so, Mrs. Monson, ma'am."

"For Heaven's sake John, call me Lydia."

After supper, Henry said to John, "I knew you'd outwit those guys. How did you do it?"

"I'm an Indian. I'm good at tracking."

January 3, 1917 I have lived in Heaven. I have listened to the breath of life drifting from the lips of my beloved Susan and it has given me new life. I have never known, nor will I ever know, a greater feeling of joy than I have now. I thank the wind, the stars, the trees, the earth, and everything on it for bringing Susan to me. There is no greater love than mine for her.

January 7, 1917 When I went to get my things out of the boarding hours, Mrs. Denning said she was sorry to see me leave, but glad I was happily married to the cutest girl she ever saw.

I am the happiest man in the world. As I sit here writing, my wife is sitting by my side. There is only one thing that would make me happier. If we were in our cabin at our homestead. I hope we can go there early this year.

January 28, 1917 Today I was treated to something I never thought of. Susan and her mother stood side-by-side, washing the dishes. Their movements were similar. The way they stood was similar. Lydia is a little taller than Susan, but from the back they looked almost identical. They wore dresses made from the same pattern. I asked them to turn around and when they did, I saw two women so much alike it was startling. Although older, Lydia has the same facial features as Susan. Lydia was a homesteader's wife, and the years of work diminished a beauty she must have had when she was younger. Dad Monson once told me he'd married the prettiest girl in town, and now I think he did. I have, too; I've married the prettiest daughter of the prettiest girl in town. They even sound the same when they speak.

John looked at the two women so long, they got a little uncomfortable. He finally asked Lydia, "Were you always so beautiful?"

"I'm not beautiful. You should have seen me when I was fourteen. I was skinny and pimply and freckled and, well, I was just plain ugly."

"Mamma, you never told me that!" Susan said.

"I guess I should have. I know how you felt when you were in high school and you didn't have a date to anything. I didn't either. But something happened to me when I was sixteen, and I started to love myself. Not just because I'd become a pretty girl. It was because I felt something inside me that told me I wasn't what I looked like before. The boys were falling all over themselves to get a date with me. Then your father came along and in him I saw a solid man. I went after him, and I got him. I knew when John came into our lives he was the same kind of man — solid. And that's why I took out the homestead in my name for him. I'm sorry for the stupid things I've said to you and to John."

"Mamma, I didn't know."

John wondered if he'd opened a Pandora's box, or if he'd helped something important to happen. "OK, you can finish the dishes, now," he said. He was happy for the conversation as far as it went.

One night as John wrote, Susan slipped her arms around his neck and kissed him on his ear. "What will you write tonight?"

"What should I write?"

"Tell your journal how much I love you."

"How much *do* you love me?"

She flung her arms as wide as she could and said, "This much!"

"Will you love me so much when we're at the homestead and everything is going wrong?"

"I'll love you even more, because I know you can make it right."

He imagined her fussing with the little things women fuss with, making changes, maybe even changing the colors, and a thousand other things. He imagined her cooking on the tiny stove, and he smiled to himself. He had to get a bigger one, and a bigger bed, too. But now, he had a wife to help him pick things out. How he longed for the day he and Susan could live together on their homestead!

February 4, 1917 I've heard the snow is still very deep in the hills, but I'd like to ride to our homestead anyway. I'm getting so anxious to show Susan our new home, I'm tempted to just quit my job and go.

February 11, 1917 Since the *Lusitania* was sunk almost two years ago, Americans seem to want revenge more and more. I hope President Wilson can keep us out of the war. Revenge is not good; it just breeds more revenge. I hate what is happening. Is there no solution? The Germans have new weapons I never heard of: submarines that move under the water and fire explosives at other ships, a poison gas that kills people when they come in contact with it. And they have airplanes. I don't know if United States has them. Has the world gone mad?

One evening John and Henry were discussing the farm. Henry asked John a question he eventually took more seriously. "How long do you intend to farm?"

"All the rest of my life. I can't imagine wanting to do anything else."

"Right now, no, but some time in the future, you might want to move on up. I think you should think about it."

"On up to what? I can't think of anything I'd rather do than farm."

"OK, John. But just think about it."

"I don't know what else I could do."

"You have a good brain. Just think about it. I can't tell you any more."

As they sat in the living room one afternoon, it occurred to John that in the excitement of last Christmas and getting married, he hadn't asked about the trip to Salt Lake. Henry pulled himself up in his chair, "It was amazing. I should have told you about it. Just forgot, I guess. Cost a lot of money, but sometimes, a lot of money buys a lot of enjoyment. And we had that."

"Oh, yes, Daddy, It was a wonderful trip. We rode the train all the way, and then a street car to the fair, and. . . Daddy, you tell him about it," Susan warbled.

"That's what I was trying to do, Susan. I saw things coming up for farmers I never thought would happen. The most interesting for me was the tractors. There were only two there. One was a funny looking thing with only two wheels, and had to have an implement attached to run straight. There were at least twenty more representatives with pictures and descriptions of their machines, but none of them could give a delivery date. They look good, but I don't think it's time to buy one. They all need more development. As far as I could see, a farmer would have to have a very large farm to pay one off. One speaker talked about using phosphate fertilizer made from rocks. There's a big area in Idaho south of us where there's a lot of phosphate rock, but nothing has been done with it, so far. There wasn't much about dry farming, but the future in the valley looks great."

Their conversation went on, Henry telling of Sam getting deeply involved with an extension agent booth just after they entered, and Susan and Lydia spending time at an exhibit of cooking and canning.

Susan spoke up. "We learned how to make jelly out of apples and currants, and raspberries, and other fruits."

"Didn't you know that already?"

"Yes, but they showed us some new processes, and some new products. We had a wonderful time."

"We have a lot of wild fruit at the homestead. You can have all the fun you can stand when we get up there."

Talk of moving to the homestead occupied much of the newlyweds' time. John worried the snow might keep them in Ammon even after the factory closed. One day Susan asked when she could meet John's mother. He told her of her death and about his twin sister. Her questions seemed endless, but John enjoyed talking about his parents and the way he lived before he came to their farm. He told her about the little rabbit skin cap his father made for his mother.

"How sweet! She must have loved your father very much."

"I'm sure she did, and it might be why she didn't tell him about my sister. She said she wanted me to have other sisters and brothers, but she could never have another baby. It's probably something that caused her death. She wasn't more than about forty."

March 8, 1917 Mr. Weaver told me today the factory should be finished for the season about the first of April, and asked me to stay on for a couple more months, but I told him I had a farm to look after. I don't think I want to work in the sugar factory next year.

March 11, 1917 I was reading a book today when Susan came and demanded attention. She was baking bread and had flour on her nose and chin and even smelled like fresh-baked bread. We went into the kitchen where she sliced a hot loaf, spread butter and honey on it and offered it to me with an impish grin. She knows I don't like much sweet stuff, so she cut another piece and buttered it for me.

Although Susan had never seen the cabin, she talked as if she knew all about it. "When we get to our homestead, you'll always have fresh bread to eat," she said.

"Not until we have a stove with an oven."

"Don't we have a stove?"

"I have a tiny stove I carried on my back from Ozone to Bull's Fork. It was made to heat a tent, and it's only big enough for one pot."

"Then I guess we'll have to go shopping, won't we?"

"We also need a bigger bed. Mine is just big enough for me."

"Then it's big enough for both of us."

"But we'll be piled on top of each other."

In a fake husky voice she said, "Yes, I know."

By the middle of March, the weather was beautiful, and the happy couple got ready to go to their castle on Bull's Fork. The road to Ozone was passable, but when the time came, so did a blustery spring day with rain, sleet, and snow.

John remembered his plan to have a small orchard when Sam opened the subject. Sam asked, "Do you think it's possible to have an apple tree with more than one kind of apple growing on it?"

John had never heard of it but said, "It might work. Why don't you give it a try?"

In another entry, he reported, "I woke up last night thinking I have to build a toilet, too. I'm sure Susan wouldn't want to do what I've been doing. There's always something else."

March 20, 1917 I hope we can get up to the homestead soon. I'm so anxious to show it to Susan. I hope she likes it.

March 24, 1917 Mr. Weaver told me today the factory will finish early next week, but he asked me to stay on till the first of April. I guess I will. I had hoped to take Susan up to the homestead tomorrow, but maybe it's just as well to wait another week. The weather has been good and when I finish at the factory, I won't have to hurry back. Susan will be disappointed, but I think she'll understand.

March 25, 1917 Dad Monson and I talked a little about the war in Europe. I don't know what Susan would do if I had to go. He told me he'd make sure she was all right, but maybe she'd have to leave the farm and come to Ammon. This is the only dark cloud hanging over me. I haven't told Susan of my own fears, and I won't until they're real. I want her to be happy as long as I can make it so.

April 1, 1917 Susan and I left early this morning in the Monson's buggy. We had a few groceries, and we were prepared to stay a day or two so she could make plans for the other things we need. We got to the homestead a little before dusk, and I drove in from a different direction so she'd see it all at once for the first time.

As soon as the buildings came into view, Susan gasped, "This is it, isn't it? Isn't it, John-Pierre?" He had no chance to answer. "Oh, it's so beautiful! Just what I knew it would be!" She threw her arms around his neck and tried to smother him. He drove looking sideways. He finally got a chance to look, too. There was quite a bit of snow in the cove under the hill, and the root cellar was still partly buried. He drove into the yard, and Susan jumped off the buggy before it stopped, ran to the cabin, flung open the door, and shouted, "I'm home! I'm home! At last, I'm home!"

After living in the valley all winter, he found the place incredibly bare, nothing but a tiny stove and a narrow bed in the room, a pot and a frying pan hanging on nails in the walls, and his eating utensils laying on a makeshift table he'd built from left over pieces of lumber. But Susan was wild with enthusiasm. She ran from place to place saying what she would put where. Things they didn't have yet, already had a permanent place.

"It's beautiful, and I love it," she said, her face alive.

John got her to stop and sit on the bed, but she continued babbling about their beautiful home. He built a fire in the stove, went out to take care of the horses, and came back with the things they brought from Ammon. "Where shall I put these things?" he asked.

"Oh dear, we don't have any shelves, do we?"

"No, all we have are four walls, a roof, a stove and a bed. Don't forget the reason we're here is to decide what else we need." He tore off a piece of the grocery wrapper, took his pencil from his journal, and told her to make a list.

Seeing her running eagerly around those two rooms was worth every bit of sweat and effort he'd put into building the cabin. He felt like a giant.

He started to put a pot of water on the stove to boil potatoes when she came and took his hands. "No, that's my job, I want to cook every meal we have here."

After wrestling with the pot of potatoes and trying to fry some eggs and sow belly, she said, "I guess you'd better show me how to do it. I'm not used to such a tiny stove. A bigger one goes to the top of the list."

"And how about a bigger bed?"

She flashed the impish grin, "Not yet. I like the idea of us piled on top of each other." By morning, she decided differently, "I'd like to have a brass double bed. Can we?"

They returned to Ammon with her list and happy hearts.

April 5, 1917 I took the wagon with Susan and her mother to Idaho Falls where we went to many stores for first a stove, and then a bed, and a wash basin and a lot of other things. Almost everywhere we went, there was talk of war. Susan was so wrapped up in making a home she scarcely noticed, but her mother looked worried.

We'll leave in the morning with a load of things I bought for the cabin. Susan's parents will go up with us. I'm glad. The stove is too heavy for Susan and me. It's got a lot of shiny stuff on it I can't see any use for. I bought some boards for shelves, and she has some more pots and pans. We also bought a lot of things like sugar and flour. She had a big list and we got most of the things on it. She jumped and squealed when she found just the right brass bed. I hope we don't need any more stuff for the cabin. I spent over $100. But making her happy has made me happy. I feel like a king. I guess I should, though; I've got a queen.

They got to the cabin in the middle of the afternoon and unloaded the wagon. Henry helped John install the stove, but it almost didn't fit. The little one was so small the chimney hole wasn't directly above the new stove. They took all the stuff they could off the new stove to make it lighter, and had barely set it in place when Susan started putting the removed parts back on and polishing it. The bed was next and Susan and Lydia put the bedding on it and stood back to look at it. Lydia asked, "Where did you sleep when you came up here before?"

"We slept on the cot, Mamma."

"Both of you?"

"Yes, of course."

"How?"

"We piled up on top of each other."

Lydia looked at her and slowly shook her head, but she seemed almost as excited as Susan about setting up a new household. Henry and Lydia stayed with the Campbells in Ozone that night.

Once again, John and his bride were alone in their new home. Susan beamed and went from place to place inspecting the same things she'd already inspected. Then she sat on the bed and asked, "Which side do you want?"

"The same as always."

"But it's a new bed. Don't you want to try something new?"

They settled on the same sides, but they did try something new.

Chapter Twenty-One
Violent Storm Devastates

Robert Burns wrote, "The best laid schemes o' mice and men gang oft agley." John and Susan settled in and their future looked bright. The field was a green sea of young wheat teased by the wind, bending with every breath. Susan had already baked a batch of steamy loaves in their new stove. They sat up late at night planning. They needed a cow, a brood sow, some chickens. She began writing down what she would plant in the garden. Both were happier than either thought possible. Then came the blow.

April 7, 1917 I learned at Dehlin post office that yesterday the United States declared war on Germany. When I think of what the white men do to each other, I wonder if he's really any better off than the Indians. As Indians we had our wars but mostly over hunting grounds that didn't belong to anybody anyway, and they were usually settled quickly. This war in Europe has been going on for a long time. When the Germans sank American ships, it was just too much, so we are now in a war. I don't know what it means but I'm sure it will have something to do with us.

He told Susan as soon as he got home. "Will you have to go?" was her first question.

"I don't know," he answered. "I guess if they call me I will but it won't be because I want to. They told me at the post office a lot of the local young men have already enlisted, and will be leaving soon."

The thought of leaving Susan in a wild land sickened him. She was strong, but couldn't do all the farm work. If he didn't volunteer, he'd have a little while before they called him.

He knew he was too young and healthy to be rejected. He was not a man of war. He was, like his Shoshoni brothers, a man of peace.

The fact of what the war might mean to them didn't sink in at first. Susan seemed oblivious and kept on happily fussing in the cabin. He sat her down and explained what might happen. She stared at him a few seconds and suddenly burst into tears.

"I know how you feel. I don't even know if I'll have to go, but it seems likely right now. Please don't cry till we *really* have a reason to cry."

"I guess I'm just confused. We just started our lives together and I'm so happy. Now you might have to leave me at just exactly the wrong time," said Susan through her tears.

"There is no such thing as a right time for war. I built this place from a piece of raw sagebrush land into a farm, and I built this cabin for you, even though I didn't know it at the time. I am proud of it all. Now, I can share it with you, and my happiness is complete. I don't want to leave you. I want to go on building. Some day we'll have our little home as perfect as we want it."

Susan cried harder. She threw herself into his arms, and wept giant tears. "Jean-Pierre, we're going to have a baby! And now you have to leave me. It just isn't fair. It isn't *fair*!"

John was struck dumb. His mind raced from Susan to the farm and then to the strange idea they'd have a baby. Susan, the farm, the war, the baby. The sequence ran through his mind over and over. Then the knowledge he'd be a father hit him.

"How? A baby! Susan, how? When?"

She looked up at him and giggled through her tears. "How? John-Pierre, you *know* how. You should have stayed on your side of the bed." Then she giggled again.

"A baby! Oh, you wonderful woman! A baby? I'll be a father, and you'll be a mother. I don't know what to say."

She nuzzled his shoulder and giggled. "Remember at the dance where we met a long time ago, and you said you'd be ready to start a family when your cabin was finished, and I shocked you when I said I wanted to help? Well, I've helped, and I'm as happy as you are. I hope it's a boy."

"I don't care if it's a potato. I'll be a father!" They laughed at his grotesque outburst.

"Believe me, it won't be a potato. As to when, I don't know for sure, but I think between seven and eight months from now."

I'm going to be a father! Imagine! Me! A father! My baby will be a fourth Shoshoni, a fourth French-Canadian and half white. "

"Your arithmetic is all wrong. It will be one-fourth Shoshoni and three-fourths white."

"I don't care if it's a potato!" They laughed again.

Reality struck. John crooked a finger under her chin and said, "Susan, you've made me the happiest man who ever lived, but we're in a war, and I see no way to get out of going. There is no place they can send me I won't think of you. No place!"

Susan changed the subject, "We've *got* to have a toilet! It might be all right for you to pee on the bushes, but I can't. Besides, I want a little privacy at other times."

The sudden pronouncement of such an ordinary thing left John holding his crooked finger under her chin with nothing more to say. Finally he stammered, "OK." He wrote, "She was right. I promised to build one tomorrow, I doubt it's much of a challenge."

April 8, 1917 We went to the Monsons today. Once, a long time ago, Dad Monson told me not to call him *sir* and asked me why I did. I told him it was because he was older and much wiser than I am. He said he was older but he wasn't sure he was wiser. But I needed to tell them. Henry agreed I should wait till called. Lydia cried because Susan is going to have a baby and I might have to leave her. We came home, had supper, and went to bed without saying much.

The next days held little joy. John walked around in his field thinking of what he could do to make things easier for Susan if he had to leave. They ate in silence, the joy they knew only a few days before was dampened by what seemed to be inevitable. He wrote, "I will be in a war and I might be killed. I might never see my child. I'll make it so Susan owns the farm and everything. After the war is over, I want to come home and live a happy life. It has not been easy for me so far, but I can see happiness coming. It's just around the war corner."

A few days later, they went to a lawyer's office in Idaho Falls and drew up the papers making Susan the joint owner of the homestead.

April 18, 1917 Today, I am very happy. The wheat is almost up to my knees and looks like a green ocean. The wind leaves swirling tracks that vanish in a second, only to reform and vanish again. We are very happy. We have no debts and we have a little money in the bank.

The next day, John started building the toilet with some helpful supervision and advice from Susan. He reported: "I started building the toilet today, but it turned out to be a bigger job than I thought. I dug a hole about a foot deep and, one and a half feet wide by about five feet long. Susan looked at it and said, "You like to dig holes, don't you?"

"No, why?"

"Well, you'll have to dig a lot of them if that's as deep as you want it. It should be about as deep as you are tall."

"How do you know?"

"I've watched Daddy dig two of them."

When he finished, it wasn't as deep as he was tall because he hit bedrock at about his shoulders. He'd spent two days on it, already. He and Susan went to Louie Franck's place and asked him how to build the house.

"About all you need now is four walls, a roof, a seat, and a door that can be fastened from the inside. It might be nice, too, if the roof didn't leak." They spent the afternoon, and Irene spent most of it on Susan's lap. Eugene and Lee were friendlier, too. Carrie insisted they have an early supper, so they stayed. John wasn't really sure how to proceed with the toilet, but he knew he needed some more lumber. "It seems there's always something else I need."

April 21, 1917 I finished the toilet this morning. The hole is almost in the middle of the seat. I tried, but by the time I'd finished sawing it, it was no longer in the middle where

I planned it to be. Susan said it's just wonderful. It should be; it took almost two weeks to build it.

During the next few days, they planted their garden. Susan wanted John to go to her Sunday school with her. "I enjoyed seeing my neighbors and meeting a lot of new people.

"I didn't understand the need for all the ritual, and some of the things they said didn't make much sense, but that's the way they do things. Everyone was very friendly and just about all of them invited us to visit."

Then a good rain fell. As they sat in the cabin, John told Susan about running naked in the rain the year before. She suggested they do it then, but he declined. After all, it was daytime.

They didn't talk about the war. Neither of them wanted to think about it. They discussed getting some livestock, at least a cow and some chickens to start with. The hay John planted was much better than last year, reminding him he needed a hayrack. Louie Franck promised to help but he was busy weeding his summer fallow ground. "Maybe Mr. Fogelsong can help me build it, but first I have to get some lumber. It seems there's always something else I need."

May 15, 1917 George Fogelsong came to my place and told me what kind of lumber I needed and how much, and I went to the sawmill and bought it, and a little extra.

On the way back, I stopped at Ozone to buy some nails. I learned there that a man named Alva Beesley skied to Blackfoot last February. A blizzard came up and he didn't make it back. He was found frozen in a deep snow bank a few days ago. I also learned Mr. Bone had been granted a post office in his store, and that it would be called Bone Post Office. Everything is changing so much.

Mr. Fogelsong and I started to put the hayrack together the next day, but when he saw me using nails to build the bottom frame, he said I needed bolts. So I rode to Ozone to buy some. Then I remembered I didn't have any way to make the holes so I had to buy a brace and bit. It seems to me that a simple thing always turns into something complicated. Mrs. Otteson told me I'd need washers for the bolts. Otherwise, when I tightened them up, they'd sink into the wood. I had also forgotten a wrench, so I bought one. I was glad when we finished. I was afraid I'd need something else. We changed the grain box for the hayrack, and now I can haul almost anything. I think I'd better buy a grain drill before I run out of money. I really need one.

May 17, 1917 Susan and I went to Ozone today to buy some more groceries. Just after we got home, the sun set, and we watched it. I couldn't help thinking of the future. Just when everything was ready to settle down, along comes a war that I'm sure will take me somewhere I don't want to go. We didn't talk; just watched, as the shadows got longer until they were swallowed up in the darkness. Is that what our future looks like?

Chapter Twenty-Two
Lightening Strikes

They say bad things come in threes. People prove it by reciting all the things they know and dividing them into groups of three. No one did that with John and Susan, but with two problems, the war and her pregnancy, it was about time for the third one.

A brilliant flash of light and violent crack of thunder rocked the cabin and shocked John and Susan awake. He ran to the door. A raging wind whipped soaring flames in all directions around the shed. He grabbed a bucket and ran out without dressing. The panic stricken horses packed the far corner of the corral seeking a way out. He tried, but couldn't haul enough water to stop the flames. Each bucketful just sizzled when it hit the fiery fury. Susan, wearing just her nightgown was beside him throwing water with another bucket, but there was nothing they could do. It just burned, and burned, and burned.

They went back into the house and sat on the bed. In his dismay, John forgot about the horses. He ran back out. They were gone. The barn was a part of the corral, and when it burned, a section of the corral collapsed and gave those frightened animals a way out.

They got dressed and in a few minutes, both Louie and George showed up. They saw the blaze, and came to help. Smoking pieces of wood lying like a pile of sticks on a bonfire remained where the shed once stood. Susan's chin was quivering and it was all she could do to keep the tears from falling. All four of them stood in silence looking at the destruction.

After a little while, Louie spoke, "John, we'll get a bunch together and help you rebuild it." A few minutes later, they left and Susan and John sat on the bed holding each other till the sun streamed in through the window.

"I'll make some breakfast," she said.

"I think I should look for the horses."

After breakfast, he went and kicked around in the smoking ashes. A piece of metal caught his eye, "Oh, *no*, the harnesses are gone, too, and so are three sacks of oats."

John started walking and whistling for Shoni. After about half an hour, Shoni showed up, leading But and Mage. It was the only bright spot in an otherwise very black day. They didn't sleep very well that night. The thought of starting all over to build a new shed plagued John all night.

Susan was strangely quiet till after noon when she said, "I'm glad it wasn't the house."

"So am I."

She came to him and sat on his lap. "John-Pierre," she started, "we'll rebuilt it, and when we do, why not add space for a cow. Maybe we could have a chicken coop, too."

"I hadn't planned those improvement for quite a while, but it's a good idea," he answered, "and what about a pig pen, too?"

He knew she was just trying to get his mind off the fire, but he accepted the idea. He sat at the makeshift table

251

and figured how much lumber he'd need. Mr. Covert said the barn he wanted to build originally would cost about a hundred dollars. If he put everything in a row, it might cost less to build.

Susan put her hand on his shoulder, "Just like Daddy, always figuring."

"He was my teacher, remember?"

"You really like him, don't you?"

"My father taught me many things, but he never taught me how to farm. Dad Monson did. I owe him a lot."

"When can we get started?" she asked.

"Tomorrow, This afternoon. Right now."

Susan smiled at the recollection. "But don't you have to have a plan?"

"I built a toilet without a plan. And I built the shed that burned without a plan. I don't think I need a plan for the new one."

But he did have a plan. He'd learned a lot when he built the shed that burned. All he had to do was enlarge it. But now he needed new harnesses.

May 21, 1917 I had to do it. There was no other way. Susan and I rode Shoni to the Monsons and I borrowed their buggy. I left Susan to visit with her family while I went into town, bought new harnesses for almost fifty dollars, and took them out to the homestead. Early the next day I returned the buggy and, after a very short visit, Susan and I rode back home.

May 22, 1917 Susan and I drove the team with the new hayrack over to the sawmill and got a huge load of lumber. We took a picnic lunch and ate it on a table that looked exactly like a big rock.

As they neared home, the wagon tracks were rough and the load bounced around a lot. Susan was sitting on it, and when she caught John watching her, she asked, "What are you looking at?"

"I'm just watching your titties bounce."

"John-Pierre, that's nasty!"

"Don't you like it?"

". . . Yes."

They laid out the new barn on the ground with stakes and a few scraps of burned boards just to see how it would look on the ground. The Francks came by and Louie told John to let him know when he wanted to start and he'd round up some of the neighbors to help. He told him he needed a load of poles for the framework, then he'd be ready. Louie promised help for that, too. "How about tomorrow?" he asked.

John looked at Susan. She looked directly at him, grinned an impish grin, and asked, "If it's a bouncy ride, can I go with you?" Then quickly added, "I could fix a lunch for us."

The next morning, Louie and George and John Snow showed up and they cut all the poles they needed in one day.

A few days later, five neighbors showed up and built the whole frame that day.

May 28, 1917 Today the barn is almost finished. All I have to do is nail the battens on. I can do that alone. I have some wonderful neighbors. Besides George, Louie, and John Snow, Dave Rushton, and Charley Muggleston came to help. The little valley with Bull's Fork rushing through it was filled with the clack of hammers, and the rasping of saws — a cacophony of friendship. I am probably happier than I was when I finished my little shed alone. But the cloud of war still hangs over my happiness.

May 28, 1917 It's finished. The corral is repaired and the barn stands as a monument to hard work by a lot of good neighbors. Susan and I walked out to look at the alfalfa field this afternoon. I think I'll have to go to work on it in the next couple of weeks.

The weather has been too nice. We could use some rain. We came back along the wheat field and saw the heads are forming well enough, but the ground is dry and there are some yellow stalks around the edges.

May 30, 1917 Today was the first really hot day we've had. Susan spent most of it out in the garden fussing with her plants. She's become quite good at irrigating it with nice straight rows. So far the only thing we've had to eat from it were some radishes. We still have a lot of things in the root cellar from last year, and she's trying to use them up before we harvest again this year.

As they ate supper that night, Susan reminded John it would be nice if they had a bigger table. A little less than $800 remained in the bank and he still needed a grain drill to plant winter wheat. That is, *if* he was there to plant it. He was reluctant to spend any more money unless it was necessary.

Susan didn't talk about the war any more, but sometimes she cried at night. John didn't ask her why because *he* didn't want to think about it either. She was always cheerful during the daytime, though.

In one entry he noted, "Now we have a place for a cow and some chickens and pigs, I think I'll start looking for some. Chickens won't cost very much and maybe I can buy half a dozen or so. A cow and a brood sow will be more expensive." Discouraged, he was reluctant to start anything he wasn't sure he could finish. Uncertainty was his new enemy.

June 3, 1917 It's getting very dry. I wish the war cloud was a rain cloud hanging over my fields. I can't even make any plans. We need so many things. I'd like to have a buggy so we could ride in it instead of on Shoni when we go anywhere. Susan needs a washtub and a scrubbing board and all the things women need to make their work easier. She could use a cow after the baby is born and she weans it, and chickens would give us fresh eggs. I don't think a pig would be useful to her, but if I could stay home, I could build a smoke house and we'd have smoked meat most of the year. I just don't know which way to turn.

Last night she told me she was very happy the way things are right now. Then she told me about the washtub and the scrubbing board, again.

Today, we took a bunch of watercress over to Fogelsong's, and paid a short visit. Lizzie, the little girl, gave us some hard-as-rocks cookies she baked. Susan asked for the recipe and the girl was overjoyed.

June 7, 1917 I bought her a washtub and a scrubbing board in Ozone. Another homesteader left and gave four chickens to Mrs. Otteson, and she asked us if we wanted them. There didn't seem to be any way we could get the washtub, scrubbing board and four chickens back to the homestead on Shoni, but Susan solved it. She asked Mrs. Otteson if she'd loan us a gunny sack. She put the chickens in the sack, I climbed onto Shoni, gave her a lift up, Mrs. Otteson handed me the scrubbing board, gave the sack to Susan and hoisted the wash tub up so we could put it over our heads to carry."

All the way home, they traded remarks about their load. It was like an armored knight with two bodies, wearing a single helmet and carrying a strange weapon with a sack full of ammunition. They made jokes about it, and when they laughed, the sound echoed around in the washtub making them laugh even harder.

At home they put the chickens in the coop and watched them explore their new surroundings. "You know something?" Susan asked. "We forgot to give them a place to roost. Chickens don't like to sleep on the ground." John looked at her with an amused frown, then found a small, fairly straight quaking aspen and nailed it across one corner of the coop. Susan beamed. "All they need now are nests to lay their eggs in." John wrote, "There's always something else."

June 11, 1917 Still no rain. I hope we get some soon. Last year was like this, and I don't want another short crop.

I wonder if they've forgotten me and won't need me to go to war. But not knowing is awful, too. I hope they can wait till I get my crop harvested and the next year's crop planted. I should plant the new one in the middle of August, a very busy time of year. I've heard there might be an elevator in Iona some time soon where I can sell my wheat. Iona might be a shorter trip.

John cut and stacked his hay with Susan's help.

By their calculations, she conceived in late February or early March and the baby would be born in November. He wrote: "She's just beginning to show. I'm probably the only one except her who notices it, but I'm so used to seeing a perfectly flat belly any change is obvious to me.

The chickens started laying. "Susan found an egg yesterday and brought it into the cabin. Her face was lit up like the sun after a summer shower."

June 21, 1917 For the past several days, I've been digging in my spring to make a cooling box, so we can store stuff that might spoil. I haven't installed the pump yet. I should do that before I start harvesting. Our garden is growing very well.

June 25, 1917 A little rain fell last Monday, but it was only a promise. It's been cloudy since then, but nothing happens. At least it's not hot.

I wish I knew about me going to war. Not knowing is worse, I think, than knowing the worst. At least, you can plan something if you know the worst.

I started today to install the pump in the cabin. It looks like a much bigger job than I thought at first. The spring is about a hundred feet from the house and the pipe has to be very deep to keep it from freezing. I started digging the trench from the house to the spring and it's very slow. Just the trench will take several days, but it'll take my mind off the uncertainty.

Susan hung some pictures on the wall. It makes the place look more homey.

June 30, 1917 This is the last day of June, and still no rain clouds. The wheat is headed out, but the heads are short again this year. The field is turning yellow. If we don't get a rain, there won't be much of a crop this year, either.

I'm afraid to spend any money. I don't know what will happen with me, and I don't know what will happen with my crop, either. Susan asked me if we could water the field with buckets of water from the spring. "Water sixty acres with a *bucket*?" I asked.

July 2, 1917 I finished the trench, but when I went to Ozone to buy some pipe, Mrs. Otteson said pipe was one thing they never did carry. She ordered some for me, but it will take a few days to get here. She also said there would be another Fourth of July celebration in Ozone on Wednesday. I told Susan about the celebration, and she was excited. She said, "I've always wanted to go to one of them here. Can we?" I started digging the hole for the pump box. That's a mess.

July 5, 1917 It was awful hot yesterday when Susan and I went to Ozone, but I think everybody in the whole area was there. I took Susan first to Mrs. Holmquist for two reasons. First, I wanted one of her roast pork sandwiches, and second, I wanted to introduce my bride so she'd leave me alone next time she found an unmarried girl. I needn't have worried about the second reason. She already knew.

Mrs. Holmquist was impressed when she saw Susan. "My, my, John Fountain. What a pretty young thing. It's wonderful to be married, ya? And she's going to have a baby! What a lovely thing. When?" But she didn't wait for an answer. "We were very happy as new weds. My man and me had a good time. It's nice to be married."

"Probably in November," Susan answered.

"What? November? I don't understand."

"We're expecting our baby in November. You asked me when it will be born, didn't you?"

"Oh, yes. November. I remember our first baby. It's a lovely time. You will enjoy it."

John thought it was time to move on before Mrs. Holmquist started to recite her past failures to get him married off. They left munching sandwiches, and hadn't gone but a few yards when they met Bishop Judy.

"Well, hello! How are the newlyweds? It's good to see you here."

"We're doing well enough, sir," John answered.

"Please call me Aaron. Or if you have to be formal, call me Bishop Judy."

"Yes, sir. . . I mean Aaron."

They talked about how things were going and the weather. Susan glowed with the joy of being somewhere outside their cabin, and joined in the conversation. John thought he detected a bit of sadness; as if she missed going to church.

They watched the same things John had seen at all the celebrations he'd been to before, but his mind was on his drying field and the war. Susan was excited about everything, and her joyous laughter filled the air every place they went. The pie-eating contest left her in stitches.

At the spelling contest, she seemed to know all the words and whispered the spelling to herself.

Although they were stopped often for conversation, they were alone in spite of the number of people there. They left to go home late in the afternoon, tired, happy and exhausted. Just before they left, Mrs. Otteson told John he could pick up his pipe, so he did the next day. He laid much of it after he got it home, and thought he should be able to finish the next. Mrs. Otteson reminded him of the other things he'd need to connect the pipe together and to the pump. "I don't know when, if ever, I'll use the wrench again."

July 10, 1917 The pump is finally working. I couldn't get any water to come out of it till I read the directions. I had to pour some water into it to prime it. Then there was plenty of water. At first, it was muddy, but after several buckets full, it cleared up. Susan is very happy with it. She planted flower seeds last spring, and they're blooming with all the power they have. The yard looks like at the Monsons. We always have flowers in the house, and it makes me feel good.

It's still hot, and every cloud bringing a promise of rain moves on. My wheat is nearly all yellow, and I doubt even a heavy rain would help it now.

On July 15, Susan seemed to be sad and John, being used to joy from her, asked her why.

"Sometimes I'd like to go to church on Sunday."

"Then we'll go. I like seeing people, and most of them are there."

A smile lit her face, and she said, "I'm sorry, I miss it. I used to go almost every Sunday, and I feel sort of left out of things when I don't go." The experience was the same as the other times he went with Susan. Everyone greeted them and treated them like old friends although John didn't know some of them very well. When they got home, he told Susan they could go more often.

July 16, 1917 It was hot again today, but I decided to disc my summer fallow land to get rid of the weeds. The dust boiled up in a suffocating cloud. It will take about four days. Maybe I should just give up on the wheat and disc it, too. I'm so discouraged. No rain. The cloud of the war. Money getting short. I keep forgetting I'll be a father. My only bright spots are Susan and the baby.

Chapter Twenty-Three
Expect Clouds

On July 19, the day after his twenty-third birthday, John's draft notice came.

July 19, 1917 Today it came. I have to report to my draft board within a week and bring the notice with me. My heart is so heavy, I can't imagine leaving my wife to go fight in a war that means nothing to me. They tell me I'll be fighting for freedom, but whose freedom? Not mine; I'm already free.

I don't think I am a selfish man, I just don't want the same things as Mr. Kaiser Wilhelm, and I have to fight him for what I want. Why? He's thousands of miles away. I don't want to fight him. I want to live in peace.

July 20, 1917 We walked again through a golden sea of dying wheat. It was like saying good-bye to myself. The crop is sick because it's dry and the only medicine to cure it is rain. But there *is* no rain. I don't know if Susan or I am the saddest but I think it's me. All I love in the world is here, not in some place I've never been and don't want to go to.

July 21, 1917 I took Shoni to Ozone for some food today. He lets Susan ride him, so I bought a bridle. It will be easier for her. He didn't like it very much,

Although sadness at John's leaving overtook them, they tried to recapture the private moments and feelings they had. They told each other how they felt at different times after they found each other in Ozone. John would never forget Susan's story of how she practiced for their wedding night.

"Our wedding night didn't turn out the way I planned it," Susan said.

"What was different?"

"I practiced getting undressed in a hurry."

"Well, it didn't work. You took forever. I didn't expect you to get undressed in *bed*."

"What I'd planned was to was stand in front of you and take my clothes off real quick and say, Come here you goddam French Indian, I've been waiting for this moment for seven years, and I want it to happen, *now*!"

Words like that from Susan took John so by surprise, he laughed, and they both laughed. "Why didn't you?" he asked.

"When we got into the room, and I knew we were alone, and what was going to happen, I got scared. Don't you remember?"

"Didn't you want it to happen?"

"Of course, dummy. I was just scared."

Together they remembered the craziness of that night. And they laughed and laughed. John thought: My Susan, my Susan, I have to leave you.

July 22, 1917 Susan and I rode to Idaho Falls to report to the draft board. She stayed in Ammon with her folks. I found out I have to report at the train station on August 3. It seems

262

so close. There isn't enough time. When I picked Susan up, the whole family said they'd be there to see me off.

August 2, 1917 Tomorrow I leave my life behind me for a time I cannot measure. I've never been so lonely. Susan tries to keep her chin up but I know she's having a hard time, too. It's been two years since I threshed my first crop of wheat. On that day, I won the world, I thought. And then a year and a week or so later, I met Susan after so many years I didn't recognize her. I didn't know it then, but I fell in love with her immediately. We were married on the first day of this year, and I knew I had won the world again.

I walked out through my field for the last time and felt heads of wheat scratch my hands. It was rough, not like Susan's touch, but I loved it. Our short life together has been Heaven. Why can't it go on? I'm a slave to one white man's insane desire to control. The Shoshonis never lived that way. I remember my mother's words, "The white man's medicine is very strong. You must go live among the white men and become one of them." I have tried, but now I wonder if his medicine is really stronger. Or is it just a difference I don't understand?

August 3, 1917 Susan and I clung to each other all night. She slept very little at first. I lay awake listening to the sounds of nature, wild nature, the world I lived in for many years and the world I love. The coyotes howled and I thought of the wonder of being free to run, jump, laugh, dance. Then I remembered something funny, except maybe just now it isn't funny. I remembered Susan had never seen me dancing around a fire. I lay thinking about it for a long time. Then I woke her.

John gently shook his sleeping wife. "Come outside."

Her sleepy voice asked, "In Heaven's name, what for?"

"I have to dance for you."

"John-Pierre, are you all right?"

"Yes, of course. I just want to dance for you."

"You told me you didn't know how to dance. And there's no band, no dance floor. Are you going crazy?"

"No, my wife, I'm not crazy. I'm going to dance an Indian dance for you, and I want to do it in the light of a fire."

"You *are* crazy!"

"Susan, please. It would mean a lot to me before I . . ."

She interrupted. "Oh, all right. But it's a weird thing to do in the middle of the night."

She climbed out of bed slowly and pulled a dress over her nightgown. Outside, John piled up some aspen branches and lit them. When the flames were high enough, he raised his arms and sang of his sadness at leaving their farm and their home and mostly her. He sang a song of love for her and the wonderful life they'd had. He sang of her sadness, and then he made drum noises with his mouth and danced. As he danced, he watched her face. At first, she seemed fearful, then she felt it. He danced and sang, and slowly her face brightened and she came to him. He put his arm around her waist and showed her the simple dance, and she danced with him. Around and around the fire they danced, and then she sang of her happiness and her sadness. They went on till the fire died.

In the morning, a ray from the rising sun made a spot on the wall opposite the window, slowly widening, it crawled down the wall, across the floor, up and across the bed, and filled the room with light. He watched it for the last time. Susan stirred and stretched her arms above her head. "That was the most wonderful thing you ever did for me. It was a part of you I didn't know anything about. Let's do it again when you come back."

As they ate breakfast, a dark cloud rolled in and big drops of life's water fell. It was too late to save much of the crop, but it cooled the air. John's train left at 3:15, and when they got to the station, it looked as if everyone in the valley was there. All the Monsons and John stood in a little clump not saying much. The emotion was too high. Susan clung to his arm till a man in uniform called his name. He struggled aboard and found an open window he could reach through. They held hands till the train jerked and began to roll and gain speed. They held to each other till she could hold on no longer. Her face was wet with tears and he watched her still waving to him till she was out of sight.

Chapter Twenty-Four
Changeable Weather

August 7, 1917 It seemed the train would never get here. Along the way we picked up a full load and by the time we arrived at Fort Douglas, there was only room to stand. A few of the guys talked in little clumps, some played cards, and two were so drunk they had to be carried off the train. The next day, we had to strip all our clothes off and a doctor looked us over asking a lot of question and making notes. We had to stand in long lines to get food that wasn't any better than the stuff I cooked for myself on Bull's Fork.

Several of the guys were friendly and wanted to talk to me, but I just didn't want to talk. We all look the same in the clothes we received. I don't like them, but I guess it's what I'll be wearing for the next few years. Few *years*? That part never really struck me until now. What if I don't get back home till my baby is married and gone from our home and I have grandchildren? I have to keep thoughts like that out of my mind.

I've already written two letters to Susan. I'll be here for about four weeks.

August 15, 1917 Mostly we've been marching around a parade ground, but today they began interviews. It seemed they wanted to know everything about me.

John patiently, sometimes impatiently, answered the questions asked by another soldier wearing a corporal's stripes. "You got a trade, soldier?" the man asked.

"I'm a homesteader, sir," John answered.

As he asked questions, he repeated the answers when he wrote. "A farmer. Where?"

"On Bull's Fork, sir."

"Where the hell is Bull's Fork?"

"About twenty-five miles east of Idaho Falls, sir."

"Idaho Falls. Married?"

"Yes, sir."

"Married. Any kids?"

"My wife will have a baby in November, sir."

"No kids. Now the next section."

There were a lot of questions about birthmarks and moles and scars and other identifying marks that didn't make any sense to John. Then he asked if he spoke any foreign languages.

"Yes, sir."

"A farmer speaks a foreign language?"

"Yes, sir."

"Which one?"

"I speak French, sir, and Shoshoni."

"A farmer from Idaho speaks *French*? You're pulling my leg."

"Yes, sir. I do speak French."

"Says he speaks French," he said and wrote.

The interview finally ended and the training continued. He had no problem with it. It was easier than lifting sacks of wheat.

August 29, 1917 There hasn't been much to write. Mostly I've written letters to Susan. I got a surprise day before yesterday when I heard my name called. I went to the place I was told and met Captain Roland Cross. He motioned to a seat across the desk from him.

Captain Cross read the interviews to select soldiers with special talents the Army could use. He started out, "According to your interview, you speak French."

"Yes, sir, I do."

He continued the interview in French and seemed quite satisfied with what he heard. He told John, "My father was a diplomat in France and I went to school there. Your French is exceptional." He handed John a book and told him to read a page from it.

"I'm sorry, sir. My father taught me only to *speak* French. He never taught me to read or write it."

Captain Cross frowned. "But you can read and write English."

"Yes, sir."

"We'll use interpreters in France, so I'll recommend we send you to a school to teach you to read and write French. You'll have two weeks to learn it, and if I'm any judge, you'll make it." Then he switched to English and said, "Come back here in an hour for your transfer papers."

The papers assigned John to the University of Utah for an intensive course in French.

September 16, 1917 My days have been filled with French. I spend most of my time learning to read the language and I was surprised many of the words I knew were written much different from the way they sound, but I'm learning to spell and write them. They were right when they told me it was an intensive course. I haven't spoken a word of English since I got here. The only writing I've done is to Susan.

September 18, 1917 Today I got orders to return to Fort Douglas to await assignment. They told me I won't be going to France soon. My files say I'm a qualified interpreter. I wonder how much longer I'll have to stay in Fort Douglas.

A letter from Susan confirmed my fears about the crop. Dad Monson said it would barely pay for the harvest. Only about $300 remained. What kind of pay is that for a year of work? I'm very glad I worked in the sugar factory last winter. She wrote that she cooked for twelve men, but didn't say anything about where they sat to eat. I hope she can get a table. I should have done that before I left. Her father planted my winter wheat with his drill he hauled up on his wagon. I owe him a lot.

She told me James was drafted and left on September 16 for Fort Douglas.

September 29, 1917 Captain Cross called me to tell me I probably wouldn't be assigned for quite a while. He said because of my ability, I'd probably be a chief interpreter. The US Army uses mostly native Frenchmen to interview German soldiers, but they have to have an American to interpret from French to English. He also said I'll be sent to another intensive Officer's Training course on October 4. It will take about six weeks.

On October 4, John left Fort Douglas for the University of Cincinnati. Captain Cross called him to wish him luck just before he left. He told John he had to show authority, and a bar on his collar was more impressive. He told John he thought he'd make a good officer.

By the time he got to Cincinnati, he was as tired as when he hauled grain all day. Four nights on a slow-moving train was the worst thing he could think of. He was assigned to a room with man named James Cotton. He was surprised he was in a school for aviation officers. "I guess they didn't have any place else to send me. I seem to be some sort of extra they don't know what to do with."

He wrote to wish Susan a happy birthday and told her he was sorry he couldn't buy her a gift.

Her response was overwhelming. It announced he had a son born on her birthday, November third, and he weighed eight and a half pounds. John went overboard to express his joy at the news. "I'll teach him everything I know and he'll ride Shoni, and drive the team, and we'll work the field together. And some day he'll have a little sister that looks just like you and maybe a brother, too. And maybe a whole bunch of brothers and sisters and I'll teach them how to ride Shoni and drive the team, and farm and use a slingshot, and they'll all go to school and learn everything there is to know, and we'll go to celebrations and eat some of Mrs. Holmpuist's sandwiches and they can get in pie eating contests and run in the races, and we'll have a wonderful family. We never talked about a name. You said you'd like to name him after me. I think I'd like him to carry Dad Monson's name, too. How about John Henry Fountain?"

The course continued, John easily comprehended the meaning of each part. But part of it still bothered him. "Here I am learning to kill people. I don't want to kill people; I just want to live the Shoshoni way."

November 30, 1917 I finished the course yesterday and I'm a Second Lieutenant assigned to the Fifth Division. James Cotton and I leave tomorrow for Camp Logan near Houston, Texas to join our outfit. They told me it's a long train ride.

December 4, 1917 We got to Camp Logan last night very late. It took forever to get here. Now I have to tell Susan where I am so she can write to me. Worse, though, I won't get any letters from her for a long time, maybe even weeks.

John's quarters at Camp Logan weren't as nice as at the university but better than at Fort Douglas. He learned the Fifth Division would be sent to France soon and diaries and written materials should be sent home, because they might fall into the wrong hands. He wrote, "I am entering a time in my life I expect my descendants will want to know as much as possible about, and that I will want to come back to sometimes. I don't know what to do. I'll have to think about it."

On December 13, he wrote a short remembrance of working in the sugar factory and getting married after some difficulty with Mrs. Monson. "Since that time so much has happened to me I have a hard time imagining there was time for it all."

The next day, he got four letters from Susan. He opened them all and laid them, ordered by date, in a pile and read them as one long one. Then he read them again and again. The last one referred to his enthusiastic response to the news he had a son. "Susan told me to slow down, John Henry won't be ready for all I have planned for him till long after I get back. She told me she was sure the baby smiled at her when she laughed at what I wrote."

While at Camp Logan, he wrote of his new friend, James Cotton. "James told me of his fear of being shot or killed, but I'm sure he's as safe as I feel. We've both talked of our lives and our families. He came from a wealthy family that raises cotton and tobacco in Kentucky (I thought it strange that his name is Cotton). His father tried to use his influence to get him exempt from the draft, but he couldn't. He told me they use negroes in the fields and they work for just enough money to keep their families, so their kids can grow up and go on working as their parents did. It seems unfair, and I told him so. He told me it was the way it always was and always would be. Just because they were slaves one time, do they always have to be slaves? James is a very nice friend and I'm sure if he could see my homestead, he'd have another idea. I told him about homesteading and he said it sounds like the world's worst job. It *is* hard work, but there are good things about it, too.

They continued to wait. Boredom is the enemy of a soldier with nothing to do. He read magazines and books, and wrote letters home, but the uselessness of what he was doing depressed him. He wrote, "I'm sick to death of this waiting!"

January 13, 1918 Wait, wait, wait. It seems all I do any more is wait. I've been assigned to a special intelligence unit and a dozen soldiers. It seems to be just "hung on" the Fifth Division, which is scattered all over United States. Only a few hundred are stationed here.

John's boredom was relieved somewhat by an assignment to translate a few things to be used to orient the troops before they went to France. Many of them were things about specific French places, and some were interesting to him. He described one of them. "For instance, one describes Paris. I read it very carefully and found a reference to the Bastille and St. Antoine district. The Bastille was torn down and all that remains is an open space. Mr. Dickens said great mobs of people stormed the Bastille, but I read there were fewer than a thousand. The real location of the beginning of the revolution was in a poor area of Paris called Faubourg St. Antoine. Reading this made the story come alive. I'm glad I read the book.

"There seemed to be a lot of little articles about Alsace and Lorraine and the Vosges Mountains, which are quite a long way from Paris, but it was interesting. I'd like to visit the area."

January 18, 1918 When will this waiting end? I thought we had a war to fight, not a war to wait. If it wasn't for the translations, I think I'd go crazy.

January 19, 1918 Waiting is at least as monotonous as working in the sugar factory, and a lot farther from Susan.

I read in a newspaper the French Army is rebelling against their officers, and the whole population of France has lost its will to fight the Germans. If something doesn't happen soon from this side, there might not be a reason for us to go. The Allied Forces have been at it for almost four years and the whole war seems to be bogged down in a morass of helplessness.

February 16, 1918 I learned today we'd be leaving for France very soon. At least something new will happen. We'll be trained in France by French trainers who have been in the fight for a long time and know what to expect.

February 19, 1918 We leave by train for New York on February 22. I have to write to Susan first to tell her what has happened. I've sent my journal to her, and I've decided to write it in Shoshoni using English spelling. I'll translate it when I return home, and write it in English.

It's like entering a new life. I don't know what's ahead of me and maybe I don't want to. I do know it might be a long time before I see my wife and son. Is everything I've worked for going away? No, it's not going away, I'm leaving it behind.

March 4, 1918 I am glad to stand on firm ground again, although sometimes it, too, seems to be moving. I was seasick most of the trip for eight days. I never want to be seasick again, but now I'm afraid of the return trip. The spring storms made the ship wallow almost all the time, and if I ate something, it almost always came back up, so I lost a few pounds on the trip. I feel all right now, but tired.

They told us we'd be put into training camps for intensive training before being sent anywhere. As I understand it, General Pershing wants the American soldiers to fight as units, not as replacements for French and British troops. They were expecting replacements immediately. Instead, the word is, we'll start training as units that will be sent to the front, possibly under French or British command. I just don't understand war, I guess.

As soon as I could I wrote a long letter to Susan. I'm sure it will be a long time before I get an answer.

At a training facility south of Paris John was put in charge of a group of twenty-two soldiers and noncommissioned officers attached to the Fifth Division. They met at the beginning of each exercise, and then the officers took their troops to the mock battlefield to sharpen them. They captured several "German" soldiers in a mock drill. To make it more realistic his interviewees were not German soldiers, but German was their mother tongue, and he was set up in a tent where he questioned them. He knew very soon what his job was, and during many sessions, he could tell if he was told the truth about something or discount the stories. His questioning skills grew with time until he knew exactly how to trip up a soldier by going through a series of questions, then returning to the first one or two. By then, if the soldier was lying, he often forgot the first answer, and said something different. One of his French interpreters named the routine "Fountain's Circus", and the name stuck.

Fountain's Circus caught the attention of his commanding officer. He listened in to one of John's practice sessions. "Lieutenant, are you a lawyer?" he asked.

"No, sir, I'm just trying to get the right information. When we get real prisoners to question, things might be different."

"Things will definitely be different. Some prisoners won't even talk to you. Most of the time you'll talk to Frenchmen. The father of a flock of kids is likely to know quite a lot about any Germans in the area where he lives."

"I've been told that, and from what I've heard so far, I hope I don't have many Germans. I know an old German at home, but I never heard him speak German, so I didn't know how rough the language is. How can anyone sing in such a language?"

"Oh, they do sing, and loud when they get a few liters of beer inside them. Actually, it sounds a lot better when they sing."

"Do you know where we'll be going?"

"Not yet, Lieutenant, but you'll know along with everybody else as soon as it happens. Good luck. Are you sure you're not a lawyer?"

"No, sir, I'm not a lawyer."

"You ought to be. Think about it."

April 14, 1918 I've seen it! Today James and I had some time off so we went to Paris. It was a lot farther than I thought, but I was able to find where the Bastille was and St. Antoine. There wasn't much there, but it was interesting to try to relive the sounds and smells that must have been there when Mr. Dickens wrote his book. It was dirty, but not the way I expected. There was just a big open space partially paved with cobblestones.

James wanted to see Versailles, so we had just enough time to go there and hurry back to our camp. It was pretty impressive and well kept, although I think it could have been better.

John's training, included not only exercises in interrogation but physical training and practice on the small arms range. His scores were acceptable, but not impressive. Once he pulled out his slingshot and hit the target dead center. "Now, that's what I call a small arm," one of his colleagues said.

Finally, on May 31, 1918, Field Order No. 1 was issued moving the Red Diamond Division (Fifth) to the Vosges Mountains in Alsace to become part of the French Seventh Army.

May 31, 1918 We left by truck and on foot for a position in German-controlled France somewhere near Strasbourg. Germany has held the Alsace and Lorraine provinces east and south of here since 1870. The French want it back. Seems to me in forty-eight years the differences would have been dissolved and accepted, but we're in a war and this war is about land.

June 4, 1918 As we bounced along in the back of a noisy truck, James asked me what I was writing and I told him.

James looked shocked and said, "That's against the regulations. You're not supposed to do that."

"I know, but this is different. I'm writing it in Shoshoni."

"What kind of language is that?"

"An American Indian language."

"I thought the Indians didn't have a written language."

"They don't, but I'm writing it using English spelling."

"What if the Germans get hold of it?"

"I'd bet my life there isn't a German in the world who could read it."

John handed him his notes and asked him to read them. The only words he understood were the names of places they'd been.

"John," he said, "I can't understand all of it, but there are words I do understand. They're the names of places. "I think even the most ignorant German could put something meaningful together. I think you should be very careful what you write."

He was right. John scratched out the names of places and used other words for them.

June 7, 1918 Some time ago, the American forces under the command of a French general entered Alsace and Lorraine for the first time. The fighting was fierce, but they secured a substantial part of the provinces. My unit was held back for two weeks while this was happening. Food got low, and the rains came, making the roads and the camps muddy. After we started to move, we had to get out and push the trucks out of mud holes, and sometimes we had to cut branches from trees and bushes and put them under the tires. As the mud holes got deeper, some of the trucks tipped over and spilled their cargo. Others detoured into the fields. My truck was close to the front so we didn't have to contend with the things the ones following us did.

We drove through the streets of Strasbourg, and people waved as we passed. Although the province was under German rule for a long time, they still consider themselves French. I saw little of Strasbourg, but it looked like a city of history. I hope I can see more of it. We drove a long time before we came to a big house in bad condition.

Chapter Twenty-Five
Clearing Skies

Things happen that couldn't, shouldn't, are impossible, or too astounding to be true. Sometimes they're called miracles.

June 17, 1918 This big old ruin is our headquarters. The rest of the division is camped in the forest about half a mile away. The house is very large, surrounded by a tangled mass of overgrown plants, many, perhaps most, of them dead. We arrived late in the evening, and were told not to show any light while we got settled. There were twenty-three of us in the house and we slept wherever we could find space. The commanding officer, a Frenchman named Captain Maurice Fargot, told us he would assign our quarters the next morning.

The house sat on a small hill at the edge of a forest. A circular driveway embraced a round, concrete, weed-filled sump which might have been the pool at the bottom of a large fountain at one time. Behind the house were low hills that John learned were the Vosges Mountains. The house was three stories high with eleven windows spaced at regular intervals across the front on each of the two upper floors. Columns supporting a half-domed shelter flanked the main entrance, and at the top of the steps on each side were the remains of statues. The roof of cut green slate was the only part of the house that was intact, although moss grew on much of it. The mostly glass-less windows announced that the building was long abandoned. Near overhanging moldings at the top of the outside walls and under the window façades he saw it had once been painted yellow. Much of the outside plaster had fallen off, exposing the building stones. John, remembering Dickens' description of gargoyles adorning the Marquis' house, was delighted to see several of the same beasts around the roof.

Inside, he gazed in awe at the scenes painted on the ceilings of the three large rooms on the main floor. To the left and right of the entrance room were large, empty rooms. The one to the right was lined with shelves reaching from a few feet above the floor to the ceiling. Huge fireplaces dominated the opposite ends of each of the rooms flanking the entrance. Across from the entrance door, twin staircases forming a loop led to the second floor. Although the ceilings in the ground floor rooms were decorated, the walls were dirty and scarred. All three rooms were about the same size with very high ceilings. A door behind the stairs led to a room that might have been a kitchen added to the back of the house.

The rooms up the winding staircases were not so elegant, but spacious. The third floor rooms were smaller and had only one window per room. Two soldiers were assigned to a room. The three officers had rooms of their own. Two French officers left after the second night.

John's first impression was whoever lived here must have been either royalty or rich beyond his imagination. He decided it was a castle for royalty.

He reported, "I wrote to Susan to tell her we're in a castle, but it's not very elegant any more. I can only imagine how beautiful it must have been. Plaster is falling off the walls on the outside and the rooms are big and cold. I don't mean cold from the weather — just cold. I hope we don't have to stay here very long, but our commanding officer said this is our headquarters. There are twenty-three of us in this place including a Frenchman, Corporal Andre Fouré. He's a nice guy from a little town near Paris. We worked together a lot during the training program before we came here. He's a couple of years older than I and an extremely handsome man. He told me his wife calls him Adonis. I had to ask him what it meant and he laughed before he told me. I had no idea who Adonis was."

John's initial work was interrogating the French people in the area to find out what they knew about German troop movements. At first, there weren't many, then they trickled in as time passed. Most said the Germans left a few days before the Fifth arrived. One old man came, stared at John intently for a few seconds, then told him there were still Germans in the forest about a kilometer behind the house. He didn't know how many. but he was so sure they were there John told his commanding officer, who send ten soldiers to investigate. They returned and reported no German soldiers were there.

The old man was back the next day. "*Monsieur*, I know your soldiers couldn't find the Germans," he said, "but they're still there."

Surprised at this revelation, John asked, "Can you show us where you found them?"

"Yes, but it is safer if only one or two go with me."

"Why?"

"Sir, many feet make a lot of noise."

"What do you suggest?"

"Can you go with me? I can show them to you."

John went to Captain Fargot and told him what the old man said, but the captain was skeptical. He was sure the old man was just after money, and might lead them into a trap. He refused to investigate further; his troops had already scoured the area and found nothing.

"May I go with him, sir? He asked me to, and I think I can handle anything he can lead me into. I'm sure he's telling the truth."

"Why do you think so, lieutenant?"

"My interrogations didn't earn the name 'Fountain's Circus' by making a lot of mistakes, sir."

The captain looked intently at John for a moment, then said, "Be back here in an hour and a half."

John was amazed at how quietly and rapidly the agile old man walked, and after a few minutes, he asked, "How old are you?"

The old man turned, put his finger to his lips, then continued along a dim trail without answering. Fifteen minutes later, he motioned John down and crouched almost to the ground, then led John silently to a brow where he lay on his belly behind a bush and pointed downward. Several German soldiers milled about on a small trampled area. John counted thirty-two soldiers and two cannon, along with several horses and supply wagons with boxes of supplies and ammunition. Either the small contingent was waiting for orders, or had been left behind. He tapped the old man on the shoulder and nodded they should return. As they approached the headquarters, the old man said, "Eighty three."

"I counted only thirty two," John said.

"Sir, you asked me how old I am. I'm eighty three."

"Amazing! How long have you lived here?"

"All of my life."

"How did you learn to move so silently?"

"I used to stalk deer in these woods. I could get almost close enough to touch them. I know these woods as well as I know my own face, sir."

"I'm sure you do. What do you know about this castle?"

"We call it a chateau. A rich baron owned it last. My father worked for him till he disappeared when I was very young."

"A baron. What does that mean?"

"A title given to him by the government. He owned much land, and many people worked for him. He had great influence in this area."

"Thank you for your help. I'll report it to my captain. What is your name?"

"Henri Barticelli, sir."

"That's Italian, isn't it?"

"Yes, sir. My father came from Treviso in Italy to work for the baron. Good-bye, sir."

The old man left and John gave Captain Fargot the information. Two days later a stronger force took the Germans prisoner. Fountain's Circus relieved them of valuable information.

Henri Barticelli didn't reappear till a week after the interrogations. He found John walking around the grounds and approached him. Again he stared at John and said, "There are no more Germans in the area."

"How do you know?"

"I have combed the baron's forest, and there are no more."

"I think you're telling the truth. How about the area beyond the forests?"

"I haven't searched all of Alsace, but there are no German soldiers within several kilometers of here, sir."

The old man continued to look at John. "Henri, why do you look at me?"

"I'm sorry, sir, you remind me of someone."

"Who?"

"I don't know sir. Just someone. Do you have any more questions, sir?"

"Can you tell me more about this house? It must have been very elegant at one time."

"After the baron disappeared, it fell into the hands of his creditors. Then, in 1870, the Germans came and took it away from them. They just let it deteriorate. The baron's family owned it and all the land around it for many generations before him. They captured several springs from the mountains and brought the water here. A huge fountain in front gave the chateau its name, and the fields were full of growing crops, forests, and orchards, and the vineyards produced a very fine wine. The beauty of the place was indescribable. It is sad to see what has happened to it." Then he left.

Several times John saw a shaped stone in front of the round sump where the road divided into the curved driveways. One corner of it was exposed under the brush growing next to it. Curiosity finally brought him closer. Something was inscribed on it, but all he could make out were the letters "ne". A growth of moss hid the rest. Pushing the bushes aside, he rubbed the moss from the stone until the words, *Chateau de la Fontaine* were visible. He brushed away more moss. Below the name were the Roman numerals MDCX. He thought: What a coincidence! My name on a stone in France. I'll ask Henri about it.

A few days later he met Henri. "Does this place have a name? I'm sure it was once beautiful."

"It was known as the *Chateau de la Fontaine*, sir."

"Then the stone in front of the fountain belongs there."

"Yes, sir, but it's almost lost in the bushes and moss. How did you find it?"

"A few days ago, I brushed away some of the moss and found the name," John said, "and I'm curious about it. Lafontaine was my last name when I was born."

The old man's face brightened, then looked puzzled. "May I ask you something, sir?"

"Yes, of course."

"What was your full name when you were born?"

"Jean-Pierre Lafontaine, Why?"

"And what was your father's name, sir?"

"I don't understand. Why do you want to know?"

"Please, sir. What was your father's name?"

"Jean-Claude Lafontaine."

"And your Grandfather's name?"

"I'm not sure exactly what his name was. He changed it when he came to Canada. I don't remember if my father ever told me."

"Why wouldn't your father tell you?"

"I think there was something in my grandfather's past he didn't want people to know. I remember once my father told me my grandfather gave up his title in France when he escaped to Canada."

"What to you know of your grandfather?"

"Only that he was a wealthy French nobleman who wrote books."

"Where did he live in France?"

"I don't know. Probably near Paris, somewhere. I never found out."

"Does the name, *Francois Jean-Claude Baron Pierre de la Fontaine* mean anything to you?"

"Some of the names are familiar. Why?

"That was the name of the owner of this place, the man who disappeared when I was a boy."

"What happened to him?"

"No one knows. Some think he was killed. He left everything in place when he disappeared. Even his clothes were left in the chateau, and his horse was left in the stall. He just vanished one day. Do you know what kind of books he wrote?"

"No. Just books. Stories, I suppose. I don't know."

Henri's face told John there was more to the story than what he'd heard, but he didn't press him.

"I will leave you to your work now, sir." Then he left.

John continued interrogating German prisoners brought from many fronts, and Fountain's Circus was often consulted during planning of military campaigns.

Three weeks after his conversation with John, Henri returned. "Have you thought of our last conversation, sir?"

"Not much. Why?"

"I've thought much about it. Would you be willing to look at a picture I have in my house?"

"A picture?"

"I went through my father's things, and found a picture of the baron."

"Henri, what is your interest in me?"

"Sir, when I first saw you, your looks startled me. You bear a resemblance to the baron. Although I was just a young boy, I remember him, and I know he went to Canada. Your resemblance to him, your name, your father's name, and that your father was Canadian makes it almost certain you are related."

"That's not possible. How could I be related to him?"

"A grandson, sir."

"Henri, you're dreaming!"

"Dream or not, sir, I'd like you to look at the picture."

"But you said you knew him when you were a little boy."

"Sir, do you remember how your father looked? If he came to you now, would you recognize him?"

"Of course, but I never saw my *grandfather*."

"Sir, first, your name, it's from this chateau. Second, it was part of the baron's name. Third, your father's name is very similar to the baron's. Put them all together plus the fact the baron fled to Canada and your father was Canadian, I think it's not just possible, it's *likely* you are the grandson of the former owner of this chateau. What else do you need?"

"Henri, what do you want from me? I can't believe I've found my grandfather. It just could *not* happen this way."

"I'm very sorry, sir. I want nothing from you. Will you come to look at the picture?"

"Why is it so important to you that I see it?"

"I am afraid you do not believe me. I must leave now. If you will, please come to my house at the foot of the hill."

Henri left, but the conversation stayed in John's mind. He thought: What if the old man *is* telling the truth? It *can't* be. Coincidences like that just *don't happen*.

He went on with his work, but the old man's words lingered, especially the coincidences of the names and the Canada connection. He thought: What will a picture prove? Then he dismissed the whole thing.

The war went on, but the number of interrogations decreased till he spent little time with questions and most of the time writing his Shoshoni notes or letters to Susan.

On the evening of July 14, 1918, John made his way to Henri's house with his mind full of questions: Why was this old man so anxious? What if my grandfather *did* own the place? What would it mean? Who would believe such a story, even if it *were* true?

Henri greeted him warmly and invited him in. He walked across the room to a covered frame and removed the cloth. John gasped, "*Mon père!*" (My father!) The old man's face burst into a smile. "Henri, how do you come to have this picture? It's almost exactly how I remember my father."

"The baron gave it to my father before he left. The University of Strasbourg presented it to the baron in appreciation for the work he did for them."

"It seems so impossible. What else can you tell me about him?"

"I remember how elegantly he sat on his horse, Kashmir. Once I did him a small favor, and he took me for a ride. I was overjoyed. I remember how wonderful the chateau and the grounds were, and I remember the huge fountain your grandfather's grandfather must have built. The family name was taken from it as well as the chateau. My father loved him like a brother and the baron gave this house to him as a gift."

John looked around the neat little house and noted it was about four times the size of his cabin on Bull's Fork. "What, exactly did my grandfather do?"

"I can't tell you all the details; it was a long time ago, but I remember he raised all kinds of crops, and he was an experimenter. He had orchards, fields, forests, and vineyards. The baron wanted to make wine from his grapes, so he went to Treviso and found my father who was a vintner, and brought him here. They became fast friends, and my father never went back. He told me of the Baron crossing different types of food crops to improve their quality. He was always in his forests, fields, or orchards, measuring growth and writing in his notebooks. He studied what was happening, season after season, and gained vast knowledge of growing plants. The walls of his library were filled with books and his notes."

Still puzzled, John asked, "He wrote books, too. When did he find time for writing if he was always in his fields?"

"Ah, my friend, your grandfather wrote *textbooks* about agriculture. They were used at the University of Strasbourg, and other universities throughout Europe. He was famous for it, and they paid him well. That was why the university commissioned the painting. According to my father, he was a genius."

"If he was rich when he left, how did he get deep in debt."

"He loved parties and people, and women. There were many parties at the chateau. Sometimes I'd sneak up and watch through the windows. People in fancy clothes danced and ate and drank wine and had a good time. It was all so elegant. His Chateau de la Fontaine wines were famous all over Europe and were always served to his guests."

"Why did he run away?"

"According to my father, he considered women God's finest creation, and should be treated that way. He never married, but many of the ladies from this area and as far away as Strasbourg would come to visit him. Count Luis de Marillat discovered his wife was one of them and challenged the baron to a duel. The count was a formidable duelist, and your grandfather was never noted for his courage in the face of physical abuse, and he just left. A few years later, my father learned he went to Canada. By then he hadn't paid any of his debts which must have been enormous and his creditors banded together, and took the chateau and land and several thousand hectares of forests. No one could decide anything, and only a few of the debts were actually paid before the Germans came and took it all. The Germans did little, and everything deteriorated. Perhaps now, the confusion will be resolved, but not soon. All of his creditors are dead and their descendants are mostly now unknown."

"I find it hard to believe I've found my grandfather, but the Canada connection and the painting, and the coincidence of the names, everything points to it. But there must be other descendants of the family somewhere."

"I know of none. The baron was the last of the family to own the chateau. When he died, it was the end of the family bearing the title. I am sure you are a grandson. Do you know of any other descendants in Canada or America?"

"My father told me he married a woman with two children in Canada, but he never told me more about them. But they would not have been related anyway. I don't know if he had any other relatives, except me."

"Whether you are convinced or not, I am. There is too much evidence I am right. You, sir, are the grandson of *François Jean-Claude Baron Pierre de la Fontaine*. I am convinced beyond any doubt."

"I like to think my grandfather was a farmer. What will you do with the painting?"

"I hung it on the wall for you to see. If you want it, it's yours."

"I'd certainly like to have it, but I have no way to get it back to Bull's Fork. It's too big."

"I can arrange to have it removed from the frame and rolled up, so it would take little space. It's about sixty by forty centimeters. I measured it before I hung it up."

"Thank you Henri. I'd like that."

John returned to his quarters, still not completely convinced, but overjoyed at the prospect he'd found his grandfather. A few days later Henri appeared with a small paper-covered roll containing the painting.

The next day John wrote, "I couldn't wait to tell Susan. I found my grandfather! I am living in his house!

He was a farmer who wrote text books about agriculture for the University of Strasbourg. He had so much land our homestead would fit into it a hundred times, maybe a thousand times."

September 10, 1918 Today I received a letter from Susan telling me her mother had the flu and Mr. Hansen in the hills had died from it. That was almost two months ago. By now she's either dead or better, and I won't know for a long time. Why does it take so long for our letters to get to each other? I'm very worried about Susan and the baby. She said she'd stay away from people and that very few people got together any more. There were no church services and the schools wouldn't open till the epidemic was over.

The flow of prisoners almost stopped as the allies pounded the German Army back toward Germany. John escaped the boredom with a visit to the university in Strasbourg to see if he could find any of his grandfather's books. On his first visit, he found a helpful, albeit ancient, librarian who was familiar with them. She told him there were none left. During the forty years of German occupation, they replaced French professors with Germans and French books with texts written in German. It was impossible any books were left after so long. Unconvinced, John asked, "Can you direct me to someone or some firm that might have such a book?"

"The original publisher was this university, and if any of those books existed, I'd know about it. I'm very sorry, they were truly works of art."

"What do you mean?"

"The illustrations were exquisitely rendered."

"By whom?"

"By the author. Are you a collector?"

"No, ma'am. but the author was my grandfather, and I'd like to have at least one of his books."

"I'm sorry. I see why you would. I can't think of anywhere you could go after so long." John was disappointed, but decided he'd been too optimistic.

The work dwindled till he was virtually jobless, and his staff of twenty-two shrank to two. Then Andre Fouré and an American, Sergeant Amos Kelley, were reassigned, leaving him alone. The Germans were losing ground fast, and there was talk of surrender.

The Red Diamond (Fifth) Division fought so consistently the Germans dubbed them *Die Rote Teufeln*, (The Red Devils).

John filled his time he with walks on the trails around the chateau, and he rode the supply truck to Strasbourg about once a week to visit the interesting parts of the city. Once, he returned to the university library. The ancient librarian spotted him and led him to an office at the back of the building. "Mr. Lafontaine, there is an example of your grandfather's illustrations." On the back wall, behind glass in a simple black frame about two feet by three feet was an original illustration showing a grafting technique. "In the back of my mind, I remembered seeing that drawing somewhere within the past few years. We seldom use this office any more, so I didn't think of it. When I did, I came here and there it was."

The old lady was right. It was a work of art, but when John asked for it. She told him no. She had no authority in the library any more. She worked there without pay to fill her lonely days.

He was relieved when a letter about Lydia's health arrived. His journal recorded, "Susan said her mother was a very sick woman. All her hair fell out and, even after she got better, she didn't go to church because she looked so funny."

October 29, 1918   I try to place my grandfather at the chateau. It seems so impossible he lived here. Impossible that I came here. I wish I could have known him, but even though I never knew him, I stand in awe of such a brilliant man.

I have to write what Susan told me in her last letter. 'By the time John Henry was ten months old, he could take a few steps alone. I had just put him on the floor where he held onto my knee. Sam sat in the chair across from me. Guess what? He just turned and walked to Sam, no help at all. But he wouldn't come back. When I called to him and held my hands out, he just got down and crawled." I want to see my son!

The war ended with the Armistice signed at the eleventh hour of the eleventh day of the eleventh month, 1918, and the Fifth Division was sent to Luxembourg a week later to guard the lines of communication for the occupation troops in Germany. John, married and a father, and no longer essential to the Fifth Division, got, a release from duty. Just before he left, he checked for mail. There were seven letters from Susan. He devoured them as he waited for his orders to return to the United States. On January 23, they came, and he reported to LeHarve where he boarded a ship bound for New York.

January 24, 1919 My war is finally over. I shall never forget the experiences I had. I made many friends and learned more than I ever, in my wildest dreams, thought I would. Captain Fargot told me the morale in the French Army and among the civilians had sunk so low after four years of fighting the Germans, some of the soldiers mutinied. The French people, especially in Paris, though the city was never occupied, gave up hope. I thought about Mr. Dickens' book, and how the citizens of France had overthrown their government, but in this case it was another government. Captain Fargot was a source of inspiration for me and we were good friends.

I remember Andre Fouré. Adonis, his wife called him, a most handsome man. I could always count on him.

And before the two of them, back in the training camp south of Paris, Colonel Sorensen who told me I should be a lawyer.

But, I think most of all I'll never forget Henri Barticelli. He's a most remarkable man. At the age of eighty-three, he is as spry as I am. When he led me to those German soldiers, I couldn't believe how silently and quickly he moved through the forest. He gave me the greatest gift. He gave me my grandfather, a man I knew so little about, I was embarrassed when he asked me about him. But to find I was living, actually *living*, in his chateau in France was the most astounding thing to ever happen to me. The experiences made my life richer, but they also gave me inspiration. I'm glad to have had them, but I want to go home.

Now, in just a few days, I'll leave the battlefield in France and return to my own field on Bull's Fork, and to my wife and to my son whom I've never seen. And then Susan and I will live the rest of our lives and we'll have many children, and I'll buy a cow and some pigs and we'll ignore the rest of the world for the rest of our lives.

The return voyage was even worse than the trip to France. John was seasick for the entire nine days. Then without a break, he boarded a train to Fort Douglas. It lasted almost a week, and he arrived on February 11, 1919, tired, drained, and homesick for Susan and John Henry and Shoni and Bull's Fork. The discharge took another four days before he was given his ticket to return to Idaho Falls.

His war with Kaiser Wilhelm was over.

Chapter Twenty-Six
The Storm is Over

February 12, 1919 Last night was the first night I slept in relative comfort since I left Luxembourg too many days ago to be conscious of. The voyage back from Europe was worse than when I went there, and I couldn't sleep because I was seasick the entire trip. I think we were on the water nine days in giant waves that flung the ship around like a feather in a windstorm. Then without a break, I boarded a train for Fort Douglas. Once again, I had no chance for decent sleep. After one night of restful sleep, I still feel tired, but I'm eager to get home. I'm a lot closer, but still many hours away from my family.

There's a lot of snow here, and I suppose Bull's Fork is snowed in. It will take a few days for the discharge process. I don't want to wait. I want to go home!

February 14, 1919 Today I got it. Tomorrow I leave on the train for home and my family. There isn't anything else to say.

John got to Idaho Falls on February 15, 1919 at 10:30 A.M. He stepped off the train carrying his bag and lit out for Ammon on foot as fast as he could. The four miles took under an hour. From a hundred yards away, he whistled for Shoni knowing he'd make a fuss. The ruckus brought the whole Monson family out before he had a chance to knock on the door.

Susan was in his arms before anyone came near. "John-Pierre!" she shouted and kissed his face furiously. Mrs. Monson came next carrying John Henry. She kissed his cheek and hugged him and handed him his son. John Henry looked suspiciously at his father, then his face wrinkled and he burst into tears. Lydia took him back to comfort him. Henry hurriedly shook John's hand and went to the barn to get the horse which ran up to and nudged John with his nose. Susan said, "I've got a story about Shoni, but not now. Let's go in the house. It's cold out here."

A few pats on the nose satisfied Shoni his master was back, and Henry led him back into the barn. Inside the house, Freddie, now eight years old, just pressed his foot on John's as a sign of the old ritual, then shook his hand. James, almost twenty-two, and discharged after going nowhere except Fort Douglas, announced, "I'm going to be married next month."

"I heard you had a girl friend. When do I get to meet her?"

"In a couple of days. She's in Utah right now."

Sam, now a husky thirteen, grabbed John's bag and carried it into Susan's room after a hearty handshake and welcome home.

There was no end to the questions, nor to the answers. The year and-a-half away from the family saw many changes, but the one John noticed most was how weary Henry looked. His normally full face was haggard, his clothes hung on him like wet rags, and he walked as if every step hurt. He said nothing of it. Susan, with both arms around his neck dragged John to the sofa and sat down, still fastened to him.

Lydia recalled reality when she announced she needed help with dinner. "It's already late," she said, "and I'm sure John's hungry. He looks like he could use a good meal."

Releasing John, Susan said, "You stay right here. I don't want to wait another year and a half for you." She flashed a smile, kissed him again, and went into the kitchen to help her mother.

Sam was holding the baby, now fifteen months old, able to walk and say a few words. Suddenly he pointed at John, said, "Dada." and struggled to get down. He walked directly to his father much to the delight of everyone in the room. John picked him up and held him at arm's length.

His voice cracked when he said, "Yes, I'm your daddy and we'll see a lot of each other." He turned to Henry and asked, "Do you have any idea how the roads are up to Bull's Fork?" John Henry settled down in his father's lap as if to stay there and watched his face as he spoke.

"Probably impassable, but I saw Ludwig Franck in town a couple of days ago, and he managed it with a team and a sleigh. You thinking of going up there before spring?"

"I've been dreaming of getting back there for a long time. Yes, I'd like to. Dad, this moment has been on my mind since I left here."

"I'll bet it has. I've never seen anyone more dedicated."

"You've helped me so much. I don't know what Susan would have done if it hadn't been for you."

"Your neighbors helped a lot, especially when Susan was there alone. Almost every day at least one of them would drop by to see if she needed help with anything.

Dave Rushton happened by just after Susan had a run-in with four Indians."

John straightened up in his chair. "Four Indians? I know them. I've had troubles with them twice already. What happened? What did they do?"

"Oh, that little girl took care of them all right, but I think it would be better if she told you about it."

Sam, appearing very anxious to get a word in, said, "John you've got a three-apple apple tree up there. I got transparent and wealthy twigs to grow on a crabapple stock. It's doing very good. I looked at it when we brought Susan down last fall, and it's growing."

"It worked, then. Good! I'm anxious to see how it produces."

They talked until Lydia announced dinner was ready. John, still holding his son who hadn't taken his eyes from his father's face, sat in his usual place. Susan sat beside him and took John Henry on her lap. Freddie asked the blessing, "Dear Lord, thanks for bringing John back to us. Bless the food. Amen."

Small talk filled the next few hours. When someone asked about the food in France, he answered, "Different, very different. At the chateau, the cook was French. Our kitchen wasn't up to much, but he prepared some good meals. Mostly, I thought they use too many sauces and it was quite rich. I didn't complain because it tasted good, but not nearly as good as this. It was much better than at the homestead, though."

"Why didn't you tell me you don't like my cooking?" Susan asked with a pout.

"My darling wife, I meant what I fixed myself. Your meals were as good as your mother's."

She looked at John. "It's been so long." A tear came to her eye.

"Next time they want me, I'll hide,"

John asked Henry, "How bad was the crop last year? Susan said you and the neighbors took care of it."

"The land is good, John, but it needs water. There just isn't enough rain to get a good crop every year. Even using a drill to plant it, the yield wasn't nearly what it should have been."

The afternoon with people he knew passed quickly. Questions about finding his grandfather filled much of the time. By the time they'd finished supper, every detail of his acquaintance with Henri Barticelli was worn out and John was ready to go to bed.

Susan said, "Please, can I have my long-gone husband to myself, now?" And she led him to her bedroom, laid the baby in his cradle, and flung herself at John.

The next morning, John found Lydia in the kitchen and asked her why Henry looked so tired.

"He *is* tired. He farmed two places while you were gone, and it got to him. He worried a lot about Susan up there alone and spent at least two days a week with her. He's tired, John. He told me last night he is so thankful you're back."

"What can I ever do to repay you? I owe both of you so much for taking care of things for me."

"There is a way, John. Just take care of Susan. We all know how hard it was to be away and unable to do anything. All we did was help."

"Good grief! All the excitement of getting back made me forget something." He went to the bedroom, opened his bag, and took out two identical packages. Then he woke Susan, "Good Morning, my queen. I have something for you."

Susan stirred and said, "Yes I know. You gave me something last night. What else?"

John opened one of the packages and took out a length of Belgian lace he bought in Luxembourg. "Here," he said, "I'm not sure what it's for, but I think it's supposed to be a collar for a dress or something."

Susan, now wide awake, jumped out of bed. "Oh, it's beautiful! Wait till I show it to Mamma."

"I have another one just like it for her. Let's give it to her."

They gave the other lace to Lydia, and her face burst into a a surprised smile. "It's beautiful! My Aunt Lucy tried to teach me to do this, but it took so long I never did much of it. Thank you so much."

John had gifts for all the family and gave them out. He turned to Susan. She put the collar around her neck still wearing her nightgown. "You look ravishing, my dear!" he said.

"Grrrr!"

Anxious about what happened between the Indians and Susan, John's frustration grew until he could take her outside in the cold afternoon sunshine. He asked what happened.

"I was never so scared in my life. I saw four men on horses several times, riding on the other side of Bull's Fork. I didn't think much about it. A lot of people ride horses over there. I was carrying water to the horses with a bucket I'd made a new handle for out of wire when all four of them showed up. I asked them what they wanted, and one of them said he wanted revenge and grabbed my arm. The bucket still had some water in it, so I swung it at him and hit him on the side of his head. He dropped to the ground with a bloody gash in his hair. I was afraid I'd killed him. Then another one grabbed the bucket and tried to take it away from me. He got hold of the wire and I had hold of the bucket, so I started to twist it and jerk on it. Pretty soon he realized the wire was twisted around his hand, and he couldn't let loose. I just kept turning and jerking on it while he yelled. The other two, sitting on their horses quite a ways away, just laughed at the two with me. The one I hit first came up behind me and held my arms. I kept turning the bucket while I stomped on the foot of the one holding my arms. The wire broke. and both of us fell backward. I think he lit on a rock. Anyway he turned me loose. I turned and slammed the bucket hard on his forehead and opened another gash. His face was bloody all over, and he backed away. I was mad and scared all at the same time. I don't know why, but I yelled for Shoni. He was running around the corral snorting and whinnying and when he heard me, he jumped over the gate and charged another Indian riding his horse toward me. Shoni ran into the horse so hard it threw the Indian into the air and he landed on his back. He tried to get up, but he dropped down again and never moved.

"The fourth one kicked his horse and aimed a gun and shot at Shoni but his horse was running and he missed. Shoni ran into his horse, too, and knocked him off. The gun came flying at me. If I'd been expecting it, I could have caught it, but it hit me on the shoulder and fell in front of me. I was so scared and blind mad, I picked it up and pulled the trigger, but nothing happened. By that time, Shoni was chasing the Indian who shot at him, and tried to bite him. One was lying where Shoni knocked him of his horse, one had a piece of wire so tight around his hand he couldn't get it off, and the other one I'd hit twice with the bucket had two big bleeding cuts on his head. He looked at me and started toward me. I didn't know how to work the gun, but I knew I had to do something to make it shoot, so I started pulling and pushing things till the thing that holds the bullets dropped out to the side. I pushed it back in and found the little thing you have to pull to make it shoot. I pointed it at him, closed my eyes, and pulled the trigger. I never imagined the noise it would make or how much it would hurt my hand, but I didn't hit him. He was too close for me to shoot again, so I doubled up my fist with the gun in it and hit him as hard as I could in the eye. Then he ran.

"The one with the wire around his hand ran, too. The one Shoni chased ran to the bushes and climbed to the top of the cove, making as much noise as a bull, trying to get out of there. The other one just lay there, so I filled the bucket with water and poured it over his head. When he woke up and saw me standing over him with a gun in one hand and a bucket in the other, his eyes got as big as saucers, and he got up and ran. Shoni took off after them. I don't know how far he chased them, but they never came back. Mr. Rushton came by in a little while, and I was never so glad to see anyone in my life. When Shoni came back, Mr. Rushton brought me to Ammon. The next time I went up there, Daddy was with me, but I stayed anyway when he left. I never saw the Indians or their horses again."

Susan was shivering. John stopped and put his arms around her. "It's probably a good thing I wasn't there. I don't know what I'd have done. I might have killed them. Last time I saw them, I told them if they ever showed up at my place again, I'd kill them all. After what they tried with you, I'm not so sure I won't. What a fighter you are! Please don't get angry with me, I don't think I could win a fight with you."

"You know them?"

"Yes, they've tried to pull some trick a couple of times. The first time they tried to steal Shoni, but he was more than a match for them. When they left, I took off after them throwing rocks at them. I thought that was the end of it, but a few months later, they cut my tent down and scattered my things all over. I took after them, and that's when I told them I'd kill them if they ever came back. I guess they watched the cabin long enough to be sure I wasn't there. I'm sure they wanted to burn it down. What happened to the gun?"

"It's at the cabin. I just put it on the floor and haven't touched it since. Daddy put it on a shelf out of sight."

In spite of the snow, John was determined to get up to his place after so many months. The next day, he and Susan left John Henry with the Monson family and headed for Bull's Fork in Henry's sleigh behind Bud and Mage. There were drifts, but they made it to the cabin about four in the afternoon. First, he built a fire and while it warmed the cabin, they unloaded the sleigh and put the horses in the barn. Then they made supper. John dug out a new notebook, and wrote his first entry in it.

February 17, 1919   I got back home again day before yesterday. I noticed first thing Dad Monson looked very tired. He'd lost a lot of weight and his clothes seem to just hang on him like rags over a wire. I didn't ask him about it, but I will if he doesn't look better soon.

They greeted me with hugs and kisses, especially Susan. She just couldn't quit, and she hung onto my neck with both hands as if she was afraid I'd disappear. And when the questions started, I was happy to answer them all, especially the ones about finding my grandfather.

Today we got back home to Bull's Fork.

Chapter Twenty-Seven
New Storm Brewing

February 18, 1919 This morning we waded in snow up to our knees. We found the three-apple tree and it looks about normal to me. The berry patch has spread filling the area with bushes. I led Bud and Mage across the frozen, snow-covered spring to where its warmer waters flowed from under the ice and let them drink. Then I fed them. Susan was with me every step, holding my hand.

She showed me where she had the scuffle with the Indians, and now we can laugh about it. One farm girl against four Indians didn't sound good for the girl, but she sent them running just as Shoni and I did twice before. She showed me the gun.

Knowing Susan had taken care of what happened let John be more objective.

"Why didn't you tell me about it?" he asked.

"I didn't want to worry you. It was all over and I was all right. What could you have done?"

"Nothing, but I wish I'd been here. They wouldn't have come to the house. I'm certain they wanted to be sure I was gone before they came. They're afraid of me, and

Shoni doesn't like them, either. Do you realize he might have saved your life?"

"Of course. I didn't think about it then, but he acted like he knew them. He ran around the corral and whinnied till I called him and he got out."

They looked over the white field where frost sparkled like scattered fragments of a shattered mirror. John turned to Susan. "I'm so glad to be back home." They gathered a few things from the root cellar and went back to the house.

They left early the next morning, stopping in Ozone to visit Otteson's store. Mrs. Otteson told them Ervin Campbell brought back a French bride named Madeline. Only a few had not come back yet, and a few others would never come back.

They got back to the Monsons just before dark.

February 25, 1919 Susan and I hope to return to Bull's Fork about the first of March. The wind comes up after every snowstorm, but the days are getting warmer and sometimes the snow melts. I want more than anything right now to see spring come to my homestead. I've always been somewhere else. I want to see the buds on the trees burst and watch the leaves creep out. I want to watch as the melting snow uncovers the sleeping earth. I want to watch the bushes bloom and smell the flavors of spring.

It's hard to believe I've been home only two weeks. It seems as if I never left. I wish I could have been here when my son was born, but there will be others. Susan says she wants to have another baby soon.

March 3, 1919 We tried to get up to Bull's Fork on the 28th of February, but a blizzard came up and we had to turn back. The wind was blowing so hard, It looked like the snow was falling horizontally. We had to stop in Ozone and spend two nights with the Ottesons. The Monsons wanted to go to the

Campbells, but we couldn't even get there. I had no idea the blizzards up here could get so furious. When we left Ozone, we just came back to Ammon and even the road back was almost impassable.

We'll try it again in a few days. I want to live at my farm for the rest of my life.

March 8, 1919 I'm sitting in my own cabin on my own homestead writing this. The Monsons helped us move back up here, and stayed overnight, then returned to Ammon.

Dad Monson insisted we bring old Flossy up for milk for the baby. He had a heifer about to freshen and didn't have space for her, so he said we could keep her till he had room. I know what that means. It means we don't have to bring her back.

Susan and I and the baby are at last alone in the place where we'll live from now on. It's not the same kind of place my grandfather had, but to me it's much more valuable. I went outside a little while ago and looked at the cabin from the barn. It's a big yellow house with many windows and a green roof with gargoyles spaced around it. A circular driveway leading up to the front door embraces a huge fountain, and eight columns hold a domed shelter at the front entrance. All around are green gardens, and vineyards, and fields and forests. It is much better than my grandfather's house because I have Susan and our son here, and in the barn are my horses, and four chickens and a cow. For supper we ate food we grew on our own land. I wouldn't trade what I've got for all my grandfather's property. This is *my* place. I am not a baron; I am a *king*.

March 10, 1919 Today was clear and bright and quite warm. Susan and I took the baby out for a walk. Although it was sometimes hard to get through the snow, we got up to the field and walked around. There are a few green places where

305

the wind blew the snow off, but there are still deep drifts in the cove. It, too, is melting fast. Winter is not over yet, and I expect we'll see more snow and cold, but we're snug in our little cabin. I read a little bit of Mr. Dickens' story to Susan and John Henry tried to say some of the words.

As John and Susan watched, spring came in halting steps, as of afraid it would make a noise if it moved too fast. As they walked along the field, John noticed some of the wheat around the edges might be frozen. The days were getting warmer, but the nights still left snow frozen hard. John noted, "Some of the willows are showing the fuzzy things some people call pussy willows. I think because they think they resemble a cat's tail. They look a lot more like the tail of a cottontail rabbit to me."

March 23, 1919 Today I went with Susan to her Sunday school in Dehlin. I like the people who come, and we enjoyed seeing them again. They were all glad I was back from the Army, and asked many questions.

Mr. Schwieder asked me if I would like to sell my farm. I told him no. He said he thought everybody would eventually have to sell out because of the drought and the crops getting worse. He said he thought the best use would be for range land for cattle or sheep. I could do that myself, but I'd have to have a lot more than one hundred and sixty acres. I think I should wait and see what happens, and then decide if I want to farm the land, or buy more for range. I certainly don't want to sell what I've worked so hard for.

I enjoyed the time there. It was important to Susan and made her happy. The people are very friendly. One of the things I noticed at her Sunday school the first time I went was they pass around pieces of bread and little glasses of water. I asked Susan what it meant. "It represents the blood and flesh of Jesus." She told me I didn't have to take it, so

I didn't. When I think about it, it sounds kind of gruesome, like a cannibalistic ritual.

March 27, 1919 We had another blizzard today. It was nice the fore part of the week, but then it turned to rain, then came a heavy, wet snow. I don't think it hurt the wheat, but it makes getting around very difficult. And messy. Susan stopped me at the door after I fed the horses and milked the cow, and insisted I take my shoes off before I came in. There's always something to complicate my life.

April 1, 1919 "Shoni's gone!" Susan shouted at me when she came into the house. I was getting out of bed, so I pulled on my pants and shoes and ran out into the icy teeth of this early April day without a shirt or coat. The cold shock sharpened every nerve. All the way to the barn I thought about the four Indians. I was shivering when I reached the door and nearly ripped it off its hinges when I opened it. I couldn't see Shoni! He really was gone! This time I'll *really* kill them! Then on the other side of Bud and Mage, I saw a black head rise and the white star stared at me. I shivered in the cold wind all the way back to the house and opened the door, "Susan, he isn't gone, he was out of sight on the other side of the team."

Gaily she said, "April Fool! Breakfast is ready."
I guess I deserved it.

April 5, 1919 For the past week, the snow has been retreating as if the sun was chasing it in slow motion. I think my wheat survived the winter kill I was afraid of, and I can expect a decent crop this year if we get some rain during the summer. That's my new hanging sword: rain. The alfalfa is already getting green.

Though their cabin supplies were getting low, they decided to wait to go to Ozone till the ground got drier. He wrote, "The mud from the melting snow reminds me of slogging through the mud in France. We'll have to wait till it dries out a little to go to Ozone. Susan made this humble cabin into a cozy home and she's always fussing with it. She has a few geraniums her mother gave her, and they're blooming an unbelievably brilliant red. It's nice, but the walls can become a prison if she doesn't get out sometimes. She's always ready to leave for a while."

April 10, 1919 I wish we had a buggy. We went to Ozone for some things today and with three of us on Shoni, it was difficult to keep things from falling off. Susan offered to stay home with the baby, but I thought we should all get away for a little while. Mrs. Otteson was happy to see us and we talked for a long time. She told us there would be a dance and a program at the Ozone ward on Saturday, the 19th.

They both remembered the dance a little over two years earlier when they met and John didn't recognize Susan as a woman. She turned to John, "Can we go? I love those dances."

"If you want to. But what about the baby?"

"We'll do what the rest of them do. We'll put him on a bench to sleep." John often helped moved the benches out of the way at dances, and watched the parents put the kids in their blankets and nightclothes to bed on them. He wondered how they slept with all the noise. He wrote, "I don't think I'd refuse if we had a dozen kids."

Some of the things they got in Ozone were wrapped in old newspapers. As he unwrapped a sack of sugar, John spotted a headline, "Crazy Horse, Crazy Woman." It was the story of three Indians who brought a fourth to the hospital in Idaho Falls, then rode away. The one they brought in had broken ribs, a broken arm, and blood from a giant bite on his rump was still seeping through his torn pants. The story said one of those who brought him in had severe cuts on his head and a black eye, another had a black eye and bruises on his face. The third, who did nothing to help the other two, had a severely swollen hand.

When they questioned the injured one about his wounds, all he would say was, "Crazy horse, crazy woman!" The newspaper was dated July 23, 1918.

John read it to Susan as she scurried around to find a recipe to prepare a potluck dish for the dance. She commented, "Oh, those poor Indians. I didn't mean to hurt them *that* bad. What can I fix for the dance that would be special?"

Susan's comment made John smile and he answered. "Why not make something up? That way it'll be new to everybody, including us."

"How in the world do you make up a recipe?"

"Every recipe was invented by somebody. You're a good cook. You can create an absolutely sensational dish."

"You're such a liar. How can I?"

"What was your father's favorite dish?"

"He loved Mamma's fried potatoes with onions."

"What will make it sensational?"

"But that's so simple."

"Then make it complicated. Make it fried onions with potatoes. Add something to it, or take something away. You can do it."

"What if it doesn't turn out right?"

"I'm not the cook. You are. It'll turn into something terrific. Try it out on me first. If it's not good we'll eat it anyway, and you can do something different."

"You make it sound so simple. How can you make fried potatoes with onions complicated?"

"Just make something right now, and we'll try it. We've still got a root cellar full of stuff from last year. You can find something."

Susan still thought she needed a recipe, but the idea of creating a new dish intrigued her. She sat at their makeshift table and began writing. And scratching. And writing. And scratching.

A few hours later, they ate a meal based on potatoes and onions with several other things. Over the top of it was a pie crust, and it was baked in the oven.

"Did you like it?" Susan asked.

"Fantastic. Did *you* like it?"

"It was wonderful. I'm so relieved. Do you think the others will like it too?"

"I've eaten a lot of potluck things at dances, but this is the best."

"But I don't have a pan big enough to make much of it."

"Then bake it in your bread pan,"

Susan worked on her potluck dish all day Saturday. John wrote, "She's got it all bundled up in a blanket to keep it warm and we're about ready to go to the dance. I hope the pan is left after the intermission."

April 20, 1919 We went to the dance at Ozone last night and had a good time. Susan finally taught me how to dance, and I found out the biggest difference between how I danced in my field and on the dance floor was the rhythm. From then on, although I made a few mistakes, it was simple.

Susan's new recipe was a sensation. I was surprised there was a baking pan left. It was clean, and a lot of the ladies asked for the recipe.

During the intermission, Ervin Campbell's French bride was called on to sing the French national anthem. She wasn't doing very well, so I helped her.

Bishop Judy announced. "We have a newcomer from France in our midst and she's agreed to sing for us. Mrs. Madeline Campbell will sing the French national anthem."

Madeline came up on the stage. There was applause, and the piano player played *La Marseillaise* somewhat inexpertly. It took two tries before the words came out, and Madeline became more frustrated with each try. She finally got it going and in a thin voice sang the first verse. John turned to Susan. "Do you mind if I help her?"

"Can you sing?"

"I don't know, but I think I can help her."

"Do you know the words?"

"Of course. I didn't spend so much time in France without learning a thing or two."

"Then go ahead. It can't beat my potato dish."

But it did. Madaline was ready to step down after the first verse, but then John's baritone started quietly, increased in volume as he walked to the stage, and boomed out when he reached it. Madaline looked shocked, then said a word to the piano player, and fell in behind John. Her feeble voice grew to a confident soprano, and she sang with all the gusto of any Frenchmen who ever lived.

At the end of the song, she said in French, "I didn't expect anyone would know that song. You must be John Fountain. I've heard of you. I was scared to death till you began to sing with me. Thank you. I love to sing, but this is a strange audience. Do you know *Alouette*?

"My father taught it to me when I was this high," John said, holding his hand about two feet off the floor.

"Then let's teach these people to sing it." They led their enthusiastic audience as they sang the simple French song over and over. They couldn't get enough of it. Later,

Susan told John, "That was so much fun. I loved it. I didn't know you could sing so well."

"Neither did I."

Then more dancing. John finally got the feeling of the rhythm and followed Susan's lead and after a while he haltingly took over. Susan forgave his deficiencies,

Finally, it was all over, and people gathered their children, their pans and kettles, and each other, to return home. Dawn had just broken and it was Sunday again when they reached the cabin with John Henry tucked in and sleeping between them.

During the next few days, Susan worked on her recipe, but John didn't think she improved it. She also insisted John work on his dancing to make it perfect. He wrote, "She hummed a tune while we wrestled around the house. I found out she knew what I wanted to do by the way I held her. It was kind of like steering Shoni with my knees, but I wouldn't *dare* tell her that."

April 29, 1919 The weather is getting warmer, and most of the snow is gone. The trees and bushes are starting to get leaves, and a few of the birds are singing. Bull's Fork has returned to normal. Two weeks ago, it was a savage, muddy flood running over its banks. My fields are a sea of green. I lost some of my crop to winter kill, but only a narrow strip along the edges. Much of what I thought was gone has recovered.

May 3, 1919 John Henry is eighteen months old today. As soon as the ground is dry enough I have to disc the summer fallow ground to get rid of the weeds. I don't know where they come from, but they're there in force.

May 12, 1919 I finished the discing today. The ground is still moist, and the wheat is growing very well. If all works as it has so far, I'll have a decent crop this year.

I never thought of the economics so much when I started to homestead, but now I've had one good crop and two near failures, and a family, I have to think more about our future. Do I have to work in the sugar factory to support my farm? I don't think that's the way it should work.

May 16, 1919 Susan and I and the baby went to the Francks yesterday afternoon and during our conversation, Louie told me the chance for enough rain this year was slim. So far, everything looks just the opposite.

May 21, 1919 We went to Ozone and bought a few things. When I lived alone, my needs were simple and not very many, but now I have a family, they've grown far faster than I thought. I thought we had all the things Susan needed for washing clothes. She uses her mother's home made soap which is very good, I guess, but she decided she needed a trouncer to make washing easier. I've watched her mother use one, and I can't disagree. It saves a lot of scrubbing on the washboard. It cost sixty-nine cents, but it makes her happy. I wonder what we'll need next.

May 24, 1919 This morning when I went to do my chores, I saw a hawk circling around in the sky. He seemed so free. As I watched, he dove toward the ground, then swooped back up, turned, and dove again. This time he hit a mourning dove so hard, it fell to the ground. He pulled the feathers off, then ate part of it, and flew away with the rest.

Freedom? What is it? In the Shoshoni village, we were as free as the hawk, and we hunted for the same reason. For food. The white man changed that. He isn't free. He's tied to a place, and can't go very far from it. I'm tied to my homestead, and I don't *want* to go far from it.

May 29, 1919 I think spring is the most beautiful season of the year. All last week, the birds sang their mating songs, and this morning Susan and I watched from our cabin as a male sage grouse ruffled his chest to show off for a hen nearby. In just a few minutes, another male showed up and did the same thing. The hen didn't seem to pay any attention to either of them.

Susan had never seen this in the valley and was fascinated by the display. "Why do they blow themselves up that way?" she asked.

"They're trying to impress the hen."

"She doesn't look very impressed."

"Just wait. In a few minutes, she'll walk away, and the males will start to fight, then they'll follow her."

"If she's so uninterested, why would they bother?"

"Oh, she's interested, all right. She just wants the strongest one to mate with her."

"What if the males just walk away instead? Would it insult her?"

"Not really. She'd just find another one or two to fight over her."

"Would you fight for me?"

"Susan, that's an unfair question. With humans it's different. They pick each other out. Men don't fight each other for a woman."

"John-Pierre, would you fight for me?"

John remembered the four Indians she fought off. "If I'd been here when those Indians showed up, I'd probably have gone crazy and they'd have been lying on the ground, either dead or wishing they were, by the time I got through with them."

314

"That doesn't sound very romantic. I'd expect more from you than violence." Luckily, he got out of that trap. Across Bull's Fork, a mother deer walked by with a fawn only a few days old. Susan pointed and said, "Oh look, a mother deer and a cute little fawn!"

They watched the deer till they were out of sight around the bend, and the fighting was forgotten.

June 4, 1919 A couple of weeks ago, we were getting four eggs a day from our chickens, but there was only one today.

June 8, 1919 Much of the moisture is gone. The wheat still looks good, but it won't for very long if we don't get some rain. My alfalfa is thicker this year than ever. I can cut it soon.

June 13, 1919 Still no rain. I wonder if Louie Franck was right. Two years ago, I thought I'd lose my entire crop, then it rained, and I got a small harvest and made a little money. I'm getting discouraged. The heads on the stalks are shorter than they should be. I'll have to cut my hay soon. It's getting dry.

June 15, 1919 We went to Susan's Sunday school today. Most of the people come comfortably in buggies. Three of us on Shoni is too crowded if we have to go very far. Susan was all smiles and the people made us feel at home among them.

June 26, 1919 We finished stacking the hay. It was slow work, and we had to take care of John Henry. The flies bit him and he scratched till he bled. He gets into all kinds of mischief, too. He spotted a mouse and ran to catch it. For a boy his age, he can run awful fast.

After they had their supper, John opened his journal. Susan came and sat on the page he was writing. She said, "I think we're going to have another member of the family."

"How come?" John asked, caught off guard.

"Do you need a lesson about the birds and the bees?"

"You're serious, aren't you?"

"I'm happy, but you don't sound very happy. What happened to all the enthusiasm when I told you about John Henry?"

"Susan, I'm very happy. You took me by surprise, and I couldn't think of anything to say. It's wonderful! Do you know when?"

Well, I've waited for two months now and I'm sure. That means probably sometime in January."

"I'm overjoyed. In January? Wow! We'll have to be careful about staying here over the winter. Maybe we could go to your folks before it's due, and stay with them."

"I don't think so. I think James and his bride will be there. My bedroom won't be mine any more. What do you want to name it? Potato?"

John remembered the day two years earlier when Susan told him she was pregnant. He burst out laughing, and grabbed her, "No, I don't think we need another 'pot'. I hope it's a girl this time, for you."

"I don't care if it's a potato," she said and grinned. In spite of the joy at her news, John was worried. What if they couldn't go to her folks for the baby to be born?

By the end of June, John was sure he'd lost his crop. Rain clouds came, but went on by. They went to the Fourth of July celebration in Ozone. It was dismal. The only ones having a good time were the children. They met and talked to Erwin and Madeline Campbell for a while. She was homesick, and thankful for a chance to speak French.

John asked her what she thought of this part of the world. "So big, and so empty! People are so far apart."

By July 10, John was convinced he'd lost his entire crop and wrote, "Still no rain. Only dry heat. I've lost my wheat crop. All I have left is my garden."

Then came a hard rain, a cloudburst, and Bull's Fork ran as full and furiously as during the spring runoff. He and Susan went up to the field while it was still raining, and got soaked. They hoped against hope the wheat would survive, but it was doubtful. It rained off an on till mid July, but he was sure he wouldn't harvest enough to get his seed back. Even the chickens had quit laying. He also commented that Louie Franck told him he would give up his homestead for a dollar an acre.

They received an invitation to James's wedding reception, opening a tiny window of joy in a dismal wall of sadness. Glad for the distraction, he and Susan went, and got some startling advice from Henry Monson.

Chapter Twenty-Eight
Troubled Weather

July 20, 1919 The wedding reception was nice, and almost everyone in Ammon was there. The girl's name is Jennifer Blair. She was very pretty in her wedding dress. James looked uncomfortable in his new suit, but everybody was very happy for them. It seemed strange that James had to meet a girl from his own home town when he was in the Army at Fort Douglas, but he explained he already knew her. He just never had paid any attention to girls before he went into the Army, and when he saw her down there, something clicked. The party was a big success with lots of potluck food.

The next day, John and Henry sat alone the living room. John asked him if he was feeling well. Henry thought for a second and said, "John I think you should find something else to do. You're a hell of a good farmer, but you're in the wrong place. And I'm not so sure you should even *be* a farmer. I've known you for a long time, and ever since you started your homestead up there, I've thought it was a mistake. You're too damned smart to be working so hard for so little. I hear the drought this year has just about wiped everyone out. What about you?"

"I think the best thing to do is just plow it under. I doubt if I could even get my seed back, it's so bad."

"Remember when you said you wanted to homestead in the hills before you left us? I told you then I thought it was a one-sided gamble. When I saw what was happening up there, I told you to think about doing something else."

"I remember, but what *can* I do? The only thing I know is farming. Maybe if I sold out, I could find a place here in the valley."

"Damn it, John, you're wasting your mind! When you and Susan married and I saw you in that suit, I thought that's the kind of clothes you should wear all the time."

John said nothing. Henry pushed on, "Damn it, John! Get the hell out of those hills. They'll kill you." And then quietly, "I don't want to lose you."

The rest of the family came into the room with James and Jennifer, and the conversation turned to something else.

They went home, and Susan collected two more eggs a few minutes later.

July 21, 1919 There's no chance to save anything. Even if I had it cut and stacked, a thresher wouldn't want to bother with it. Too much effort for too little return. I wonder if Dad Monson is right. I wonder if I should get out of these hills. If I did, what would I do? I know only one thing, being a farmer. And I love it. Dad Monson was positive I could do something else, but what? I am at a loss.

July 25, 1919 A hot wind dried everything left, completely. Even the weeds look sad. I can't imagine what I've built here should be left behind. It's a part of me. I'm almost afraid to tell Susan what her father told me. But I have to. She's a part of this place. I built it for her, too. It was to be our home, and it has been our home for months. I *can't* just quit.

July 27, 1919   We went to Susan's Sunday School this morning. Although, as usual, everyone was very friendly, they all talked about the drought. I've never heard these people talk so discouraged. All their prayers were to make next year better. They've given up on this year, just as I have.

Whether it was what Henry told him about leaving the farm or his realization his father-in-law was right, John was deeply troubled. To leave what he'd built seemed impossible. By August, he was so discouraged, he wrote, "Four years ago, I harvested a pretty good crop. This year there's nothing. Then Susan reminded me I can prove up and get title to my farm. I guess I should do that. At least I'll have something. We have less than $200 in the bank, and a baby is coming. So is winter. I wanted to spend this winter on the homestead, but I guess that's not possible now. With James and Jennifer living with the Monsons, we have no place in the valley. I don't know if I can rent a house in Lincoln and work in the sugar factory again. I don't *want* to work there."

Then John remembered "I have to pay for the homestead. A dollar and a quarter an acre! That's $200. More than I have in the bank."

Most of his neighbors plowed their crops under, and he spent three days turning his under, too.

August 9, 1919   I came into the house after discing, all covered with dust. It's so dry, I can't plant anything and expect it to grow. Susan brushed me off with the broom, and then said she had something serious to talk to me about. I've never seen her that way before.

Susan didn't say anything till after supper and Johnny was in bed. She sat across their table, still with a serious look that troubled John. "Something is really bothering you. I know what it is, but I want you to say it. What is it?"

John told her what her father told him.

"While you were in the Army, Daddy told me often he was sure you had to work far too hard for the little return you were getting. I've expected you say something, and I've been afraid you would. He also told me you didn't belong on a farm. I didn't want to believe it, but he finally convinced me. He was here so often and sometimes for so long, I felt sorry for him. When he came to plant the wheat last fall, he worked from dawn till he couldn't see before he came into the house for supper. One morning I called him for breakfast, and he was still out working. John-Pierre, he worked all night to get the wheat planted. He told me he changed teams and worked in the moonlight to finish. After breakfast, he drove his own team back home. James was in the Army, too, and Sam just couldn't handle all the work there was to do, so he had to get back to his own place.

"Daddy loves you like a son, maybe even more than his own, and that's why he tried to take care of two farms at the same time, even though they were more than twenty miles apart. He worked so hard. One time he told me you should get out of these hills, and you could do almost anything else. That's why he told you what he did."

This was the most earnest thing Susan ever said to John and his thoughts ran in circles. "But Susan, what else can I do? I have only an eighth grade education. I didn't even go to high school. You did. What else can I do except work in the sugar factory? I *hate* that kind of work. That would kill me sooner than anything."

"You wrote me one of your officers said you should be a lawyer. Why not?"

"Why not? How can I get into college without a high school diploma?"

"Go to high school."

"You're not serious."

"Oh, but I am serious."

"You can't be. Do you know how long it will take? And besides, what will we live on if I have no income? No, it's just impossible."

"It was also impossible that you found your grandfather."

"That was purely coincidence. There's little chance a coincidence will give me a high school diploma or pay for college or keep my family alive."

"No, coincidence won't, but I'm sure you can work out something. I don't want to leave what we. . . what *you've* worked so hard for, either. I know when the crops are good, you're very happy. But the crops have been getting worse each year, and now you don't have one. Isn't it worth a try to find something else? For me, for John Henry, for Susanna Marie?"

"Who's Susanna Marie?"

"Our daughter, of course."

"You're sure it's a girl?"

"Not absolutely, but I have a hunch."

"Susan, that's another thing. The baby is coming. I have to be able to provide for my family. I just don't know what to do. The only thing I can think of is to work in the sugar factory again this winter, but we'll have to find a house in Lincoln."

"And you can study to get a high school diploma."

"Susan, please, I just don't want to hear any more about going to school. There isn't any way I can do that

322

and provide for a family." Susan looked disappointed, but smiled. They didn't talk about it any more.

John's frustration grew. "It seems there isn't a green leaf left anywhere in the field. I certainly can't plant anything in this dust. I still can't stand the thought of working in the sugar factory again. I've thought a lot about what Dad Monson said, but it seems impossible."

He went with Susan to her Sunday school again, and thought he'd never seen so many discouraged people. But there was a bright spot.

August 20, 1919   Susan and I helped Johnny pick chokecherries today. We took them off the bushes and he picked them out of the bucket. They were very ripe and hung like clusters of grapes, especially those near the spring. At first, we didn't pay much attention to what Johnny was doing, but when Susan started to wipe the red from his face, she noticed his mouth was full and told him to spit them out. He just looked at her and swallowed.

We had a washtub full, and Susan couldn't wait to start cooking them. I hope her mother comes so we can get rid of some of them. I like chokecherry jelly and syrup but I don't think I'll need all we picked today.

September 2, 1919 I feel as if I've played a game and lost to an inferior player. I am so discouraged. And I keep thinking about what Dad Monson told me. Johnny and I went up into the field this afternoon and walked around. Every time I kicked a clod, Johnny kicked a clod.

They walked in silence, John's mind torn between the reality of drought, his desire to stay on his homestead, and by his conversations with his father-in-law and Susan. "Why kick the dirt, Daddy?" Johnny asked. He wondered, too. Why *did* he kick the dirt? Maybe it's frustration, or anger, or maybe just because it's there.

He answered, "Because I'm a farmer, Johnny, and farmers are *supposed* to kick their own clods." John smiled at him and said, "Come on, let's go for a ride." John hoisted his son onto Shoni, then swung himself up. Up on the road, he realized he hadn't ridden his horse at a fast run for a very long time. He let out his Indian yell. Shoni knew what he should do. The wind in Johnny's face made him turn his head as the horse's hooves hammered out a familiar rhythm on the road. John's thoughts turned to his son's future, his daughter's future, Susan's future, *their* future. He knew he had little to offer them in the hills. I've *got* to do something else, he admitted to himself.

September 5, 1919 I thought back to the camp near Paris, to Fountain's Circus, and to the words of my commanding officer, "You ought to be a lawyer." I did enjoy what I was doing, though.

John's thoughts turned into action. He decided to look into what he could do. He told Susan He was going to Idaho Falls and would be back before dark. He didn't go to Idaho Falls; he went to Ammon and looked up Miss Edwards. She had married the principal of the Ammon High School and was now Mrs. Sommers. Two teachers in the same school named Spring and Sommers made him chuckle.

He told her of his conversation with his commanding officer and later with Henry, and asked her what she thought about getting a high school diploma and maybe going on to college to become a lawyer.

"John Fountain, you can do it!" she said so firmly he believed her. Still he held back. There were a lot of unanswered questions.

"When I was in the Army, my interrogations got the name "Fountain's Circus', and I think it was the way I asked questions. I could soon tell if a person was lying."

"Then you'd be good in a court room. John, I've watched you. You were a star pupil, and I've kept track of you. I taught the girl you married for four years, and you've got a very good wife. She'll be behind you, no matter what you want to do. That's the number *two* reason why you should go back to school. The number *one* reason is you'll be wasting a wonderful mind if you don't."

"But I've worked so hard to build my homestead. What about that?"

"John, I won't advise you any further. I've probably said more than I should already, but *think* about it. You've got a little boy now, and there will be others. Their futures are in your hands, too."

September 9, 1919 Susan wanted to go visit her parents yesterday. I didn't want to leave the hay lying in the field, but she pointed out there was little chance rain would hurt it, so we went. I figured something was going on that involved me, but I just kept quiet.

Freddie answered a knock at the door soon after they arrived. Mrs. Sommers came in with her husband. John was sure he was in for some pressure. The talk naturally turned to education, and soon the pressure started, though not the way John expected.

"Ethel talks a lot about you," Mr. Sommers said. "She told me about your conversation a few days ago. Now, I have a proposition for you. I don't want you to answer, now. I want you to think about it. Take your time. You're twenty-five years old. You've been in the Army. You've created a farm, and I think you know a lot more than you realize. I have some high school final examinations you can take. We have to know what else you need to know to get a diploma, and I think you can make it with some help. I won't guarantee anything except the help you need is right under your nose.

"We'll find out what subjects you need to know more about and teach them to you. When you can pass the high school graduation requirements, we'll grant you a diploma."

"But Mr. Sommers, sir, I'm not sure I want to do that."

"I don't want you to answer now. Just think about it. Ethel told me you'd probably make an excellent lawyer."

"With all respect, sir, I've been successful at farming except the weather has been my enemy lately."

Henry Monson added, "John, you *are* a good farmer, but you're wasting your time. Like I said last time you were here, get the hell out of those hills!"

John looked at Susan and she smiled. "All right, Mr. Sommers, sir. I'll think about it. All of you have more confidence in me than I have in myself. But one important thing we haven't talked about is my wife and son and, according to Susan, a daughter on the way."

Lydia spoke up. "Susan, you didn't tell me."

"Of course not, Mamma. We just got here. And I wanted to hear what Mr. and Mrs. Sommers had to say. I didn't think of it."

"First things first." Henry said, "We only cross bridges when we come to them. Let's wait to see what John has to say about Harold's offer. Then we'll take the next step."

John pondered what had happened during the past few weeks. He wrote, "I thought a lot about Mr. Sommers' proposition. I've worked hard to get to where I am now, but where am I? I love the morning sounds, and the smell of nature. It would be very hard to turn my back on it. But

I hear more and more talk of giving up and moving to the valley. I don't want to!"

September 18, 1919 I took Shoni and Johnny out for a ride today. As soon as I got on and Shoni started out, Johnny yelled, "Eeyaha!" and was disappointed when Shoni just kept walking. We rode down Bull's Fork and up Pipe Creek. It looks pretty dry, but it looked like the people in the Pipe Creek area had a harvest, at least. I love this life, but nature doesn't love me, and it's proven it doesn't love me over and over. If only it were just a little bit friendlier.

I owe it to Susan to at least try.

Chapter Twenty-Nine
Sunshine Ahead?

September 21, 1919 It finally rained. Not a hard rain, but it wet the ground quite deep. Now, if we don't have a heavy freeze before it snows, I'll have a crop next year. I borrowed Dad Monson's drill and planted my winter wheat a week ago. I've got my fingers crossed because it was so late. I'll know more when the first snow comes.

The rain encouraged John, so he decided to see about proving up his homestead. A land office had opened in Idaho Falls, and he was surprised and no little relieved that the payment requirement had been lifted because of the drought. The inspector was impressed by his work and readily approved it saying he'd hear from them within a week or so. Encouraged, he decided to take the tests Harold Sommers offered. He was almost resigned to leaving his homestead, anyway. His preoccupation with his decision took his thoughts away from everything else.

October 4, 1919 Tonight at supper, Johnny was playing in his mashed turnips with his spoon, when I thought of the new baby. I guess I've been so preoccupied with leaving the farm, I haven't thought of much else. Susan is showing quite a bit, but what came to me was the name she picked if it's a girl.

While John was writing, he stopped and asked Susan, "Where did you get the name 'Susanna Marie' for a girl?"

"Don't you like it?"

"Yes, I love it. I just asked where it came from."

"Remember the song, Oh, Susanna?" and she sang a snatch of it. I always wanted to be called *Susanna*, but Mamma and Daddy said my name was close. Some of my friends called me *Susie*, but I didn't like it. Marie is my mother's middle name. We named John Henry after you and Daddy, so I thought I should have my name and Mamma's for our baby girl."

At Sunday school the next Sunday, the atmosphere was very gloomy. He wrote, "All the sad talk about crop failure made me think more about what my future holds. I'm glad I decided to take the tests." Still not sure, he asked Susan after supper one night, "Do you *want* to leave this place? You've arranged for me to take the tests, and I will, just to see, but I have a fear you want to leave here."

"I love this place. I told you I'd follow you to the end of the earth, and Bull's Fork is almost there, but I love it. You built it with your own hands for me. This is my first real home. It's what I dreamed of for years — you and I in our own home, together. Then she grew pensive. But I think Daddy is right. You should look into something else. I don't care what it is. I'll follow you to the other end of the earth if you decide to take me there. I am happy now, and I know you'll make a decision that will be good for all of us."

"OK, let's go see what Mr. Sommers has."

"When?"

"Right now, this afternoon, tomorrow."

Susan giggled, then her face grew sad "I don't want to leave this place, either."

October 10, 1919 It's been a week full of things happening. First, my grain has started to grow, and we had an unusually warm rain, but if we don't get some snow to cover the new plants, it could spell disaster.

I took the tests. Some of them were very easy, but there are a lot of things I have to learn. Mathematics is a strange world I don't know anything about. A lot of history is something I wasn't familiar with except for the little bit of French history I learned from Mr. Dickens' book and while I was in the Army. I know some of American history because I've lived it.

The results of the tests left John wondering if there was any chance he *could* get into a university. There seemed to be so much to learn. Harold Sommers thought he should start as soon as possible and asked how much time he had.

"I have a crop in, and winter will be here soon. There is little to do on the homestead during the winter, so I could spend a lot of time before Susan has to come to Ammon for the baby to be born. Then after we return, there'll be time. I've dreamed of living on my homestead for a winter ever since I started it. I've had to work in the sugar factory every year except when I was in the Army, and now both Susan and I want to spend a winter there. I don't have much money left, but we had a good garden and stored enough food. I know we can survive out there."

They returned to Bull's Fork without taking any texts. Susan was disappointed but tried not to show it. She expected him to start studying as soon as the tests were over.

October 16, 1919 The past days haven't been good. Susan tries to be happy and show me a smiling face, but I know she thinks I might not go on with Mr. Sommers' idea. Dad Monson says I'm a good farmer, but I've been up against the weather, and last Tuesday, the weather showed me what kind of enemy I have. My grain was coming up and looking very good, but the frost got it.

John was doing his morning chores when he saw the spring frozen over. He ran to the top of the cove. It took only a glance to find out his wheat was also frozen. He worried when he planted it so late it might not grow enough before frost, but he had hope. The only thing left was to wait till spring and plant it again. His bank balance of $82.37 might carry them through the winter with most of their winter's supply of flour and sugar and the like on hand but they'd still have to buy some things. The stuff from the garden filled the root cellar. With only a little more they could survive.

Survive? Is that all? Dad Monson's words rang in John's head, "Get the hell out of those hills! They'll kill you!" He could already feel their fangs.

That was the turning point. John surveyed his field every day hoping for a show of life, but found none. The second crop was wiped out. He wrote, "I have to start studying. I have to get out of these wonderful hills. I *have* to. I don't *want* to."

October 20, 1919 We woke up to a blizzard this morning, but by ten o'clock, the sun was shining and water was running from the melting snow. The afternoon was warm, and I took Johnny, all wrapped up in clothes getting too small for him, out for a walk along Bull's Fork. He's almost two years old, now and seems to know how to get into some kind of mischief. He threw rocks almost constantly, so I pulled out my slingshot and showed him how to hit a big rock with it. I let him try. He got the little rock to whirl around his head just once, but it wound around his face and shoulders down to his waist. On the way back, he pulled his hat off in the sunshine and revealed hair just a little bit darker than Susan's. His skin was much lighter than I'd noticed before, and when I called to him, he turned and flashed a smile just like Susan's. But his nose is a lot like mine.

October 31, 1919 We went to Ammon day before yesterday and talked to Mr. Sommers. He suggested I study only one weak subject at a time, then take the test. I brought three history books home: *American History*, *Ancient History*, and *History of Modern Europe*. They are old books, badly worn and some of them have writing around the margins, but the information is still right. I started reading the ancient history first. How do we know what happened so long ago? There weren't even books printed then.

John's interest had been kindled. He wrote a condensed version of the ancient history text, perhaps just to refuel his memory, but one of his most interesting comments was written just after he finished the book. He wrote, "Ruins of cities and roads, and giant temples. We were primitive. There doesn't seem to be any other way to describe it. We never built anything like that." And later, after reading about half the European history book, he wrote, "It's kind of funny that Europe was so far advanced in every way when my Indian ancestors were still in the Stone Age. Why? I wonder."

November 21, 1919 This morning when Susan was fixing breakfast, I notices her belly was swelled a lot. She insists it will be a girl and talks all the time about Susanna Marie. I hope she gets her wish. I think it would be nice if Johnny had a sister. I wonder what my sister would have been like if she'd lived.

November 22, 1919 Susan reminded me next Thursday is Thanksgiving, and she would like to have a small turkey to celebrate. We haven't had much meat for a long time, so I told her I'd go to Ozone to get one. Mrs. Otteson didn't have turkeys, but I knew the Monsons did, so I went to them. Of course, I had to stay for dinner, although they'd already eaten. I started back with a young hen with her legs tied.

It wasn't a simple thing for John to bring the turkey home. He laid it in front of him and all went well till he passed Kep's Crossing. There, the turkey began flapping her wings and struggling, so he brought her up in front of him, and let loose of her legs, holding her with his arms around her. It worked for a little while, but just as they reached the top of the hill, she flapped her wings again and got loose. With her legs tied, the only thing she could do was hop and fly through the snow with John in hot pursuit. To himself he thought: It would be easier to chase a rabbit. She dodged, flew, stumbled, and hopped always just out of reach. Finally, she landed in a snowdrift and, with her legs tied and useless, she stopped just long enough for him to grab her tail feathers. Before he could catch her with the other hand, she flapped her wings and flew off leaving him with a handful of feathers. With no tail she couldn't fly very well, but it took ten minutes more before he caught her. The rest of the trip home was uneventful except she decided after the chase, it was time to empty her bowels, and she did. Right in his lap.

He got home just at dark. Susan was worried about him, but when he turned that hapless creature loose with the chickens and Susan saw the turkey without a tail, she began laughing. John changed his pants and told her the story. She said, "I wish I could have seen it."

"So do I. It would have been better to watch than participate."

December 2, 1919   I started the American history book today. I think I like history. So many unpleasant things have happened in the past that happened a short time ago, I wonder why they happen the second time. I like learning new things.

December 9, 1919   Susan's old storybook has come in handy. Johnny listens with wide eyes to every story, and she reads them the same way my mother used to tell me the Shoshoni legends, with lots of hand movements and changes in voices. Tonight she read him *Little Red Riding Hood* and I thought, what a shame anything so wonderful as a wolf should be so portrayed. Then I thought of the wolf that died near my tent years ago. I got out the skin that was supposed to be a part of a winter coat, and brought it to Johnny, and told him what it was.

When the wolf skin was laid out in front of the boy, he shied away, frightened. "Daddy, wolf is bad. Take him away." John told him the story of the wolf and how they became friends. He listened, then looked at his mother, "Mamma, why did the wolf in the story want to eat Little Red Riding Hood? Daddy had a wolf friend."

"Johnny, *Little Red Riding Hood* was a story written a long time ago, before your daddy even lived." Susan answered. "Then, people were afraid of wolves, but wolves are really afraid of people."

"Why was Daddy's friend a wolf?"

John told him more. "Johnny, wolves usually stay away from people, The old wolf that came to my tent was hungry and very old, so I fed him. He didn't want to eat me,

334

but he ate the bread I gave him. We weren't friends like a dog would be, but we were friends."

"Can I have the wolf skin?" He slept under it.

December 13, 1919 Yesterday was sunny, but not especially warm. At about one in the afternoon there was a knock on the door. The Monsons stood there in the bright sunshine with giant smiles. Freddie was with them. He hugged me like a real brother.

He and Dad Monson disappeared to their sleigh and came back with half a frozen pig. That was our Christmas present. We spent the rest of the day together, and Susan and her mother made pork roast for supper. With bread hot from the oven and mashed potatoes from the root cellar, we celebrated.

John finished reading the history books and was ready to take the test, but reported, "The snow is up to my hips on the level and there are drifts as high as the cabin in other places. It's impossible to go to Ammon."

Then the spring froze and no water came out of either the pump or the outlet where John watered the animals. By Christmas day, his routine was fixed: haul snow, melt it, haul more snow, melt it. There were no Christmas gifts. "Susan and I agreed we'd postpone our gifts to each other for another time. but I made an Indian flute for Johnny."

For several days, Susan cut fat off the pig and rendered the lard. The cabin smelled of rendered pork and they sat in the evenings crunching cracklings at each other. On January 1, 1920 Susan woke John. "It's been three years," she said.

"What's been three years?"

"It's our anniversary, John-Pierre."

"Has it *really* been three years?"

"You disappoint me. Have you forgotten our wedding?"

They relived the lunacy and tenderness of their wedding again and laughed until Johnny woke and broke up the party.

He wrote, "We're beginning a new year in our own cabin on our own homestead. Susan is getting very big. We discussed when the baby would come, and decided it would be about the 23rd. We'll leave a few days before to go down to Ammon and I think we can stay with her folks. Jennifer's folks invited them to their place. We plan to have Mrs. Hyatt deliver the baby, and Lydia will be handy to help for a few days before we come back to Bull's Fork. All three of us will ride Shoni. I'll have to come back a couple of times to take care of the animals. Flossie's not giving much milk so I think I can milk her every other day, night and morning and she'll be all right. The biggest problem with them is water. I'll have to work something out.

"I've thought a lot about this year. It could be a turning point — a radical turning point — in our lives. When we go to Ammon, I'll take the history tests and pick up some more of the books for things I need to know. I like the challenge of learning something new, but I'm not sure I like what might come of it. I don't want to leave my homestead, but after finding out what my average profit on the farm is, I can't believe I should work so hard for so little. I went through all my journal notebooks and found out my profit per day was seventy-three cents. That's far less than I earned in the sugar factory, but it includes everything I've spent on the cabin, barn, horses, and equipment.

I love my farm, and so does Susan. What am I thinking of? The weather is my enemy. I can't fight an enemy like that. I watch it, but it tells me nothing. I can't see it. I can't outmaneuver it. I can't even guess what it will do. If I think about what it has done to me, I have to think there *must* be something better on the horizon for both my family and me. The big question now, is WHAT? I've decided to find out what.

January 6, 1920   I can't believe the snow that's fallen. Today it's clear and cold, and this morning when I went to do the chores and chop some more wood, there were giant ice crystals on top of the snow and the sun shining on them made me feel as if I was invading a sacred place where I shouldn't be. I had to wade in snow up to my hips to get to the aspen grove where I chopped down about a dozen dead trees.

Chapter Thirty
Sudden Change in the Weather

January 16, 1920 Last night, Susan woke me up and said, "The baby is coming!" We weren't ready to go to Ammon yet, and the wind had picked up and was blowing snow so heavy I couldn't even see the barn. She told me to stay in the house and help. So I did. It was a baby girl — just what she said.

Susan and John went to bed as usual, about 7:30 in the evening. John was very tired after chopping wood and melting snow all day. He said he thought he had enough wood to last the rest of the winter and he was glad he wouldn't have to wade through deep snow any more to get it. The wind had blown all day but not too badly until just at sundown when it picked up and turned into another raging blizzard. But they were snug and warm in their cabin.

During the afternoon, Susan felt something, but it was far too early for labor pains, so she dismissed it. Later in the night, she was sure she had a labor pain but decided she wouldn't get excited. Maybe in the morning, the wind would have stopped and they could go to Ammon.

Well after midnight the real pains started and she knew the baby was coming. She woke John. "John-Pierre, I think the baby is coming."

"It can't, it's too early."

"I *know* the baby is coming."

"How do you know?"

"I just know. You've got to help me."

"I'll go get Shoni. You take care of Johnny."

"I mean *now*. The baby's coming *now*!"

"I'll hurry. Shall I wake Johnny?"

"There isn't time. You have to help me. We can't go anywhere. The baby is on the way."

What Susan was saying finally sunk in. John jumped out of bed and stood next to it, wringing his hands. "I don't know what to do. I don't know what to do."

"First, see if there's some warm water in the reservoir on the stove."

John started automatically to the door to get some snow to melt.

"Damn it John-Pierre, in the *reservoir*, on the *stove!*"

"Oh, yeah." He hurried to the stove, opened the firebox, realized it was the wrong end of the stove, went to the reservoir and opened it. "There's a little bit."

"Get some in the wash basin. Then get some of Johnny's diapers and bring them to me."

"Where's the wash basin?"

"Where it *always* is. On the counter."

He found it and brought it to Susan. She reminded him, "Get... some... water... in it... out of the... reservoir on... the... stove." Another pain came. "Hurry, Get the diapers here fast."

He just stood dumbly, looking at her. "Where are they?"

"In the box next to the cradle. Hurry, I think the baby is here."

John set the wash basin of water on the stove and ran to the box.

"How many?"

"A big handful. Hurry!"

He rummaged around and dug out a double handful of diapers, then ran to the stove with them. He stood with his hands full of diapers, looking first at the washbasin, then at his full hands.

"Over *here*, John-Pierre, over *here*! Hurry, Hurry!"

"What do you want me to do with the water?"

"Forget the water. Bring the diapers!"

Another pain, very hard, and Susan yelled. John looked at her, his face frozen in the same agonized way as hers. He couldn't move. "John-Pierre, *come here*!"

He approached her almost in fear and held the diapers out to her. Quickly she raised herself and shoved most of them under her. A gush of liquid poured from her, and another pain brought a little head covered with black hair into view. John, still frozen in place, stood with his face a blank and his mouth open.

"It's coming out John-Pierre. Catch it!"

John raised his hands and waited. Susan yelled, "I'm not going to throw it to you. Come over *here*!"

"Where?"

"Right in front of me! Catch the baby when it comes out."

"With what?"

"With your hands, dummy!"

"I don't know how."

"Damn it, get over here!" Susan put his hands into position. "Now, wait till it comes out." Another pain and it did. A slippery little body covered with slime dropped into John's waiting hands. "Is a boy or a girl?" Susan asked.

"I don't know."

"Well, *look*."

"Look where?"

"You idiot! Between its legs!"

"Oh, yeah. . . I can't tell."

"John-Pierre, if it looks like you, it's a boy. If it looks like me, its' a girl."

"I can't tell which of us it looks like."

Susan, damp with sweat, exhausted, and exasperated beyond anything she'd ever experienced shouted at John, "Is. . . there. . . something. . . sticking. . . out?"

The baby coughed and began screaming and squirming and John almost dropped it on the bed. "No, I don't think so."

"Bring her to me. Then get the washbasin and a couple more diapers and bring them to me. Can you remember all that?"

"Uh, I guess so."

John handed his daughter to her mother, ran to the box containing the diapers, and bought another handful.

"Here," he said, relieved.

"And the wash basin?"

"Uh, oh yes."

"Now, John-Pierre. listen carefully. We're not done, yet. We have to cut the cord."

"The cord?"

Susan pointed. "Yes, the cord, right there. Can you see it?" John nodded. "Now go to the cabinet where I keep the string and bring it. The scissors are right beside it."

John went and retrieved a small ball of string and the pair of scissors. "What's this for?"

"You, my dear, confused husband, are going to separate me from Susanna Marie."

"You're already separated."

"Not quite. Now, take a piece of the string and tie it around the cord a few inches from her belly. Do you understand me?"

"Uh, I think so."

"Then do it. Tie it very tight."

John timidly pulled the string around the umbilical cord close to the baby's belly and formed the first loop of a knot. Susan could see it wasn't tight enough and said, "Tight, John-Pierre, very tight." John's shaking hands pulled the ends of the sting, and his face screwed up in a grimace as he finished tying the knot.

"OK, now tie it again a few inches away, toward me, I mean."

"Isn't one enough?"

"No, now tie it just like the first one."

"Won't it hurt?"

"No, it won't hurt. Just tie it."

John tied the second knot.

"That's fine. Now cut us apart."

John just stood transfixed. As if he was mindless.

"Cut between the knots, John-Pierre."

"Uh, What with?"

"With the scissors or your knife or the butcher knife from the kitchen. Just *cut* it."

Holding the scissors he'd used to cut the strings, John looked at Susan, agony in his face. He moved the open scissors to the cord. His shaking hand was almost out of control. "Won't it hurt?" he asked. But he didn't hear the answer.

The man who'd ridden a wild bucking horse and tamed it, the man who'd cleared 160 acres of sagebrush-covered land with his own hands, the man who'd nearly cut his toe off and bandaged it himself with his own pants leg and rode eleven miles for help, the man who wanted to become a white man suddenly turned an ugly gray, his eyes rolled back in his head, and he slumped to the floor in a dead faint.

Susan, nearly exhausted, got the scissors out of John's hand and cut the cord, got the wash basin and cleaned the baby, delivered the placenta herself, and took the noisy baby, wrapped in a clean diaper, under the bed covers and rested.

It was several minutes before John revived. "Susan, are you all right? Did I cut it?"

Susan answered through chattering teeth, "No, I did it. I'm awful cold, John-Pierre."

For the first time John noticed the house was cold. He was shivering, himself, and soon had a fire blazing in the stove. Sheepishly, he sought Susan's eyes, "I don't know what happened. I just couldn't close the scissors. I guess I passed out."

"You did that, all right. I'm so tired. Pull these wet diapers out from under me and cover me up as much as you can. I'll feed the baby as soon as I can." For the first time he realized a faint cry came from under the covers. He turned them down just enough to see the tiny head again. He removed the diapers and got their winter coats and laid them over Susan. He had finally regained his ability to think. The baby quit crying in a few minutes, and about an hour later, with the cabin cozy and warm again, Susan woke and fed her new daughter.

John, wide awake, stayed up keeping the fire going, and in the morning cooked some oatmeal for his wife. As he fed her by the spoonful, he told her about the first time he cooked oatmeal over a campfire in a bean can. "I had no idea how much it would swell. I had to keep taking some out. There was enough to feed a whole tribe of Shoshonis."

Even in her weakened condition, it struck Susan so funny, she had to quit eating to laugh.

January 19, 1920 The storm finally stopped yesterday and it's bright and sunny. My daughter is four days old today. She looked at me for the first time and seemed to know who I was. Well, I think she knew who I was. Susan has a huge supply of food for her, so I doubt the baby will go hungry. She's up and around almost the same as before, but she still gets tired in the afternoon.

January 22, 1920 I forgot to write about the snowdrifts the storm made. One of them almost covered one side of the barn, and I had to tunnel to the root cellar for some carrots and potatoes, and a pumpkin last Sunday. The trench I dug through the snow to the barn in most places is deeper than I am tall. Johnny runs back and forth in it having a wonderful time. I had to shovel at least three feet of snow off the haystack to feed the animals. The sun has been shining without a cloud in the sky anywhere, and the contrast between the hills buried in white snow and the blue of the sky looks unreal. Susan is very strong, and the baby is good and healthy.

Chapter Thirty-One
Improving Conditions

February 1, 1920 For two days last week, the weather was warm like a day in spring. All the paths I shoveled flowed with water from melting snow, and the snowdrifts are now about half as high as they were. Two nights ago, it got bitter cold, and everything froze so hard I could walk on top of the snowdrifts. I looked out over the country and saw a few bare spots, but only a few. My field is mostly buried in snow even though the wind blew some of it off during the storm. It would be good if there was a crop to receive all that moisture.

By the middle of February, John had to go farther and farther to get snow to melt for water. He wrote, "I've carried almost all the snow from around the house and barn into the cabin to melt. It's getting to be a very tiresome job. I tried the pump again, but nothing came out."

Supplies were getting low and the roads were still blocked. The days were sunny but cold and it froze hard at night. He wrote, "As the ice crystals on the snow grow bigger, sometimes I think it should be left alone."

John worried, not only about his routine, but about not being able to get Susan and the baby checked over. They seemed all right but he wanted to get to Ammon. "We're almost out of sugar and we're getting low on salt and flour. Flossie doesn't give much more milk than Johnny drinks. The next warm day, I think I'll try to get to Ozone."

The weather refused to cooperate. There was no warm day. In fact, a storm came up and he couldn't get to Ozone to buy groceries till the end of February. George Fogelsong broke a road through with his team and sleigh and took John to Ozone where they bought supplies. John noted, "My bank balance is down to sixty dollars."

March 8, 1920 The wind blew for more than a week, but there wasn't a lot of snow. I'm even running low on snow to melt. The weather turned cold, again and the snow freezes so hard I have to cut up big blocks of it into small pieces to carry into the cabin.

March 13, 1920 We've had a few rather warm days, and more of the snow has melted. I climbed up and looked at my field this afternoon, and all I saw were frozen wheat stalks where they were exposed. I have to plant as soon as it's ready, but I can't plant too soon or it might freeze like it did last fall.

Johnny stares at the baby a lot. Yesterday, he tried to get her to blow on his flute, the one I made for him for Christmas, but put it too far into her mouth and she gagged. Susan was scared, but nothing happened except she cried a little bit.

March 16, 1920 A lot of the snow is gone, but I'm sure winter is not over. I walked up to the road yesterday and saw that several sleighs have passed, so I know it's open.

Susan baked again today, and we had pork side meat with it. While she baked, I melted snow for the animals. We got only one egg today, and Old Flossie is giving less and less milk. There's barely enough for Johnny to drink and some for oatmeal for breakfast. Susan doesn't skim the cream any more, but we have quite a lot of butter left.

March 18, 1920 I love my daughter. Today she smiled over and over when I looked at her. I was holding her while Susan fed Johnny, and she watched my face all the time. I was reminded of Henri Barticelli when I looked at my grandfather's picture and recognized my father in it.

That reminds me, I haven't had the picture framed again. I pulled it out and looked at it again. That time seems so long ago. It was in a very ornate gold colored frame, and I'd like to have it framed the same way, but not until I have a lot more money. I wonder if the day will ever come.

By March 24, the weather was better, and John thought about going to Ammon to have Susan and his daughter checked over. Although he finished reading all the history texts, one thing still bothered him, seemingly because he couldn't understand it. "I'm still amazed the American Indians were so far behind the rest of the world. I've thought a lot about it and I think we just concentrated on survival, while much of the rest of the world had enough and could spend their energy on things not related to survival. Besides, they were probably in centers of population with more people to do specialized things. As far as I am concerned, I think I could do a lot of other things, too, if I didn't have to work all the time to make the farm."

His preoccupation with his new found interest in learning had sparked a new interest fueled long before in France. "I wonder what it would be like to be a lawyer," he wrote.

Finally he could get Susan to Ammon. She was pronounced healthy with no complications and while he was there, he took the history tests and felt confident he'd passed them. Before leaving he picked up algebra and geometry texts to continue his studies.

April 1, 1920 Susan went out this morning to gather eggs. She came back all excited. "The spring is flowing!" I ran out to the outlet of the spring. It was still frozen solid, but there was a sign of a trickle, which I was sure was from melting ice, so I went back in and said, "No, Susan, the spring isn't flowing. It's still frozen."

"April Fool!" she said. Johnny also said, "Apurrrl Fool!" I hadn't tried the pump for a long time, so I tried it. Muddy water came out. Then more muddy water. After a few more pumps, clear water came out. The spring really was flowing!

"April Fool!" I said, and Johnny repeated it. Later, the flow from the outlet increased substantially, and I knew my snow melting days were over.

April 4, 1920 The wind has been warm and dry for the past few days and the snow has almost all melted from the field. I dug down into the soil and it's very moist. I have to get Dad Monson's drill and some seed and plant it again. If I can get it in soon, and it snows on top of it after it's planted like it does sometimes, there should be enough moisture to keep it going for a long time. But I have to have seed, and that means I'll have to get a loan at the bank. We don't have enough money left to live on till harvest time, so I'll have to borrow some for that, too.

I've been doing the algebra problems in the book. They don't seem to be so difficult after I read the text. In fact, I like doing them. The answers are in the back of the book, so I know when I've done them right. Only problem is I've run out of paper, and I have to use the only spare notebook I bought for my journal, and the one I'm using is almost full.

With spring coming, John didn't want another missed opportunity, so he borrowed Henry's grain drill and returned Flossie. "Old Flossie had dried up completely, so we took her back. Dad Monson still didn't have room for her, so he 'loaned' a heifer to us. I went to the bank and borrowed $150 to get us through the summer and for seed wheat."

Even with the help of Louie Franck, John had difficulty unloading the grain drill, and it fell between the planks he laid out to roll it off the wagon. They couldn't put it back on, so he called Susan to help. "I called for Susan, and when she came we were able to get it straightened out and off the wagon. I had no idea how strong she is. She could almost lift one side of that thing by herself.

"Early the next day, I got started planting. I think everything will work out now. I have about a fourth of the field planted." John finished planting his wheat by mid April, and returned the grain drill. Susan went with him and picked out some seeds for their garden. A few days later, they planted it. John was optimistic again, "I dug up a few wheat seeds. They're swelling, and they look good. I think I'll have a good crop this year. The moisture should last till about the first of June, and if it rains then and a couple more times in June, I'll have a crop like the first one."

April 22, 1920 Today it snowed and rained and the wind blew. I studied my algebra book and worked the problems. It seems so easy. I think mathematics is a language all by itself. I'm nearly finished with the book. I'll start the geometry book next.

I wish we had a buggy. Four of us on Shoni isn't a big load for him to carry, but it's awkward for us. Johnny sits in front of me and pretends to drive. Susan holds Susanna Marie in front of her. But I've got to have a buggy. They cost almost $50 for a simple one. Maybe I can find a used one. There is always something else I need, no matter what I have. But a buggy will have to wait at least till I harvest this fall. Maybe I won't need one at all if we leave.

April 25, 1920 We came to Ammon yesterday, and today Susan went to her Sunday school with her parents. I stayed here with Johnny and Susanna Marie.

Last night I talked with Dad Monson, again and he told me he was glad I'd decided to finish high school, and I was wasting my head on the homestead.

We talked a long time about what I'm doing and he told me again to get out of the hills. He knows how I feel, but what he told me makes sense. I think he hit the nail on the head when he asked me how much money I was making on a daily basis. I had to admit it was much less than a dollar a day. When I told him that, it hit home. Hearing myself say it to him, made me realize even that small amount was not a sure thing. The last thing he said has troubled me ever since. He said, "I know the feeling of having done something great. I built my homestead from nothing. But think John. Are you chasing a dream or facing reality? I think up there you're chasing a dream, and that's the reality."

April 26, 1920 We got back to Bull's Fork about noon. Susan knew I had a problem and asked me what it was. I told her what her father said. I don't want to leave my farm.

April 30, 1920 My grain is starting to grow. I look at it and think of what Dad Monson told me. How can I leave this place? I know my crop this year will be good. I just *know* it.

May 2, 1920 Susan talked me into going to her Sunday school. Everybody seemed happy to see the baby and us. It's the first time most of them have ever seen her. Almost everybody expects this year to be a good year for grain.

May 5, 1920 I've been thinking of what I should do ever since I talked to Dad Monson last time we were in Ammon. I think he's right. Maybe I should look into something else for a living. I know if it weren't for our garden and the root cellar, we'd run out of food and money.

I passed both the algebra and geometry tests in Ammon. Now I have one new book about how the United States government works.

He was reading his new text book after supper, when Susan came up behind him and playfully bit his ear. "I think Daddy is right. You're smart, and I'm sure you could learn a new job. I'd be proud if you went to college."

"I'd like to, I think, but let's look at it: What would we live on? How would we pay rent? How could I pay the college? I think I'd like to go, but I just can't see how I can."

"When we got married, and I helped you buy your new suit, I thought you belonged in it. I didn't ever want to see you without it. Last Sunday, you looked so handsome, and distinguished. I think you should wear it all the time."

"What about the farm? And the horses?"

"We could sell them."

"I'll never sell Shoni. And that's another problem. If I go to college, where will I keep him?"

"There have been lots of times we didn't know what to do, like when you went to war. I never told you how

351

scared I was. But we made it with Daddy's and neighbors' help. We survived, and now we're just looking at a new challenge."

"I guess that's one of my problems. I haven't really finished this challenge. If I quit now, it's like giving up something that's very important to me."

Although John had resigned himself to leaving the farm, there were still doubts. He had so little experience outside his farm and the sugar factory, he couldn't be sure of anything, and now with a family, his doubts about leaving the farm increased. At least, on the farm, he knew where their next meal would come from. Susan, never having known anything other than living in a farming community, was also concerned, but more optimistic about John's ability, and their future if they left.

She responded, "It's important to me, too. I love this place. I loved it from the first time Mamma told me about it, and when I saw it, I knew it was exactly what I wanted. You remember when I came the very first time. I yelled, 'I'm home!' I *was* home! And it's *still* my home. I love this place. I love it with all my heart, but there's a power far greater than we are, and it's not always friendly. In the five years you've been here, you've had only one good crop. Daddy used to say, 'Don't whip a dead horse.' I think that's what we're doing."

"OK, Susan. Let's look at the problems we'll have if I leave here and go to college. What will we live on? I don't know how much I could sell the place for, nor do I know who would buy it. Even if we sold it, we might be able to live on the money for a while, but what happens when it's gone and I don't have any income?"

"When you cut your foot, you managed. When you went to war, we managed. When the barn burned down, we managed. Last winter when the spring froze up, we managed. Damn it, John-Pierre, *we'll manage!*"

John was stunned. He looked at Susan. Her face told him more than her words. There was a tear in her eye, and her lower lip quivered.

Tearing up the roots they'd planted on Bull's Fork wouldn't be easy, but it wasn't easy when his mother sent him to live among the white men. It wasn't easy leaving the comfort of the Monsons' home to homestead. It wasn't easy leaving Susan when he went to war. They looked at each other for a long time, his mind ran in circles between the life he had and a future he had no idea about. Finally he said, "Yes, Susan, yes. We'll manage."

Chapter Thirty-Two
Uncertain Weather Clears

May 10, 1920 I feel as though a huge burden had been lifted off me. I've thought a lot about those days of interrogating German soldiers in France and Fountain's Circus. The idea of being a lawyer appeals to me. Susan is happy, and I know I've made the right decision, and she agrees with it.

May 11, 1920 My wheat reaches my ankles. This year's crop is bound to be good. A nice shower wet the ground today. A decent harvest will help when I start college. I like the text about the United States Government. I've read it twice and I think I know everything in it.

Susanna Marie is moving quite a lot. She rolls over onto her belly, and kicks and moves her arms. When she finds out she has to have them under her, she'll start crawling around. I love my family.

May 15, 1920 The weather is warming up. Today we all went for a walk down Bull's Fork. It was so pleasant, we went without coats. The grasshoppers are coming out and Johnny wanted to fish.

Susan looked at me and said, "I hope we can find another place like this some day." So do I.

May 20, 1920   When I finished doing my chores this morning, I walked into the cabin and met the wonderful smell of fresh-baked bread, and eggs were sizzling in the frying pan. The baby was fussing a little bit, so I finished the eggs while Susan nursed her. We sat down at the table and ate oatmeal, eggs, bread and fresh butter, milk, and chokecherry jelly. I want my life to be like this forever.

The decision firm, and final, John and Susan went to Ammon so he could take the American government test. He wrote, "It would be a lot easier if I had a buggy to go to Ammon, but I haven't, and I guess I won't need one, now. We got here early in the afternoon yesterday, and I took the test this morning. It seemed almost too easy. Sometimes I wanted to write more than the questions asked for, but I thought it better if I just answered the question. I finished quickly, and I'm sure I passed it."

The next day both Mr. and Mrs. Sommers came with the test and a high school diploma. He missed only one question, but it was a part of another one.

With the way to go to college now open, Mr. Sommers asked, "Where do you plan to go?"

"Probably University of Idaho to study law."

"I doubt you'll be sorry, and neither will your clients."

Mrs. Sommers changed the subject, "John, a long, long time ago, I gave you a notebook to keep a journal. Have you done it?"

"Yes, Miss Edwards, I have." John got it and handed the last notebook to her.

She read briefly the last few pages and looked at him. "Your decision to leave your homestead was really difficult. Do you ever read it? By the way, I'm no longer Miss Edwards, you know,"

"Yes, ma'am, I know. I was just going back a few years to when you were my teacher. Yes, I read it sometimes. It's kind of like living my life over again. Sometimes it's fun, and other times, it's not. And sometimes, I don't know why I wrote some of the stuff I did.

"And how about Dickens? Did you read it?"

"I read most of it twice while I was reading it the first time. Some of it was a little hard to understand at first, and it took about two years because I worked so much of the time.

June 2, 1920 We returned to Bull's Fork last Friday. My grain is looking good and the heads are forming. Now all I need is rain to keep it growing. Around the edges of the field, it's a little dry and a few stalks are turning yellow. If I don't lose any more, it won't matter.

June 17, 1920 Still no rain. All the leaves on my wheat are yellow and the only green is the stem and the heads.

I took Johnny down to Bull's Fork to fish. He was so enthusiastic, I forgot for a little while what my wheat looks like. It's such a pleasure to see his startled face when a fish bites. Just like last time, when he felt something pulling on the end of the string, he threw the pole in the water and looked scared. But I gave it back to him, and he squealed with joy when he pulled a fish out of the water. He caught two, both small, but when his mother cooked them for him, she had to make him wait till she could take the bones out.

After supper, I sat for a long time watching my family. Susan was nursing the baby, Johnny was watching as if mesmerized. This is my family, my responsibility, my future, and my life. What am I offering them? Wheat turning yellow from lack of rain. Suddenly, I'm more ready than ever to leave it all behind. I've already decided where to go, but what I don't know is how long it will take to get there, and what problems will come up along the way. My confidence lies in what Susan said, "We'll manage."

June 20, 1920 Yesterday, a huge black cloud rose over the horizon and boiled furiously. Lightening stabbed the earth and thunder roared through the hills, but nothing fell except a few drops. It was still cloudy this morning when Susan took me to her Sunday school. As usual, the neighbors were friendly, gushing over Susanna Marie, and patting Johnny on the head. During the service, which seems to me to be a repeat of every other time I've been there, I looked around me. I think most of the people were looking out the window to see if it was raining. I like these people and we all depend on rain. Every one I talked to told me the same story, which was the same story I told them. The wheat is headed out, but turning yellow.

They returned to their cabin and Susan fixed dinner. Just as they finished eating, a clap of thunder sent them to the door, and Johnny started to cry. Rain fell in giant drops from boiling black clouds. They stood there just a moment, then ran out in it. John took off his shirt and yelled with joy. "At last! Rain. My crop is saved." Susan followed, and the two of them ran around, letting it wet them. Johnny came to the door, still crying, and watched them. Then he began laughing and ran to join them.

John took Susan by the waist and Johnny by the hand and began to dance while he made drum sounds. Water splashed as they stomped the ground, rain lashed their faces. They laughed and danced, and laughed and danced some more.

Later as they sat in the cabin, the coal oil lamp lit, they listened while thunder ricocheted around the hills, and lightening slashed through the clouds and the rain made music outside. They were still a little bit wet, but who cared?

Susan turned. "Remember when we danced around a fire the night before you left to go to war? I said we should do it again when you came back. Well, we just did!"

June 23, 1920 My crop wasn't completely saved, but it will be better than I expected a week ago. The heads were just green enough they're trying to fill out. I might have a crop as good as the second one.

The rain lasted two days, and everything got a good soaking. Even my hay has started to recover. I was about ready to cut it to save the few leaves remaining, but now I think I'll wait for it to start growing again.

July 6, 1920 Susan and I went to the celebration in Dehlin yesterday. It was delayed one day because the fourth was on Sunday. Mrs. Holmquist was there, telling the same story about the pigs in Norway. I bought two sandwiches and Susan shared hers with Johnny. The atmosphere was both celebration and despair. The rain was almost too late.

July 10, 1920 My wheat has almost recovered. The kernels on the tips are shriveled and the crop will be much less than I thought when it came up this spring. I was so hopeful then, and so sure of a good harvest. Nature has not been my friend again this year.

July 18, 1920 The baby has learned to crawl. Yesterday Susan and I watched while Johnny played with her on the floor. I didn't see what he did, but she started to laugh and then Johnny laughed. For several minutes they took turns laughing at each other. It was so funny we laughed. Neither of us could see why the kids laughed so much. I guess that's what made it so funny for us.

July 20, 1920 Susan and I looked at the apple trees this morning. They're all doing well, but they're just sticks with leaves now. If we had more rain, I think we'd have been able to build a very nice place. I regret leaving it, but I think I've known for a couple of years I was "whipping a dead horse" as Dad Monson told Susan. I just didn't want to admit it, even to myself.

July 23, 1920 I got two pieces of good news today. Louie Franck brought an application from the University of Idaho from the post office. They start classes on September 20, and he told me about the harvest arrangements.

Louie told John everybody was ready to start the harvest. The headers were due at his place in two days, and the thresher shortly afterward. Nobody expected much, but the grain is really ready.

And there was more good news. A man named Walter Scocroft, offered to haul the wheat on his truck. A truck could haul three or four times as much as a wagon and make two trips a day. There was another development, too. John wrote, "We were on Dave Rushton's place when Arthur Schwieder showed up. We had just stopped for the night, and he came to me. "I hear you've decided to leave and go to college, John. Do you plan to sell out?"

"Yes, sir. But I haven't done anything about it yet."

"I'd like to buy your place. It's a little far from where I am, but I can use it. I think I can get together a good sized farm including yours. I thought it might make good range at first, but I think if I change methods, I can make it as farm land."

"Mr. Schwieder, thank you for your offer, but I have no idea what it's worth right now. Let me get the harvest out of the way and ask a few questions around, and then we'll talk about it."

On July 30, the thresher got to John's place and finished in two days. He wrote, "The ground where the stacks were was covered with a layer of wheat kernels that fell out of the dry heads and it was one or two inches thick. I'm sure there were twenty-five or thirty bushels lying there. We shoveled it into the threshing machine, so most of it was saved, but there was still a little bit mixed in with dust.

"Susan fixed a wonderful dinner. We still don't have a decent table, so men were eating on our makeshift kitchen table and out in the yard seated on a log and some of them were standing up."

Altogether, John got 910 bushels, and the price was $1.55 per bushel. He decided to use the Scowcroft truck to haul his grain to Ammon even though it cost him about $30, but it saved him the worry and work of hauling it by wagon. After all the bills were paid, he had about a thousand dollars left. "I hope it will be enough. We'll probably have to buy everything we eat from now on."

It seemed everybody knew John was leaving the farm, but no one offered to buy it except Arthur Schwieder. Everyone wished him well.

He helped four other neighbors finish harvesting, and it was time to get ready to leave. "It feels funny that I'm not going to plant my winter wheat."

The next Sunday, John suggested to Susan they go to Sunday school. She asked, "Why? You never asked to go before."

"I can visit with more people in a couple of hours there than if I spent two weeks riding from place to place. I want to talk about selling out. We have to do that, you know." His reason disappointed her but she agreed.

After church, people gathered in little knots to talk about their problems. Most of the farmers there were thinking about getting off their homesteads and onto something more dependable, something that didn't depend on the weather. He heard of one homesteader with 320 acres who offered to sell it for ten cents an acre. There were several homesteaders who borrowed money from the bank to buy more land, then couldn't pay it back and lost everything. Another said he wouldn't take less than ten dollars an acre for his. Most said they thought their land was worth between five and ten dollars an acre.

Harlin Loveland cornered John. "I wondered how long it would take you to use your brain for something besides fighting the weather. You've done better than most of us, and I think its because you think different. I am surprised you've decided to go to law school, though. I pictured you in a farm implement store."

August 4, 1920 I don't know why for sure. Maybe just to look at what I have. I went up to the top of the cove and looked down on my yard and tried to imagine what it would look like if I could stay here and finish what I've started. What *do* I have? I've got a cabin, the root of a bigger barn, a disc and a harrow, a corral, Shoni, Bud and Mage, and harnesses for them. New harnesses. I have a borrowed cow and four chickens that will probably have to be turned into chicken stew. I've got a wobbly wagon, a decent hayrack, and a grain box that won't last much longer. I've got an orchard that won't bear fruit for several years. I've got a wonderful garden and a spring for water. I've got a root cellar that works much better than I thought when I built it.

Built. Yes, I've built the whole thing myself.

What do I need? I need a derrick to stack my hay, and a mowing machine to cut it and a rake to rake it. I'll probably need a new wagon. I need a buggy. Shoni has carried all four of us every place we've gone for a long time, and when we have a bigger family, there won't be room for all of us. It's already crowded. I need a grain drill. I should have bought one long ago. If I get a buggy, I'll need a shed to put it in. And I'll need runners for the winter, or a sleigh. I need a table for the kitchen, and we need more chairs, and we could use some sort of bench for just all-round use. I need another room on the cabin, and if the family gets even bigger, I'll probably have to have a fourth room. I need a brood sow, so we can have more fresh meat in winter and a smoke house to cure some of it, and I should have my own cow, maybe two or three to produce milk and butter and things we can sell. And I could use the extra calves for meat or to sell. I need a bigger corral, and I should have a shed to keep all my farm implements in like Dad Monson. And when Johnny gets big enough, he'll want a horse to ride to school. I'd like to finish building a bigger barn, too. It wouldn't hurt to have a hand plow to plow the garden. And maybe even a car. Several people around here have them. I don't think any of them could beat Shoni in a race out here, but they have more room for a family.

Then I began thinking about the future. I wanted my farm to be a success, so I could get the things I need and live comfortably. That seems unlikely the way things have been going. I've chosen to become a lawyer. But when I look the future in the eye, I can't see anything. It was the same when my mother told me to go live with the white men. I looked to the future, but I couldn't see anything then, either. I've already made the decision. I have to do it.

I went back to the cabin with a heavy heart, but Susan cured it. She said, "Guess what Susanna Marie did this afternoon."

"What?" I asked.

"She said, 'Mamma.'"

My heart is lighter now.

362

August 9, 1920 I feel lost. I won't plant any winter wheat, and making improvements wouldn't be worth the effort. When I think of what I've heard homesteads bring, I'm dismayed. Ten cents an acre! But if my homestead would bring ten *dollars* an acre, I'd take it. But what about the other things? Who needs them? The cow isn't mine. Susan could make chicken and dumplings out of our hens. That pretty well takes care of the livestock, except for the horses. I will never let Shoni go.

August 12, 1920 We got a big surprise today. The Monson's came to visit us. All of them. The first thing Sam did was go see his apple tree. Freddie explored the place from top to bottom. He was gone over two hours. James and Jennifer, who is just beginning to show her pregnancy, walked down along Bull's Fork, but came back in an hour or so. Susan and I sat in the cabin and talked to Dad Monson and Lydia while Johnny went from one to the other wanting attention.

The conversation dwindled slowly and John and Henry went outside. John asked Henry how much he thought his homestead was worth.

"I don't know much about dry farms, but land is valuable. I think you should ask for between five and ten dollars an acre. You might be able to get something more for the improvements and the equipment you have, but I don't know. Have you talked to anybody about it yet?"

"Arthur Schwieder told me twice he wanted to buy it. We haven't talked about the price, though."

"I know how you feel about this place. I feel the same way about mine. Just don't set the price too high."

About ten the next morning, Arthur showed up. After introductions, John and Henry took him outside. Arthur spoke first. "John, you've done a great job here. I admire your decision to go to college, and I know it will cost a lot of money. I'm ready to give you four dollars an acre for it."

"That's $640. I was expecting more."

"Have you talked to anyone else?"

"About selling? No. I can't fight nature, and it's been pretty tough on all of us out here so far, but I have so much effort invested here I think it's worth more."

Henry bit his lower lip and said, "The land itself is probably worth five to ten dollars an acre. Then there's the cabin, the barn, the equipment, and the location. And it has a spring on it. Those things add value. What do you plan to do with it?"

Arthur looked surprised, "I know a man can't make a living out here on 160 acres. I can't, and neither can anyone else. A few years ago, I went over to Martin's Flat and saw a combine that cut a twenty-four foot swath. It was an amazing machine, and most of the time it worked, but it took thirty-three horses to pull it. I thought it needed more manageable power, like a tractor. I've been looking into tractors for about two years now, and I think they've reached a stage where they can really be more economical and reliable than horses. I envision a spread of several thousand acres that can be farmed by very few men, maybe even only one. I like this place because it could be a part of it. I've looked over the whole area of Dehlin and Bull's Fork and other areas, and I think it can be done. I'm not a risk-taker, but I can see a future out here, maybe several years away, but I think I can make it work." He turned to John and said, "Let's just cut this short. I'll give you a thousand dollars."

John and Henry looked at each other. Henry said, "How about the improvements and the equipment and the horses."

"I can use the horses, especially the riding horse, and the disc and harrow, but the house and barn and other things hold no value for me. How about another $100?"

"Mr. Schwieder, Shoni is not for sale. He'll be with me for the rest of his life. I won't sell him for anything."

"I didn't think you would. How about it? Eleven hundred dollars for everything, and you keep Shoni."

Henry turned to Arthur. "I'm still a little in the dark. Your plan sounds pretty big to me. Aren't you a afraid it might be a little bit too grand?"

"Well, I've watched my neighbors and I've gone to other places, and seen what they do. I think most of them are just too small, and they don't really take advantage of the weather. If I can get big equipment in here to do the work faster and at the right time, I think by plowing and planting on the contour of the land instead of just back and forth, I can conserve more of the moisture and beat the drought. Maybe not every time, but enough to make it profitable. I'm convinced of it, but it can't be done on a small scale. Think about it, John, I'll drop by next Monday."

August 16, 1920 Mr. Schwieder came by early this morning and we shook hands on the deal. I'll meet him at Mr. St. Clair's office in Idaho Falls next Friday.

I am both happy and sad.

August 20, 1920 Today, this morning, in Mr. St. Clair's office in Idaho Falls, my farm became Arthur Schwieder's farm. When I signed my name, I had to try two or three times before the pen touched the paper. I sold something I cherished. The only other thing important to me is my family. Their joy and love I will always cherish. The uncertainty I feel is in just a few words. "Will Fountain's Circus live again?" I got back home in mid afternoon. Susan, carrying Susanna Marie, and I and Johnny walked down Bull's Fork and through the field for the last time. We didn't talk very much. Neither Susan nor I wanted to say what we felt, but it was there. I chose a path I have to follow to its end to know where it leads. On Monday, we'll say good-bye to this land that made me a white man and the cabin and Bud and Mage, and to our wonderful neighbors, and perhaps we'll never see any of them again.

About The Author

Mr. Hansen grew up on a farm in Lincoln, Idaho, attended Lincoln school, Idaho Falls High School, and graduated from Idaho State College with a degree in Geology. His professional career exceeded thirty years, ending with a five year contract with the United Nations in Vienna, Austria. Working for UN afforded professional travel to many exotic places in the world.

He retired in 1993, published his life story for his immediate family in 1996, and started a career as a freelance writer. He has published articles on many diverse subjects in several magazines. This is his second book.

He presently lives with his wife, Hilde, in a beautiful valley in the Southern Alps in Austria.

Printed in the United States
128845LV00001B/4/A